Praise for Mary McNamara and
Oscar Season FEB 2011

"Glitz, gossip, and suspense . . . cheeky, engaging . . . It's the perfect type of read for a nonstop flight between LAX and JFK and it's smarter and better crafted by leagues than any Jackie Collins paperback . . . you can't help but enjoy McNamara's pithy dialogue, fast pacing and trenchant observations . . ."

—Samantha Dunn, *Los Angeles Times Book Review*

"Eminently worth reading . . . a witty, well-observed piece of social satire."

—*Daily Telegraph,* UK

"[McNamara] paints a disturbingly accurate picture of life, love and publicity during the industry's most electric awards season."

—Christina Kinon, *Daily News* (New York)

"In the category of 'deliciously fun reads,' Mary McNamara definitely gets a Best Newcomer little gold guy."

—Joy Tipping, *The Dallas Morning News*

"A scandalous look behind the velvet rope."

—Martin Zimmerman, *The San Diego Union-Tribune*

"Agatha Christie meets *Hollywood Squares* in journalist McNamara's glitzy debut . . . McNamara's self-assured, tabloid-fueled narrative—simultaneously sexy, scandalous and suspenseful—will appeal to fans of authors like Jackie Collins and Harold Robbins. McNamara insightfully portrays life on the other side of the velvet rope . . ."

—*Publishers Weekly*

ALSO BY MARY MCNAMARA

Oscar Season

the Starlet

a novel

Mary McNamara

Simon & Schuster Paperbacks
New York   London   Toronto   Sydney

Simon & Schuster Paperbacks
A Division of Simon & Schuster, Inc.
1230 Avenue of the Americas
New York, NY 10020

First Simon & Schuster trade paperback edition June 2010

SIMON & SCHUSTER PAPERBACKS and colophon are registered trademarks of Simon & Schuster, Inc.

For information about special discounts for bulk purchases, please contact Simon & Schuster Special Sales at 1-866-506-1949 or business@simonandschuster.com.

The Simon & Schuster Speakers Bureau can bring authors to your live event. For more information or to book an event contact the Simon & Schuster Speakers Bureau at 1-866-248-3049 or visit our website at www.simonspeakers.com.

Designed by Meredith Ray

Manufactured in the United States of America

10   9   8   7   6   5   4   3   2   1

Library of Congress Cataloging-in-Publication Data
McNamara, Mary.
  The starlet : a novel / Mary McNamara.
    p. cm.
1. Motion picture actors and actresses—Fiction. 2. Motion picture locations—Fiction. 3. Murder—Fiction. 4. Tuscany (Italy)—Fiction. I. Title.
  PS3613.C5859S73   2010
  813'.6—dc22

                                                    2009051616

ISBN 978-1-4391-4984-3
ISBN 978-1-4391-5808-1 (ebook)

For Danny, Fiona, and Darby,
my very own models of excellence,
with much love and admiration

THE STATUE AT THE center of the fountain was much higher off the ground than it looked. It was also slipperier, with far fewer footholds than a person might be led to believe. At first glance, the mottled bronze tangle of knees, hands, hips, and tails—there were a couple of mermaids involved—seemed to promise an easy climbing experience. Halfway up, however, she began to question the motivation and wisdom of her decision, not to mention the depth of the water. What was she doing here anyway? She couldn't remember, but there had to have been a reason. A good reason. There always was. Well, usually. Most of the time.

The girl pulled herself up another twelve inches, and became temporarily distracted by her knee, which appeared to be impaled on a trident. The pain cleared her head for a few seconds and her breath came fast and labored. She just needed to get to the top. That was it. She was climbing so she could get to the top. Simple. If she got to the top, she could really see things—clearly, for once—and then it might turn out that the past week hadn't happened at all. Lloyd was not dead. How could he be dead? Here she was in the middle of a beautiful Italian city climbing a fountain. That was not something you did if your lover had just died.

There, she knew there had been a reason. She would just get to the top of King Triton here and wait until enough time had passed to erase the time that had gone before, and then she would dive and obliterate its vision of Lloyd on his knees, the cord around his neck. It would be a baptism of sorts, a symbol of a life begun again. Water always meant rebirth. Characters submerged, touched death, then reemerged with a new understanding of reality. Who had told her that? Someone. People were always telling her things. Explaining why she was doing what she was doing until she wanted to scream. So why was no one here helping her get off this fucking fountain?

Whisked numb by cocaine, her nose was icy cold even under the warm April sun and seemed to provide a wide-open passage from the sky directly to her brain. For a moment everything seemed sharper, yet somehow more distant, a world in which the cinematography was perfect but the sound guy had dozed off. For a while, the drugs and alcohol had worked in perfect harmony, had carried her down the street—several streets actually—and lifted her up this far. But now the euphoria was shredding like wet tissue paper, leaving her exposed and ridiculous. She was ridiculous. She was ridiculous, and probably bleeding. She needed another bump, another pill, another drink. She needed it all to stop. It was something she had chanted to herself every hour of every day, especially since Lloyd had died and left her alone. *Please make it stop.* Maybe if she got to the top of this god-awful, slippery mess of a fountain everyone would just leave her the hell alone. Maybe when she hit the water she could make things change.

Because there they all were, below her, swarming the fountain, filling the street like a zombie plague—the cameras, all those cameras, the thousand-eyed beast that followed her wherever she went. She smiled down at it because that was what you did with the beast, you smiled at it, stroked it, kept it calm with sounds of affection, with little sugarplum kisses, but really she was scanning the horizon for someone to tell her what to do next.

Because this climb was not working out; her foot was slipping, her hands were frozen, and the festive clarifying force of the cocaine was surrendering to the alcohol, which lifted her up and over as if she were on a Ferris wheel. In just a few minutes she would probably black out, and who knew what would happen then.

That could not have been the plan; blackouts were never part of the plan. Below, people were calling her name, telling her to dive, smiling and laughing and telling her to dive. Was that why she was here? She looked around at all the faces, trying to find Lloyd. Maybe he could tell her; he understood a lot more than she did about how things really worked. But Lloyd was dead, naked and dead, which made no sense at all, and around her she saw only what she always saw—cameras and strange faces calling her name. For a minute she thought she heard a voice she knew. Far away, on the other side of the beast, a woman stood up and said something, something that made her look angry and worried. It was a look the girl knew very well, had seen on many faces all her life. She gave the woman an apologetic glance and did what she always did—she followed direction.

Chapter One

MERCY TALBOT HAD BEEN famous since she was eleven years old. Her mother had certainly made every effort to have it happen sooner. As the story went, Mercy had announced at age four that she wanted to be an actress, had clamored for auditions the way other girls demanded Barbies and kittens. That was back when the Talbots were still the Groplers and Mercy was Tiffany Dawn. The name change came with the move from Michigan to Los Angeles—Angie, Mercy's mother, took the family's new surname from her then-favorite store; "Mercy" came from all the hours Angie spent on her knees, offering prayers for her daughter's success. "Have mercy," she would murmur, lighting candles in front of various saints, "have mercy." It seemed a natural enough transition. It would become one of Angie's favorite stories to tell during interviews; she called it "fate" and never explained why her daughter required mercy in the first place.

Angie was a dance instructor who had spent two years with the Joffrey before being sidelined with a knee injury. Or so she said. In Los Angeles, she enrolled Mercy in one of the hundreds of children's acting classes designed to fan the hopes of parents in exchange for regular payment by cash or credit card. Still, there was something undeniable about

Mercy, even in those ridiculous classes, even at age seven. A directness in her gaze, a natural huskiness in her voice. She had hazel eyes so light they were almost golden and an ability to transform in front of an audience that impressed even the highest rung casting agents. It also scared them to death. At seven, eight, nine, Mercy Talbot was clearly a natural-born actress, capable of playing a pint-sized Blanche DuBois should the need arise. Unfortunately, that was not what anyone was looking for. Cute, perky, smart-ass, or wide-eyed were much more desirable. No one knew what to do with those golden eyes, that sharp, vixenish chin. None of the kid shows would touch her. Mercy could not even get a juice commercial because, her mother was told, her rasping contralto made her sound like she had a cold.

But she never gave up, or if she did, Angie refused to notice. While Don Talbot (née Gropler) sold insurance, then real estate, then opened a specialty coffee franchise, Angie and her daughter never missed an audition, even when it was a cattle call. Good thing, too, as those later profiles always made clear. Because it was while standing in line at an outdoor mall in Woodland Hills, sizzling under a ruthless early May sun, that Mercy Talbot got her big break. Not from the producer who was holding the audition, looking for an unknown to play the best friend in the next American Girl movie, but from his college buddy, an indie director who had tailed along. He was hoping to find a girl to appear in his film—a small, stylish ghost story—and he certainly could not afford to hold an audition like this. Also there was free food. But after five hours of terrible readings and bland chicken curry salad, David Neilsen gave up and made his way toward his car. As he passed the endless line of sweat-glazed, fretful girls and their grim-faced, iced-latte-swilling mothers, he saw Mercy, straight and slim, looking like she had some sort of internal air-conditioning. From the top of her white-blond head to the patient arch of her sandaled foot, here was a girl who could do some serious face time with a ghost.

Sweetly Sleeping became an indie phenomenon, selling out of Sundance for an unheard-of $10 million. It was the number one movie for the entire month of June and picked up countless awards, including three Oscars, one for Mercy as best supporting actress. When she gave her acceptance speech she was twelve years old. Angie stopped shopping the Talbots sales and began wearing Dolce & Gabbana, and Mercy never had to go on a blind audition again. There were small films and blockbusters; an urban-girl drama created just for her ran for three years and won her two Emmys. For a good three, maybe even four years she was perhaps the most beloved star in America. Cameras followed Mercy's every move—birthday parties, trips to Hawaii with her family, the day she got her driver's license. She was clear-eyed and charming in every interview, never turned down a request for an autograph or a picture. The only product she would endorse (outside those associated with her movies) was milk.

Mercy was not afraid of becoming the next burnt-out starlet, she said, because she had a normal family life and an abiding faith in God. (The Talbots were staunch Catholics until Mercy's publicist suggested that Catholic didn't play so well these days among the gay community, who just loved Mercy. So they became staunch Episcopalians.) Mercy smiled for the cameras, she wore clothes that were appropriate for her age, she lived with her parents in South Pasadena so she could go to public school when her schedule allowed. And she was clearly very talented. After years of searching for the next big megastar, Hollywood had found the real deal.

Things began to change when Mercy turned sixteen. Taller now but still slim as a switch, she suddenly seemed too old for children's parts but too young for adult roles. Angie got her breast implants and convinced her to do a provocative shoot for *Vanity Fair*. The half-naked cover kept the media, and middle America, buzzing for weeks; when things finally calmed down, few people noticed that Mercy had quietly had her implants removed. Puberty, kept at bay by Mercy's strenuous work schedule, had finally struck, and now Mercy could rely on her own breasts, and deny that she had ever had implants.

But for better or worse, Angie's ploy had worked. Mercy was officially an ingénue, and although she worked more than ever, the paparazzi, which had once been her friend, turned predatory. The same hormones that granted her curves also gave her thighs, and Mercy's weight became the subject of public conversation. At seventeen, she took up smoking to control her appetite and combat the between-takes boredom; images of her lighting up filled the Internet as everyone from Perez Hilton to the American Lung Association denounced her as a "poor role model." Her parents divorced. When Angie claimed poverty, Mercy paid her father a multimillion-dollar settlement that included a privacy clause. He promptly married one of Mercy's tutors, who just as promptly gave birth to a baby girl. Mercy severed all ties.

She and her mother moved into the family's Malibu beach house, where there were plenty of places for the paparazzi to hide. Soon every cigarette, every embrace, every ill-timed hitch of her skirt was instantly posted everywhere. Magazines paid bartenders for the dregs of Mercy's drinks, then reported that Mercy, still underage, had a fondness for Jack Daniel's. She began hooking up with other young stars, since the attention made it impossible to date, or even befriend, anyone else, and followed the time-worn pattern of breakups and occasional scandal. There was a hateful video on YouTube of one ex deriding her sexual talents. There were rumors of an abortion, of feuds with other young stars. There was a DUI, then another, there was an accident on Wilshire in which her mother was injured—she claimed Mercy had been driving erratically because she was fleeing paparazzi. Mercy lost her Malibu house to a fire, which many of the celebrity websites suggested she started herself, either for the insurance or after passing out with a cigarette. The websites chronicled her on an almost daily basis; her name entered the ranks of Britney, Paris, and Lindsay, though film critics and the mainstream press still liked to point out that her talent put her more on par with Bette, Joan, and Spence.

Despite all the bad press, Mercy never stopped working, because she could still open a movie. Whether because of a true love of the profession or the tyranny of Angie, Mercy Talbot always delivered a performance worth remembering. If anything, the tension between her personal and professional life made her an even bigger box office draw. People came to her movies wondering if this would be the one in which the bad behavior finally caught up with her. They inevitably left in a state of baffled and exhilarated admiration when it was not. There were Golden Globe wins, multiple Oscar nominations, Team Mercy T-shirts. Every film left the public more besotted than before, and every fall in between seemed to take her closer to the brink.

Mercy Talbot is twenty-three years old. She has been famous since she was eleven.

She never stood a chance.

So thought Juliette Greyson as she sat stirring her cappuccino in a small café in Florence. She was trying to decide if she really needed to interrupt a very pleasant afternoon of shopping to save the young woman drunkenly climbing the statue of Neptune and his daughters from the middle of a wide but not terribly deep fountain on the Piazza Cordova. She was not at all certain. As the head of public relations for the Pinnacle Hotel in Los Angeles, Juliette knew more about the inner workings of movie stars than she ever thought she would, or wanted to. She spent her days, and nights, anticipating their needs, analyzing their motives, and minimizing their crises in a way that had made the Pinnacle Hotel *the* Industry hotel in town. At the Pinnacle, no desire was too great, no whim too petty; the staff was there not to judge but to serve. If Juliette had been home, this particular situation would have been a no-brainer—not a single paparazzo had ever so much as taken a snap inside the Pinnacle. If she were at home, she would be summoning whatever security staff was available, pushing her way through the crowds right now, climbing up after Mercy, and carrying her to safety if necessary.

But she was on vacation. A long and lovely and much-deserved vacation from the Pinnacle, from Los Angeles, from her life. Juliette was in Italy to figure out What To Do Next. And that did not involve rescuing troubled young starlets, not even the ones she liked. A few moments ago, when Juliette heard the metallic insectlike clatter of photographers on the move, she thought she must be hallucinating. Surrounded by slender high-shouldered buildings of russet and rose, silver-gray and cream, she had felt utterly unmoored in time, deep in a fortress of fairy-tale beauty cradled by ancient streets, each lined with flower-fringed storefronts and front stoops dappled with sun. Over her shoulder loomed a slice of the rose-colored Duomo, as if to remind the city's citizens of their higher aspirations. There were no limos, no Hummers, no celebrity and his entourage, no television cameras, no twentysomething publicists in pointy shoes. Instead, as if conjured from a dream, a trio of nuns, in full habit and wimples, turned one corner, skimmed along the outskirts of the piazza like large lost seabirds, then disappeared through a stone-arched alley.

But then the buzz had become a roar and the paparazzi had appeared, grubby men in dark jackets and sweat-stained polo shirts, pouring down a small side street like ants racing a flood. So now, instead of contemplating lovely nuns and geranium-laced window ledges, Juliette was watching Mercy Talbot slip and sway twenty feet above a fountain. Mercy. It had to be Mercy. How much attention did this girl need any-way? Plenty. Juliette knew this from firsthand experience. Mercy Talbot and her mother had stayed at the Pinnacle for three months while their Malibu home was being rebuilt after a devastating fire. By the end of the first week, the staff had been ready to personally rent them another Malibu beach house. Hell, they'd *buy* them one if that's what it took.

But Mercy developed an attachment to the Pinnacle, and Juliette had to admit that, when assessed separately from her mother, Mercy was no more, or less, demanding than the typical guest. And there was something about her, a radiance, an incandescence, that made her impossible to resist. Unfortunately, no one ever got Mercy without getting her mother; Angie had recently taken to dyeing her hair platinum so they would be a "matched set."

So where was the dreaded Angie now, when she could actually be of use? Mercy was going to kill herself now if she wasn't careful, or at least break something important. Surely she would climb down, surely someone would arrive to help her climb down. A bodyguard, a publicist, an adoring fan. Lord, Juliette thought. Wasn't she supposed to be in rehab? Juliette was certain that a week before she left L.A. she had heard that Mercy was "doing well" in rehab.

"*Prego, prego,* over here, over here, *bella, bella,* Mercy, Mercy, over here, no, no, *bella, si, si,* in the water, dive, Mercy, dive."

Juliette felt the unpleasant and unfamiliar sensation of panic spin a web within her chest. It was impossible that this young actress was going to be allowed to break her neck in the middle of the day in a Florentine fountain. Juliette scanned the crowd for that platinum head, for the man with the earpiece and the sunglasses. But she could see only paparazzi, the shifting, sweating, yelling, hooting paparazzi. At the table next to Juliette's, two women snapped photos with their cell phones. Mercy's foot slipped. She gripped the top of Neptune's head, leaned forward, and closed her eyes. A hush fell, but it was not a helpful hush, not the pause in which everyone realizes things have gone too far and steps should be taken. Instead it was excited, anticipatory. Looking around her, Juliette realized the crowd expected Mercy to fall. They were, in fact, *waiting* for Mercy to fall.

Furious, Juliette stood up and called out her name. Mercy straightened, took one hand off the water god's crown, then the other. Juliette thought of a painting she had seen once of Saint Joan of Arc, moments before flames were kindled beneath her. Mercy's face held the same glorious tension between surrender and soul-rattling fear. For one brief moment their eyes met, and without thinking, Juliette stepped over the café's low hedge of potted geraniums and into the street. But it was too late.

With a small hopeless shrug, Mercy dove.

Juliette felt as if her heart actually stopped, though whether because of fear and horror or simple admiration, she could not say. It was a flawless dive, a thing of utter and miraculous beauty. Mercy's small light body hit the murky water like a kingfisher, disappeared, and then the girl instantly emerged, pushing the hair out of her eyes and laughing. The cameras went wild.

Grinding her teeth, Juliette pushed her way through the crowd until she was at the edge of the fountain. In just one minute the actress would stand, the white cotton shift she was wearing would be reduced to translucence, and fortunes would be made. Because Mercy was famous for eschewing undergarments of any sort.

"Mercy," Juliette yelled above the Italianate din with all the authority she could muster. The necessary irritation came naturally. "Mercy Talbot. Stop that right now."

The young woman's head turned, her big, wet-lashed, golden eyes blinked once, twice, and she sat down suddenly in the water like a child in a tub. Juliette had no idea if Mercy had recognized her or if she was just responding to the authority in her voice, but frankly, it didn't matter.

"Now get out of that fountain this minute," she snapped.

Startled, Mercy obediently began to rise. "No," Juliette yelped, suddenly seeing what she knew she would see, which was pretty much everything. "Wait, wait, I'll come to you." Slipping off her shoes, she grabbed the only thing she had handy—a tablecloth she had bought that morning—and, over the protests of the men around her, waded into the fountain. Shielding Mercy with her body, she wrapped the young, dripping-wet woman up in ten feet and $300 worth of hand-woven Florentine linen.

"*Andare a casa,*" she snapped at the photographers as they crowded around her, pushing their cameras literally into Mercy's face. "Go home to your mothers and tell them what you have been doing. Shame on you. *Vergognati, vergognati!*"

"I do know you," Mercy said happily, as if they were two friends meeting on the street. "You work at the Pinnacle, right? I thought that was you. I have a photographic memory. Or I do sometimes. Juliette, right? How weird. This is Italy, you know."

Juliette nodded, trying to get her own shoes on, gathering up her parcels, and already greatly regretting her actions.

"Did you see me dive?" Mercy said hopefully, looking around, smiling now as if there were nothing unusual about being steered through a crowd of photographers while wearing a tablecloth and no shoes. "I thought I was going to die. Seriously. I never in a million years thought it would work, though I read in a book about someone doing it, diving into a fountain. I think it was a book. Maybe it was a movie. I hope they got it—the dive, I mean—but probably they just wanted more pictures of my tits."

"Yes," Juliette said. "Undoubtedly. Now just shut up for one second and let's see how we get out of here. Do you have a car?"

"I don't feel so well," Mercy said suddenly, and without further comment she leaned over and vomited on the pavement right in front of Juliette's feet. "I really want to lie down now," she murmured, leaning heavily onto Juliette's shoulder and giving every indication of doing just that.

"Jesus," Juliette said, digging her fingers into the girl's alarmingly thin arm and steering her toward a main street where she could see salvation in the form of many taxis. "Jesus." Hollywood had indeed gone global; ten thousand miles away from L.A., and it was like she had never left.

In the cab, Mercy began to shake uncontrollably and ignore Juliette's questions. She was staying at the Medici, she finally admitted after the cab had driven aimlessly for twenty minutes, but she didn't want to go back there, if she had to go back there she would kill herself. Her mother and the director were still in Rome. They were both looking for her, she supposed, but she had thrown her phone into the Arno and if she had to see either of them right now she would kill herself. "I mean if they don't kill me first," she said, "if they don't literally suck the blood right out of my veins and then sell it on eBay." She didn't remember really what had happened over the past couple of days, or where she had been, and she didn't think it was anyone's business, and if Juliette kept bugging her, she would kill herself. She didn't know what she had taken, thought maybe some meth, probably some Oxy, definitely some coke, and Juliette could smell the alcohol rising through her pores. "Don't make me go back," Mercy said over and over. "I'll die if I have to go back."

She began thumping her head against the window, so Juliette rolled it down. Mercy wouldn't explain what she meant and Juliette could not imagine that she was referring to the Medici, which was a perfectly lovely hotel. Mercy, however, was becoming slightly blue around the lips and genuinely hysterical, so Juliette rolled the window back up and called the hotel, hoping to get some answers and, with luck, find out where the private entrance was. While Juliette was dialing, Mercy began pawing at the front of her dress and miraculously produced a vial of pills, two of which she quickly swallowed. Juliette grabbed the bottle out of her hand and shoved it deep into her purse. Mercy's shaking subsided and she leaned against the window of the cab, one pale thin hand absentmindedly stroking the hair of the driver, who smiled into the rearview mirror as if such things were a natural part of his job.

As it turned out, Juliette knew the assistant general manager of the Medici, a guy named St. John with whom she had worked years ago in L.A. Juliette was amused to note that since she had seen him last, St. John had developed the vaguely snooty accent preferred by many hoteliers and which Juliette's boss, Eamonn Devlin, commonly referred to as Piano Bar Continental. St. John had some answers but was not at all willing to tell her about their private entrance because he did not want Mercy Talbot anywhere near his hotel. She had been there three nights, he said, and they had had to resuscitate her twice, and, as they had told her this morning, they regretted the fact that they would no longer be able to accommodate her—the hotel was now fully booked. "Naturally, she is distraught over the recent tragedy, as are we all," St. John said, "but I am afraid there is nothing we can do. I have taken the liberty of booking her at the Ritz."

"Wait," Juliette said. "What recent tragedy?"

There was a pause of almost audible disbelief.

"Surely you must know: Lloyd Watson overdosed last week," St. John said. "Where on earth have you been? He and Ms. Talbot were shooting a film in Rome and apparently he pulled a Heath Ledger. He's dead."

Juliette was shocked. Lloyd Watson was a young actor with a string of indie hits and film festival awards. Handsome and affable, he had recently had a baby with a former costar. The two did not marry but they seemed friendly enough. There had been rumors of drug abuse, but the birth of his son had sent Watson into rehab, where he had, supposedly, cleaned up his act.

"I didn't know," Juliette said. "I'm on vacation. Jesus, that's terrible. Jesus. What was he? Like twenty-eight?"

"Twenty-seven, and Ms. Talbot seems to have been quite . . . affected."

Filming of their movie, St. John said, was postponed indefinitely while the producers tried to replace Watson, but they were reluctant to let Mercy go, for obvious reasons. This left Mercy trapped in Rome with her mother and nothing much to do. So she had fled to Florence, where she had proceeded to host nightly parties with guests of rapidly declining social and economic status.

"I thought she was in rehab," Juliette said, a bit desperately, glancing at the slight figure now slumped beside her. "When I left L.A. she was in rehab."

"Well, yes," he said. "At Resurrection. But"—St. John's voice dipped to a more gossipy and American intonation—"you know that place. Too many loony stars to keep track of. Apparently she escaped. Or she left to do this film. Either way, it didn't work. I mean really didn't work. Though"—he caught himself so quickly, Juliette assumed a supervisor had walked by—"no doubt Mr. Watson's death was quite a shock. We have been in contact with Mrs. Talbot," he continued, back in professional mode. "She is flying in this afternoon. If you like, you can pick up Miss Talbot's bags at the front desk, or we can send them to the Ritz. Please give her our kind regards and tell her we hope to see her again . . . as soon as her health permits."

He hung up just as the cab pulled in front of the hotel. For a moment Juliette was tempted to just push Mercy out of the cab and dump her on the steps; she was on holiday, for chrissake, she didn't want to have to deal with a junkie starlet on a bender. Beside her in the cab, Mercy had either fallen asleep or passed out. Her hands, which lay palms-up on her lap, were still shaking. God, she was thin, Juliette thought, looking at the childlike wrists, the bony bruised knees. How these women remained so thin without collapsing more often was one of the great mysteries of Hollywood. What was wrong with the movie business, that it consumed so many of its young? "Too much money, too many neuroses, and an overreliance on the service industry," Devlin had once remarked as they waited for paramedics to arrive at the Pinnacle. "Also, I believe it is physically impossible to get through a press junket sober."

But you couldn't blame the entertainment industry for everything. Juliette, who grew up in Connecticut, remembered when her own knees had looked like Mercy's. When she had been Mercy's age, Juliette had known very well what it was like to pass out in a cab, to try to piece together the shards of a lost day or night or week. She knew the endless spine-rattling cycle of fear and thirst and shame and desire. Just thinking about it made her scalp tighten, her heart flop like something torn loose. Although it had been years since she had reached for a bottle or a line, she could feel it all again, that primal, propelling need to feel better, some way, any way, the fierce and dedicated hopelessness of it all.

Sighing, she sent the driver in to collect Mercy's things.

Chapter Two

ALTHOUGH SHE KNEW IT was probably not a good idea, Juliette took Mercy to Cerreta. About an hour from Florence and just north of Siena, Cerreta was a two-hundred-acre farm estate that had been owned by Juliette's family, on her mother's side, for centuries. What had begun as a single tower from which the Delfino family could survey and protect their land was now a true *castello*, complete with a villa and a group of farmhouses, aproned by olive groves, vineyards, and green fields. High on a hill surrounded by woods, it was invisible from any road save the one that led to it. Even then it took five bumpy, oil-pan-thumping minutes through forest, field, and pasture before the bell tower and villa of lovely mottled gold stone appeared, etched against woods and sky like a medieval painting. Over the years, it had moved through the generations until, beset by debt and disrepair, it had come to rest in the hands of Juliette and her cousin Gabriel Delfino.

Gabriel had lived there for almost ten years. Both only children, he and Juliette had been, once upon a time, as close as brother and sister; now they rarely saw each other, and geography was not the only divide. Though Gabriel was stockier and darker than Juliette, who had her father's red hair and fair skin, they were clearly related. When they argued, Gabe's hazel eyes went as green as his cousin's and their faces mirrored each other with stubbornness as much as bone structure. And when they argued, which was often, it was almost always about Cerreta. Over the years, Juliette had suggested they sell off some of the land and turn the castello into a Tuscan resort, a haven for the quietly rich or successful artists. At such times, Gabriel told her that when she had spent more than fifteen minutes of her adult life on the property, he would take her opinion under advisement; until then she could shut the hell up.

It was an effective argument. Juliette didn't like to think much about Cerreta. Even the sound of its name—*Cher*-ta—seemed sad to her, a word that one should sigh rather than say. The hills, the woods, the castello, the drowsy smell of lavender, rosemary, and burning wood, were all too closely tied in her mind with things she'd rather forget. For centuries Cerreta had endured without her; without her it could guard its hillside for a few more years. Meanwhile, her marriage, her divorce, her survival from her divorce, and, of course, the Pinnacle, took priority. So slowly but surely Gabe did exactly what he wanted. Which was to restore the farm and create a self-sustaining Eden, free of serpent and judgmental deity. Over the years, he had sent Juliette endless photos and emails about the gray-water and black-water reclamation systems he had installed, the organic garden he had planted, the regionally significant breeds of pigs and sheep he was single-handedly saving from extinction, the state of the olive harvest.

Receiving them, Juliette could not hit delete fast enough. Slopping pigs and harvesting olives, even under the Tuscan sun, was not what she envisioned for her future, and she could not understand how Gabriel lived among the ghosts. Yet, when her life in Los Angeles seemed battered beyond recognition, when she could not imagine what she was supposed to do next, she had gotten on a plane and come to Cerreta. Found her cousin tanner, balder, healthier than she had ever seen him, running a not-quite-profitable bed-and-breakfast and, with the aid of a small international group of students, something approaching a farm and winery. As a peace offering, she handed him the money she had gotten for the house she had bought with her husband—first ex, now dead—to pay off the back taxes on the land. For almost three weeks, she had slept and read and walked, had tended the vineyard and slopped the pigs, eaten enormous quantities of imperfectly formed but delicious organic produce, brushed up on her Italian, and watched, amused, as her cousin and his interns worked the land and each other with the same casual pleasure.

Now, bumping up the road to the castello, Juliette looked at the still-trembling and occasionally twitching form of Mercy Talbot, the perfect embodiment of everything that Cerreta was not. *Gabriel,* she thought matter-of-factly, *is going to kill me.*

But first he had to help her get Mercy out of the car. Transferring the starlet's semi-inert body from the taxi to the car that Juliette had parked outside Florence had been hard enough, even with the taxi driver's help. Pulling into the courtyard of the castello, Juliette was grateful to see it was empty—the last thing she needed was a bunch of twenty-year-old farmworkers and their digital cameras. She could hear the sounds of laughter and guitar music coming from the other side of the villa, where, she assumed, dinner had been cleared away. As she attempted to drag Mercy's dead weight from the backseat, Gabriel ambled out from the villa, his round glasses glinting in the dying light. When he saw Juliette's arms were full of something, he headed over to help her. When he saw that something was actually a young woman, he headed over faster.

"What happened?" he asked, his face flushed with concern as he slid his arms under Mercy's shoulders and knees. "Is she hurt? Are you hurt? Was there an accident?"

Mercy turned toward the sound of his voice and groaned. Juliette had had to stop three times on the road from Florence and the smell of drunken vomit was undeniable.

"Oh," Gabe said, his voice losing its edge of panic and concern. "Great. Is she one of ours?"

"Not exactly," Juliette started to say, tugging him away from the car, but it was too late. Mercy's head lolled back, and even in the twilight the sharp chin, the fine bones, not to mention the white-blond hair, were unmistakable.

"Jesus Christ," Gabriel said, looking for a moment as if he would drop her where he stood. "What is Mercy fucking Talbot doing in your car? And why did you bring her here? God almighty, Jules, you were only gone for five hours! Where did you find her? George Clooney, I hear, is installed at his villa on Lake Cuomo; will he and your superstar boyfriend Michael O'Connor be joining us, too?"

"Shut up," Juliette said, shoving him now into Casa Padua, one of the houses that was part of the castello. Anger always brought out the Boston in Gabe and his voice bounced off the stone of the courtyard like a brawler in a bar fight. "Everyone will hear you and the next thing you know, you'll be a download on TMZ. And," she added, punching him in the shoulder that did not cradle Mercy's head, "Michael O'Connor is not my boyfriend."

"That's not how you were talking a few nights ago after you got a few shots of limoncello in you." Gabriel kicked at her feet in response to the punch but followed her.

"God, why do I tell you anything? No, upstairs," she said, motioning to the uneven stone steps that led to two of the bedrooms. "I had slept with him once—well, twice—but then things got complicated."

"If you hang out with complicated people," he huffed, unceremoniously dumping Mercy onto the bed, "that will happen."

"Says the king of the olive groves?"

"Says the king of the olive groves," he agreed, nodding. "She looks terrible," he added, surveying Mercy with a clinical gaze. "What's she coming off of? Meth? Coke?" He lifted up her wrist and felt her pulse. "Thready, but she seems to be breathing okay. She's cold, though," he said, feeling her arms, her cheeks. "I'm telling you, if this girl goes belly-up here," he said, straightening Mercy's legs, putting a pillow under her head, and piling blankets on top of her, "I am going to be totally pissed. Someone's going to have to sit up with her," he added, putting an ear to her chest. "And it isn't going to be me."

"She's fine," Juliette said, steering him out of the room, trying not to think of St. John's story of the double resuscitation. "She'll be just fine."

"She better be," Gabe said, following her down the stairs. "But I ask again, what in the hell is she doing here?"

In as few words as she could, Juliette described the afternoon's events. Gabe groaned. "What, you couldn't take her to the Four Seasons? Call her damn mother? Seriously, Jules, I don't want some drug-addled starlet rattling around here, having the DTs, and mugging for the paparazzi. These people never travel alone. They don't understand the concept of alone. This isn't the Pinnacle."

"I know this isn't the Pinnacle," Juliette snapped, her own exhaustion and agitation catching up with her. "If it were the Pinnacle, I could just call Promises or Resurrection and have them send the rehab cab for her. But it isn't. And she, okay, she's famous and a big mess, but she's also just a kid. Who was in a bad situation and needed some help. Last I heard," she said, glaring at her cousin, "looking out for drunks and addicts was your prime directive."

"Primary purpose," Gabriel said, taking a seat on the window frame in the living room. "If you're going to quote the Big Book, at least get it right. Though how you know the lingo is beyond me, since you don't even go to meetings. Because, of course, you still drink. Not that it's any business of mine."

"Recovery is a personal journey," Juliette said. "And I may still drink, but I've been clean two years longer than you, so don't lecture *me*."

Gabriel shoved his hands in his pockets and snorted. Along with Cerreta, she and her cousin had shared, for a time, a New York apartment and a fondness for, then dependence on, cocaine. Gabriel's abuse extended to alcohol, crack, and finally heroin, before he dragged himself half dead to an AA meeting. Over the years their habits, and then the breaking of those habits, had shaped and threatened their friendship. Juliette still drank occasionally because drinking had not been a problem for her, except when paired with drugs. But in the world according to Gabe, addicts were addicts and she was living on borrowed time. Although she was very happy her cousin was sober, Juliette found his hell-and-brimstone devotion to abstinence—from everything, including aspirin—just another example of his lifelong tendency toward zealotry.

"Shit," Gabriel said now, rolling his eyes. "Tell me you did not bring Mercy Talbot here so I could lead her to sobriety. Because I do not have that kind of time or patience."

"I did not, as a matter of fact," Juliette said testily, "and I would appreciate it if you would keep your platitudes to yourself and just leave her be. She's been through every recovery program on the planet. I don't think you in all your shining glory will provide the defining moment.

"Sheesh, Gabe," she went on more gently. "I brought her here because she was having a nervous breakdown in public, because the Medici wouldn't have her back, and because I couldn't think of any better place to take her. She can sleep here, and maybe eat something. If she wants to get loaded, she'll have to walk down three miles of gravel road and hitch another five into town, where no one speaks very much English, and frankly I don't think she has the appropriate footwear. Seriously," Juliette said, putting her arms around him and leaning her forehead against his, "it will only be for a few days. Then her mother can come get her. Or her manager. Or whoever the hell is in charge of her. But she's a nice kid, I think, or she was, underneath it all."

"Underneath all what?" he asked, briefly submitting to her embrace before shaking her off and heaving himself from the sill. With his scruffy beard and what was left of his brown curly hair, Juliette thought he looked like an overeducated, severely pissed-off shepherd. "She didn't have more than three stitches on, and if she weighs ninety-five pounds, most of it's teeth and collarbones. Do what you want," he said airily, waving his hand, "it's your house. But if she croaks during the night, I don't want to know about it. Just drag her over to the quarry and heave the carcass in. And you better go through her luggage, if she has any. I don't want any of that shit here, and I do mean that."

"Okay, okay," said Juliette, palms up. "Don't worry. It'll be fine. She'll be fine."

Gabriel stood in the doorway and shook his head. "Little Juliette. You always think you can fix it. Still. After all these unfixable years." He smiled at her then, fondly and just a little sadly. "Just promise me," he said as he stepped into the fragrant dark, "that this isn't the start of a long line of horrifyingly famous people and their assistants demanding sanctuary and much better towels than I have on hand."

"I promise," Juliette said, laughing at the resigned set of his shoulders as he crossed the silent courtyard under a high, clear crescent moon and a ridiculous number of stars.

Mercy did not die during the night; she didn't even wake up. Though unwilling to sit by her bedside like some Jane Austen character, Juliette slept on the wide window seat across from the bed. The walls of Casa Padua were thick and she didn't want the girl to pull a Jimi Hendrix and choke on her own vomit. But aside from a few moans and the occasional thrashing, it was a fairly quiet night, and when Juliette woke the next morning, Mercy was nowhere to be seen. Following the smell of burning coffee, Juliette found her sitting at the small wooden kitchen table, dipping pieces of bread into a jar of honey and looking out the open window. Clouds moved steadily through a bright blue sky like celestial commuters, their bottoms pressed flat as if they were sliding on glass. On the stove, the espresso maker bubbled and hissed, smoked and boiled over.

"You're supposed to put the water in the bottom," Juliette said, snatching it off the burner. Mercy turned at the sound of her voice and smiled. Radiantly.

"Oh," she said. "It really is you. When I woke up and saw you there, I thought I had dreamt you up. There was a fountain and three nuns, a bunch of cameras, and then you. And you brought me to a castle in the woods. Which also seems real."

"Yes," said Juliette gravely. "And I tucked you into bed, fed you bread and honey, then took all of your drugs and flushed them down the toilet. Just FYI."

Mercy shrugged, ripped off another bit of bread, and dragged it through the honey.

"That's okay," she said. "I didn't really want them."

"There were an awful lot of them not to want," Juliette said. "I didn't even recognize half of them, but then I haven't been in the market for a while."

"I'm not even sure how I got them," Mercy said, taking another tiny bite of bread. "People are always giving me things. And then I had them, so I took them. Because why not, when there's nothing else to do? But here," she said, gesturing toward the window, with its view of the vineyard and the forest and, on a far-off hill, the ruins of an abbey, "it looks like there's lots of things to do." She gave Juliette another wide-eyed smile, but her hand shook as she toyed with her bread and her face looked raw and bruised in the morning light, flesh clinging to bone as if for dear life. A wave of what Juliette assumed was nausea seemed to sweep over her, and she put her hand to her forehead.

"Did you really chuck the Oxy?" she asked, abandoning for a moment the childish singsong. "Because that was a real prescription, you know. I have joint-pain issues."

"This is an Oxy-free zone, I'm afraid," Juliette said. "But help yourself to Advil. And I'd drink some water. Water is very good for the joints."

Mercy sighed. "Oh, well," she said with a tiny smile. "One day at a time. Again."

"Yes, indeed," said Juliette, dumping the contents of the espresso maker. "And the first thing we're going to do is call your mother, or your agent, or whoever you call at a time like this. This isn't a hotel or a rehab center and I'm not a sober buddy or a star-sitter. I'm a private citizen on vacation and I don't need your people or *Us Weekly* or a bunch of producers accusing me of aiding and abetting you going AWOL."

"I'm not AWOL," Mercy said, examining her fingernails. "I'm supposed to be shooting a movie in Rome. Except crazy old Lloyd Watson had to hang himself in search of the perfect orgasm." She flicked Juliette a tiny sliver of a look.

"Hang himself? I thought he overdosed."

Mercy rolled her eyes. "That's what they're saying, because the truth is too embarrassing. And whenever one of us goes down, it's always all about the toxicology report. I mean, he might have overdosed, too. But he definitely hung himself. I should know. I found him."

She paused for a moment and there was that look again, that swift flash of golden eyes, gauging Juliette's reaction. Juliette steeled herself and waited.

"It looked like it was an accident," Mercy continued, "like he was whacking off, you know? Autoeroticism? That's what the police said anyway. But I didn't buy it. We fucked a few times and he was pretty vanilla. You couldn't even touch his hair because he had so many plugs, and he was always worrying about bite marks and *bruising,* for godsake. So I really don't see him putting a noose around his neck. I tried to tell the police that, but my mother was afraid they'd only care that I'd fucked him. Sell it to the tabloids or something. It was pretty awful, actually."

Shaking her head, Mercy returned her attention to her bread and honey.

"I can't imagine," Juliette said, refusing to react at all to this strange welter of information. It was way too early in the morning to cope with such things, and anyway there was a fairly good chance Mercy was lying. Or exaggerating. Or trying to impress her somehow. The whole rant had a scripted feel, as if Mercy had been sitting here, just waiting for Juliette to show up so she could deliver this monologue. Juliette wondered how loaded she still was.

"Really?" Mercy blinked. "But your husband was murdered a few months ago, wasn't he?"

"My ex-husband," Juliette said automatically, refusing to show the surprise she felt. Somehow she felt she had to keep control of this conversation, that if she did not, she would never regain her footing and Mercy would run amok and bring down the very walls of the castello.

"Right, your ex-husband. They found him in the park right before the Oscars, didn't they? With his throat cut."

The way Mercy innocently enunciated the words made Juliette's teeth clench; the coffee began to boil, so she turned the flame off.

"So you know, right? How awful it is, the police asking you things and the people looking at you like you know something . . ."

Images rose up in Juliette's mind, images she had flown thousands of miles to a whole other world to forget. Once again she felt Devlin's arms around her, holding her up as he told her Josh was dead; once again she saw the implacable look on the police detective's face as he asked where she had been that night, once again she watched Michael O'Connor lie and say she had been with him. That night when everything changed and her life became unrecognizable. She had not killed him, but in a way, she was the reason he had died. If he had not left her, he would probably be alive today. And she would not be here.

Mercy mistook Juliette's silence for anger and seemed to realize she had crossed a boundary. Led by her shoulders, her body began to wilt.

"Sorry. It's been a tough week. I guess I went a little off the rails," she said, laying her head down on her arms.

"A little," Juliette said stiffly. She actually did know what Mercy was talking about, and knew also how much worse the gauntlet must have been for the girl. Not only did she have to cope with the shock of the death and all the questions, but then there was a whole other level of scrutiny and cover-up. Juliette remembered all the damage control and spin that surrounded Josh's death, and he had only been a screenwriter. It made her woozy just to think of what insanity had swirled around Lloyd Watson. All she would have to do was click on the Internet to get sucked right into it all once again.

For a minute she wondered how quickly she could get the young woman on a train to Rome, but, glancing at her, she relented. With her head tucked down, Mercy looked like a schoolgirl punished for talking in class; her hair lay on the back of her neck like the tail of a pale heart, making her seem incredibly young and vulnerable.

"Mercy," she said with an exasperated rush of sympathy, "I'm sure whatever happened was pretty terrible. But I don't think running away to Florence and snorting your weight in cocaine is the best option. Why don't you just go home for a while? Take some time to, I don't know, regroup. Preferably without the drugs you say you don't care about. I can't imagine that filming is going to resume anytime soon."

"That's not what Bill Becker says," Mercy said, speaking into the fortress of her arms. "He told me to stay put and he'd have someone cast in a week. Two at the most. He sounded fairly confident. But I didn't like Rome. Everyone seemed to be watching me. Like I had something to do with it. Like I gave him drugs and made him crazy. Which is pretty funny, considering. I was trying to help him, you know? Which is why I think he got in trouble. You really flushed everything?" Mercy asked, raising her face, now flushed and slightly sweaty. "You didn't keep anything? Not even for yourself? I'd totally understand if you did—"

"Wait," Juliette said, ignoring Mercy's words, which still seemed studied in the way she rattled through one digression to another. "Wait, so Bill Becker's company is making this film?"

"Um, yeah," said Mercy, frowning; this was not the response she had expected, but she quickly adjusted accordingly. "Ol' Bounceback Bill. It's an international thriller, sort of like *The Da Vinci Code* only with flashbacks. A detective and an art historian who fall in love just like an artist and a nun did, only there's a murder involved. Or something like that. I haven't read the script all the way through. Why? Do you know Becker? He has a fairly high creep factor—the whole thing with the cigar." She shuddered delicately. "But he seems to know it, and I like that about him."

"Oh, I know him, all right," Juliette said, reaching for the bread and the honeypot, thinking of the last time she had seen Bill Becker, how Bill Becker was another big reason she had fled to Italy. Bill Becker and Michael O'Connor, with his wide-screen charms to which she had been mortifyingly susceptible. "Now we're definitely calling your mother."

"No," Mercy said, closing her eyes and grabbing the arms of the chair as if Juliette were going to drag her away somewhere. After the previous meanderings between self-pity and cheerfulness, Mercy was suddenly quite focused. "I just won't. I can't. Not now. Please, Juliette, seriously, I'm begging you," she said, her voice teetering on the edge of hysteria, her fingernails scoring the inside of her arms. "I'll wind up like Lloyd if I let them near me. I just need a break. Just a tiny little break. So I can figure out what to do. Regroup. Like you said. Here. I can regroup here. I know I can."

"I said I was going to call your mother," Juliette said. "Not the police."

"I wish you *would* call the police," Mercy said. "Like the *American* police. But it's probably too late. I'm sure everything in that room is now up for sale on eBay. But there's no way my mother would allow me to talk to the police now. The woman is about spin. Don't you see?"

Mercy turned her attention once again full force on Juliette. "I just can't deal with her right now. Or those sober buddies she keeps hiring. Or the rehabs she keeps shoving me into. She sucks all the joy and meaning out of everything. I'll die if I have to go back." Mercy pulled herself into a small bony huddle, wrapped her arms around her legs, and rocked. "I'll just die."

"Oh, for godsake," Juliette said, her head pounding against the young woman's relentlessly disjointed commentary. She reached for a pan of milk she had been heating on the stovetop. "Stop saying that. The only thing that will kill you right now is your own stupidity. You're not a minor anymore. Get a new manager, tell your mom to back off. Quit the movie. It's your life. It's your career. You're a grown-up. Act like one."

Mercy shivered. "Your mom must be dead," she said.

Juliette started, scalded her hand on the milk she was pouring.

"I'm sorry," Mercy said, "but she must be, because if she were alive, you would know. You can't fire your *mother*. It doesn't work that way, not even in Hollywood."

"Fine," said Juliette, angry at the burn, which really hurt, and the reason she got it. "Here's an idea: Why not give sobriety a shot? If you want people to stop treating you like a spoiled, strung-out starlet, stop acting like one. If you want people to stop treating you like a drug addict, stop being one."

"What a great idea," Mercy said, just as sarcastically. "Why haven't I thought of that? Where do you think I was for three weeks before I got yanked over to Rome, a week early because, you know, suddenly Lloyd Watson's schedule changed? You think I've been holed up at Resurrection because I like eating off a tray? 'Go to rehab,' everyone said. 'Go to Resurrection, they've helped so many people.' So I went, and you know what?" she said, her face going gray. "It wasn't any different than anywhere else."

Juliette paused, and swallowed a derisive comment—she was not a fan of posh rehab centers, and Resurrection was one of the poshest. It was run by Steve Usher, a former rock star who had surrendered his guitar and party-boy ways during the late nineties in favor of a meditative lifestyle that revolved around a memoir/recovery guide he had nicknamed the Little Book. Usher had long straggly rock-star hair and an unfortunate habit of showing up at even the most formal gatherings wearing loose linen tunics and no shoes. Resurrection was located halfway down a cliff in northern Malibu; it had its own mini-tram and a gift shop. But still, Juliette thought, a person like Mercy couldn't exactly show up at some local AA meeting without causing a furor. Usher, by all accounts, understood the particular perils of getting sober in the limelight quite well. If reports were true, he had actually helped quite a few A-list celebrities, not to mention many more of the still rich but less notorious.

"You can't blame rehab, Mercy," she began a bit more gently. "Really, you can't. It's hard to get sober, the hardest thing you can do."

"Jesus, you sound just like them," Mercy said contemptuously. "It's a terrible place, Resurrection; you have to be out of bed by nine and eat in the dining room with everyone else. And they make you ride horses and call it therapy. I hate horses," she said, her voice rising to a childish singsong. "Let me stay here. Let me stay with you. I'll do whatever you want, I promise. I won't drink or talk to anyone. I'll pick grapes and do the dishes and learn how to make coffee. It's nice here, and I don't take up much room."

"First of all," Juliette said, smearing butter on her burned hand, "you are not going to seriously talk to me like you are five years old. That's just bizarre. And second of all—"

As if on cue, her BlackBerry rang. Juliette's BlackBerry had not rung for weeks. Before she left L.A., she had changed her number and given it to only two people: Eamonn Devlin, the general manager of

the Pinnacle, and Michael O'Connor, who, while the rest of the world
thought he was doing location work, had spent the previous January and
February receiving chemotherapy at the hotel. Both had contributed,
in their own ways, to Juliette's decision to escape to Cerreta. She had
left L.A. to find a little breathing room, and both men had honored
her intentions. Neither had called, or written, or emailed since she had
arrived. Not that she had checked. All that often.

This call, her BlackBerry informed her, was from Dev.

"Hello?" she said, turning her back on Mercy and walking into the
living room. "Hello, Dev?"

"What the hell is going on over there, J.?"

If Juliette had expected her first post-vacation conversation with
Devlin to be tender or emotional or even kindly, that went right out the
window. "There are photos all over the Internet of you fishing Mercy
Talbot out of some Florentine fountain, did you know that? Her mother
just called me, demanding to know where you were, exactly, and what
you had done with her daughter, exactly, and it's two in the morning
here, J. Two in the morning."

"Sorry, Dev," Juliette said, stung by his tone. "Lovely to hear from
you, though, and I certainly hope she didn't interrupt anything. Or anyone."

There was a pause that stretched on until she thought perhaps he had
hung up, and then Devlin laughed. Softly, gently, as if at some private
joke, and for the first time since she had left, Juliette thought about
going home.

"Only beautiful dreams, J. Only beautiful dreams," he said. As the
tension left his voice and her neck, she could imagine him rolling onto
his back in bed, could almost see the dark eyes twinkling beneath his
bedside lamp. "How are you anyway? Drawing strength from risotto and
good red wine? I thought I might get a postcard, but no, the first word I
get is off Defamer. You look as lovely as ever, of course, though I cannot

say the same for our Mercy. I suppose you know about Lloyd Watson. Some people are wondering if it wasn't suicide, that the idea of working with Mercy was just too much for the poor man to bear."

"Oh, come on," Juliette admonished—it was always disturbing to see the speed with which the death of a celebrity became fodder for jokes. Also she could feel Mercy's eyes on her. She stepped out onto the wide front porch and watched a handsome blond intern trundle a wheelbarrow full of kindling across the courtyard. How did Gabe get these amazing-looking young people to do all this work for room and board? The allure of Tuscany was powerful indeed.

"I'm not joking," Devlin said. "Rumor had it they were involved and she was the one who knocked him off the wagon. But what I am most interested in is how you come into it. I thought you were 'getting away from it all.' I hope that didn't mean you were just getting away from me. Among all those young and handsome Italian men."

Juliette felt her scalp get hot, just as if Devlin had caught her admiring how the intern's shoulders flexed beneath his burden. Instead of answering, she recited the previous day's events, not that she had to explain much—all she had to say was Mercy, fountain, and paparazzi and Devlin completely understood. "Well, good for you," he said finally. "She's a handful, but good Lord, she comes by it naturally enough. That mother is a horror. You should have heard her grilling me about your background and what you thought you were doing, what I knew about Lloyd Watson and how the Pinnacle was prepared to 'deal with the situation.' Mostly she wanted to know where you were. Fortunately, I could honestly tell her I did not know or she'd be on your doorstep as we speak."

There was another small pause. Juliette had not told Dev where she was going, at least not exactly, and he had not pressed her. "You know where I am, J. Just give me a shout when you're ready," he had said during their last conversation before she left Los Angeles, the conversation in which he had also told her he loved her, though God only knows what that meant. Juliette had known Devlin for almost twenty years, during which time he had loved a lot of women, a few of whom she had actually met once or twice. But she had never mentioned Cerreta to him, though out of habit more than secrecy; it was not something she discussed with anyone. Now she felt shy about explaining herself. Over the phone, and in this context. Cerreta was family, part of her past, and she never discussed either family or past. Not with anyone. Not even with a man she had known and trusted for so long.

"I told you, I'm in Italy," she said. "Tuscany, if you want to be more precise. But if I had told you more than that, you'd have told me where I should stay and where I should eat and who I should scout out for a job at the Pinnacle, and I just want to rest . . . for a while."

"For a while," repeated Devlin. "I like the sound of that. As long as it isn't too much longer 'a while.' You had a lot of vacation accumulated, J., but at some point corporate will be calling."

She didn't say anything because she had nothing yet to say. She still had not decided if she ever would return to the Pinnacle, or Los Angeles, for that matter. She had sold her house and neglected to buy or rent another; as of this moment, she had no place to live, save Cerreta.

"All right, all right," he said. "I'll leave that for another day. Keep an eye on Mercy, though, if you can bear it. She's a lovely girl, you know. Troubled, but lovely."

"Would you like to speak with her?" Juliette asked sarcastically. "I can put her right on."

"God, no." Devlin laughed. "I've had enough Talbot women whispering in my ear for today. But maybe you can talk some sense into her. She'll wind up dead if she's not careful, and that would be a damn shame. Meanwhile, I told her mother you were an ideal and most discreet companion for anyone in need, so maybe she'll leave the poor girl alone for a few weeks anyway. Although it won't be nearly that long if

Becker has anything to say about it. From what I hear, he'll have a new leading man before all his various permits expire, if he has to convince one at gunpoint. Which we both know he is perfectly capable of doing. So she should be out of your hair in no time. Your long and lovely hair," Devlin said with a stagy sigh; now she could definitely hear him settling back into a pillow and grinning his wide and knowing grin. "I should have asked you for a lock before you went. To wear beside my heart."

Juliette laughed at his melodramatic tone and a sudden tender memory of his bed, where something had once almost happened, but in the end, in the probably quite fortuitous end, did not. "I do miss you. There, I've said it. But that doesn't mean I'm coming back."

"I understand, J., I understand. Well, Tuscany's not such a big place; perhaps I'll come to you. Maybe it's time I got out of the hotel business altogether."

"You should get some rest. You sound delirious. I'll talk to you soon, though, let you know how things are going."

Devlin laughed and murmured a farewell that might have been fond or even suggestive, but Juliette did not quite catch it because Mercy had suddenly appeared just behind her.

"'Dev'? Is that Devlin?" she asked. "Can I talk to him?"

"It was, and no, you can't, because now he's gone," she said, hanging up and drawing Mercy back into the house just as a pair of German tourists, dusty backpacks in place, passed by. "Your mother woke him up in the middle of the night looking for you."

"I would have loved to hear that conversation," Mercy said, throwing herself down on the long sofa that lay in front of the huge stone fireplace. "He's why we stayed in the Pinnacle after the fire, you know. Eamonn Devlin," she said in a tone usually reserved for James Bond. "He's got such a crazy-great reputation—I heard he used to work for the IRA or run guns in South Africa or something sexy like that." She sent Juliette a glance searching for confirmation, then smiled a small secret smile when Juliette refused to even acknowledge the words. "Still, my mother's a match even for Devlin. I bet he told her to let me stay here, though, and I bet he told you to let me stay here, too. He's one of the few people in L.A. who actually likes me. Which is good," she said, pulling a blanket over herself. "Because he's one of the few people in L.A. whose opinion I respect. They say he killed a man," she added, in a surprisingly decent impersonation of John Wayne. She shifted uncomfortably.

"You really flushed the Oxy?" she said. "Because now I think maybe I'm getting my period, and I really do get terrible cramps."

Juliette nodded absently. "I told you, there's plenty of Advil," she murmured, hefting her BlackBerry, wondering what her life would be like if she really never went back to the Pinnacle or saw Devlin again, thinking that she should call him right back and tell him all about Cerreta and her parents and Gabe, or maybe just ask him what he meant, exactly, when he had said "I do love you, J.," and then let her go to Italy without another word.

But it all seemed so big a change in plan, so definitive and dramatic, and she just couldn't bring herself to do it. Besides, what would he say? Nothing that would make anything any clearer. She, Juliette, had to decide what she wanted next, how she felt. About him, about Michael, about what sort of life she wanted, what sort of person she wanted to be. She had spent too many years of her life letting other people, with all their tempting problems and tantalizing needs, shape who she was.

And anyway, it was two o'clock in the morning there; she wouldn't want to wake him up again.

When Juliette turned to tell Mercy she could stay, for a few days, a week at the most, Mercy had fallen asleep.

Chapter Three

LIKE MOST PROFESSIONAL WAIFS, Mercy Talbot had a remarkably high threshold for self-abuse. She slept a lot the first day and when she finally showered and dressed, she looked so thin and drawn that Juliette would not let her leave the house before she ate. "Carbs," Mercy said happily, grating drifts of parmesan onto an alarmingly large portion of linguini. "They're the only real drugs in Hollywood. If I could have bread even once a week, I wouldn't need cocaine."

"I thought I read in a magazine that you ate whatever you wanted," Juliette said, her mouth twitching at the corner.

Mercy rolled her eyes. "Yeah, the rest of the sentence being 'as long as it has no fat, sugar, or taste. Or if I barf it up on command.' This one model always tells the press she eats a candy bar every day. Only it's one of those mini-mini candy bars and that's all she eats all day. Me," she said, shoving another forkful in, "I've always been a savory girl."

Once she had eaten, it was as if her Florentine bender had never taken place. She flung herself out of the house and wanted to see every inch of Cerreta, hear every story of every house on the property, every room in the villa. For all the sophistication of her young life, Juliette realized, Mercy had really never traveled except for work. And then she had always

been in the controlled environment of the set. But when Juliette offered
to take her back to Florence for some nonmedicated sightseeing, Mercy
shook her head. She had never been anywhere more beautiful, she said,
she was never going to leave Cerreta if she could help it.

"This is yours?" she asked over and over again as they walked in the
gardens, the vineyards, then into the woods, following trails to the
ruined abbey, the Etruscan excavation site, the half-finished castle abandoned deep in the forest. "I can't believe this is yours. Why would you
work in a hotel when this is yours? Why would you ever live in Los
Angeles if you could live here? It's a castle, you have your own freaking
castle. Why are you putting up with whiny movie stars like me when
you have your own freaking castle?"

Wandering through the villa or out into the *fattoria,* amid the tangled
flower beds and well-tended vegetable gardens, Juliette had to admit that
there was a peace here, a droning, lavender-infused calm that draped
itself around the doorways, along the sun-warmed stone wall, and hung
like the amber evening light that stretched limitless and unquestioning
over the hills. The world seemed far away, somewhere over the billowing
waves of trees, and not terribly important. She could imagine staying
here, if not forever, then for a long time. And in the still-practical part of
her brain, she could certainly imagine a lush but still authentic sanctuary
that would keep Gabe in all the interns and traditional farm implements
he could ever need—eco-friendly travel was the hottest trend going, and
Gabe was so green you could practically steam him and serve him with
brown rice. Why not use all her hard-won experience at the Pinnacle to
help them both create a sane and lovely life?

Standing just outside what remained of the castle that so impressed
Mercy, Juliette tried to explain why she had stayed away for so long.
Her father had been a college professor, and when she was a child, her
parents and Gabriel's had talked endlessly of leaving Connecticut, with
its bitter winters and the endless demands of university life, and living

in Tuscany year-round. Until Juliette was in high school, most of her summers had been spent here, painting and planting and learning how to mortar stone walls, harvest the olives, and keep the aging generator and water pump from shutting down permanently.

"But then I got older," she said, "and . . ." She paused, almost finished the sentence, then didn't. "I don't know," she said. "I lost interest."

"They died, didn't they?" Mercy said matter-of-factly. "Your parents. That's why you jumped that time I said your mother must be dead. How did they die? Car wreck?"

Juliette's mouth went dry. Mercy was standing on a crumbling staircase that rose along a stone wall that enclosed what must have once been the beginnings of a formal garden. Now it ran wild with chestnut trees and ash, raspberry thickets and sudden riotous spills of orange poppies. With the sun behind her, Mercy's hair shone like a halo, and her eyes were gazing at something over Juliette's shoulder, something far away in the distance. In her hand was a wild iris she had picked, and with her pale and strangely peaceful face, she looked like a medieval saint, wrought of stained glass or marble.

"How did you know that?" Juliette asked harshly. Juliette never spoke of her parents. Ever. "Who told you that?"

For a moment Mercy didn't answer, just stood there as if she were listening to distant music or lost in a far-gone memory. "Well, it's the only thing that makes sense," she said reasonably when she at last turned her attention back to Juliette. "You and Gabe own this now, so your parents must be dead. Only something fairly traumatic would make you lose interest in a place like this, so I figured it must be something tragic. I guess it could have been a plane wreck or a murder/suicide, but car accidents are much more common."

"Their car was hit by a train," Juliette said suddenly, stung by the word "common" and the casual way Mercy had used it, the casual way she was talking about the most guarded part of Juliette's life. "They were coming home from a party and there was a fog and they took a side road that ran over train tracks where there was no crossing and they got hit by a train."

Mercy nodded, as if she had known all along, but she said nothing.

"The radio was on," Juliette continued, uncertain why she was doing so. "The police said the radio was on. And they were driving very fast. There was snow on the ground but it was getting warmer and there was a mist, a thick blue mist . . ." Her voice trailed away, and around her the sun and forest vanished and she saw the road as it had been, narrow and winding through the uneven farmland, the mist rising from the snow, the car's headlights hitting it as if it were a wall, the world reduced to a small muffled frightening space. "Anyway, after that," she continued, already wishing she had not spoken, had made up some other reason for her various life decisions, "I didn't think about this place so much. When Gabe decided to move over here, I was happy, because that meant I didn't have to worry about it for a while."

Mercy nodded again. "Sometimes," she said, "running away works. A lot of people say it doesn't, but they're wrong."

Juliette fought the urge to argue with her; she was not running away. How could she be running away when she was here? The place she had run away from?

"There's supposed to be a Giotto here, you know," she said instead, quickly, drawing Mercy into the dark interior of the ruined castle and away from any further discussion. "According to family legend, he spent summers up at the villa and as a thank-you to the contessa—she was like my twenty-greats great-grandmother—he painted a fresco on the property. 'In the place only God knows.' Or at least that's what she wrote in a letter to her sister. This castle is the Castiglion Che Dio Sol Sa, which means the Castle That Only God Knows, so we always figured it was here somewhere. Gabe and I searched and searched for years, but we never found it. My dad found out later that the castle was not around in Giotto's time."

"Cool," Mercy said, and the conversation moved seamlessly to other, less disturbing things.

Mercy quickly fell in love with Cerreta, from the damp fragrant wine cellar, its ceiling strung with curing meats and drying herbs, to the family library with its six-foot-high shelves of journals and Bibles and books of local history. Juliette led her through the family chapel, its linen altar cloth and silver chalice still in place. Here mass had been said each week for all the inhabitants of Cerreta when it was still an estate worked by dozens of families, and confession was heard once a month in a small, carved-wood confessional. Juliette could remember hiding there as a child, crouched on the worn velvet kneeler, while Gabriel counted to fifty in the courtyard below.

Together the two women climbed the stone steps of the campanile, through the storerooms, some still stocked with grain and firewood, some filled with Gabriel's pottery rejects and a few old watercolors done over the years by Juliette's mother and her aunt. From the top you could see, far in the distance, the fortress walls of Siena and the hill town of Montalcino. In between was a swaying sea of forest, broken only by fields, vineyards, and the crumbled remains of various centuries-old houses and holy buildings.

"We should shoot the movie here," Mercy said as they sat between the battlements, absorbing the impossible shimmering silence of the countryside. "I think the love story part is supposed to take place in the country, and it's even more beautiful here than in *A Room with a View*. We could even add in the bit about your missing Giotto. And," she added practically, "there's plenty of room for the trailers."

"God, don't let Gabriel hear you," Juliette said with a horrified laugh. "That is his worst nightmare. Cortona barely survived that Diane Lane movie—tour buses still block the roads every summer with people on the Tuscan movie tour. Gabriel won't even let me put pictures on the website—*Bon Appetit* did a story on a bed-and-breakfast two towns over and now you can't even walk through the market for the tourists, he says."

"Still, I bet you and Devlin could do wonders with a place like this," Mercy murmured dreamily, watching the swallows. "Make it expensive enough and you won't have to worry about tour buses. And Gabe can keep his organic olive grove—sell the bottles for a hundred bucks a pop." She gave Juliette a look of such keen-eyed mischief that she had to laugh. It was a conversation Juliette and Gabe had had more than once, and fairly recently.

At first, Gabe had kept his distance. He seemed to think Juliette was using Mercy as some sort of focus group—to see how the rich and famous would take to Cerreta. He checked in now and then with Juliette but gave Mercy no more than a stiff nod and a wave, and he certainly never addressed her by name. At his request, Juliette did not bring Mercy to the villa for meals, but if the small population of students and staff recognized her when she sidled over to politely bum a cigarette or hover at the edge of a group gathered around Gabe as he played guitar, they gave no sign. Although many of the interns were American, most of the guests at the villa were German or Australian, hikers more accustomed to hostels than luxury hotels, and they, too, only smiled and nodded on their way to meals or daytime excursions. For them, Gabe and his tours of the property and occasional narrated hikes through the nearby hill towns remained the only star of Cerreta.

"It's so nice how everyone acts so normal around me here," Mercy said after she had chatted with a group of students on their way to repair a wall on the property. "I get so tired of all the fuss and the pictures and the autographs."

"Oh, they probably don't know who you are," Juliette said. "And if they do, they don't care."

Catching sight of Mercy's face, Juliette burst out laughing.

"Don't worry, Mercy," she said. "You won't shrivel up and die. It doesn't mean they don't find you interesting. It's just not everyone worships at the altar of celebrity. There are still some parts of the world where people live in quiet ignorance of your splendor."

"Now I know you're just teasing," Mercy said with a quiet smile, "because that's not possible."

Eventually, when she tired of exploring and watching others work, Mercy announced that she wanted to "do something." So Juliette introduced her to the pigs and the sheep, to the endless weeds in the organic garden, the joys of composting and fence repair, the villa's laundry room, and finally its kitchen. She kept waiting for Mercy to object, to ask to use the phone, or to borrow the car, to complain about the lack of a clothes dryer or about Juliette's refusal to let her try any of the vineyard's wine. "You can drink all you want, you just can't do it and stay here," she said firmly. But Mercy never complained. Occasionally she joked that other stars would only weed gardens if they got their own television show, but for the most part she seemed perfectly happy to shadow Juliette like a little sister, and Juliette was surprised at what an easy companion she was. Once she was not strung out, Mercy rarely spoke of Hollywood or herself; she was far more interested in hearing about Juliette's life or her visions for Cerreta than in discussing Lloyd Watson or the film she was going to make. Sometimes Juliette would catch Mercy watching her with a knowing look, as if she understood more of what Juliette thought than Juliette did herself.

"She's playing you," Gabriel said dismissively. He and Juliette were standing over the huge oak table in the study of the villa, going over the renovation plans for one of the half dozen houses on the property. Ancient maps and dim portraits of Delfinos long dead hung on the walls, three dusty wild boar heads glared down from above the fireplace; one wore a party hat. The stone floor was cool even through Juliette's sandals, but the fire was cheerful and a cluster of lamps threw a cozy circle of light. "She wants to stay and so she's playing the role she thinks will please you. No one ever said she wasn't a very good actress."

"Well, I don't see what fabulous benefits she is reaping from being here. It's not like I can advance her career, or even get her a good seat by the pool."

"You're not her mother," Gabe said, making notes in the margin of the plans. "Which seems to be a fairly valuable asset."

Gabriel officially softened his position on Mercy during the second week, when he watched her spend the better part of a day digging trenches around the roots of the olive trees. The only way to prevent the boars from eating the roots, Gabe had found, was to bury fences around them. It was backbreaking, mind-numbing work, but Mercy kept at it long after Juliette had abandoned her spade for her laptop. At the sound of Gabe's wide-open laugh, Juliette smiled, and looked up from her work. From the small garden behind her house, she could see Mercy's white-blond head shining amid the silver-green of the olive leaves. Her hands were moving gracefully in front of her as she struck a pose and gestured, illustrating whatever story she was telling, while Gabe threw back his head and laughed again. Then their two heads drew close together as they knelt in the dirt and stretched the wire fence between them, lowering it bit by bit into the circular trench. Mercy wiped the sweat off her face with the back of her hand but did not pause. The two worked together until the sun had dipped far below the forest line and the light bled from crimson to a dim hazy peach.

"Gabriel says we should come to dinner tonight at the villa," Mercy announced as she walked in the door and headed toward the shower, stripping off her dusty clothes. "I like him. I like how he talks about you, like he's your brother. I wish I had a brother or sister. I'm glad he didn't kick me out that night."

"He can't kick you out," Juliette said, not looking up but still amused to discover that Mercy had apparently not been completely passed out that first night. "No matter what he says. Ask him at dinner why he can't kick you out. I'm sure he'll be happy to tell you."

"I can't kick you out because Juliette owns the controlling share of Cerreta," Gabriel answered when Mercy dutifully asked the question later, in between bites of stuffed zucchini and white beans.

"That's not what I meant," Juliette protested. "I meant you wouldn't kick her out because you understand what she's going through. I thought you'd give her your primary-purpose talk."

"And the reason Juliette owns the controlling share of Cerreta," he said, ignoring her entirely, "the extra one percent that makes it impossible for me to tell her to take her washed-up movie star friends back to Los Angeles? Because on an October evening about—what, Jules, eleven years ago? twelve?—I was in great need of much cocaine. But I had no money. So I turned to my lovely cousin Juliette, who was still in the cocaine business. Alas, she was not as generous as she is today. And at this point I had nothing, no car, no guitar, no stereo, no watch, nothing but a bottomless need for cocaine. So I had to trade the one thing I had left in the world, my equal footing in our inheritance—one percent for half a gram. I thought it was quite a deal at the time." He took a long drink of water and another bite of zucchini.

"Wow," said Mercy, looking at Juliette. "Only half a gram? That was harsh."

"Very harsh," Juliette said. "Especially since my plan was to sell the whole thing out from under him. But he was a mess. You should have seen him."

"And you were a picture of health? You weighed about seventy-five pounds and you smelled like a nightclub floor."

They were sitting at one end of a long trestle table out in the courtyard of the villa. Around them, the B-and-B guests and what staff were not serving the meal chatted in Italian and German and English, sun-flushed faces moving in and out of the soft circles of light thrown by candles on the tables and hung in nearby trees. The spicy fragrance of jasmine and rosemary, sun-warmed stone and yellow dust, stirred in the dark, retreating when a new platter of food came out sizzling from the kitchen, or a new bottle of wine was opened. Mercy watched Gabriel closely, her face bright and expectant, her whole body canted toward him.

"Fortunately, Juliette sobered up before she was able to sell our birthright," Gabriel said, now too focused on his own story to notice the look on Mercy's face. "A year or two later, I sobered up, too. And over the years, she has offered me my one percent back. But I'd rather leave things the way they are. Because I need to be reminded just how stupid I am when I'm left to my own devices. So stupid I would have traded this place," he said, motioning around him, to the high stone walls and the flowering hedges, the acres that rolled away into the dark, "all of it, for a day's worth of drugs."

Juliette watched him, too. He was a compelling speaker; even though she knew the story and the punch line, it still left her a bit choked up. She remembered that night vividly, how triumphant she had felt, thinking what a junkie Gabe was, how she would never let herself get that bad. She remembered, too, the years that surrounded it, the clubs and the men and the twitching nights, those horrible hours just before dawn when sleep seemed a myth and the darkness threatened to suffocate her. She remembered lying on the fetid couch in her dealer-boyfriend's apartment while he met with his "clients," feeling her heart pound almost out of her chest, her skin crawling as if it would detach itself from her body and slide out the door. Those nights she drank vodka from the bottle like it was medicine, a vain attempt to placate the hyped-up wrath of the cocaine, and wondered if a person could die from shame and the mocking dark of four a.m.

Juliette looked at Mercy and wondered if she had ever felt that sort of fear, and the mortification that inevitably followed day after day after day. But Mercy only had eyes for Gabe.

"This would be a lot to lose," Mercy said now, softly. "And I know why you told that story," she added. "You want me to realize I have a lot to lose, too. And I do. But it's not like what people think. I'm not like what people think. It's not my fault that things happen the way they do. I just want to do my work and have fun. It's everyone else, all the people who want something more. They push and they push and then things just go crazy."

"We've both been through what you're going through, Mercy," Gabe said. "That's all I'm trying to tell you. You're not different. You're not alone."

"But I am," she said earnestly. "I *am* different. I *am* alone. You don't know. You have this, and you have her, and you have what you can do, and all these people. All I have is *me,* and people are fighting over who has the controlling share of *me.*" Her voice was low and clear, and in the candlelight her skin was so pale it seemed transparent. She kept her eyes on Gabriel.

"But you can't let them do that," he said firmly. "You need to take care of yourself, make a commitment to yourself. Even if it means you don't make a movie for a while. Even if it means you ditch Hollywood forever. You can't give what you haven't got."

"That's what they said at Resurrection," Mercy said, shaking her head. "But they didn't mean it. They just meant they wanted me to commit to *them,* to letting *them* have control. The staff was always slipping scripts under my door, or inviting people like Bill Becker to these bogus 'interventions,' just so they can make contacts, or get you attached to their projects. Which is why my mother put me there in the first place. How do you think I finally got on the picture I was doing in Rome? They had these tea dances, which were basically pitch meetings, and half the people there were stoned out of their minds. Lloyd said—"

"You can't expect to find real sobriety in a celebrity recovery spa," Gabriel interrupted. "Those places are worse than useless. They're part of the problem."

"I know," Mercy said excitedly. "They are. That's what Lloyd said, though I don't think it was the same for me as it was for him."

"Some of those places aren't so bad," Juliette said, not liking Gabe's tone, how it gave Mercy an excuse she was only too ready to use. "You get out of them what you take into them."

"Please," Gabe said dismissively. "Those places are just extensions of the Pinnacle. The people who run them treat sobriety like it's just another sort of pampering, something you can order up off the menu. I had a guy last year who wanted to buy Cerreta because he thought it would be the perfect place for a 'spirituality-based resort.' I swear to God, those were his exact words. Yoga and wine-tasting is what I believe he had in mind. Like he'd never heard of Napa." Gabriel drenched another piece of bread in olive oil and shoved it in his mouth.

"You never told me that," Juliette said accusingly.

"What? Like that's something we would seriously consider? Please."

"Yeah, but still, you might have mentioned it. Any other offers you've turned down lately?"

"Oh, come on, Juliette," Mercy said quickly. "You wouldn't ever sell Cerreta. Not really."

"No," said Juliette, still looking sideways at Gabriel, who was nonchalantly digging into his pasta. "Not now, at any rate—we're finally almost on top of the taxes. Now we just need to figure out a way to pay for all the things to be fixed. There are ten lovely houses on the property; if we could rent them out during the spring and the summer you could expand the vineyard and the olive grove and actually sell some wine and oil. Then you could have all those classes and projects you keep talking about."

"We'll get there, we'll get there," Gabriel said, winking at Mercy. "Jules never had much patience, even as a little girl. As soon as she thought of something, she wanted it done. You have to learn to appreciate the process. It's all about the journey; isn't that what all your L.A. gurus tell you?"

"I would if I understood which process exactly was going to pay the bills. If you're going to turn this place into an educational retreat, you need a place for people to stay and food for them to eat and staff—"

"Here we go," Gabriel said, "and we'll end up with three massage tables, a lap pool, Egyptian cotton sheets, and a five-star restaurant."

"What's wrong with a five-star restaurant?" Juliette said, but even she had to laugh; Gabe's grin always was irresistible, even when he was being a jerk, and he seemed so solid and reliable in his blue work shirt, the sleeves rolled up to reveal thick capable arms and wide callused hands. He was like a figure from some WPA mural somewhere, an artistic emodiment of Honest Labor; just looking at him made Juliette feel slight and shallow.

"I could help," Mercy said, looking from one to the other. "I could make an investment. Or a contribution. I really admire what you're trying to do here. There's no reason this couldn't serve as a model for other agricultural reclamation projects, other conservation initiatives. Though I think you're right to keep things small, take things slow. Overreach, and the whole thing could so easily collapse."

Juliette stared at her. One minute she sounded like a little girl complaining about the mean kids at school, the next a spokesperson for Greenpeace. Even the way she held herself was suddenly different, more adult. More self-assured. Gabriel noticed, too; now he was watching her as she had watched him. A frown hovered over his glasses, but Juliette could see a shift in the way he looked at Mercy, as if he were considering her as a grown-up.

"Well, thanks," he said. "But the patronage system didn't work out so well in the long run. I was thinking about setting up a foundation, but it's complicated."

Mercy shrugged and leaned back in her seat. "Well, I could always call Bono. Or George Clooney," she said, with that same mischievous grin Juliette had seen on top of the campanile. "I'm sure they'd love it here. And they could bring all their friends. A string of horrifyingly famous people demanding stacks and stacks of very good towels."

For a moment Gabriel looked startled, then indignant, then a little guilty as he realized Mercy had heard every word he had said on the night she arrived. Watching her handiwork make its way across his face, Mercy laughed, a sound as bright and distinct as her hair, and soon Gabriel was laughing, too. Like the tumblers of a safe, Juliette felt the conversation click into place—Mercy was seducing him. No, not exactly seducing, but doing reconnaissance, figuring out what tact to take—wounded bird, defiant child, saucy benefactor. For a moment, Juliette felt the searing prod of envy—how easy it was, always, for people like Mercy to get what they wanted, which was mostly attention. Even from men like Gabe, who must have been so tantalizing in his initial disinterest.

Still, there was something satisfying about the startled look on her cousin's face; Gabe was always so certain of himself, always so sure he knew the best way of handling anything, always so condescending toward Juliette about Hollywood and the Pinnacle. A few days after she arrived, she had tried to tell him about Michael O'Connor, about how the star had secretly stayed at the Pinnacle during his cancer treatment, about the intimacy that had grown between them during the events surrounding Josh's death, about the essential humanity that made him not just another movie star. And Gabe had reacted with a callousness just short of contempt.

"I don't know why you want to waste your one and only life taking care of terminal narcissists, Jules," he had said with a sigh. "If you get off on making people happy, at least pick people who are capable of happiness."

Watching Gabriel finally notice the wicked elfin beauty of Mercy's famous face, watching as words failed him at last, Juliette couldn't help smiling to herself. A fling with Mercy would probably be good for him; it would certainly be good for Mercy. It didn't get much realer than Gabe, who didn't think twice about discussing the exact nature of black water over breakfast.

Glancing at the girl, however, Juliette was startled by the look on her face. In mid-laugh, she had frozen, her eyes glued on something just over Gabriel's shoulder.

"Mercy?" Gabriel said, and he and Juliette turned together. A woman stood in the doorway who looked, for one moment, like Mercy's twin. Same face, same hair, same slight build, but, Juliette quickly realized, years older—her figure was thicker, her face fuller, the white-blond hair carefully styled. When she caught sight of Mercy, her silhouette shrugged with impatience; as she headed toward the table, her high heels made small quick clucks of disapproval against the flagstone. "Tell me you're not actually eating that," she said, nodding at Mercy's plate of tiramisu. Mercy did not answer. In the time it had taken Angie to walk ten feet, Mercy had simply shut her face down. As if it were a window gone suddenly dark and silent. In the now-sullen features, Juliette could barely recognize the person who had been sitting across from her just a moment ago.

"Hello, Mother," Mercy said, putting a huge forkful of dessert into her mouth. "What the hell are you doing here?"

"Have you completely lost your mind?" Mrs. Talbot said, pulling the plate out of her reach. "You look like you've put on six pounds, and you know what the wardrobe situation is—the gowns for the flashbacks took weeks to finish and they're very fitted. Have you been taking your medication? Your vitamins? Do you even have your inhaler? I cannot believe you are eating dairy. You know how dairy makes you bloat."

"Inhaler?" Juliette asked, startled. "I didn't see an inhaler. Do you have asthma?"

"No," Mercy said, "I do not have asthma."

"Not technically," said Mrs. Talbot, fingering her daughter's hair with obvious disapproval. "She has a preasthmatic condition that we control with steroids and an inhaler. You look awful, sweetie, just puffy and awful," she said, eyeing Mercy as if she were a used car she might buy. "But never mind, I suppose you've been through a lot. And we have three days. We're shooting in Siena now. Apparently the permits ran out in Rome, but Siena will do just as well and Bill says it's cheaper. I've booked us a suite at La Coronet. It's small but it's owned by the same company as the Pinnacle, so I'm sure we can find someone who does pores and colonics. Perhaps Juliette could help us. Hello, Juliette," she said, finally acknowledging the presence of anyone except Mercy. She extended her hand. "Thank you so much for all you've done. Such a strange coincidence you being here, isn't it? But Devlin said you'd take good care of our girl and it looks like you have. Good Lord, Mercy, what have you done to your hands?" She lifted her daughter's right hand, gazing in horror at the calluses and ragged nails. She closed her eyes with a pained expression. "I don't even want to know. Do we owe you anything?" she asked, opening her eyes and returning her attention briefly to Juliette. "No? Well, then, darling, if you're done, we can be on our way before it's too late. The driver almost hit some sort of vaguely prehistoric creature—he said it was a porcupine—on the way up and it was quite upsetting. Is there luggage?" she asked. "Shall we call someone?"

Juliette sat there, frozen. She could not think of one single thing to say. Angie Talbot had barely paused to draw breath and now she stood, her face a Botoxed blank, fairly vibrating with disapproval and anxiety, her desire to leave rolling off her like waves.

"And suddenly it all becomes astonishingly clear," Gabriel murmured.

"I'm not going anywhere," Mercy said flatly, finishing the tiramisu with a fork-swiping flourish, avoiding both her mother's eyes and Gabriel's. "So you might as well just get back in your little rental car and drive away."

Now it was Angie's turn to freeze, though only for a moment.

"Didn't you hear me? Production is back on. You're due on set in three days."

"So I'll be on set in three days. Meanwhile, I'm staying right here."

Angie stared at her daughter. "You can't be serious," she said, her voice losing whatever lightness it had attempted. "Listen, my dear, you've had your little vacation in the country, I get it, that's fine, Lloyd was a lovely young man, but now you have to get back to work. Think of how hard we fought to get you on this project. A costume drama. Finally. It will take you to a whole new level. Meryl won her first Oscar for *The French Lieutenant's Woman*."

Mercy gave no sign of hearing her, so Angie increased the volume. "I cannot believe how selfish you are, Mercy Talbot. You're not the only person who was upset by Lloyd's death, you know. And while you pulled a disappearing act, who do you think had to cope with the reporters? Do you have any idea what I've been through trying to keep your little midday swim out of the mainstream press? I had to get Becker to agree to shoot a fountain scene so we could pass the photos off as location shots, but it's been hell. Even your sober buddy quit after you left Rome; she claims you spiked her orange juice with Ambien. Did you?"

Mercy shrugged. "Now, how on earth would I get Ambien, Mother? You count yours every night."

Angie ignored her. "She'll probably sue, which is just what we need. You're teetering on the brink of being uninsurable, do you know that? *Uninsurable*. I spent hours on the phone with Bill Becker promising that I'd be there every day, that I'd make sure you'd be up and running on time every single day. Steve Usher had to write an affidavit. You can just imagine how much that cost me. If you're not careful, you'll wind up having to pay your own way like Downey."

"He's doing okay," Mercy said defiantly. "He's doing just fine."

"Yes, now, but it took him ten years to get his career back. You're a woman. You don't have ten years."

Mercy crossed her arms, and drew her knees up and settled back into her chair. Her mother sighed. "Fine. I see you are running a bed-and-breakfast here," she said, turning to Juliette. "I'd like a room. With a phone. And," she added with a little shiver, "a bathroom, if that's possible."

With a swift movement, Gabriel rose from his chair. For a moment Juliette was afraid he would bodily eject Angie from the property, and she had to admit she would certainly do whatever it took to help him.

But when he spoke it was with all the Italian charm, and accent, he could muster.

"I am sorry, signora," he said, taking her hand. "My cousin, she is very rude. I am Gabriel Delfino and I run the Villa de Cerreta, where we would be more than happy to accommodate you. If only we were able to. But as you see,"—he swept his hand around, gesturing unironically toward the dozen or so guests—"we are fully booked. Tuscany in springtime, it is very popular. But the Coronet is a fine hotel, and Siena is only twenty minutes away. I would offer you coffee, but"—he glanced at his watch—"they do close the gates to the city at eleven and I am afraid if you do not hurry, the only room I will be able to offer you is with the sheep."

"Good night, Mother," Mercy said. "If you go peacefully," she said, relenting, "I promise I will come to the hotel tomorrow morning. And get a new cell phone. And answer it if you call. All right?"

For a moment Juliette thought Angie would simply explode with anger and frustration and whatever chemical was currently fueling her—she had that tightly strung look of a Pilates and ephedrine addict. But Angie was also apparently shrewd enough to take a graceful exit when she saw one. Heaving a quick, martyrlike sigh, she then swooped in and kissed her daughter's cheek. "Oh, all right, Mercy," she said, making a great effort to smile indulgently. "If that's what you want. Just do try to get some rest. We're weeks behind, so it's long days ahead and we don't want you getting sick or dehydrated." She made a move to caress Mercy's hair, but Mercy jerked away and Angie's hand tugged at the bottom of her linen jacket. "Well, the car's waiting. *Bonne notte,* Juliette, Mr. Delfino. I'm sure we'll see each other again."

"Oh, I certainly hope," Gabe said, putting his hand on his heart. "*Arrivederci.*"

With something between a smile and a grimace, Angie turned on her heel and, spine erect, clacked her way back the way she had come.

"Not bad for a boy from Boston," Juliette murmured.

"Oh, Mercy," Angie said, turning in the doorway as if she had forgotten something. "You'll never guess who Bill got to play Inspector Huddle."

"Who, Mother?" Mercy asked, her face still motionless and seemingly bored. "George Clooney?"

"Even better," the older woman said with a satisfied smile. "Michael O'Connor."

Mercy started packing the moment they got back to Casa Padua.

"What are you doing?" Juliette asked. "I thought you were staying here."

"Did you see the look on his face?" Mercy asked, tears thick in her throat, as she threw one thing after another into a suitcase. "He was horrified. And he's right to be horrified. She's horrifying. I'm horrifying." She sat down on the bed and wept into her hands.

"Good Lord, Mercy," Juliette said, sitting down beside her. "You're totally overreacting. Gabe got rid of your mother, not you. Believe me, if he was horrified by you, he would have sent you off, too."

After a few moments, Mercy nodded, grew calmer. "I know," she said, defeat tugging her voice down half an octave. "I know. The problem is, my mother's right. If I have to be on the set in three days, then I do have to lose six pounds. I do have to stop eating wheat and dairy and unclog my pores. I do have to focus, at least start reading the script."

"Wait, you really haven't read the script yet? I thought you were joking."

Mercy shook her head. "I only read the treatments. My mother says when I think about a part too much, I lose it. So it's better if I don't read it until we're close to shooting. She says my process is that I have no process. Which means," she added bitterly, "I just memorize the words and say them. Half the time I don't even know how they're going to come out. Mother says it's all in my subconscious, that my neurological system does most of the work. She says it's all about my relationship with the camera and has been since I was a baby, practically. Everyone seems to think it's some great gift, except the part that makes me such a freak."

Juliette looked at her doubtfully. It did not seem possible that Mercy Talbot just regurgitated lines, or that her performances emerged whole and intact from some synaptic fluke. On-screen she was a wonder; the critics invariably fell all over themselves praising her ability; her "dedication to craft" was one of the most-cited reasons for the Industry's patience for her other, less professional qualities.

"It's okay, Juliette," Mercy said, seeing her frown and smiling kindly. "You did your best. You talked to me like I was a real person, and I appreciate that. It doesn't happen all that often anymore. And I made my little stand tonight, which is something. Something I've never done before." She looked around the room wistfully, at the high ceilings and white stucco walls, the window seat with its built-in shelf full of books. "This has been a lot of fun, and maybe you can come visit. Hold my hand when things get rough. Michael O'Connor," she said, and shook her head. "Shit. That's just what I needed."

"What?" Juliette said, mortified to realize that just hearing his name made her chest grow warm. "He's good. I mean, he's a good actor."

"Of course he's good," Mercy said, with a small look of disgust. "But I've heard he's hell to work with, like a total control freak, a perfectionist. And he already hates me. I mean, I tried to get a part in that mobster movie he did three years ago and he said, 'No way.' That he wanted a 'grown-up' in the role. A grown-up to play a teenage hooker. Whatever. He's a dick. And now I have to spend the next three weeks kissing him. Yay for me."

"Well . . ." Juliette hedged, trying not to bristle at Mercy's dismissive tone, not to mention the thought of her kissing him. "He's not so bad, I don't think. And that was a while ago, and this was your project first, so he wouldn't have come on board if he didn't want to work with you."

Mercy rolled her eyes. "Yeah, right," she said. "He's been MIA for a year now; I heard he was sick. His last two movies tanked. So I don't think this has anything to do with his suddenly wanting to work with me. God," she said, brightening, "I bet the screenwriter is shitting bricks right now. I mean, O'Connor's like eighty-five years older than Lloyd."

"Oh, come on," Juliette said defensively. "He's not that old. He might not be able to play twenty-eight, but he could play thirty-five. Or at least thirty-nine."

Mercy looked sharply at her and smiled. "Oh," she said, suddenly sounding like a child again. "You like him. Do you *know*-him like him, or just like-him like him?"

Juliette felt her hackles rise at the implication that she was just another fan, but she wasn't about to exchange girlish confidences with Mercy Talbot. The time she had spent with O'Connor, including those few scattered hours of passion, now seemed unreal. Like Mercy, O'Connor lived in an alternate universe of fame and wealth and possibility. While you were there with him, it seemed almost normal, but when you returned to the real world, it took on the qualities of a dream, which made it more tantalizing and yet unreliable. Many things had been said, and pointedly not said, when they had parted—Michael had left L.A. even before she had, to finish his treatment in peace. He had promised to call her as soon as he was done, which by Juliette's calculations should have been a week or so ago. What was he doing, signing on to this already troubled film so soon?

"He's an acquaintance," Juliette said, attempting indifference. "A guest at the hotel."

"Really?" Mercy said, with that keen-eyed look, that viciously infectious laugh. "A 'guest at the hotel.' Michael O'Connor . . . well, well, this will be interesting. A Tuscan reunion." She fell backward onto her pillow. "Maybe you can keep him the fuck off my back."

Juliette spent much of the next week pretending that she was not waiting for O'Connor to call. Mercy called. Seven or eight times a day for

the first few days after she left. While this was not particularly condu-
cive to work or relaxation, Juliette was relieved. She had driven Mercy
into Siena but Mercy would not let her come into the hotel, would not
let her speak with her mother. Watching her disappear into the stately
dim recesses of the Coronet, Juliette remembered the shrill desperate
expectation in Mrs. Talbot's voice, and she felt, if not fear for Mercy,
then certainly trepidation and not a little pity. But Mercy sounded fine.
She was busy, she was irked—by a change in cinematographer, by the
director's judgmental eyes, by her mother's insistence she talk to Steve
Usher every night—but she sounded sane enough.

"Tell Gabriel I said hi," she invariably said as a sign-off. Juliette dutifully told Gabriel hi, each and every time Mercy requested it. "Is she still
sober?" he just as invariably asked. "Because there are plenty of meetings
in Siena, and I'll be happy to take her to one." And Juliette could see that
her cousin's defenses were firmly back in place.

That O'Connor didn't call and didn't call became a heavy chain she
dragged around day after day. She could not imagine that he did not
know she was here; Juliette could not imagine Mercy keeping such
information to herself, although knowing the actress, she had probably
offered suggestive commentary as well. Maybe that's why he didn't call.
Mortification turned her stomach to acid while scenes from their past
filled her head in vivid, breath-shortening detail. Knowing he was less
than a half hour away made it too easy to conjure the feel of his breath
on her neck, of his mouth on hers. How could he just not call?

Disgusted, she threw herself into physical labor in the hopes of
exhausting herself. She had known the dangers of falling for an actor,
had steeled herself for the charming dismissal, the unexplained silence,
the vaguely enthusiastic greeting should they run into each other back in
L.A. But still. He had said he would call when his treatment was done,
when he no longer needed her help. He had to know she was a half hour
away . . . how big a sonofabitch was he anyway?

"Will you stop?" Gabriel said to her one evening when she was mechanically forking hay into the sheep stalls, ignoring the burning in her shoulders, the blisters on her hands. "Enough," he said, wresting the pitchfork away from her. "If you want to see him so badly, just go down there. I'm sure he's staying at the Coronet too. There's no other really posh hotel around."

"I don't want to see him," Juliette said petulantly. "I flew halfway around the world so I wouldn't have to see him. And anyway, I'm sure he is very busy. He has a movie to film, you know. That he just signed up for. And he hasn't been well. And if he wants to see me, he can come here."

Gabriel rolled his eyes and thrust the pitchfork into the hay with such force it startled a nearby ewe. "See, that's exactly what I'm afraid of," he said. "That he'll just show up here one day, with his entourage and his camera crew, just show up and ruin everything."

Michael O'Connor did not show up at Cerreta, and when he did finally call it was certainly not for the reason she had expected.

"Juliette, my darling," he said without greeting or preamble, as if they had just spoken the day before. "I had grandiose plans that involved a white horse and an enormous number of roses, but everyone around me is either an idiot or nineteen years old and a non-English speaker. And now I'm afraid you will have to come to me. Because Mercy Talbot overdosed last night."

Chapter Four

To WITHSTAND THE ONSLAUGHT of brigands and armies, the city of Siena was built on a series of hills. At the height of its power, it was a bitter and defiant rival to nearby Florence, bristling with walls and the bell towers that each important Sienese family built to maintain its status and power. Now, as she passed the endless spring-green rows of sunflowers just rising, the fields edged in cherry blossoms, Juliette wondered how the ancient city would fare against more modern invaders. It remained a medieval fortress-town. Winding narrow streets climbed and crested the hills, leading inevitably to wide plazas that vanished the moment you turned a corner; on the hour bells rang out from the neighborhoods' many churches, invisible amid the complicated pattern of the streets. Even with the Coronet and a few equally high-end hotels and restaurants, she couldn't imagine how it would accommodate the demands of Hollywood. For one thing, there was almost no parking. And in Juliette's experience, filmmakers required a lot of parking. No one but residents could drive within Siena's walls, and even then there were restrictions. As with other major hill towns in the area, a large parking lot had recently been built at the bottom of the hill outside Porta Caterina. From it, tourists rose to the city by a series of escala-

tors; Juliette could not see all the grips and gaffers and electricians hauling the literally tons of equipment they needed up a bunch of escalators.

She herself refused to ride an escalator into Siena on principle.
She had been coming here since she was a child and couldn't treat the
ancient city of artists and saints as if it were some medieval-themed
mall. Instead she crammed her rented Mini Cooper into a space along
the side of the road leading to the Porta San Marco, which, with a small
lot and scenic overlook, served as a drop-off point for tour buses. And
indeed, there stood a large bus, huffing and hooting like a sounding
whale, disgorging an American tour group just as Juliette entered the
city. The visitors adjusted their matching red fanny packs and gathered
around an overly made-up woman bearing a yellow banner. Juliette
murmured a silent prayer to the Madonna, who, crowned with gold
stars, smiled wistfully down from the corner of a nearby building. As a
hotelier, Juliette had nothing against tourists; she even understood the
economic and emotional need to travel in packs. She just wished, fer-
vently, for a world without fanny packs.

After entering the city, she made two quick turns onto a series of
ever-narrowing streets that led her silently past several more watchful Virgins as well as a string of fruit markets, cafés, patisseries, wine
bars, and churches, until finally she saw the small maroon awning of the
hotel. From the doorway she could hear the hum of tourists as they made
their multilingual way down the Via di Città, the curve of Siena's central
thoroughfare, in search of gelato and leather goods, pottery and shots of
the cathedral and campanile. For a moment she remembered coming to
Siena on a long-ago winter's day during a year when her parents decided
to spend Christmas at Cerreta. The streets had been filled then only with
shadows and moonlight and a few Sienese shopping for the holiday. For a
moment Juliette could taste marzipan and feel the warmth of her father's
hand. She could not remember anything else about that Christmas, but
there had been that one lovely evening anyway.

Closing her eyes against the memory, she stepped into the hotel. The past slid away into the air-conditioned, velvet-and-wood-paneled hush of the present, and she was ashamed to feel her heart babble quickly in her chest. Her conversation with Michael the previous night had been limited and odd. He seemed concerned about Mercy, but agitated as well. He spoke as if she, Juliette, were somehow responsible for not only Mercy's well-being but the future of this film. Just as she began to set him straight about this, he had sighed. "You would think, after all these years, I could handle a difficult costar and a psychotic director all by my lonesome, but it seems that I cannot. Oh, Juliette," he said, filling her name with the clipped consonants that fell on her ear like small kisses, "just please come."

Now, squaring her shoulders and clenching her jaw to prevent any shy or joyful smile from betraying her, she stepped through the door and scanned the small lobby. But Michael was not there.

At the front desk, she was told that Mr. O'Connor had left a message that she was to meet him on the Campo, which was currently being used as a movie set. For a moment she was distracted from her mission, even from the thought of seeing Michael again; the Campo was Siena's main plaza, the sight of the Palio, the city's famous biannual horse race, the heart of its tourist draw. On any given day, the many overpriced cafés and bistros that ringed it were full of non-Italian speakers; the more hearty, and less wealthy, tourists sat and lay on its cobbled stones, watching the clouds and the pigeons, the bell tower and the gorgeous border of palazzos stretching against the sky. "The Campo," she said. "The entire Campo has been shut down?"

"*Si*," said Silvio, the chief concierge, a tall thin man with a dark head of Pre-Raphaelite hair. "For two days."

"Unbelievable," Juliette said.

"They did the same for that James Bond movie," he countered with a shrug. "Our wise officials think the economy has kept Americans away, this will bring them back. Like *The Da Vinci Code* did for Paris."

"Unbelievable," Juliette said again. Bill Becker really could do anything. Except, it would seem, control Mercy Talbot. For a moment, Juliette felt a thrill of pride in that—at least someone refused to issue the proper permits. "Would you ring Mercy Talbot's room?" she asked. "Tell her Juliette is here."

"Yes, Signora Greyson," the concierge said. "We know who you are. But Signora Talbot is also on the set. I will draw you a map."

"On set?" Juliette was shocked. "I thought she . . . I mean I heard she was . . . ill," she finished lamely, realizing she had been gone from the Pinnacle just long enough to forget momentarily its cardinal rule: Never offer information about anyone.

"If you call being brought back from the dead 'ill,'" said one concierge in Italian, her voice low, her eyebrow raised. "If you call being a drug addict 'ill.'"

"Many people do," Juliette answered, also in Italian. "And surely you are not referring to any guest of this hotel . . ." she glanced at the woman's small gold name tag. "Isabella. Because that would not be . . . policy."

The young woman flushed and hurried away; Silvio, deciding the best way to avoid conflict was to ignore it, began giving Juliette directions as if nothing had happened. "I know how to find the Campo," she said, cutting him off. "Is there someone in particular I need to find to be allowed past security?"

A few minutes later, she was introducing herself to a man who, after consulting with his walkie-talkie, graciously moved aside a wooden barrier and pointed down one of the side streets to a café. Even across the gentle slant of the sloping plaza, her eyes dazzled for a moment by the sun and the palazzos that rose in gracious angles of russet and cream and golden ocher above the awnings, she could see the familiar silhouette of Michael O'Connor's head and shoulders as he talked and laughed with a woman in an apron who was applying his makeup. Juliette approached slowly, suddenly reluctant and conscious of each careful step, of the gentle swing of her hair down her back, the tug of her jeans on her hips, the shallow breath in her throat. He caught sight of her and smiled, that wide, mischievous, irresistible smile that had carried him through four marriages and three decades of stardom. Something heavy lifted from her shoulders and all thoughts of Mercy Talbot vanished.

But not for long.

"Juliette," Michael exclaimed, not rising, "Look at you. I would crush you to my manly bosom except it has taken six very disagreeable makeup artists three hours to render me presentable as 'a brilliant but troubled detective in his late thirties.'" The two young women who hovered around him laughed softly and murmured obliging disagreement. "Personally, I don't see what's wrong with early or even mid-forties, but when you have a leading lady who can so easily appear to be twelve, concessions must be made. Concessions being highly preferable to confessions, which I tend to avoid. Just ask Juliette," he said, taking one of her hands. "A woman who rarely concedes anything and has nothing to confess. You look wonderful, my Juliette, even in this fine but unforgiving light, so far from your natural habitat. But then, you always look wonderful."

He paused, his head tilted to one side, and offered her the full effect of those endlessly blue eyes, wide under their hitched-high brows. He did look years younger than when she had seen him last, though whether this was the makeup or the fact that he was not currently wracked with chemo, she couldn't say. He exuded health and the faint tang of lemons and was undeniably, almost regrettably, handsome, with his short dark hair perfectly mussed, his shoulders thrown back and broad. But to save her soul, Juliette could only smile a little and shake her head. *Is this really how he is going to do it?* she thought with surprising disappointment. After everything that had happened, and almost happened, he was going to greet her in High Movie Star-speak and expect her to, what? Giggle like the stylists and fall onto his lap?

"Mr. O'Connor," she said gravely, answering with the formality of her own profession. "You're looking well. It's a pleasure to see you, as always. I understand there is a situation you would like to discuss with me. I can give you"—she looked at her watch—"twenty minutes. Are you comfortable here, or shall we walk?"

His laughter rang down the street, bouncing along the buildings, their windows tall and wide above flower boxes and balconies like the surprised eyes of watchful doyennes. "How is Devlin surviving without you? I can hear the Pinnacle collapsing from here. But by all means, let's walk," he said, springing to his feet. "Can I offer you anything from the craft services? A Fiji Water? A granola bar? Mr. Becker has provided us with our own version of Americana right here in Siena. I seem to remember you liking cashews."

"I'm allergic to cashews," she lied.

"You are not," he said, steering her into a small side street, and gripping her on either shoulder. "Juliette," he said, his voice losing some of its professional pitch. "Don't be angry. Why are you angry? Aren't you a little happy to see me? Don't lie, because I've been lied to by the best and I'll know."

Juliette had heard that line before; hearing it again made her feel both tender and impatient. She chose impatient. "Where's Mercy?" she said abruptly. All the anticipation, the giddy thought of seeing Michael again, all those days spent imagining their reunion, then denying the images, had vanished, leaving behind a solid headache and the desire to be done with this errand. What had happened all those months ago had been a fling. This was real life. "Last night you made it seem like life and death, but here she is, on set, working, so I'm not sure why we're here. What is it you expect me to do anyway? I don't quite understand. I'm not a starlet whisperer."

"Talk to her," Michael said seriously, ignoring the sarcasm and everything behind it. "I have never seen a set wound up this tight and she's just a bender away from bringing it all down. I don't know what exactly happened with Lloyd. Everyone's talking about it but no one's saying anything. But I do know the director, Ben Golonski—"

"I know who the director is," Juliette interrupted, trying not to snap.

"Okay, then you know he is a spoiled brat and at this point he'd strangle Mercy in her sleep if he thought he could get away with it. Not that she ever sleeps; she's up all night with the crew, which Ben is ready to fire, only it would take too long to replace them here. All of which would be fine, none of my affair as the geezer costar, except she's late, she's unprepared, she and her mother are at each other night and day . . ." He made a motion to pass his hand across his forehead, then stopped himself, unwilling to smear his makeup. "We've got to finish ten pages by midnight tonight because the city fathers are throwing us out then. Ten pages! In two time periods! It's logistically impossible to begin with, and I . . . well, I feel like Clark Gable on *The Misfits*. And that movie *killed* him."

He paused and, glancing at Juliette, his face softened. "Look, I realize I'm an asshole for asking you to do this, I know this is not how or why you wanted to hear from me. If you ever wanted to hear from me." He looked at her expectantly, but she was not about to answer this bit of verbal fishing, so he went on. "I'd certainly rather not be asking you for help, once again. But from the way she talks about you, Mercy seems to admire the hell out of you. Which"—his voice dropped to more intimate levels—"means we have at least one thing in common."

Juliette made a soft mocking noise of disbelief, and O'Connor caught her by her shoulders. "Come on, Juliette. Why do you think I took this crazy movie? About a thousand people sent me the footage of you hauling her out of that fountain; three seconds later, Becker's got my agent on the phone making plane reservations. Tell me that's not the universe sending clear direction. Tell me"—he put his hand on his heart and threw back his head—"that's not fate."

Against her will, Juliette smiled. Here was the O'Connor she recognized. He was so close she could feel the warmth of his body, hear the quiet sound of his breathing, and—as if her very muscles remembered the rise and fall of his chest beneath her hands, the beat of his heart against her cheek—she felt the muscles in her jaw release, her shoulders relax.

"Mr. O'Connor. You always did say the nicest things."

But before the moment could go anywhere interesting, a young man appeared, yelping, "Found him," into a cell phone. "Mr. O'Connor," he said with a gulp, "Mr. Golonski needs you on set? Like five minutes ago? Someone was supposed to come get you? I'm so sorry, but we have to go"—he took a deep breath and swallowed the upswing—"like now."

"Juliette," Michael said in appeal, holding up his palms.

She shook her head ruefully but smiled. "Where is she?"

"Anthony, take Ms. Greyson to Ms. Talbot's trailer," Michael said. "I can find my way to the set."

All the trailers were parked in and around a small paved and sheltered marketplace near the easternmost entrance to the city. Walking down the steeply inclined street that led to it, Juliette marveled at how strange it was to see the long white Star Waggons snuggled against each other like larvae, with the high peaked roofs and street-corner Madonnas gazing serenely over it all. A beige golf cart zipped by, a woman in what seemed to be fourteenth century costume clinging to its open backseat while a young man with a violet mullet drove with one hand, texting with the other. Juliette idly wondered where they had found such a thing. Italians were not big on golf. Becker must have had them shipped over. How much did something like that cost? she wondered.

Anthony's discreet knock brought Angie to the door. "Ms. Greyson is here to see Ms. Talbot?"

A look of angry displeasure crossed Angie's face. "Mercy is resting," she said, pointedly, not looking over at Juliette. "Tell her we'll call her. When it's convenient."

Before Juliette could speak, or turn around and leave in disgust, she heard her name called from within the trailer. Angie's mouth pressed itself small and pale, and with a sound of impatience she withdrew.

"Juliette?" In a moment Mercy appeared at the door, all but leaped down the steps, and threw herself into Juliette's arms. "I'm so glad you're here. Why didn't you call first? I had no idea you were coming."

"I came," Juliette said, disentangling herself from the young woman who smelled of fresh cigarette smoke and old tequila, gently pushing Mercy back so she could look at her, "because Michael said you were . . . sick yesterday."

Mercy rolled her eyes. Her hair, crowned with extensions, was a mass of flyaway ringlets. She, too, was in makeup, much of which was now smeared on Juliette's neck and blouse, but there were blue circles under her eyes and she looked as if she had lost ten pounds since Juliette had last seen her. Mercy wore only a small cotton shift. Beside her, Anthony dropped his eyes and melted away.

"Oh, that," she said, tugging Juliette up and into the trailer and shutting the door firmly behind her. "I don't know why everyone is making such a big deal about it, I'm fine."

"He said you overdosed, Mercy," Juliette said. "People tend to make a big deal about things like that. Frankly, I don't know why you're even working today. I don't know *how* you're even working today."

Mercy threw herself down on a red velvet sofa. Angie was nowhere to be seen, and the inside of her trailer looked like a Moroccan prince's tent two minutes after the harem departed. Dresses of lace and angelic linen were strewn on velvet sofas and silken chairs that waited provocatively beneath filmy curtains and hangings of jewel-toned beads and golden rope. "Jesus," Juliette said, whisking aside a bit of purple tulle, "do you charge by the hour?"

"I know, isn't it great?" Mercy said. "I'm playing a modern woman who may or may not be the reincarnation of a painter's virginal muse, so I thought I should get in touch with my inner call girl. And it wasn't an overdose, I don't know why everyone keeps saying that." On a table beside her right shoulder, an army of bottles were amassed, some prescription, some brown plastic with the label of a famous L.A. health store on them. Absentmindedly reaching for one, Mercy shook loose an alarmingly large yellow capsule and swallowed it with a swig of green tea. The action did not cause even the smallest pause in her monologue. "I just had a little trouble waking up, that's all. I took a few Ambien last night"—she poured herself three more gelitan caplets, green this time, and swallowed them—"and okay, probably not the best idea to do shots with the best boy, but it's not like Ambien are real drugs, and it always pays to make friends with the crew. Especially when the director despises you. So I was asleep—okay, majorly, deeply asleep—but next thing I know, some guy is pumping me full of adrenaline." She finished her green tea and reached for a can of Red Bull. "Today everyone's looking at me like they're afraid I'm going to kick it like Lloyd, but you want to know what I think? I think that bastard Bill Becker told them to do it so I could finish the seven hundred scenes I have to do today, because shooting me up with adrenaline costs less than paying for the permits so we could go into tomorrow. Do you want a Diet Coke or what?"

Juliette surveyed the young woman dispassionately. In the days she had spent with Mercy, she had never seen her this agitated, never heard her talk so manically.

"What are you on right now, Mercy?" she said, glancing at the table. "What is all that crap and what did you just swallow, while I was standing right here looking at you?"

"Nothing," said Angie, appearing from the depths of what Juliette assumed was a bedroom. "Oil of evening primrose," she added, picking up one of the bottles. "For premenstrual bloating. Some flaxseed oil and Omega-3. Mercy has to take care of her body and we follow a strict, doctor-approved herbal regimen. Not that it's any of your business . . ."

"It is very much my business when the star of this movie calls me because he's afraid your daughter is going to kill herself." Juliette had not planned to take this tone, but Angie always did bring out the worst in her. "You would be amazed at the many, many other things I would rather be doing right now."

"First of all, Michael O'Connor is not the star of this movie," snapped Angie. "And you shouldn't believe everything you hear. I would think with your experience you would know that. There is a conspiracy on this set to paint Mercy as some sort of drugged-out troublemaker, and has been from the very beginning. Ben Golonski has been nursing a grudge against Mercy since she wouldn't star in that horrible movie he did about Jamestown. And while I've certainly always been a fan, Mr. O'Connor seems bound and determined to convince everyone that he stepped in at the eleventh hour like some shining knight to save this film. As if we don't all know where he's been for the last few months and why, and that if he doesn't get back in the game with a hit, he'll be doing lame-o comedies like De Niro."

"Golonski, too," said Mercy idly, stroking a small silky terrier that had emerged, yawning, from beneath the sofa. "Becker got him for cheap because no one else will touch him—his last three films have bombed and that book he wrote didn't help matters."

Right, Juliette thought, suddenly remembering the details of Golonski's fall from grace. A few years ago, he had gotten some absurd amount of money for his autobiography—he was all of forty-three—in which he managed to insult virtually every studio head in Hollywood. At the time he was the Industry darling, riding a megahit wave that left him unassailable; even those people he had trashed competed for his pictures. Until, after demanding total creative freedom, his movies began to tank. One after the other. Becker always did know how to leverage a man when he was down.

"So here we all are," Mercy said, kissing the dog between its ears and lapsing into a babyish singsong, "a bunch of screwups trying to prove we can still make a movie without dropping dead in the process. Isn't that right, Cupcake?" she cooed, fondling the dog's ears. "Do you think we can do it without killing each other? Do you? Do you? Did you meet Cupcake, Juliette?" she asked, tearing herself away from kissing the animal long enough to display him proudly for Juliette. "I got him at Resurrection. They encourage pets as therapy, which is about the only constructive thing they do at that place."

"Mercy!" said Angie. "How can you say that when Steve Usher has been so supportive of you, so protective? He called only last night to see how you were doing."

"Shut up, Mother," Mercy said. "Just because you slept with him doesn't mean I have to embrace him and his ridiculous Little Book."

"Watch your mouth," Angie said. "You don't know what you're talking about."

"What did you tell Mr. Usher?" Juliette said, to interrupt what was clearly a well-worn mother/daughter exchange. "Or was this before she had to be injected back into consciousness?"

"You have absolutely no right to speak to me or Mercy that way," Angie said hotly. "Who the hell are you anyway? You work in a *hotel*. Where, I am pleased to inform you, we will certainly never be staying again. And if I see one word of this alleged overdose appear on any website or in any magazine, I will personally sue you and your boss for defamation."

"Mother, for godsake," Mercy drawled in a bored voice. "No one even listens to you when you talk like that. This isn't a road show of *Gypsy*." She raised her eyes from behind the dog's white fur, looked directly at Juliette for perhaps the first time since she had arrived. A word flashed into Juliette's mind just before Mercy laughed and shook Cupcake off her lap.

"Juliette," she said. "I'm fine. You can see I'm fine. Except that— spoiler alert—my mother is a professional bitch and things are a little tense because Bill Becker thinks we should be shooting twenty-seven pages a day to make up for the money he lost when Lloyd . . . wound up dead. And I should be in costume, because in about three seconds someone will knock on that door, demanding that I be on set. Again."

"Thank you for coming," said Angie, pouncing on the moment and steering Juliette to the door, but not before Juliette could see how slowly Mercy walked as she started for the bedroom, see her hands shake as she reached for an inhaler. "And do tell Michael we appreciate his concern, especially considering his own, well, his own set of health issues. It was such a relief to see that his hair had grown back in," she added maliciously, opening the trailer door and all but propelling Juliette into the sunshine.

"Well," Juliette said, adopting a measured tone that she did not feel, "I certainly am glad everything is okay. But Michael said I could hang around a bit and watch the filming," she added disingenuously, raising her voice so Mercy could hear, "so I think I will. See you on the set." She flashed a wide smile into Angie's anger-frozen face.

As maddening as the whole thing was, Juliette had no intention of leaving. Because the word that had run through her mind when Mercy had raised those golden eyes to hers was "beseeching."

Chapter Five

MAKING HER WAY BACK to the Campo, Juliette wondered if any movie ever got made without one form of insanity or another occurring off-camera. Location work was particularly fraught. Away from family, familiarity, and what little media-enforced moral order there was in Hollywood, the cast and crew lived in their own little biosphere for weeks, sometimes months, simmering in a creative rue of lust and jealousy, artistry and boredom. Long hours under hot lights in a strange place, and boundaries melted away, revealing the more basic instincts of human nature. Love affairs bloomed like orchids in a hothouse and rivalries easily exploded. Over it all dripped money, like a poisonous glaze, highlighting the food chain—who had the biggest trailer, who went into makeup last, who had a private chef on set—and intensifying the pressure to get it right and get it done as quickly as possible. Minutes were worth millions. On a film set, everything and everyone was rented by the hour; no matter how complicated the contracts might be, it had the same basic economics of a back-alley tryst, which could explain why it so often turned into just that.

What happens on location, stays on location, or so the Indusry mantra went. Except, of course, when it didn't, as Juliette knew only too well. She had lost her husband to location. Six weeks into the filming of his first successful script, Josh, the man to whom she had been married for ten years, the man whose writing career she had supported emotionally and financially, had left her for the kohl-eyed leading lady, with her Oxford accent and Pre-Raphaelite hair. Juliette's heart broke so fast and hard it was weeks before she could breathe normally, months before she could sleep or smile or feel anything except the raw and bloody pulse of pain and disbelief. A year later, Josh was dead, murdered for reasons Juliette still didn't understand.

"Don't go loving him again just because he's dead," Devlin had said more than once at the time. "Dead or alive, he's still a right bastard."

Thinking of Devlin, Juliette smiled. He had been right, of course, about both things. Josh's death had wiped away the protective layer of anger she had slowly acquired after he left. How could you be angry at a man murdered in his thirties? Even if he had cheated on you. In the weeks after his death, Juliette couldn't help but dwell on the possibilities—if he hadn't died, perhaps Josh would have realized the stupidy of his choice, of his actions, come back to her on his knees. Perhaps she could have found a way to forgive him and they could have resumed their lives as if nothing had happened . . .

"Right bastard," Devlin would say in passing if he caught her with a certain look on her face, and even in the midst of catastrophe it made her laugh.

"Right bastard," Juliette repeated to herself now, though she had a suspicion she was not speaking only about Josh.

Guided by a growing cavalry of golf carts, rivers of black wire, and the sound of shouting, she considered the forces at work in Siena. Though she did not buy for one minute the idea that O'Connor had come onto this film to be close to her, neither did she believe he had had to beg, as Angie had suggested. Even with a couple of nonstarters and a few months' absence, he was a multiple Oscar winner and still one of the most bankable stars around. Although Juliette knew his battle with cancer was not exactly a secret among the inner circle of Hollywood, where nothing was a secret, it had not leaked into the entertainment press or even the tabloids. But she certainly did not put it past him to position himself as a savior, just as Angie suggested. Although she had seen him, during his illness, accept humility with a grace that astonished her, she had also seen the opposite—an arrogant assurance of his place as one of the universe's masters that allowed him to pass judgment on just about everyone. Certainly he seemed more annoyed by how Mercy's drug problems might affect *him* than concerned with her actual well-being.

Ben Golonski she did not know personally; she had seen him hold court at the Pinnacle, had watched his familiar but still amazing trajectory from unknown to the top of the power list and back again. When his book came out, she and Devlin had shared a laugh over it, marveling that no matter how many stars had crashed and burned around them, the people currently dwelling in the heights of Hollywood never seemed to think the ground could give way under them. Until it did.

Juliette wondered why on earth Golonski would agree to keep filming after Lloyd's death, when Mercy was so clearly in danger of going off the rails. As she began sidling through the crew members ringing the set, she got her answer.

"I beg your pardon," said a light and musical voice, as a small hand bit into her shoulder. "Who the fuck are you?"

The woman who turned Juliette to face her was so beautiful that for a moment Juliette froze, unable to process the various bits of emotion and information that were assailing her. This woman was manhandling her, which was infuriating, and questioning her as if she were a suspect in something, which was unacceptable. But her hair was the precise color of honey and fell about her face in perfect Breck girl waves that set off wide gray eyes and skin so perfect, so milky smooth and soft, that Juliette had the childish urge to reach out and stroke it.

"I ask again," this vision of loveliness said, "who the fuck are you?"

The repetition gave Juliette just enough time to gather herself, to perfect her posture, set her own not-insignificant jawline and, with great formality, pluck the woman's hand from her shoulder.

"My name," she said quietly and carefully, as if speaking to a mentally challenged child, "is Juliette Greyson. And you are . . . ?" She tilted her head to one side and watched with great satisfaction as that ivory skin flushed, those big gray eyes darkened like thunderclouds.

"Security," she snapped.

"You're security?" Juliette asked.

"Security," the woman repeated, at which point Juliette noticed she was wearing a Bluetooth. "There's some crazy redhead on my set. Come deal."

"Wait, wait, Carson, hang on one second." The ever-shifting sea of electricians and production assistants parted and O'Connor emerged, clad in a black raincoat over an artfully rumpled sweater. "Hi, Juliette, sorry, Juliette," he said, throwing a placating arm around her shoulders. "Carson, this is Juliette Greyson, remember I mentioned I was going to have her come down and talk some sense into Mercy?"

Never had Juliette seen a woman's face shift so quickly, the irritated line of her mouth instantly curving into a welcoming smile, the hard and dismissive eyes lighting up with pleasure.

"Juliette," she said, extending the hand that had moments before gripped her with such ferocity, "of course. I should have known, all that gorgeous auburn hair. I'm Carson Cooper, I work with Bill Becker and I've heard so much about you. From both Bill and Michael. You'll have to forgive me," she said, waving away their initial meeting with a lovely deep-throated laugh. "Things have been a bit tense on the set, as I'm sure you know. And with Michael here, and Mercy, of course, we've had a fair number of fans infiltrating the ranks." She took Juliette's arm and began steering her through the crowd. "Not to mention all those hor-rible photographers."

Juliette shot a glance at O'Connor. Was he really buying this? The thrilling little laugh, the accent that was suddenly vaguely Continental? Michael was smiling slightly but in a way Juliette could not read. Meanwhile, Carson continued to murmur in her ear with sudden girlish intimacy.

"It has been so difficult since Lloyd died, and we thought all was lost until I was able to convince Michael here to step in, our knight in shining armor." She paused to give O'Connor a blinding smile.

"How *did* Lloyd die?" Juliette said abruptly. "Was it an overdose, or something else?"

Carson came to a sudden stop a few steps away from where a small number of black canvas chairs were arrayed around a group of monitors; Juliette could see Ben Golonski deep in conversation with a tall gray-haired man whom Juliette recognized as an award-winning cinematographer.

"Something else?" Carson asked, and her tone was a bit less dulcet. "What else could it have been? The toxicology report could not have been more clear—Lloyd had a dangerous mixture of painkillers and sleeping aids in his bloodstream. He had been plagued with insomnia for years," she added, falling into what was clearly a prepared text. "Just last month he complained about it in an interview in the *Los Angeles Times*. It appears he was self-medicating and accidentally overdosed. Why?" she added, peering into Juliette's face. "What did you hear?"

"That it wasn't quite as clear-cut—"

"How is Mercy?" O'Connor interrupted. "Or how did she seem to you? She's due on set in two minutes."

"She seems terrible," Juliette said bluntly. "She looks like she hasn't slept in days and she's obviously strung out on something, though I suppose it could just be some of those Chinese herbs all you people are so fond of. She says she didn't overdose last night, that she was just deeply asleep and someone shot her full of adrenaline just so she could get through however many scenes she's supposed to get through today."

"Right," Carson said, and with an exhalation of exasperation abandoned her attempt to charm Juliette. "Because that's something I'd certainly authorize, something I want to have to explain to the insurance company. Fuck me. You know what, though," she added with a bitter laugh, "if I thought that would work, I would do just that. A shot in the ass is just what that girl needs. Mercy Talbot has been an actress for the better part of a decade now and she knows exactly how it works. She's caused more than enough trouble already. So you do what you need to do, honey, but she's working today. All day." At that moment Golonski raised his head and gestured; without a word, Carson stalked off.

"Wow," said Juliette. "I can't imagine why Lloyd was having trouble sleeping. Who in God's name is she? Why have I never seen her before? Or heard of her? She's a nightmare. Is she Bill Becker's love child? Or did she just spring full-grown from his head like Athena from Zeus?"

O'Connor chuckled. "She's like two years out of NYU film school," he said. "Masters program. I think her father knows Becker or something. She's actually not that bad. You can't afford to be nice when you're running a freak show like this. She talks tough because if she doesn't, everyone will roll right over her. She's actually a lot like you, Juliette. She knows how to do her job."

"When I start sounding like some summer stock actress channeling Helen Mirren," Juliette retorted, "you have my permission to shoot me in the head. She is very pretty, though," she added, "which certainly must help."

"In many ways," O'Connor agreed benignly. "Ah, here's Mercy," he added. From one corner of the Campo, Mercy approached, stylists and wardrobe assistants following her like a royal entourage. She scanned the crowd and gave Juliette a small but definitely happy smile. "Upright and seemingly functional. You are a miracle worker, my Juliette. Take a seat if you like and pray we get through the next twelve hours alive."

* * *

The cast and crew may have, but Juliette did not. She hung in for eight, partly because she wanted to keep an eye on Mercy, partly because every hour or so Michael would dart over and promise that he'd be on break soon so they could grab coffee, and partly because when the scenes were being run, it was fascinating to watch. Though she had spent many, many hours with him while he was ill, she had never seen O'Connor work.

As the hours passed, however, it became much less fascinating, and by the time the sun sank, Juliette was so exhausted from just watching the filming that she worried she would not be able to find her car, much less drive it home. Hour after hour, take after take, scene after scene, the action moved from the Campo to two separate side streets; there were costume changes and lighting changes as the story passed from day to night and back. Some scenes were shot repeatedly from every conceivable angle, while others blurred by in one take or two. At one point new pages of dialogue were passed around, fresh from the writer, who was holed away somewhere, still frantically trying to adjust the script for a lead who was at least twenty years older than the character had originally been conceived.

Juliette had been on movie sets before, but she had never seen anything like this level of intensity, this pressure to produce. Beyond an occasional wave, she didn't get to speak to Mercy again. No matter what he promised, whenever there was a break, Michael was instantly surrounded, by makeup people, the lighting people, the cinematographer, the director, everyone fussing and talking and generally acting as if the city were under siege and he the only hope of defense.

Still, whatever Ben Golonski felt about Mercy or this film, he seemed, at least from a distance, to treat her with unfailing patience and admiration. He had good reason. Watching the action unfold on the monitors in increments of two minutes or five, Juliette was struck by just how good Mercy was. Her role, as far as Juliette could tell, was actually two women: a modern-day art historian full of secrets and feisty one-liners, and the beatific young sixteenth century nun who haunted the dreams of O'Connor's jaded and celebrated but still struggling painter. He, too, had double duty, playing the painter and also a modern American detective investigating a series of murders staged to look like famous paintings. Both created characters that were easily differentiated yet also subtly related, but with Mercy the shift bordered on the miraculous. Her art historian had a hopeful cynicism that Juliette recognized as completely modern, while her novice was a luminous blank slate, a woman who somehow shone with a clear light that seemed to come through her rather than from her.

When Golonski yelled cut, Mercy occasionally staggered to her chair, angrily pushing aside the hands that inevitably reached out to adjust her hair, her costume. Her mother was never more than two feet away, handing Mercy various pills that she fished from a black leather satchel, or urging her to use the inhaler. Whether because she was exhausted by the work or Angie's ministrations, Mercy came close to tears on a few occasions and had to be coaxed back into frame. But as soon as the cameras were rolling, she was a wonder to watch. If anyone was slowing down filming, it was Michael; more than a few times, he asked for another take, demanding it if Golonski tried to demur, pushing himself, and Mercy, to try it another way.

But even so, the only real tension Juliette saw was that of a group of people working very hard to get things right.

"See?" said Carson, appearing behind Juliette's chair after one particularly long scene during which the chemistry between Mercy and Michael, in their Renaissance roles, was almost unbearable to watch. "See what she is capable of if she just acts like a grown-up and focuses on her art? Sometimes it doesn't seem right that all that talent got put in such a messed-up package."

"Maybe talent like that has a hard time staying in any package," Juliette said. "Maybe if she knew people would love her even if she didn't make them millions of dollars she wouldn't be so messed up."

Carson made a sound like spitting. "That's the only reason she gets away with being who she is, Juliette," she said. "But she's doing great today. I mean, look at them." She motioned to the monitor, where Michael and Mercy were consulting with the director, watching each other's faces and nodding as he spoke. "It's like the age difference doesn't exist. Kindred spirits, maybe, though I'd much rather deal with his issues than hers." Carson caught herself, as if she had forgotten who Juliette was. "Thank you, by the way, for whatever you said to Mercy. It obviously had a huge impact. If every day could go this smoothly, we'd be just fine."

"I didn't say much of anything," Juliette answered. "And you need to be careful; she isn't as sturdy as she seems."

"She's fine," Carson said dismissively. "She just needs someone to set some boundaries for her. That's the trouble with becoming rich and famous when you're a child." Her eyes narrowed. "You think the world revolves around you."

Juliette could barely suppress a laugh. Hearing such a sentiment from a beautiful woman who could not be much older than Mercy but was overseeing a multimillion-dollar film set bordered on the ridiculous. But Juliette knew from long experience that in Hollywood no matter how lauded or successful you were, there was always someone who seemed to have the better deal, the easier life, the less-deserved fame. Envy drove the Industry, even more than ambition.

As the sun sank behind the hills and towers, shadows filled the city, rising from the corners until the streets were silent rivers of chilly darkness. Soon the moon rose high and bright and Juliette thought if she had to sit or stand still for one more minute she would scream or pass out. After attempting, in vain, to have a moment with Mercy, who seemed to have disappeared somewhere that was not her trailer, Juliette contented herself with waving to Michael and pointing to her watch. He blew her a kiss and turned back to his conversation. It was all very anticlimactic, she thought, as she followed the winding streets back toward Porta San Marco. Light shone from lamps anchored on buildings that lined each street, the iron arms decorated with the symbols of Siena's sixteen neighborhoods—the snail and the porcupine, the elephant with its tower, the unicorn. She followed the jaguar until it gave way to the giraffe. The night above her was blue-black and a mist rose from the cobblestones, turned archways and doorways into tableaux, possible scenes of romance, or murder.

The danger of Hollywood, she thought, was that if you spent too much time around it, everything seemed like a movie.

When she returned to Cerreta, she was surprised to find Gabriel sitting on the low stone wall outside the Casa Padua, playing his guitar, all alone except for two young cats batting at shadows in the grass at his feet. It looked as if he were waiting for her.

"So, cuz, how was it being back?" he asked as Juliette got out of her car.

"In Siena?"

"In Hollywood. Back among the corrupt and restless hearts of the entertainment industry." He punctuated every other word with a hard dramatic chord.

"It was weird," she said, choosing not to be provoked. "I don't know what I was doing there, exactly. Michael is back to being a full-time movie star, which is good, I guess. He looked like the chemo worked anyway. But the shoot's a nightmare, and you cannot believe the bitch of a producer they have on set. It's understandable that he's worried Mercy is going to screw up."

Gabe tilted his head to one side and blinked with great exaggeration as his fingers plucked an overly melancholy tune. Juliette had to laugh.

"Okay, okay," she said. "It wasn't the romantic reunion I had hoped for, but I have experienced disappointment once or twice before in my young life. Anyway, Mercy's a mess again but she won't admit it, and no one really cares as long as she keeps doing what she does."

"Your Mr. O'Connor cares. At least enough to call you. Or was that just a ruse to see you again?"

"Hardly. He cares, I guess, but mostly because he doesn't want to have to deal with it. I don't know, maybe he really does; the two of them are two of a kind in a way. And I have to say, watching them do what they do, that part, really was amazing," Juliette said, gazing up at the stars, leaning against the wall and into the fragrance-stirred silence. "To see her go from fucked-up kid to this sort of luminous presence in a matter of moments. She really is something to watch. And the camera loves her."

"If no one else does," Gabriel finished with a playful twang. He paused a moment; Juliette expected him to make some sobriety-related pronouncement about Mercy, but surprisingly, he didn't seem to be interested in Mercy at all. "I was thinking, Jules," he said, carefully leaning the guitar against the wall as if finally getting down to business.

"Never a good idea, Gabe."

"No seriously, I was thinking that you should stay. Stay here. Be part of *here* for a while, not just a visitor, not just some absentee landlord."

"Hey," Juliette protested, pulling herself up onto the wall and shoving him with her shoulder.

"No, I mean it. You shouldn't go back to that place, those people. You're too susceptible to soul-sucking narcissists. Well, you are," he said, as she began to object. "Look at who you married. The tortured writer who couldn't lower himself to ever get a job, who had no problem living off you for years, and then the moment things turn around . . ." Juliette shoved him again. "Okay, I'm sorry he's dead. A little sorry. And God knows you come by it naturally enough, your endless need to fix things. All right, all right, don't raise the drawbridge, I'm not going to talk about the past. At least not right now. But you know Hollywood was never your dream. It was Josh's. Even your job, which I know you're very good at, was an accident."

"A lucky accident."

"Well, yes, sure, for a strung-out junkie thief to wind up with a career in luxury hotel management may indeed be the ultimate definition of 'lucky accident.' But is it really the life you dreamed of? Meeting the needs of a bunch of overly entitled, marginally talented basket cases?"

"It's not always like that," Juliette protested. "Some of our guests are very talented and some of them are even nice."

"Okay, okay," Gabe said. "But the work, Jules, is it the work you want to be doing? Glorified child care?"

"Oh, I don't know, Gabe," she said with a sigh, hitching herself up onto the wall beside him, feeling the tension of her shoulders release as she arched her back, as the smell of grass and warm stone, of rosemary and apple blossom, filled every breath she took, erased all the emotional frenzy of the movie set. All those people scurrying around like ants, the anxiety and the pressure, the forest of equipment, the countless crew. They were probably still at it, and for what? A movie that would play in theaters for a couple of weeks. It was absurd when you thought about it, such a long-odds business. Even when a film was successful, it was often forgotten in a year. Only one in a million made any lasting impact on people's imaginations; *Casablanca* was still more famous than most films made in the last fifty years.

But here, at Cerreta, was something that did not change, that was not ephermeral. Across the courtyard, the villa stood as it always had, glimmering pale in the darkness, a few squares of light running along its top floor where guests were reading or making love or poring over travel guides. She could hear the gentle clash of dishes being washed in the students' quarters, hear their voices raised in song and laughter as the wine took hold. Behind her lay the fields and vineyards, the endless swell of forests, the green and golden allure of Tuscany, with its hill towns and bell towers, its storybook streets and hidden piazzas, a place at once under siege, by tourism and the modern world, and unassailable. She did admire Gabe. At least he was taking a stand, trying to create, if not a utopia then some sort of testament to a different way of living, a different way of treating the beautiful and moving and miraculous. Beauty is so dangerous, Juliette thought, because desire is so dangerous. So many trampling feet, so many grasping hands, and soon the very thing that drew them was broken, obliterated. For a moment she could see Mercy as she stood on the wall of the Castle That Only God Knows with the iris in her hand, lovely and unknowable, saying things that sounded so significant because she made them sound that way.

"We need you," Gabe was saying beside her. "I need you. Cerreta needs you. It's home. You know it is, Jules, the closest thing either of us have to home."

"You're doing fine without me," she said, shivering at the sound of the word "home." It made her think of closed doors, dangerous silences. Home had never really worked out for her. "You're doing better without me. I'd just try to make it like the Pinnacle, get rich people to come, and you'd hate that."

"I would," Gabe admitted. "But"—he paused, and the pause was so unlike him that Juliette was instantly uneasy—"maybe we could figure out something that was not quite so drastic. Something midway between the Pinnacle and the pitiful, which, I have to admit, is what we've got right now, at least financially. We need to do something. Or we will lose the place." The last sentence came out of nowhere and hung in the air with no need of dramatic guitar accompaniment.

"What are you talking about?" Juliette demanded, though she knew she was just buying time. Gabriel never lied, and he rarely exaggerated; his tone was calm but final. He meant precisely what he said. "I just gave you a half a million dollars to settle the taxes. How could we lose it? Who would we lose it to?"

Gabe shrugged. "You gave me four hundred fifty thousand dollars," he said. "Which is about three hundred thousand euros. Which settled the taxes. But there are loans, Jules, outstanding bills, some going back to when our parents were alive. Our folks, they weren't exactly cut out for business, none of them, as you well know," he said bitterly. "Sometimes I wonder if they were ever really serious at all. It was all about the wine and the sun and the drama, their twisted version of romance—"

Juliette held up her hand. "Enough," she said. "Just tell me what we need."

Gabriel shrugged again and said bluntly, "We're about two hundred grand in the hole, to various banks and tradesmen. We need a new generator, like yesterday, and I am beginning to think we're going to need a new well—four hundred years is a lot to ask, even with the blessings of Saint Bernardine."

"Shit, Gabe," Juliette said incredulously. "Why didn't you tell me this sooner?

"I did tell you some of it, like the taxes part," he said. "And I've emailed you some of the information over the last year. But mainly I just thought if I kept paying things down one day at a time, I could stay afloat. But the diving dollar is killing us, the villa's practically empty, in case you hadn't noticed. I never envisioned this place being some huge moneymaker; I just want it to be self-sustaining."

"Yeah, well," Juliette snapped, "you'll have to sell a lot of honey and olive oil to get on top of a debt like that."

"Just so you know, olive oil is a huge money pit," Gabe said. "I'd give it up but the trees look so nice and the guests expect an olive grove."

"What about selling some of the property?" she asked. "Most of it's woods now anyway; you could cut the acreage in half and still have a nice little *agriturismo*."

"We can't," Gabe said miserably. "Remember when I applied to become a national reserve? I thought it would help us preserve the integrity of the landscape, which it does, but it also means you can't sell it to anyone but the government, and they have no reason to buy it now, since there is no threat of development."

Juliette groaned. Although she had never loved Cerreta the way Gabe had, neither did she want to lose it, and certainly not to financial default. For all her knowledge about what it took to run a hotel, she had somehow managed to assume that even if Cerreta was not profitable, it would still limp along as it always had. In the hands of the banks or local developers it would soon be turned into some sort of historical tourist trap, with pottery depicting the inevitable cypress trees and Tuscany refrigerator magnets for sale in the villa and overheated Americans flipping through *Lonely Planet* guidebooks and wolfing down gelato.

"Well, what do you think I can do about it? How much time do we have?"

"I don't know, a few months, maybe six. I think if we make some sort of significant gesture, at least to the banks, we could buy more time. I don't know. I thought maybe offer it up for events? Weddings? Retreats? Hook up with a university? Maybe we should think about starting a foundation; I've gotten a few grants, but they were small and specific—it's how I keep the interns, how I paid for the black- and gray-water systems. We need something bigger and more long-term. I figured you'd think of something. You always do."

"I wish you had told me this a year ago, or even when I first got here," Juliette said, her voice rising. "It takes time to do things like that."

"I was afraid you'd turn around and drive away," Gabe said simply. "Or say we have to sell it. I was afraid you just didn't care. And I was ashamed that I couldn't do it all the way I wanted to. It makes so much sense in my mind, but I can't seem to make other people see this place the way I do."

He sounded so miserable, so self-recriminating, so unlike the Gabe she knew that Juliette felt her anger evaporate. Gabe, and his arrogance, was one of the few cornerstones that remained of her family life. If she lost that, she would be completely adrift.

"Don't," she said, putting an arm around him. "We'll figure it out. It's only money. There's plenty of money in this world and you can always get some of it if you try hard enough. You just have to figure out how to do it without selling too much of your soul. Maybe I should start selling drugs again," she said with a laugh. "I think I could drum up some business on a certain film set."

"That's not even funny," Gabe said.

"I'll call Dev. He's good at money. Or I'm sure Mercy would write you a check tomorrow." She laughed. "She's got a thing for you, or she did before she went back to movieland hell. You could work that angle easily enough."

"That is the last angle in the world I want to work," said Gabe, reverting a bit to his old self. "Taking money from an addict is never a good idea. For one thing, you can never be sure where it's been."

When she finally climbed into bed, Juliette stared out the window at the high round moon. A part of her was wallowing in self-pity—was there nowhere she could go that didn't somehow require her assistance? Nowhere she could just *be* for a few weeks? But deeper within her, a small but more essential voice was murmuring to itself in satisfaction— here was a problem to be solved, something broken that could be fixed. Let Michael and Mercy and Carson worry about their egos and their precious movie; as it turned out, Juliette actually did have her own life to live. Her own problems to solve.

I was pretty much born to be the girl who saves the farm, she thought as she turned out the light, and though she meant it as a joke, she knew it wasn't.

It was three a.m. when a creak and then a crash in the living room woke her. Picking up a broken piece of marble that served as a bookend and would do just as well as a weapon, Juliette crept down the few steps and hit the light switch. There, rubbing her hip where it had collided with the sofa, stood Mercy, wearing a long black cape, eyes huge, body shivering all over.

"I had to come," she said, her mouth working, her hair standing on end as if she had been electrocuted. "Didn't I? Because you saw, right? My mother and Ben, Michael and his pretty bitch Carson. They killed Lloyd, didn't they? And now they're trying to kill me."

Chapter Six

THE FIRST CAR ARRIVED at seven a.m. It was hot-rod red with a gold stripe down the middle and as it pulled into the courtyard, spraying gravel and dust, Queen was blasting even though the tinted windows were rolled up.

"Queen," Gabriel said to Juliette. "Who even still listens to Queen?"

"I'm going to go with Angie," she answered. "She probably picked that car to match her nail polish." The two were sitting on the front porch of Casa Padua, drinking café au lait and waiting. They had been there for more than an hour. Juliette had actually expected the onslaught to begin much earlier; her BlackBerry had been ringing almost continuously since five a.m.

"You don't have to stay," she said to Gabriel. She had dragged him out of his bed the moment she was certain Mercy was finally asleep, as much in warning as to confer. "I can't imagine it's going to be pretty."

"Oh, I'm staying." He leaned back in his chair.

Juliette laughed. "You look like you should have a shotgun in your lap."

"There's one over the fireplace in the villa," he said, his eyes brightening. "I'll go get it if you think it will help."

Juliette did not have time to answer. In a perfumed rattle of gold bracelets and matching earrings, Angie was upon them.

"Where is she?"

"Asleep," Juliette said.

"Well, wake her up," Angie said, starting toward the doorway. Gabriel sprang up, but Juliette quickly barred the way.

"Your daughter is a guest here," she said, "and she expressed a wish to not be disturbed. I'll be happy to get you some coffee if you like. Or you can join the villa guests for breakfast in the dining area. Our cook makes a lovely frittata."

"Cut the crap," Angie said. "I want Mercy, in the car, right now. This is absurd. She's got a whole movie production stalled because she seems to think she's in Tuscany for a vacation."

"She doesn't have the production stalled," Juliette said coolly. "She worked sixteen hours yesterday; she's entitled to twenty-four down. It's in her contract. And the only thing stalling the production is Carson Cooper's failure to secure permits for the next series of scenes. That and the fact that the rewrites have been so extensive that no one is quite sure what the next series of scenes should be. At the moment, I would imagine both Carson and Mr. Golonski are much less concerned with Mercy's whereabouts than whether or not Bill Becker is currently on a plane from Los Angeles so he can fire them both in person. Something you might want to consider as well."

Juliette smiled serenely into Angie's outraged face. She had indeed called Devlin as she told Gabriel she would, and though he hadn't been able, or perhaps willing, to instantly produce a business plan to save Cerreta, he had filled her in on some choice Industry gossip. Bill Becker had been overheard by half of Hollywood screaming at Carson via cell phone in the Pinnancle dining room.

"Have some coffee," Gabriel said, taking Angie by the elbow and guiding her into the seat. "And a brioche. Try some of our very own honey."

"Coffee is fine," Angie said, viewing the rolls and honey with disdain. "Is she all right?"

"Pardon?" Juliette asked, helping herself to another brioche.

"Is Mercy all right? I don't know how she even got here." Even around huge gulps of coffee, the edge in Angie's voice was obvious. "Did she walk or hitchhike or what? She wasn't feeling herself when I saw her last night. I told Ben it was too long a day, and those costumes are so heavy and hot. And that Michael O'Connor takes his sweet time preparing for a scene. Mercy almost fainted several times waiting for him."

"She's fine," Juliette said evenly, thinking of Mercy's wild accusations and her subsequent collapse into virtual incoherence.

"Fine if you consider being dehydrated, exhausted, riven with anxiety, and clearly addicted to drugs and alcohol fine," Gabriel added, leaning back in his chair again. "Which apparently you do."

The instant outrage and denial that flooded Angie's face never made it into words. As she spluttered, another Ferrari pulled into the courtyard, this one black and silent and proceeding at a much more sensible speed.

"Mr. O'Connor, I presume," Gabe murmured. Juliette tried to ignore the blood pounding in her throat.

Michael got out of the car, sunglasses on, glancing around with a wide and delighted smile as if he were returning to a favored vacation spot. Juliette felt immediately exposed, almost naked.

"Is this where the party is?" he called out, approaching the porch. Two female interns, hoes and garden shears over their shoulders, appeared from the far corner of the courtyard and, catching sight of him, stopped midstride. He offered them a small wave, a brilliant grin, and then moved quickly up the stone steps and offered Gabe his hand.

"Michael O'Connor."

"Gabriel Delfino," Gabe answered, ignoring Juliette's warning frown. "I'm Juliette's cousin."

"As anyone could see," Michael said. "All this is yours?"

"Ours," Juliette and Gabe each rushed to answer, both then laughing awkwardly, like children caught competing for attention.

"It's a family property," Gabe explained. Juliette smiled and tried not to look as if she wished she could unravel every life choice that had led her to this moment. "We are the last survivors of a proud and ancient dynasty," he added gravely. "As you can see."

"Indeed," Michael said with a grin. "You are a woman of much mystery, Ms. Greyson. I would have never suspected there was a romantic Italian estate in your background." He gave her a look full of mischief but also appraisal. "Perhaps you could give me a tour."

Juliette was spared having to answer by the appearance of a third Ferrari, this one silver.

"What, did you all get a special deal?" Gabe asked.

"Product placement," Michael answered matter-of-factly. "My character, or the modern one, drives a Ferrari, a fact that is somehow mentioned more than once during the course of the film. So our rental needs were provided for. Bill Becker thinks of everything."

"Except providing an associate who knows how to keep control of her production," Juliette murmured.

"How very ungenerous of you," Michael murmured right back. "Not everyone has your breathtaking talent for personnel- and time-management."

"What the fuck?" said Carson as she slid from the silver Ferrari. Tall and slim in a white linen suit, she strode toward the group, but instead of joining them, she stood looking up at the porch, her arms held out from her sides in exasperation.

"Where in the hell am I and why? Where in the hell is Mercy and why? Is there a reason I am chasing my cast through the fucking Italian forest instead of doing what I am paid to do, which is make a movie? Does anyone bother answering their phones anymore? Does anyone speak to their PAs anymore? The only reason I even know where you are is that I have my navigator wired to your navigators because somehow I just knew this was going to be an issue."

She paused, drew breath, and looked around.

"What is this anyway? Heaven? How gorgeous is this place?"

"Welcome to Cerreta," Gabriel said, standing and looking down at her, "a sixteenth century *tenuta* that is currently used as a learning center and bed and breakfast. To exit, you just follow the same road you came in on."

"Carson," Michael called down, "Juliette was just about to give us a tour. Join us. Mercy's fine," he added, "she's just asleep. Which I'm sure is all she needs."

"Sleep?" Carson said, folding her arms. "That is a custom with which I am not familiar. Me, I have to spend all night tracking down my fucked-up leading lady because her mother is too busy worrying about who's going to get the biggest trailer on the next set that doesn't even exist to keep track of her. Hi, Angie," she added pointedly. "Enjoying the view?"

Beside her, Juliette could feel Gabriel vibrating with words that would certainly not help the situation. "Come on," she said, taking Michael's arm and leading him back down the steps toward the producer. "I'll be happy to show you both around. Then, before you leave, perhaps we can all have breakfast in the villa."

She took Carson's arm as well, and steered them toward the vegetable garden and the path that led to the vineyards and the remains of the old quarry. "I understand you're looking for a location or two," she said to Carson as if they were meeting in the lobby of the Pinnacle. "I'm pretty familiar with the area; perhaps I can help you. Meanwhile, why don't we just take a minute and enjoy this perfect morning?"

Never before had Juliette been as aware of the loveliness of the landscape that surrounded her. The wild crocuses dotting the grass at their feet, the dim gold stateliness of the villa, the neat green lines of the grapevines that undulated over the hills it overlooked, the ancient stone walls that hemmed in orchard and garden, the spills of geranium and lavender and rosemary, all conspired to do what no human could have done, which was calm Carson down. Quietly but with no room for interruption, Juliette explained the history of the estate, how the tower had been built in the twelfth century to defend the Delfino family from the perpetually warring armies of Florence and Siena, how the villa had been added when it seemed they had succeeded, then revamped in the sixteenth century when the Roman ideal of a country house had swept the Italian countryside. "There's even a ghost," she added, "of a banished noblewoman, who's mentioned in Dante. Down the road, you'll see the bridge she crossed on the way to the prison her husband constructed when he suspected her of adultery."

As they walked past Casa Torre and Casa Regina, she explained how all the other houses on the property, including the one she was staying in, were built to house the tenant workers, sheltering as many as six families in two or three bedrooms. How the most lucrative crop of the *tenuta*—of the region, actually—was for many years not wine or oil but charcoal, the main source of fuel up until the 1950s. She told them of the count, her great-grandfather whom she remembered vaguely from early childhood, and how he had expected the farmworkers to doff their caps when he went by even though he barely had enough money to feed himself. By the sixties, most of the farmers had left the country for factory work, or to become part of the growing tourism industry in Tuscany.

"When I was a child," Juliette said, "this was still considered the middle of nowhere. Italians couldn't believe when people decided they'd rather visit hill towns, or even Siena, than Florence or Rome. It was as if everyone started visiting New Jersey and skipping New York. When our parents, Gabe's and mine, talked about turning this place into a bed-and-breakfast, everyone thought they were crazy. Now practically every villa, every farmhouse, every abbey with a single wall still standing is an *agriturismo* or a hotel."

Soon enough, Carson was leaning against a wall, overlooking the splendid mass of forest, pocked here by an abandoned quarry now choked with morning glory and gorse, there by the outcropping of a nearby ruined abbey, drinking in the cool and silent morning air. Swallows swooped overhead and she watched them dart and flutter toward their nests beneath the eaves of the carriage house, the arch that connected the storage shed to the main part of the villa.

"So beautiful," Carson said softly. "So unbelievably beautiful." The sun washed her hair gold and her eyes were misty gray as she took in the colors and contours of the buildings, the landscape. For a moment Juliette wondered if maybe all the tough talk *was* just a ruse, a mask to hide behind. Juliette knew more than a little about that.

"So we could probably put trailers down in that field over there," Carson said, with an imperious gesture toward a pasture where a horse and her colt now grazed. "We can shoot some of the smaller buildings at an angle to create a street scene, use that tower for the clock-tower scene, and those steps will be quite believable as convent exterior. We can probably bring in enough greenery to turn this"—she swept her arm over the walled-in area in front of the villa—"into a formal garden; the view is to die for, and maybe we can fill that quarry for the lake scene. You don't have a lake on the property, do you?" She whirled to face Juliette. "No? But you do have a castle, right? Mercy said there was a castle."

"Yes," said Juliette doubtfully, her head swimming, "but it's in the middle of the woods."

"Perfect," Carson said. "We'll see that next. Oh, and the vineyards. Those look too small, and there are no grapes . . ."

"It's May," Juliette said. "There won't be grapes until August."

"That blows. Well, I'm sure our computer geeks can fix that."

"Wait," said Michael. "Slow down, Carson. You want to shoot *here?*"

Carson looked at him as if he had asked if the earth was round.

"Of course I want to shoot here. What the fuck do you think I'm doing, walking around in the grass and dirt? Enjoying myself? Learning a little something about Tuscany for the Italian history final I'm taking next week? Mercy mentioned this place about a hundred times as being ideal for some of the outdoor work, and for once she wasn't huffing a pipe. We'll be in and out in three weeks, four at the outside."

"Three weeks!" Juliette exclaimed. "Never. Gabe would never let you do that. Not even for three days. I've seen what happens to places used for location work. The people who live there barely survive. No way is Gabe going to let you drag your trucks and lights and endless amount of trash around here. You'd have to use electric trucks, you'd have to agree to recycle everything, you'd have to compost, for godsake. He won't do it. I promise you."

Carson eyed her narrowly. "You own the controlling share of this property," she said. "It's not up to him."

Cursing Mercy, Juliette frowned. "Cerreta is our property, but it's Gabe's home. He calls the shots." She held up empty hands. "So sorry."

"It wouldn't have to be as bad as all that, Juliette," Michael said slowly. "It's not like the scenes require a cast of thousands; we've done most of the extras' work back in Siena. Mostly the scenes are just Mercy and me, and a few supportings. It could work out really well, for everyone. I mean, Mercy certainly seems to feel comfortable here, and I, well, it would be a bit like old times for you and me," he said with a grin and a hitched-high eyebrow.

Juliette stared at him.

"Is this some sort of conspiracy?" she asked. "Is this why Mercy showed up? Why all of you showed up?"

"No," Michael said quickly, even as Carson shrugged and looked away. "No, not at all. This is the first time I've even heard it discussed. I didn't even know this place existed until this morning, when Angie told me where Mercy had gone. I mean, I knew you were staying somewhere nearby, but I didn't know it was a place like this and I certainly didn't know it was yours. We're not trying to bully you," he said, putting a hand on her shoulder. "If you really think it's a bad idea—"

"Look," said Carson, turning her attention back to Juliette. "What do you need to make this work for you? This place is lovely but it's obviously falling to pieces, and that Gabe guy is adorable but doesn't look like he's exactly a business ace. So I'm sure that whatever we might break, we can fix to everyone's satisfaction and general improvement. We're not talking about the rest of your life, we're talking three weeks and a high-profile motion picture. This is a bed-and-breakfast, right? We'll add the name of the place in the credits; you'll have business coming out of your ears. You got a learning center? We'll set up a foundation, have *Condé Nast* do a big spread before the movie opens. Meanwhile, I have a budget and a boss who can actually say your name without screaming, which puts you on a list with about two other people. What I don't have is any time to waste dicking around over the imposition of renting out your moldering farm for a big bad movie shoot. So you tell me what you need and let's get the fuck on with it."

At first Gabe just laughed. Juliette found him still on the porch, deep in conversation with Mercy, who was seated on the top step with her legs drawn up under her chin, looking ten years old. Gabe was doing most of the talking, much of it with his hands. Mercy still looked drawn, though not as pale as she had when she showed up in Juliette's living room. She was nodding, but with the sort of frown that precedes an objection; whatever Gabe was saying so intensely in her ear, Mercy wasn't quite buying.

"But it's not as simple as you make it sound," she was saying as Juliette approached. "Juliette, explain to your cousin why it isn't always possible to tell the truth in every situation. Tell him about the mythical land we call Hollywood."

"Oh, come on," Gabriel said. "Don't make me sound stupid. I was just talking about my personal experience with keeping secrets. How quickly they fester and eat right through your soul, take over your life—"

"Well, yes," Juliette interrupted, not liking the direction of this conversation at all, but wanting to agree with Gabe enough to keep him from becoming angry, or angrier than he was going to be when she presented her news. "I think when you keep something secret, it can make it seem worse than it really is. But that doesn't mean you have to go around telling everyone every single thing."

"Sometimes things only get worse when you tell the truth," Mercy said.

"Things never get worse when you tell the truth," Gabriel said. "Sometimes there are *consequences,* which might seem worse, at first. But they aren't really. Not in the long run."

Mercy grinned wickedly as she interrupted him. "Okay, so you tell the truth. Why do you live here all on your own? Why aren't you married and raising adorably eco-friendly bilingual children?" she asked. "Because I'd totally marry you, if I weren't, you know, *me.*"

For once Gabe was brought up short. Though Mercy was clearly teasing, she also wanted an answer. Juliette could see his thumb worrying the ring he wore on the middle finger of his left hand; it was one of Gabe's few tells. Despite herself, she, too, waited for the answer.

"Well, that's no secret," he said, meeting Mercy's eyes straight on. "I'm totally fucked up. Just ask Juliette. Some damage is permanent."

"You know," Juliette said quickly, "it's way too early in the morning to be discussing the meaning of life, Gabriel. Especially when we need to talk about other things." With a small jerk of her head, she motioned Gabe off the porch. Gabe raised his eyebrows but otherwise did not move, observing her with that benign expectation that Juliette found so infuriating. "Okay. Carson wants to shoot here. For three weeks. And I think we should let her." Though she spoke with some measure of defiance, Juliette took a step backward, anticipating a certain amount of rage.

That was when Gabe started laughing. Juliette explained that this was his chance to fix everything and make enough money to get out of debt and he laughed even harder.

"What is so funny?" Mercy asked, as he wiped his eyes and leaned against the stone wall. "It's perfect. It's a totally perfect idea. I should know, I was the one who suggested it to Carson."

"See, this is the thing about God," Gabe said, when he was finally able to draw breath. "He has such a great sense of humor. Not to mention timing. I mean, what can I say? It's a total nightmare from hell, but I put it out there, didn't I? I finally broke down and asked the universe, not to mention my crazy cousin, for help, and then, bam, in a matter of hours, help is at my door. But it couldn't be some nice quiet millionaire with a degree in Italian history or Al Gore looking to fund a little piece of sustainability, or even our long-lost Giotto." Gabe was laughing so hard again it was difficult to quite understand him. "No, it's a three-ring blockbuster circus with a carbon footprint bigger than King Kong's."

"It's not that bad," Mercy said earnestly. "We do have recycling bins. And the golf carts are electric. I think."

At this Gabe went off in another gale of hysteria, while Juliette shifted from one foot to another and tried not to roll her eyes.

It took an hour or so to hammer out the terms, by which time Gabe wasn't laughing anymore. In exchange for allowing the film crew to use Cerreta for not more than three weeks, Carson would pay to repair any harm to the landscape or buildings done during shooting, also for a new well to be dug and the generator to be replaced. To create the interior sets, the production company would renovate two of the more dilapidated farmhouses, the villa's cellar, and the third floor of the tower. Bill Becker would also personally make a large onetime donation to the newly created Cerreta Foundation (which had the benefit of being tax deductible).

After signing a makeshift contract in the study of the villa, he and Juliette stepped out onto the patio outside the front door. From here the front half of the estate spread out before them, an explosion of forest and field and meadow and the rich red earth of the vineyards. Surveying so much beauty, even Juliette quailed for a moment; what would it all look like three weeks from now?

"Promise me one thing," Gabe said quietly, putting his hand on Juliette's wrist. "Promise me you aren't doing this, we aren't doing this, just so you can have some sort of Italian idyll with Mr. Movie Star over there." He jerked his chin to where Michael and Carson were huddled in conversation with each other and their respective cell phones.

Taken completely by surprise, Juliette yanked her arm away. "Jesus, Gabe," she said irritably. "I just solved all your money woes and that's what you have to say? *You* promise *me* you won't sleep with Mercy, then hound her into taking a blood oath on the Big Book."

"Seriously, Jules," Gabe said, "don't go from one needy narcissist to another. Sleep with him if you want, but don't go falling in love with him. He's not . . . real. Or rather, he's too real, in that endless-pit-of-perpetual-need way you seem to like so much." Gabe sighed. "He's just like Josh, only with more money and slightly better packaging. Okay," he added with irritable envy, "much better packaging."

She followed her cousin's gaze to the *fattoria,* where Michael stood talking to Carson. The producer was smiling and for once showed no signs of needing to be anywhere else, despite the keys in her hand, and it was easy to see why. O'Connor's eyes were on hers, shining above that white and ready smile that made whoever it was directed toward feel like the wittiest, smartest, and/or most beautiful person in the world. Even at a hundred paces, he gleamed with self-confidence. Certainly Carson's face was as happy as Juliette had seen it, gazing up into his and clearly willing to do so unto all eternity. For a moment Juliette hated him. As if he felt her eyes on him, Michael turned and looked straight at Juliette, his left eyebrow raising itself suggestively.

Startled and feeling she had been somehow caught, Juliette stepped back and redirected her gaze to the view.

"What are you going to tell your interns?" she asked. "And the guests?"

It was Gabe's turn to shrug. "Nothing," he said. "I think it will be fairly self-explanatory. I'm sure everyone will be very excited," he said with mock enthusiasm, "to be part of such a fabulous project. Look at them," he added, unable to contain his disgust as a group of dusty students, recently returned from moving a group of pigs from one field to another, surrounded O'Connor with shy smiles, extended hands, and questioning glances. "You just can't get good help anymore."

Chapter Seven

IF JULIETTE HAD SAID yes to Carson's plan in the hopes of spending time with Michael, a thing she certainly wasn't about to admit even to herself, she soon realized how ridiculous that would have been. Within moments of getting a final okay from Becker, Cerreta exploded into activity. By noon, the dirt road that led to the castello was an ever-shifting river of dust and exhaust as trucks and cars and trailers crept their way along the bumps and curves, following hastily made signs to the courtyard, a logging road, and a lower field that Gabe had let run to grass and wildflowers. Michael and Mercy vanished into a conference with Golonski, who had commandeered the villa's library. Juliette, meanwhile, was trying to figure out where everyone would sleep and how they could feed them. The carpentry crew produced bunk beds seemingly out of thin air and Casa Torre soon looked like a dormitory for the camera crew and electricians. Still, sheets had to be found, blankets and towels, and Juliette was on the phone to the local laundry service and a cleaning crew. Craft services moved into the kitchen, much to the consternation of Cerreta's presiding chef, Rosa, bringing with them boxes and bushels of nonorganic food and a list of food preferences and allergies from Angie and Mercy. Juliette took one look and tore it up, step one in negotiating a truce between the two kitchen staffs.

All day long, men and women in cargo pants, belted with pliers and box cutters and every color of electrical tape imaginable, heaved and carried, carted and rolled the copious and wildly diverse equipment required to make a movie. The first scene was to be shot outside the carriage house, which would be dressed with flowerpots and window boxes to look like the exterior of a painter's studio. The archway that connected it to the villa became an alley leading back to a street. Lights sprang up like a grove of young trees, the dirt of the courtyard soon crawled with thick black wires, while the set designer and her decorators picked through flatbeds of hedge bushes and flowerpots, rose trees, and even a selection of young willows.

"What's with all the colored paper I keep finding everywhere?" Gabe asked, shoving an eggshell-blue sheaf into a recycling bin. "Are they doing finger-paint therapy or something?"

"That's for the rewrites," Juliette said. "Every time the writer changes something, they pass out pages of a different color so no one gets confused. You can tell how rough a shoot has been by how many colors there are in the final working script."

"Great," Gabe grumbled. "Now we have to worry about dyes as well as wood pulp. Um, are we still supposed to be in Italy here?" he asked as he watched with horrified fascination as the set dressers moved plants this way and that. "Because there are no gardenias in Italy. Excuse me?" he called to the woman in black who seemed to be in charge. "No gardenias. In Italy."

"Where is the production manager?" Juliette asked an electrician who was about to climb a ladder. The young woman pointed to a man in a red flannel shirt. Juliette grabbed Gabe and together they walked toward him.

"Hi," she said. "This is the man who owns this place and he is a great resource when it comes to knowing what sort of plants are indigenous to the area, or what sort of stone or paint, or just about anything. And he's more than happy to help."

"Great," the production manager said, "perfect. Because we have no fucking clue what the director wants here, and frankly I don't think he does, either. So anything you can do to help us not look like complete idiots would be greatly appreciated."

Gabe shot her a vindictive look, but as she left, Juliette noted with amusement that he was already explaining something with considerable animation to a small crowd of people.

By the time the sun went down, Juliette was tired like she hadn't been tired since Oscar night at the Pinnacle. She and Gabe had arranged for Rosa and the interns to orchestrate the making and baking of fifty pizzas in the wood-fire oven that stood in the corner of the courtyard beside the entrance to the winepress and the cellar. Glazed with sweat, Juliette headed back to Casa Padua to change. There she found Angie working an iPhone beside a stack of Louis Vuitton luggage on the front porch. "I wasn't sure which room was mine," said Angie, finally looking up. "Mercy said she doesn't want to share, and so I thought I'd give you a chance to move your things first . . ." She gave Juliette a winning smile.

"You're not staying here, Angie," Juliette said wearily, pushing past her. "Mercy can, I guess, if she wants, but you have a lovely room in the villa. Just down the hall from Mr. O'Connor. With its very own bathroom." She pulled out a walkie-talkie someone had given her and barked into it. "Can someone come get Angie Talbot's luggage and take it to the villa?"

Behind her, Angie began spluttering her objections, but Juliette was just too tired to listen. "I'm sure you will be much more comfortable over there," she said firmly, stepping into the blissful silence of her own room and closing the door.

By the time Juliette had finished showering, Angie and her luggage were gone, replaced by Mercy, who sat cross-legged on Juliette's bed, poring over a script.

"You must be feeling pretty pleased with yourself," Juliette said, as she towel-dried her hair. Mercy looked up at her, startled. "I mean, it's not every star who can get a whole film production to follow her to the location of her choosing. That's got to move you up the power lists a few notches."

Mercy shrugged. "It's not about feeling pleased with myself," she said. "I just feel safer here. With you and Gabe around. He's bound and determined to save me," she added with a small grin, "from whatever it is he thinks I need saving from."

"From yourself," Juliette said, opening drawers and preparing to get dressed. "Gabe believes that sobriety is the cure for all ills."

"Don't you?"

It was Juliette's turn to shrug. "It depends. I don't think being strung out or loaded all the time makes life any easier, but I think drinking and drugging are usually symptoms of something else, and if you don't fix that . . ."

"Is that what you did?"

Juliette stared at herself in the mirror and tried to remember those early days, when she had shaken and sweated and puked for ten solid days, emerging with the knowledge that no matter what else happened in her life, she would never ever go through such a thing again. She remembered how she had thrown herself into the frantic but still stately dance of life at the Plaza, where the general manager had, for reasons she still did not understand, created a job for her. How ensuring the comfort of guests and the efficiency of the staff became a wonderfully exhausting problem to solve, her own personal endless algebraic equation. That was what got her high now, doing the sorts of things she had just done today.

"Something like that," she said.

"Gabe says you're only as sick as your secrets," Mercy said, lying back onto the pillows.

Juliette snorted. "He would know. He's had some pretty sick secrets."

"Me, too," Mercy said sadly. "But most secrets usually aren't just *yours*. They usually involve other people."

"I don't think Gabe means you share them with, like, Katie Couric," Juliette said. "And I don't think he means things like 'I slept with Lloyd.' I think the idea is to tell a trustworthy person the things that keep you up at night, and yes"—she ran a brush through her wet hair—"I do think saying things out loud can make them seem less terrible."

"My mother thinks I should sleep with Michael," Mercy said in what was clearly a diversionary tactic. She watched the reflection of Juliette's face from the mirror above the dresser. "She thinks it's time I had a relationship with an older man. That it would make me seem more serious, more settled. Like he's settled. Settled like Henry VIII. He's been married, what, five times?"

"Four," Juliette said, rummaging around for earrings, not daring to meet Mercy's eyes.

"My mother doesn't even know Michael O'Connor except from his movies, but she thinks I should sleep with him. She thinks it would play well in the press, distract everyone from Lloyd's death. Don't you have any cigarettes in here? Like for guests?"

"No, I don't," Juliette said. "And you can't smoke in my bedroom. Go sit on the porch or drape yourself on the stairs if you have to smoke. Get up anyway, it's almost time for dinner. Or are you back on your starlet skeletalization program?"

"Don't worry," Mercy said, not budging. "I'm not going to. Sleep with Michael. I don't trust him, for one thing. Don't you think it was weird how quickly Carson and Becker were able to get him for this role, how he just *happened* to be *immediately* available? He and Lloyd did not get along, you know. Lloyd thinks—thought—he was a washed-up old diva, ever since they were in that big espionage picture together. You know, the one with Clooney and that British woman who looks kinda like a man?"

"Well, we'll ask him all about it at dinner," Juliette said, leaning down and tugging Mercy out of bed. "Now get up."

"Don't," Mercy said, grasping Juliette's arm. "Seriously. Don't say anything about Lloyd at dinner. You have to promise. Seriously. It's just . . . it's a very touchy subject with everyone. I was just"—she smiled that bright angelic smile—"trying out Gabe's theory. With a person I trust."

"Okay," Juliette said, startled by the girl's intensity, and her grip. "Okay," she repeated, peeling Mercy's fingers off her arm. "But I don't think you should say things like that. It makes it sound like Michael is somehow profiting from Lloyd's death, when I think he was just trying to help out a friend."

"Why does having him here rattle you so much anyway?" Mercy asked. "Do you want to sleep with him? Do you *not* want to sleep with him?"

"It's got nothing to do with sleeping with him." Juliette's voice was much louder than she intended it to be. "It's just there are things in your life, or my life anyway, that need to be kept separate, and it suddenly feels so . . . crowded here. *He* makes it, me . . . I just feel crowded."

A look of pity crossed Mercy's face.

"You can't amputate the past, you know," she said. "Even if you think you have, it still aches, like a ghost limb."

Standing in the living room, Juliette once again felt tricked, by this young woman's green-golden eyes, by her throaty voice, by her ability to seem one sort of person and then be quite another. Right now she was looking at Juliette as if she knew precisely the slippery mixture of pleasure and fury Juliette felt having Michael here, watching him be seduced by the dreamy landscape of her childhood, her poor, knotted-up, long-neglected childhood. She wanted to be alone with him, but she knew then he would ask her questions, like Mercy had asked her questions, and she didn't want to answer any of them, not even the easy ones. She had tried to amputate the past for good reason. There was nothing but pain in the past, pain and loss and cold unforgiving confusion, and even so, it had chased her through most of her life, through her drug-addled twenties, through her marriage, then her divorce. And

Michael O'Connor was certainly not the solution she was looking for, no matter what she had felt, or thought he had felt, those months ago. She needed a new sense of stability, some sort of systematic plan, and he would bring her nothing but constant disruption and confusion. Only in the steady, complicated waltz of work had she found security. Safety.

Suddenly Juliette missed the Pinnacle so deeply she could have wept. She missed the smell of the inexhaustible bouquets of lilies, the hush of the lobby, the scent of good coffee, and the murmur of voices and laughter rising like a mist from the bar. She missed the logic of it all and the people who made it work so smoothly, who met any crisis, any request, with an unflappable mien and simple step-by-step solutions. Another room would be prepared, another seamstress brought in, another bottle, gown, nanny, impossible-to-get ticket would be procured. But more than that, she missed Devlin. Who always seemed to know what to do and never, ever asked her one single question about her past. Because he didn't much care. God, what she would give to have Devlin here, to see him come sauntering in this room right now, explaining how all this was going to work. Then she would know she hadn't made an enormous mistake by not just throwing Carson out on her ear.

Before Juliette could even attempt to put any of this into words, Angie appeared in the doorway with a male figure in tow.

"Mercy, Mercy, look," she said, sounding positively giddy. "Look who's come to see us through all this insanity!"

For a moment Juliette felt her heart lift; like Gabe, she had wished for something and here it was. But instead of Devlin's familiar dark hair, she saw a head of wispy blond baldness, an aggressively mahogany tan, the gleam of a self-satisfied smile, and a lot of white linen.

"Steve! Steve Usher," Angie said, as if announcing the Second Coming of Christ. "All the way from Malibu!"

✶   ✶   ✶

Halfway through dinner, Juliette had to admit that Usher, despite his rather plummy British accent and rock-star swagger, might not be as terrible as she had previously thought. He was certainly not as terrible as Gabe thought.

"Are you kidding me?" Gabe had hissed into her ear as she slid into her seat once the necessary introductions were made. "We have to sit here and listen to this charlatan? This was not part of the deal." Juliette just shook her head, while Angie chattered on about how Steve had so generously agreed to visit because he had meant to come when they were in Rome but then Lloyd had died.

"I was on my way to London, so I thought I'd stop by and see if I could be of any use . . ."

"He needs a new travel agent. On what map is Italy located between Los Angeles and London?" Gabe hissed again, wedging himself between Juliette and Mercy, almost directly across from Usher.

"It being such a sad thing, such a difficult time," Usher continued just as if he hadn't heard Gabe, which was physically impossible, "for all of us." He reached over and patted Mercy's hand. She drew it away and stared at him as if he were speaking another language. "I will be leading an early morning meditation, if anyone is interested. And, of course, I brought a few copies of my Little Book." He produced a copy from the frayed woven wool satchel he had slung around his shoulders and held it up as if he were an author being interviewed on a morning talk show. "And some of my herbal Work Through It packs—they've become quite a hit on sets back in L.A., you know, all organic, of course, and I'll throw in a copy of the solo album if you need a laugh. God knows I've got enough of those left to build my own villa. Nothing like a healthy dose of public humiliation to keep you sober." He smiled winningly as he laid the book and the box of herbal supplements down on the table.

Glancing down the table, Juliette could see the smug smile on Carson's face. Michael was seated beside her and she had her arm draped around the back of his chair. He seemed to be laughing to himself, though Juliette could not tell if the source of his amusement was Usher or the strange and tense group eating pear and gorgonzola pizza together under a purple sky. Ben Golonski was there, sporting a carefully groomed five-day stubble and baseball cap. He was holding forth on balsamic vinegars and the many things he had learned about winemaking from his good friend Francis Ford Coppola.

"There's nothing you can do here that you can't do in Sonoma," he said airily. "Regionalism is dead."

For a moment Juliette was extremely grateful for the presence of Steve Usher; if Gabe had heard Golonski, who clearly knew nothing about any of the subjects he was discussing, blood would have been spilled.

Next to the director a slight pale man was wolfing down his food and continually looking at his watch; this could only be the writer, Juliette thought. What was his name? Joseph something? Something Joseph? Devlin had said something about him, that he had almost come to blows with Golonski when Michael was brought in because the star's age and large personality had required the rewriting of key scenes. The writer had been pushing Brad Pitt. Watching Joseph devour an entire pizza, folding the pieces over New York style, which was a very messy way to eat the thin-crust Italian version, she had to admit he did not seem happy. When he wasn't eating, he was venting loud frustrated sighs.

It was just the sort of situation that Michael reveled in, a sort of Hollywood-living-up-to-its-reputation moment. Sitting between Carson and the production manager, O'Connor was busy reminiscing about the various gangsters he had played over the years, and the mobsters he had befriended so he could learn their ways.

"This one guy was missing three fingers and an ear and walked with a horrible limp," he said. "He had been kneecapped but his capo kept him around, treated him like a lapdog, as a reminder of what could happen if you didn't follow orders to the letter."

As he recounted a conversation he'd had recently with "Marty and Jack," Juliette almost laughed. On the one hand, he was clearly offering the table a performance; on the other, he was very much in his element. She accidentally caught his eye as she thought this and he smiled what seemed like a Juliette-specific smile, as if the two of them were complicit in the orchestration and enjoyment of the scene around them. Despite herself, she felt vital pieces of her internal construction begin to soften and wobble. Down the table, Angie and even Mercy were laughing. Juliette wrenched her gaze away from O'Connor to hear Usher mid-anecdote.

"So there I was," he was saying. "No knickers to speak of, and the camera's rolling. Thank God I play the guitar. If I had just been on vocals I don't see how Her Majesty could have ever invited me back.

"What a gorgeous place this is," he said when the laughter had died down. "I mean, simply amazing. I am amazed. And Angie tells me it belongs to your family." He looked inquiringly at Juliette.

"I do wish we could somehow get Steve into one of those wonderful little villas down among the vineyards," Angie said. "Away from all the craziness." She motioned away from the patio to where the set work was still proceeding. "I think it would be best for Mercy if she had a place she could go, some quieter place to talk, or whatever it is Steve feels she needs to do."

"Mother," said Mercy. "I am sitting right here. The woman who is paying for *Steve* and pretty much every other plan you come up with. Right here."

"Those villas," said Gabe, not allowing her to launch whatever remonstration she had in mind, "are farmhouses. Villas were for the rich; farmhouses, on the other hand, housed as many as six families at a time, families who worked this land for subsistence wages. Nowadays, if you believe all the inns and bed-and-breakfasts, it would seem there were only landowners and no workers in Tuscany. This is the villa, where the aristocracy, the historical equivalent of the rock stars, lived. So I'm sure Mr. Usher will be far more comfortable here, though Siena remains quite convenient for any and all who find their rooms less than satisfactory."

Silence rang around the patio as everyone stared at Gabe. Juliette hooked her feet around her chair so she would not kick him, but Gabe calmly helped himself to more pizza. Watching him, Mercy laughed in delight and he looked up, startled, and smiled.

"Your new well," Carson said into the seemingly interminable pause. "They'll begin work tomorrow. As we agreed. And Steve will be staying with us as long as he can, for the duration of the shoot, I hope. His presence alleviates so many concerns." She smiled brightly at Mercy.

"We should probably have a little ceremony before they start," Juliette said quickly, to change the subject. "Or else Saint Bernardine might curse us or something. Right? Saint Bernardine is the monk who found the well. He was preaching to a bunch of the tenants . . . well, you should tell them, Gabe. Tell the story of the well."

"Tell us," Mercy said quickly. For a moment it was almost painful to see how much she wanted everything to work out. "Tell us about the well. And Saint whatever his name is. Please, Gabe," she said, pitching her voice low and irresistible. Juliette saw a glance pass between Steve and Angie.

For a moment Gabe wavered between his irritation and Mercy's eager smile. The smile won. "Saint Bernardine was a monk who lived in Siena during the Middle Ages," he said with a sigh, beginning what was obviously an oft-told story. "He was a bit of a celebrity himself, actually, a man of rare rhetorical gift, and as his fame grew, whenever he chose to preach, hundreds, sometimes thousands would gather. Even so, Bernardine was a bit of a wet blanket; he was a great moralist, no surprise given his job description, but he was also a teetotaler, which was a bit unusual for an Italian, even an Italian monk."

At this, everyone laughed, and Juliette smiled, remembering all the stories he used to tell her when they were children, walking through the woods or picking grapes or sitting hidden behind one stone wall or another. Stories from history and stories from his own wild imagination.

"One day he announced he would preach at Cerreta and all the tenants, some four or five hundred, showed up. You know that little pull-out in the road on the way up? That's where he stood, with all the peasants on the hill surrounding him. On this day, he chose to preach about the evils of alcohol, of wine in particular, how it ruined men's health, their families, their ability to work, how it interrupted their relationship with God."

Gabe pointedly ignored Usher, who glanced around the table and twitched his mouth knowingly, leaning back a bit as if acknowledging that Gabe was telling this particular tale in honor of him and his work at Resurrection.

"Now, as much as everyone loved the monk, this didn't go over so well with a crowd of people who had little pleasure in their lives besides the wine they drank at lunch and dinner . . . and breakfast and before siesta and . . ." More laughter. "So, finally, one fellow spoke up and told the monk that it was easy to speak of such things, but here at Cerreta there was very little water, only a small stream. It was a lot of work to tote the water back to the houses, and when they did, it was brackish and unhealthy. They drank so much wine, the man explained, because they had no water.

"The monk considered this for a moment and said, 'I understand your life is hard, my brother, and I will do what I can to aid you.' And he climbed the hill into the crowd of peasants, and after walking a hundred yards or so from the road he picked up his staff and smote the ground. Once, twice, three times. And from the place he struck, a spring appeared, bubbling, then gushing with clear, clean, cold water. And that is where our well is now and where everyone who lived at Cerreta has gotten their water ever since." He paused for a moment. "It must be said that as impressed as those peasants were by the miracle they witnessed, the winery continued to flourish. But the Cerreta farmers became well known for their personal cleanliness."

"That's a great story," Golonski said loudly amid the laughter. "An unbelievably great story. So authentic. I love that story." He took a big swallow of wine. "We should work that into the script. Can we work that into the script? Have, I don't know, the well stand for the girl's untapped sexuality. Maybe some little priest could tell it. Or a tour guide. We could just use that guy," he said, lowering his voice, but not enough. "He's like a tour guide, isn't he?"

With a small wry smile, Steve Usher came to the rescue. He raised his glass of water in a toast. "*Salut,*" he said. "To a Tuscan oasis with a long history of sobriety. Which is even stranger than finding sobriety in Malibu." And he laughed so self-deprecatingly that even Gabe had to join in.

"To Saint Bernardine," Gabe said. "I hope he takes the new well in the spirit in which it's dug—desperation."

"Steve Usher is here because he very kindly offered to be here," said Carson, when Juliette caught up with her after dinner. There were several other people she would rather be talking to, and at least a dozen other things she would prefer doing. But in answer to Mercy's look of anguished defiance, Juliette felt obligated to find out if Steve had been Angie's idea or Carson's. Now she and Carson were walking quickly down the villa steps, heading toward the carriage house, where, to Juliette's alarm, a shower of sparks indicated the work of a blowtorch.

"Somehow," Carson added pointedly, one eye firmly on her iPhone in a gesture Juliette found unnervingly familiar, "news of Mercy's latest exploits made it back to L.A. and our friends at the insurance company. Who yesterday threatened to nullify Mercy's policy under some pertinent clause or other that requires she not ingest so many drugs that she actually kills herself. They want some sort of safeguard, beyond the obviously ineffectual efforts of her mother, because they're the ones who have to pay if Mercy wigs out. Which they would rather not do, having already written a sizable check for the production costs incurred by Lloyd's death. So Steve Usher is here and here he will stay, at Mercy's own expense, or this will be the last movie she ever makes."

"Okay," Juliette said, at once filled with admiration for Carson's efficient understanding of a rather alarming and complex situation, and repulsed by that admiration because she found Carson so deeply unlikable. "I understand your—their—need for that kind of reassurance. But Steve Usher? Don't you think that may wind up making the situation worse? Mercy doesn't seem very happy about having him thrust on her." Juliette met Carson stride for stride and tried not to obsess about the blowtorch, which was really sparking now. "I think perhaps—"

"You think perhaps what?" Carson stopped and faced her. "You think now that she's here among the lavender and the grapes she'll be happy? You think if she's happy she won't take drugs, drink herself insensible, and fuck whatever happens to pass her door? Because that's just stupid, and you don't look stupid. The only thing that girl has to be unhappy about is the fact that she's a drug addict who continually refuses to get help even when that help is 'thrust on her.'"

In obvious disgust, Carson began walking again and Juliette grudgingly noted her ability to quickly navigate the rocky ground while wearing four-inch heels. "She should be grateful Usher's taking the trouble. Frankly, she should be grateful *you're* taking the trouble. But she isn't. I can guarantee that. When something good happens to women like Mercy, they think they deserve it and just a little bit more, and when something bad happens, they think everyone is out to get them. You may have the time and inclination to cope with personalities like that, but I sure as hell don't."

"Then you, my dear, are very much in the wrong business." Michael's voice glimmered out of the darkness just three beats before he appeared.

He approached Carson before she could reach the ring of light spilling from what was now the set, positioning himself between the two women. "Because you've just described almost every actor, director, screenwriter, and producer I have ever met. Including myself. Especially myself."

Carson laughed and was suddenly beautiful again. "Not you," she said flirtatiously, "never you. You are the only thing that is making this movie work. You're far too easy to please and when you ask for something, you always remember to say thank you."

Juliette turned away, attempting to turn an inadvertent choking sound into something approximating a cough.

"Not always," Michael said gravely. "Only when I think it will get me . . . just a little bit more." He gave the producer a mild, self-mocking leer. "And speaking of the less-than-thrilling aspects of your job, there seems to be an argument brewing between camera, lights, and action over yonder that may need your diplomatic skills. Sorry, boss," he said when Carson made a sound of impatience. "I'm just the messenger."

"You're kidding me, right?" Juliette said as she watched Carson's long slim back grow smaller and more shadowy. "'You always remember to say thank you?' God, it makes me embarrassed to be a woman. Is that the way women treat you, in general?"

When Michael responded with only a shrug and a mildly amused look, Juliette hurried on. "And what is her problem with Mercy? I mean, okay, Mercy is a huge pain in the ass, but Carson's getting what she wants."

"What do you mean?" O'Connor asked carefully.

"I saw the footage from the other day and it was amazing. You and Mercy are so . . ." She paused for a moment, trying to figure out a way to say what she meant without echoing words he had heard and read a million times. "Well, you're just very good at what you do. Which is not surprising, I guess, but so is Mercy, which kind of is . . . considering."

"So you don't find it strange that I'm one hundred and fifty years older than she is?" Although Michael's tone was light, Juliette was surprised by a small undercurrent of anxiety. Anxiety was not an emotion she had ever associated with Michael O'Connor. "I don't look like some sort of craven old movie star desperately trying to hang on to a romantic lead for which he is clearly unsuited?"

Juliette couldn't help laughing. There he stood, all six-foot-one of him, and yes, there were lines around the famous blue eyes, dug in around his mouth by a million trademark grins. But still he was one of the handsomest men she had ever seen, and more than that, he radiated that indescribable quality that almost literally forced you to look at him. Juliette had seen senators and CEOs stutter in his presence, watched as women drew themselves straight and leaned toward him when he entered a room, like flowers following sunlight. And he was worried he looked too old for Mercy.

"Oh, my God," she said, still laughing. "You're serious. How can you be serious?"

"Don't laugh," he said sheepishly. "I am exposing my greatest fear and humility. I figure you can take it, considering you've seen me bald and thin and vomiting, with embarrassing regularity."

"Does that bother you?" Juliette asked curiously. She had wondered if that was the reason he had not called, had not written. She had seen all that, and worse, had seen him so altered he was unrecognizable. It had been difficult for him to find his footing with her after that. Men like O'Connor could not stand being seen as merely mortal.

"Enough," he said. "But not as much as the very real possibility that I made a mistake saying yes to this film. That after my . . . hiatus, I will return to the public eye making an absolute fool of myself. Not that I haven't made a fool of myself before," he added, "but the bounce-back factor, like so many things, diminishes with age."

"You're being ridiculous," Juliette said simply. "And you know it."

When he looked down at her, she found it suddenly difficult to breathe. He was impossible, she thought. An impossible man to be with, an impossible man to love. This whole thing was just . . . impossible.

"Even Carson says you two look perfect," she said quickly, taking a step backward. "Not that Carson is exactly the person I would trust to tell me the truth. Doesn't she know that's how it works in this business? If your movies make money we treat you like gods, and then complain when you act like them." She shook her head. "If everyone was easy to get along with, I would be out of work."

"And that is why we behave the way we do," O'Connor said. "Demanding our toast slightly burnt, our sheets warmed in the winter and chilled in the summer, and our water from glass bottles. Because we want you, Juliette Greyson, to remain gainfully employed at the Pinnacle. So we will always know where to find you." His voice was low and he stood quite close, looking down at her with bright, expectant eyes. "You have no idea the trouble I had to go through to find an excuse to visit Tuscany."

"You're beaming," Juliette said. "Quit beaming at me. It's never a good sign. Why does Carson hate Mercy anyway? Or does she hate everyone . . . who isn't you?"

"Oh, I suspect she will come to hate me, too," he said, raising his hand to tuck a bit of hair behind her ear. Juliette swatted it away. Why should it always be so easy for him anyway? As if he could read her mind, he laughed softly. "Carson hates Mercy for the oldest reason in the world—Mercy slept with her husband and broke up their marriage; and to make matters worse, she doesn't even know she did it."

"What?"

Michael grinned. He might be in midseduction, but like all movie people, there was nothing he liked better than gossip.

"Carson was married to one of the producers who worked on that film Mercy did about the girl who gets pregnant by her English professor and then falls in love with his wife. Launched the mercifully brief career of that screenwriter with all those facial piercings? Anyway, at some point in the proceedings the star screwed the producer. He thought it was *lurve*, ditched Carson, but when he presented himself as a free man to Mercy, she didn't even remember sleeping with him. He tried to crawl back to Carson, but she was having none of it. Which was the only possible response—adultery one can forgive, utterly forgettable adultery requires damnation. To this day, I don't think Mercy has made the connection. As you may have noticed, she is an admirably self-centered young woman."

Juliette was speechless. Whatever fondness and sympathy she had felt for Mercy began to evaporate, while she suddenly saw Carson in a much more forgiving light. Juliette knew well the feeling of rage, the sense of overwhelming injustice, that curdles so easily into hatred when someone who seems to have everything decides the one thing she's missing is your husband. Juliette could still see the tragic figure Anna Stewart made of herself after Josh had been killed, how she had paraded herself like a widow in front of everyone, including Juliette, as if somehow her scant months with Josh replaced the ten years of Juliette's marriage to him.

"Lovely," she said now. "Well, that certainly explains a lot. But why would Becker send Carson out onto this project with a history like that? And don't tell me he didn't know; if you know, he knows."

Michael shoved his hands in his pockets. "Who better to keep Mercy in line? You see how sympathetic she can seem. Just a poor little misunderstood waif . . . who just happens to be shutting down a multimillion-dollar project and putting many people's quite ordinary jobs at risk. Carson wants the big-time enough to make sure that, no matter what, she delivers a good picture. That's all she really cares about, and that's all Becker cares about."

"And you?" Juliette asked. "What do you care about? Doesn't any of what's happened bother you? Doesn't it bother you, walking into a situation like this? The guy you're replacing overdosed, your costar seems on her way to following suit, the director is an egotistical moron who seems intent on killing his own writer, and the producer who's supposed to keep everything running has a personal vendetta against her female lead."

O'Connor's mouth twitched at the corner. "And your point is?"

"Oh, come on," Juliette said. "Every movie has its tensions, but this is insane. I know everyone thinks Mercy is a joke, but Jesus, Michael, Lloyd Watson is *dead*. And even if Mercy is a selfish little husband stealer, someone should help her before she winds up dead, too. Don't any of you people care?"

Michael sighed. "God, Juliette, if I could save an addict simply by showing that I cared, I could retire to the sanctity of my holy mountain already. Do you think she's the first drugged-out, semi-suicidal costar I've ever had? Mercy Talbot is going to make her own choices no matter what anyone, including the rapidly aging Michael O'Connor, says. I can only try to limit the damage she inflicts on this project. Which is exactly what Carson is doing. Which is exactly what you would do if you were her."

Hearing herself compared to Carson again, Juliette stiffened. What had been wavering inside her righted itself. "How can you make the sort of movies you do when you're so cold-blooded about the people you actually know? Why does everyone say they know addiction is a disease but when they have an addict in front of them, they act like it's just some form of über-brattiness? As you keep pointing out, she's just a *kid*. A kid who won't live long enough to be married four times if something doesn't change pretty soon."

Her hands were all but on her hips, she was so angry. At Carson and Mercy, at the cheating husband whom she couldn't even name. At Josh and herself for moving to Los Angeles and thinking they would somehow survive. At Michael, especially at Michael, for all those weeks with no word, though he knew she was worried, for coming to Tuscany and then only calling when he needed help, for the desire that closed her throat and twisted her stomach just the same. He had told her long ago how demanding he was while he was working, how impossible to live with, but she hadn't believed him because at the time it hadn't seemed possible, not when he seemed the only person who wasn't afraid to say things that were true. But he was an actor, after all, and the number one rule at the Pinnacle, and all over Los Angeles, was: Never fall for an actor.

Juliette was so busy working herself up in righteous indignation that it took her a minute to realize Michael was reaching up to cup her face in his two hands, sliding his fingers underneath her hair, behind her ears, tracing her jaw with his thumbs, holding her as if she were something delicate enough to break.

"Look at you," he said in a low, quiet voice. "Just look at you. Trying to fix all our problems for us when really all you have to do to make the world better is just stand there."

For a moment Juliette paused and considered the stars, entire constellations of them, and the small white roses climbing up the archway of the wall near where they stood. She felt the day's warmth rise from the stone, heard the rustling swoosh of leaves disturbed by lifted wings off in the dark.

"You are a natural-born liar," she said, kissing him anyway because of course she was going to kiss him, she had known she was going to kiss him from the moment she heard his voice on the phone, from the second she had seen him across the Campo at Siena. Why else was he here? Why else had she gone when he called, said yes when Carson had asked, why else was she allowing all this insanity to happen, if not so she could kiss Michael O'Connor under ripe, low-hanging stars?

His mouth settled against hers as if it had only been a day since they had last stood like this, and his hands slid under her shirt. Taking slow backward steps, she led him into the shadows that lapped along the villa wall and leaned against the rough warm stone, offering no resistance.

He tasted of red wine and rosemary and the salty tang of mozzarella and she laughed quietly as she felt her flesh press against the ancient rock of her ancestral home. Though he was stronger and broader than he had been when she last touched him, he was still as familiar to her as the earth and the flowers and the fields of this place that she had hidden from her heart for so long.

Clinging to him with mouth and arms, thighs and hands, she moved him along the wall, under the archway, and down a few worn steps. Now they were invisible in the dark, sheltered from all eyes by the villa itself. Buttons gave then, and seams, until skin met skin and desire loosened her hips, her knees. Her head banged against the wall, scraped against the stone, but still she could not pull him close enough, could not open herself wide enough. His body covered her, erased everything that had happened before, pinned her firmly against the present.

The smell of new wine crept out from beneath the wooden door to their left; here was the entrance to the cellar, with its cool dirt floors, its long low shelves. She felt for the great metal ring to open the door, but then his hands were sliding down, raising her skirt, his fingers slipping under and up and in, and she answered his brief, inquiring smile with a breathless nod; with a shudder she found his belt, his button. As her hand closed around him, he murmured her name into her ear and at the last crucial minute, only the strength of his hands and a small ledge allowed her to remain upright as he drove inside her, her shoulders raked against the stone, and every bone in her body dissolved in pleasure and relief. Almost silently they shivered in the night, fingers clutching, muscles rocking, another restless creature in the dark.

"I understand there are beds in this establishment," Michael said later as they buttoned and zipped, tugged and brushed each other down. "I noticed at least one in my room."

"Indeed," said Juliette, who felt so giddy and astonished she almost choked. "This place is, in fact, lousy with beds."

"They might make an interesting alternative, in the future," he said, gingerly flexing his knees.

"Feeling your age?"

"Not me," he said, pinning her once again. "I've always done my best work with my back against the wall. Oh, wait, that was you."

"Stop." She laughed, kissing him, then pushing him away, then kissing him again. "No, seriously. Seriously," and, laughing, she stumbled up the steps and onto the lawn, dragging him by the hand.

"My place or yours?" he said. "Oh, come on," he protested when she hesitated. "Everyone here is an adult, at least by the legal definition. And it's no one's business who's in my bed, or yours. After all"—he grinned wickedly—"we're on location."

"I am so not the right person for that particular argument," Juliette said, but she was loath to part from him, and the thought of spending one uninterrupted night together, something that had yet to happen, was very appealing. "All right, mine. Mercy's at the house but her bedroom is upstairs. And it's still more private than the villa. We'll see how it goes, Mr. O'Connor."

They skirted the cameras and wires that now filled the courtyard. As they approached Casa Padua, Juliette could see Gabe hurrying down the porch steps toward them.

"There you are," he said impatiently. "Everyone has been looking all over for you. Mostly you," he said, motioning to Juliette, "and mostly Mercy. But Carson was also expressing concern about your whereabouts." He nodded toward Michael with a less-than-approving glance. "Because they seem to have confused me with the concierge, they sent me to find you. They're all over at the villa, the whole grisly lot of them, in the main living room," he explained, turning them around and propelling them back toward the villa, "drinking some of my best wine.

God, Juliette, look at the state of you," he exclaimed, catching sight of her back and immediately brushing off the gritty streaks of dust from her blouse and skirt. "What the hell have you been—Oh, nice. Lovely. What is this, day one? You know there are beds at Cerreta," he said, directing the last comment at Michael.

"So I've been told. In fact, we were just on our way."

"Well, I'm afraid the Love Boat has hit an iceberg." Gabe all but pushed them through the side entrance, through the winding warren of halls that led past the kitchen and the stairway that led to the bedrooms and library, through the dining room, and up a few steps to the main hallway. "Because there's a detective here from Rome and he seems to think that maybe your friend Lloyd Watson didn't kill himself after all."

Inspector Di Marco was a slight, silver-haired gentleman wearing a very nice suit that Juliette could not immediately place, although she suspected Armani. He had basset-hound eyes, a small smile that shone like an apple slice from under an equally circumspect mustache, and he could not have been more polite. New evidence had surfaced; no he could not share what it was, but some questions had emerged from various sources regarding the cause of death, and the investigation was being—here he groped for a word, before turning to Gabriel and muttering in Italian. "Revisited," Gabe said.

"Yes," the inspector said. "Revisited."

He turned and surveyed the group before them: Mercy curled small and childlike in an armchair, with Angie draped protectively around her. Steve Usher sat beside her on a straight-backed chair, his elbows on his knees, his fingers steepled under his nose, and a look of serene attention on his face. Golonski leaned back into the corner of a sofa with a self-consciously amused smile on his face, legs spread wide in the classic position of alpha male, while the writer whose name was, indeed, Joseph Andrews, sat perched on the edge just beside him, nervously jiggling his foot. Carson leaned against the large oak table, her posture impeccable, her face unreadable as she glanced repeatedly at Michael, who sat on a low bench beside Juliette. Gabe hung in the doorway, his eyes straying more often than not toward Mercy.

We look like the climactic scene in an Agatha Christie novel, Juliette thought. *Any minute the lights will go out and a shot will be fired and then Hercule Poirot will explain everything.*

But nothing more dramatic occurred than the inspector explaining that he simply wanted to review the information that was given to his colleagues on the day of Lloyd's death. He was sorry to arrive so late, he had gotten terribly lost on his way to Cerreta. He understood, he said with an ingratiating smile, that many present were on their way to bed because of the early hours required by Hollywood. He was happy to come back tomorrow to speak with those who had been present on the day of Lloyd's death, at their personal convenience.

"Meanwhile," he said, "if you could consult your memories to see if there was anything at all unusual about the day of and the day after Mr. Watson's unfortunate death, I would be extremely grateful. And I should speak to you," he asked, motioning to Carson, "to set up my little interviews?"

"Yes," said Carson, lifting herself from the desk and signaling that the meeting was now over. "I—we—will be happy to help you in any way possible. But as you say, it is late and there is a six a.m. call tomorrow, so I'm sure we would all be grateful for the opportunity to retire."

"Yes, yes, of course," said the inspector. "Though I was wondering, or rather hoping you could . . ." He dug around in his suit pockets and produced a small notebook, which he flipped open. "Mr. O'Connor," he said, finding the page he wanted. "Would you mind?" He offered Michael the notebook and a pen. "An autograph? For my wife Lucia. She is your biggest fan."

"Soooo," Steve Usher said when they all made their way out of the living room, "that wasn't too bad, not too scary. I must admit that even after all these years I get a bit twitchy when the law is *en prémisse*. Patting the old pockets, don't you know, wondering if I've disposed of the stash. Second nature, I suppose, after so many years of criminal behavior." With the last two words he carved quotation marks in the air with his fingers, laughing in an all-inclusive way. "I remember this one time in Liverpool . . ." His voice trailed off as they all emerged into the night and clearly no one paused to listen. "Oh, well, so I'll see you at five-thirty, then, Mercy. For a little meditation and a consult?"

"You will not," said Mercy, stopping, then turning to face him. "Look, Steve, I appreciate you fulfilling some insurance requirement by being here and I'm happy to pay for you to have a little Tuscan holiday. But I think the less we see of each other, the better. You didn't seem to do Lloyd that much good," she added nastily.

"Mercy," Angie admonished.

"It's all right, Angie," Usher said with a conciliatory hand over his heart. "I totally understand. Lloyd and Mercy were sharing a journey and Mercy's feeling bitter, disappointed in her friend, perhaps even in me for not having been a better guide. Not surprising. But you know Lloyd made his own decisions. I urged him to turn down this project, to focus on his sobriety, and his new family, but he was determined, mostly"— here he placed the slightest, merest, most deadly of pauses—"because he so wanted to work with you, my dear." The shot went home. Even from twenty paces, Juliette could see Mercy slouch, feel the heavy waves of guilt. "Of course, it is entirely your own decision," he concluded. "I am completely at your disposal." He made a small bow and began walking back to his room at the villa.

"She'll be there, Steve," Angie called. "Five-thirty sharp." And with an impatient twitch, she thrust her iPhone into Mercy's hand. Mercy glanced down and fury crossed her face, quickly replaced by resignation.

"You really are such a bitch," she said, almost sadly, as she trailed away, "Mother."

* * *

Whatever flame had been rekindled between Michael and Juliette seemed at least temporarily extinguished. Though he joined her in Casa Padua, their attempts to recapture what had moved them earlier in the evening were soon thwarted by the sound of muffled sobs coming from Mercy's room. *Why is she crying?* Juliette wondered, distracted for a moment even from Michael's mouth and Michael's hands. *Is it because the detective had shown up? What had been on Angie's iPhone?*

No, she thought firmly, *I cannot fix that, I will try to fix this,* and she closed her mind to everything not physically connected to him.

For a moment her efforts were fruitful, but then:

"Jesus," Michael said, rolling onto his back.

"I'll go talk to her," Juliette said.

"No, you'll just make it worse. And that's probably exactly what she wants. Why are you even letting her stay here?"

"I don't know," Juliette answered, exasperated. "Because that's what you do when someone is in the kind of trouble she's in?"

During those weeks when she had finally given up drugs, Juliette, too, had wept for no reason she could have explained. And Alex, her first real boss, the man who gave her a job and a future, let her stay with him for almost a month. He never shushed her, never yelled or lectured. Instead, he had brought sugary tea and pieces of toast, homemade lemonade and scones. Juliette believed that Mercy wanted to get well. She was just too afraid to let go of the things that had fueled her life for so long. And that Juliette understood, even if no one else here did.

"Unbelievable. Fucking unbelievable," Michael groaned. "It's like living with a child. Listen to her." He motioned toward the closed door. "Through stone walls a foot thick. No wonder her mother pumps her full of sleeping pills. If she doesn't stop, I'm going to give her a dozen

Ambien myself. Oh, my God," he said looking at his watch, "it's past midnight and we've got a six a.m. call. She'll be an extra hour in makeup already, just for her eyes!"

With another groan, he lifted himself out of bed and reached for his pants.

"You're going," Juliette said flatly.

"Darling," he said, leaning over and kissing her. "You are lovely and miraculous but I will never sleep here. And I have to sleep. I am over fifty, you know, and we'll be at it another thirteen hours again because somehow I sense my costar will not be in top form. You are certainly more than welcome to come with me, but sleeping will occupy most of the agenda."

In the next room, Mercy's sobbing took on a spasmodic quality and Juliette could hear drawers being pulled open, things falling to the floor as the girl searched for something. Michael drew on his shirt, then sat down and put on his shoes and looked up at her inquiringly.

"No," Juliette said. "I should stay, I guess. Make sure she's not in there washing down pills with tequila, or whatever did her in last time around. It was fun while it lasted," she said, getting up and following him to the door.

"And will be again," he said hurrying out the door. Watching him go, without a backward glance, Juliette fought the urge to follow. Instead, she padded up the stairs to comfort Mercy, who refused to explain why she was crying and did indeed quiet down the moment Juliette gave up and just crawled into bed beside her. Or maybe, Juliette thought as she, too, finally drifted away, it was just the Oxy finally kicking in.

Chapter Eight

THE FOLLOWING DAYS WENT by quickly, propelled by the tense and constant beat of the shoot. The sound of construction stilled only when filming began, and resumed the minute Golonski yelled cut. The rewrites were contant; they had gone through three shades of pink, four of green. Even the weather seemed anxious and uncertain. At times the air went brassy and lightning flashed at the edges of the steel-gray storm clouds.

Below, so much work was going on in so many places that Juliette, who had always prided herself on her ability to multitask, could not keep track of what was going on. Only the script supervisor, a woman in rimless spectacles who shadowed Golonski with an open script and a pencil, and the production manager seemed privy to that information, but they, like everyone else, were speaking in a language Juliette did not quite understand, moving in a pattern she did not quite recognize, and after a day or so she simply stopped trying.

"It's impossible," she said during another phone conversation with Devlin. "I mean, I thought what we did was complicated. But these people, they just whittle entire cities out of nothing. Seriously. They've managed to make this small corridor between the villa and the carriage house look like a city street. At least from a certain angle. And they've got electricians and carpenters who show up on time. Every day! Do you know how impossible that is, especially in Italy? It's unheard-of. I keep waiting for them to get arrested for violating the Italian slacker law."

Devlin chuckled appreciatively. "Carson Cooper understands that the main job of a producer is to produce," he said.

"Oh, great, another Carson fan," she said. "Do you know her? How is it I have never heard of her? She seems like a person I would have heard of."

"We were . . . briefly acquainted," he said. "In New York."

"Oh, dear God," Juliette said. "So you slept with her. Of course you slept with her."

"This was years ago, J.," he said reassuringly. "Years. I believe her husband had just left her, and it was only one night. Or two."

"Stop. Just stop." Juliette put her hand to her forehead as if to prevent an image from forming there; was there any woman living with whom Devlin had not been "briefly acquainted"? "It's none of my business. It was certainly not the purpose of this call. I was simply hoping you could tell me why the Roman police are suddenly reopening the Lloyd Watson case."

In as few words as possible, she told him what Di Marco had said. "Meanwhile, Mercy keeps making these mysterious little comments about Lloyd being killed and I just wondered if you had heard anything over there."

"I will certainly ask around," Devlin said gravely. "And do tell Carson I said hello."

Juliette ground her teeth and said nothing.

"And of course our dear Mr. O'Connor," he added.

"You are a canny idiot," she said, laughing despite herself. "And I . . ."

"What? You what? You'll be returning home as soon as the picture wraps? I am allowing myself to be encouraged by this sudden spate of phone calls, even if you are just pumping me for information."

"Call me if you hear anything," she said, laughing again.

*   *   *

Along with the business of making the movie was the business of running Cerreta, or what Cerreta had become during the past week, and that was one job Juliette did understand. Which was fortunate because many of the interns were suddenly expressing lifelong interest in filmmaking, jockeying for extra work or just hanging around with the crew, many of whom were very good-looking Italian men. Gabriel, now happily ensconced as on-site historical consultant, barely had time to notice that his interns had deserted him or that the farm manager had suddenly produced three lovely daughters, all of whom, miraculously, had head shots. Juliette was both amused and relieved. Not only could she revel in the sight of Gabe mesmerized by the business he so often disparaged, but this meant she could run things her way. She took full and shameless advantage of the film budget, ordering new linens, an upgraded refrigerator for the salami, and air-conditioning units for the chapel and library, which had always been prohibitively stuffy by early spring.

She hired some local women to clean and help in the kitchen, and offered one of the interns a job as guest-relations manager. Mainly, she wanted someone who spoke good English to answer the phones. Mercy wanted a massage therapist, Michael needed a facialist "who really understands steam," and Juliette found, to her alarmed surprise, that a small army of day spas had cropped up around the more touristy hill towns like San Gimignano. The woman she finally hired was also a licensed aromatherapist from Rome who did facials, waxing, and nails, and, as luck would have it, who also knew a former nurse who performed colonics.

"She has her own facial mister," she told Michael, "which is apparently the hallmark of a true professional. And the Romans practically invented steam."

Soon some of the local merchants got wind of the shoot and trucks full of cheese and pastries, leather goods and silk, perfume and local pottery began making their way up the road, turning the courtyard into a tail-gate market day. Angie spent two hours picking through the handbags that filled one white van before announcing peevishly that she wanted one made by a certain Sienese cobbler named Marcello whom she had read about in *Condé Nast Traveler,* and why hadn't Juliette invited him to Cerreta already, since Angie had noticed that Juliette's bag had been made by him?

Without missing a beat, Juliette summoned Marcello, who was bearded and handsome, with two gold earrings like a pirate, and caused quite a stir as he made his way through the courtyard. Angie apparently wanted new shoes as well, along with a purse like Juliette's and an Italian leather bag for Usher, to replace the ratty wool satchel he carried with him. Silent and smiling, Marcello made his way from one trailer to the other. Michael was next, then Golonski; Mercy spent so much time cloistered with him that for a moment it looked like the Sienese cobbler would shut down production until he agreed to come back the next day.

"That's what I imagined Roberto would look like," Mercy sighed as he drove away, referring to the sixteenth century painter Michael was playing. "So young and handsome; he's even handsomer than Lloyd." She was standing in the wardrobe trailer with the costume designer and two assistants pinning and stitching her into a silver evening gown. Juliette saw them exchange the exhilarated glances of "gossip received" and she wanted to slap them. "Oh, Juliette," Mercy said teasingly, "of course Michael's wonderful and he's making the movie so much more . . . interesting. But just imagine the shoemaker in a linen tunic and leather breeches. Marvelous. God," she said, twitching herself away from the busy hands, "maybe I should sleep with him instead. That would drive my mother absolutely insane."

When she wasn't procuring goods and services for the cast and crew, Juliette was trying to run interference between Golonski and Gabe. On his second night at Cerreta, Golonski tried to lecture Gabe about his various environmental credentials, which included, apparently, trips to the rain forest, the Sudan, and to view melting ice caps in Antarctica, all of

which he narrated in life-or-death heroic detail. Beyond asking the director what he estimated his personal lifetime consumption of jet fuel to be,
Gabe kept his mouth shut. But when Golonski later began a conversation
that seemed to place him as the founder of the slow food movement in
California, Juliette had to bodily remove her cousin from the area. That
evening, as everyone was gathering for dinner, a shrill scream shot through
the dusk; in a few moments, Golonski appeared at a dead run, spluttering something about prehistoric beasts. Juliette looked accusingly at
Gabe, who raised his shoulders innocently enough. After a few minutes of
Golonski almost incoherently describing the sight of a herd of enormous
clanking creatures shuffling across the road, comprehension dawned.

"Oh," she said. "They're just porcupines."

"But they were huge," Golonski said. "As big as sled dogs, and they
hissed and"—he shivered—"rattled."

"It's their quills that rattle," Juliette said sympathetically, while Gabe
shook with silent laughter beside her, "and they do hiss. They are bigger
than you think."

"Especially if you've only seen them in cartoons," Gabe said. "You
should just be grateful you didn't run into any wild boars. They can kill a
man, you know. One of our interns," he added, with a perfectly straight
face, "lost his leg last year. I never leave the villa without my .45."

After that, Golonski never ventured anywhere without two young personal assistants on either side—"boar bait," the crew came to call them.

Juliette rarely saw Michael; he was either on set working or in his
trailer reading, in makeup or wardrobe. He didn't eat breakfast, was too
preoccupied to talk at lunch, and often was too exhausted even to show
up at dinner. One night Juliette knocked on his door, and when she
entered, he looked up from his script as if he didn't know her. Even in
those moments when he was just sitting between takes, while his stand-
in took his place, O'Connor was either furiously marking up his script
or so lost in thought that it seemed out of the question to approach him.

"Maybe I could have dinner with the stand-in," Juliette murmured to Gabe as they stood for a moment in the villa's library looking out the window down at the day's set. Chris, a tall, broad-shouldered man with thick dark hair, had flown over from Los Angeles; he was O'Connor's regular stand-in.

"He's probably a much nicer guy," Gabe said. "Though he needs to get a real job. Who on earth are these people anyway? Mercy's stand-in looks like she's fifteen and she's got half the camera crew wrapped around her little finger. If Carson's not careful, she's going to have a statutory rape case on her hands, now that the police are officially installed here in little Los Angeles. Is the aromatherapist still around? Our detective looks like he could use a little ylang-ylang for energy."

"He does not appear to be going anywhere soon, does he?" Juliette said, glancing over at Inspector Di Marco, who was engaged in amiable conversation with Joseph Andrews. It had been three days since the detective began "revisiting" the cast and crew's memory of events preceding Lloyd's death, and he seemed to have no problem waiting hours on end for whomever he wanted to speak with next.

"Dev says the insurance company pushed the police to reopen the case," Juliette continued. "They don't want to pay out for accidental death, so they're trying to get it changed to suicide. Apparently somebody called in an anonymous tip about the forensic evidence. Not enough to change the verdict, but enough to pressure the Roman police into sniffing around. Or so," she finished, faltering a bit, when she saw the look on Gabe's face, "Devlin says."

Her cousin shook his head. "I thought you guys were in the hotel business. But whenever you talk about Devlin you make him sound like a combination of the Buddha and Remington Steele."

"Remington Steele?" Juliette snorted. "Jesus, Gabe, when was the last time you watched television? Devlin has an interesting past—"

"By which you mean he was once a drugged-out thief, too?"

"No. By which I mean . . . well, I don't really know what exactly I mean. Let's just say he's had a past that makes him very tolerant of other people's life experiences. You would be amazed if you knew the background of some of the Pinnacle staff. Seriously. They make you and me look like model citizens. Dev says he has the most trustworthy staff in the business because they all actually understand the consequences of betrayal."

Gabe shot her a look of keen appraisal. "What?"

"Nothing. It's just nice to see that you are capable of loving a man who isn't a bloodsucking egomaniac. Platonically, at least."

"Oh, my God," Juliette said, turning away from the window and heading toward the door. "We are not going to start this. You are not going to start this. I don't *love* anyone, and if I did, you certainly wouldn't understand the first thing about it—"

"Oh, that's healthy," said Gabe, following on her heels as she clattered down the stairs. "You don't love anyone. Right. I'm just saying that if instead of spending so much time helping Mercy sift through all the shit she is so clearly carrying around, you might want to start sifting through your own."

"You really are a poet, you know that? The Holden Caulfield of our generation," Juliette said, slamming into the kitchen, and methodically dumping every dirty glass, dish, and piece of cutlery into the sink. "I simply cannot understand why I don't want to follow your every step and piece of advice. Because you're so healthy, living here in eco-isolation a million miles from home, surrounded by a bunch of students who you can screw at will because you know they'll be on their way in six to eight weeks."

She turned to face him, panting slightly.

"Okay, okay," Gabe said, his palms up. "I'm not saying I'm some sort of example. But you are not me, Juliette. If you worked at it, you could probably become almost sort of normal."

✱ ✱ ✱

When the cameras weren't rolling, Mercy became silent and with-drawn. There were no more tears, and she did join Steve Usher for early morning meditations, which seemed to subdue her, if not fill her with serenity. Carson and Golonski were ecstatic. Their star was punctual, prepared, and focused. Gulping the multihued gelatinous pills from the seemingly inexhaustible pick-up pack supplied by Usher, Mercy at times took on a luminous, almost ethereal quality, as if she were indeed inhab-iting two separate time frames. Seeing her swathed in a black cape over her novice whites for the flashback scenes, Juliette thought she looked like she had stepped from a painting, a forgotten Botticelli or perhaps the lost Giotto. The detective had not interviewed Mercy yet, which Juliette thought strange, considering she was the one who had found the body. Instead, Di Marco seemed content to just watch the young star, a smile of pure pleasure tucked into his face. For her part, Mercy ignored him almost pointedly, though Angie occasionally drifted over to remind him that Mercy was quite busy but would be happy to help when she could. Invariably the inspector shook his head and continued watching. Juliette found his behavior odd. She began to think he was just another movie fan, milking his chance to be on set. She even called Rome, only to discover that he was precisely who he said he was.

Making her way through all the equipment and crew, Juliette edged herself toward the monitors, where Golonski was sitting, talking with Carson. As she approached, he gave her such a hostile look that Carson turned, and Juliette could see she was about to tell her to get lost. But a few yards away, O'Connor caught sight of her and grinned. He looked over to Carson and held his hands over his ears—a signal for Carson to give Juliette earphones—and immediately Carson's demeanor reversed itself. With a pleasant smile, she acquiesced, then offered her a chair. It was a modern scene, taking place in front of the villa/convent. Juliette laughed when she realized several of the interns were milling around in the background as "extras." As the action began, she was struck by how stark and unlikely and overlit the set looked, how stagy the dialogue and acting seemed, yet when she watched the scene unfolding on the screen, it looked wonderfully moody and emotional, and just like a movie.

It was a long scene, fueled by tense expository dialogue about the meaning of a certain painting and full of romantic tension as the two characters fought what was obviously a troublesome but undeniable attraction. Over and over Mercy and Michael ran the scene, with subtle changes here and there, and increasingly Juliette was struck by a sense of déjà vu in the . . . what? Not the lines, but something in Mercy's delivery, in the way she tipped her chin, in the emphasis she put on this word or that, how her air of expertise and efficiency dissolved at one point into bright laughter and a wary sidelong glance, all reminded her of someone she knew.

"That's weird," Juliette murmured to herself, wondering why it seemed so familiar.

"No. Not weird," said Carson, taking off her earphones. "You."

"That's a wrap," shouted a young man standing next to Golonski. "And that's lunch."

"What?" asked Juliette as everyone around her began to move.

"She's doing you," Carson said. "At least for the Roxanne part. I realized as soon as I met you. Probably why she was so intent on spending so much time with you. Courting the muse. Or maybe just getting that thing you do with your chin. It makes sense," she added, "since Roxanne's basically a love-starved control freak hoping someone will save her from herself. And please feel free to join us for lunch."

Turning, Juliette saw Michael and Mercy heading toward her, both of them, miraculously enough, smiling, but even as they reached her, Inspector Di Marco appeared. He took Mercy's arm as if he were her prearranged escort, asking if he might borrow a few minutes of her time.

"I—I don't know," Mercy stammered. "Have you talked to my mother?" She looked wildly around for Angie, in the hopes she would intercede, but Angie was strangely absent. "I guess so. We were going to lunch, though," she said, suddenly inspired. "I have to eat something; we have six more pages to get through and I haven't been feeling very well."

"No?" said the inspector. "I'm sorry to hear that. It does not show, of course. Your performance is inspiring. I told my wife about the movie and she and I can hardly wait for it to be. Perhaps I might join you, for lunch?"

Squaring her shoulders, Mercy seemed to settle back into character. "Certainly," she said, with a small nod Juliette recognized as her own. She shot a look at O'Connor, but his eyes were on the inspector.

It was perhaps the oddest lunch Juliette had ever endured. Watching Mercy answer the detective's questions while still in a modified version of the Roxanne character, Juliette felt strangely exposed, as if she were looking at herself naked in the mirror with everyone watching. God, did she really put her head to one side like that? But no one seemed to notice, or if they did, they gave no sign. For once, she wished Michael would play the megastar and request his lunch be served in his trailer; she even went so far as to suggest this, but he only smiled and shook his head. "I don't have enough time to eat and be in my trailer alone with you," he answered with a friendly leer. "Besides, one of the stylists is having her birthday and she wants me to cut the cake."

He motioned to one of the craft services tables, where a very American-looking sheet cake stood, festooned with frosting rosettes and loopy writing. Juliette had to laugh: no matter how famous or admired a star was, he or she was expected to preside over crew birthdays, and baby showers, and engagement announcements, choking down stale grocery store cakes and raising toasts. Some refused, of course, but then they were considered "difficult," and not even the most cushioned on-set nest created by the most thorough agent could totally protect a star from a resentful crew. Especially on location. O'Connor would sing "Happy Birthday" as many times as Carson or Golonski asked him to, and kiss the birthday girl, or boy, if that, too, was required.

Looking weary and slightly troubled, he asked Juliette how Gabe was bearing up, if the crew was composting rigorously enough, what Gabe had in mind for the place if it should indeed survive the filming. Juliette answered truthfully, explaining about the money problems and how she and Gabe differed on the future of Cerreta, but though he met every new piece of information with an appropriate comment or question, Michael clearly had his eyes on Mercy.

"Is she still doing me?" Juliette said finally, not bothering to turn around.

For a moment Michael looked surprised, then illumination dawned over his face and he threw down his napkin and laughed.

"That's what it is," he said. "I have been trying to figure out why these scenes have been so easy. For a minute or two I was afraid I was—" Now it was Juliette's turn to raise an eyebrow. "But I knew, of course, that wasn't possible. I mean, she's a child, not to mention a mess, but still . . ." He glanced back over at Mercy and laughed again. "Good Lord, it's uncanny. They can say what they want, but she really is brilliant, that girl. She's a much better actor than I ever was, though if you tell anyone I said that, I'll deny it." He gazed at Mercy with frank admiration. "Did you know?" he said, finally returning his attention to her. "I mean, did she ask you? It makes perfect sense. The character is brilliant and capable but with her own hidden wounds."

"Carson says the character's a control freak looking for someone to save her," Juliette answered flatly.

Michael laughed again and said nothing, which was not the response Juliette was hoping for. She wanted to know that Michael saw Carson for what she was—pathetically ambitious and manipulative, not to mention phony. "Your cousin," he said instead, deftly changing the subject, "does not like me very much."

Juliette opened her mouth to make a cutting Carson comment, then closed it again. Experiencing jealousy was bad enough; exposing it would be fatal. "He doesn't like most people very much. He thinks you're just another needy man in a string of needy men that I feel compelled to save because of my . . . hidden wounds."

Juliette had meant to speak lightly, perhaps ironically, but the words did not come out that way. The hardest thing about being at Cerreta, about having all this play out at Cerreta, was Gabe. After years in Los Angeles and at the Pinnacle, Juliette was used to a tacit tendency toward indulgence. That filmmaking was important work was just a given, and those who succeeded in that work were granted immunity from many social and business mores because, the thinking went, they had earned it. Gabe began at the other hand of the spectrum, with the assumption that filmmaking itself was an indulgence and everyone involved was, by extension, shallow, corrupt, and lazy. It was such a shift in perspective, it left Juliette feeling slightly nauseous.

Gabe always made her feel so *accountable*. It was one of the reasons she had stayed away for so long. He had never liked Josh, though when Juliette had married, Gabe was in no position to judge anyone. Over the years, he made it clear he was just waiting for her to come to her senses and leave so she could address the issues that had led her to fall in love with Josh in the first place. So there had been some pride-swallowing involved in her decision to come to Cerreta. And although Gabe had been, for the most part, respectful of her refusal to have a heart-to-heart about the past, she knew her cousin was not going to let her leave without some sort of emotional showdown.

But more than that, this was the first time in a long time that she had ever lived her life in front of someone who was an essential part of her past. She found herself comparing the person she was with the person she had thought she would become when she was young. Too many of the lines didn't match. When she and Gabe were running wild in New York, they had each prided themselves on being nonconformists, and though much of that was just an excuse to drink and do drugs, some of it was not. Juliette had never imagined herself becoming a member of the service industry, no matter how elite it might be. Seeing her choices through Gabe's eyes, which he made all too easy, it was hard not to wonder how she had wound up running interference for movie stars. And although she knew it was absurd, she blamed Gabe for how she felt. It wasn't pretty, and she didn't feel pretty thinking about it.

She swallowed hard and tried to look nonchalant, but when she shifted her eyes from the horizon, she found O'Connor looking at her.

"Don't," she said, almost unconsciously, turning away from the bright blue gaze and banishing her own thoughts back to her unconcious. "I think"—she cleared her throat—"the only person Gabe currently likes is Mercy. And *he* rags on *me* for being a martyr."

When she looked back, Michael's face was gentle and amused.

"He has work cut out for him," Michael said, nodding toward the inspector, who was, at that moment, refilling Mercy's very large glass of wine.

"Oh, great," Juliette said, both exasperated by and grateful for the distraction. "Where the hell is Usher? I thought that was what he was here for. And where's Angie? How is it that Mercy has been left to cope with the cops unattended?"

"Well, I don't think a glass of wine is going to kill her as long as she isn't using it to wash down whatever it is she washes down. Usher was last spotted tailing after your cousin. And maybe Angie thinks it's time Mercy learned to take responsibility for her actions."

"What is that supposed to mean?"

Michael shrugged. "I happened to see Angie chatting with our friend Di Marco and she seemed to be apologizing." He glanced up as one of the young PAs came hurrying over. "When I spoke with the inspector he said he was acting on an anonymous tip. My theory? Mercy called in some half-baked accusation or other just to stir up trouble. Or at least that's what her mother seems to think." Leaning over, he kissed

Juliette warmly just behind the ear. "I have to go now, darling, but alleg-
edly we'll be done by nine. Perhaps another moonlit stroll?" And with a
wicked grin, he was gone.

Whatever Mercy and the inspector had discussed had a definite
impact. He left shortly after the conversation with the implication that
he would not be returning. Mercy disappeared into her trailer and when
she finally arrived on the set, an hour late, she was spacy and lethargic,
easily distracted by a light she thought misplaced or a line she found too
preachy. They were shooting a flashback scene—the pages were now a
dull orange—and using the golden distance of her eyes and the halting
nature of her words, Mercy certainly evoked a woman untethered by
her love of God, so for the most part Carson and Golonski were happy.
At least they were happy when she didn't flub her lines. But in between
scenes, Mercy seemed barely able to communicate except to argue or
complain, which slowed the shoot to a crawl. The cinematographer was
beside himself; every minute the sky grew darker and the lights had to
be readjusted. They were, he kept saying, in danger of losing the entire
day. O'Connor, tired of trying to humor his costar, flung himself down
in a chair and began to do a crossword puzzle.

Finally, Mercy threw off her cloak, which she claimed was irritating her neck, and stalked off to her trailer, which she then refused to
leave. While Usher spoke to her soothingly through the locked door
and Carson threatened Angie with legal action, the storm that had been
threatening for days claimed the sky all at once. As lightning flashed
and thunder boomed, the crew cursed and ran around like a swarm
of angry bees, moving armloads of equipment into trucks and buildings and under balconies as icy fat raindrops pelted the olive groves
and the vineyards and the uninterested stone walls of the villa. Juliette
ran and lugged and heaved with the rest of them; though she could not
touch any of the film equipment—"union rules," the best boy shouted at
her when she tried to help. She and Gabriel wrestled shovels and rakes

and wheelbarrows into the carriage house, unlocked whatever doors stood before rooms that could provide shelter. By the time she stopped, Juliette was soaked through, her hair plastered to her face, her pants lashed with mud. With a wave to Gabe, who stood in one doorway of the *fattoria* with an intern on either side, she ran to Casa Padua.

Pieces of Mercy's costume, damp and rumpled, led to the closed door of her bedroom, which was shut and, as Juliette discovered, locked. "Leave me the fuck alone," was the only response Juliette got, so eventually she did just that. As the lightning and thunder cracked, she made her way around the house shutting windows and doors. For a long moment she stood on the porch, breathing deep the mineral-rich air that rose from the newly wet stone all around her—rain on rock made her mouth water. She looked over at the villa, where a light shone from every window as all the guests dried off and drew baths and prepared to wait out the storm.

Sighing, she made her slightly squishy way to her room. She was halfway through stripping off her wet clothes when a voice said, "So it is true, then; it's an ill wind that doesn't blow someone some good."

Fully clothed and perfectly dry, O'Connor was lying quite comfortably on her bed. Without a word, Juliette dropped the dripping blouse she was holding onto the floor and shut the door.

The crash of breaking glass followed the screech of something heavy being shoved against the floor, and Juliette was instantly awake. Outside, the moon shone high and clear; the storm had passed and no clouds blurred the stars. From the next room, she heard a low laugh and Mercy's voice softly calling her name. She glanced over at Michael, who in his sleep had rolled on his side and clutched the covers under his chin like a child. Juliette whispered his name but he did not stir. Outside, Mercy called again, and Juliette could hear the big iron bolt sliding open, the heavy wooden front doors pushed apart.

She emerged from her bedroom in time to see Mercy stumble onto the porch, down the stairs, and into the wet courtyard, laughing softly as she went. Exasperated, Juliette followed her. No matter what her state of sobriety, it wasn't safe for someone like Mercy to go prowling around Cerreta in the dead of night. The gray-water swamp was a few hundred yards away from the house and hidden well by reeds; barbed wire and electrified fence ran along many of the fields behind the *fattoria,* and adjacent to the olive groves yawned the old quarry, its dangerous depths obscured by a cushion of morning glories that swarmed along the bottom and up its sides. Not to mention all that mud.

But Mercy wasn't heading for any of those dangers. Watching her pale form glimmer across the courtyard, Juliette hesitated. Maybe the girl was just keeping some midnight assignation, maybe, Juliette thought with a smile, even with Gabe. But she doubted it. The day had not unfolded in such a way as to provide for midnight assignations. And before she could get to the back entrance of the villa, Mercy veered to the left, heading toward a small door cut into the bottom of the bell tower. Even at that distance, Juliette could see her throw a glance over her shoulder, before she reached up above the doorway, found the key Juliette had showed her, and disappeared.

"Crap," Juliette muttered, and hurried after her. "It really is like having a child." Entering the base of the tower, she could hear Mercy's footsteps running up the wooden stairs, lightly and surprisingly surefooted. For a minute Juliette was tempted to leave her there, maybe even lock the door just to show her what a brat she was being.

"Come up, Juliette." Mercy's voice floated down and it had never sounded so innocent, so sweet. "Come up the stairs and see the stars, how lovely they are after the rain."

I've seen plenty of stars, Juliette thought. *I'd rather be back in bed.*

When she got to the top, the moon was so bright and clear, the light dazzled her at first as she emerged from the darkness of the tower. But when her eyes adjusted, her heart turned over. Mercy was standing on the low wall that surrounded the top of the tower, her arms raised high above her head. Remembering the fountain in Florence, Juliette froze.

"If I were you I would bring my bed up here," Mercy said. "Then you would be sleeping right next to the angels."

"Mercy," Juliette said quietly, still not moving. "Please come down from there."

"Why?" she asked, swaying slightly in a way that might have been intentional but turned Juliette's throat to ice.

"Because you might fall."

"So?" Mercy laughed. "Don't you think I'm going to die soon anyway? Steve Usher tells me that I will, if I don't change my ways. And I know my mother thinks I will; that's why she's trying to make every penny she can off me before it's too late. I hate my mother." As she spoke, she kept turning her head to see Juliette, which made her sway even more. Juliette quickly moved to be in Mercy's line of vision.

"What about if you just sit down? Just sit and we'll talk."

"About mothers?"

"About whatever you want."

"All right," said Mercy, and she sat so quickly, Juliette thought she had fallen. When she could catch her breath, Juliette moved toward her; instead of sitting with her legs on the inside of the wall, Mercy was still facing outward, high above the courtyard. A bit more stable, but not what Juliette had had in mind.

"Come sit with me," Mercy said, patting the stone wall beside her.

"I can't," Juliette said. "I'm afraid of heights."

"You are? How funny." Mercy swung her legs and leaned over to look down. "I'm not."

Juliette choked back a yelp and slid her backside onto the wall, so that she sat next to Mercy, though in the opposite direction. Her hand hovered near Mercy's wrist. From here she could at least look into the young woman's face, could see her eyes wide and huge, the pupils dilated, could hear the breath coming fast and ragged, see the perspiration on Mercy's face.

"What's wrong, Mercy?" she asked quietly. "Why are you so upset?"

"My mother told the police that I was the one who called with the tip about Lloyd."

"Were you?"

"Yes," Mercy said impatiently. "Of course. But I didn't think my mother knew. But she knows everything, or almost everything. Not quite everything. Was your mother like that? Always watching you, wanting to know everything you thought, wanting to know everything you'd done?"

"No," Juliette said shortly, willing away the image that rose in her head, her mother laughing and sitting right here, on this wall, lifting a glass of wine that shone like a jewel in the summer sun.

Mercy sighed. "I think my mother fucked Lloyd just because I did, though I don't know for the life of me why he fucked her. Maybe he was messed up and she pretended to be me," she added dreamily. "She does that sometimes."

Seeing Juliettte's face, Mercy laughed.

"Poor Juliette. You should see how shocked you look. You think you know the worst, don't you? After all those years at the Pinnacle, covering up for this cheater and that thief. You don't know the worst." Mercy reached down her shirt, pulled out a vial, popped the lid off, and had swallowed a pill or two before Juliette could even blink. "Where do you think all the pictures come from, all the dirty details of my life? Like when I OD'd last year? Or the stuff about the fire and the accident? Remember that picture of me with blood running down my face? You know who took them? My mother. You know who sold them to those websites? My mother."

"Oh, Mercy," Juliette said. "That doesn't even make sense."

"Not to a normal person, maybe," Mercy said. "But she says it's better to be proactive. That those things are going to come out anyway, so we might as well profit from them."

Juliette looked at her doubtfully. She certainly considered Angie capable of many things, but it didn't even make financial sense for her to exploit Mercy that way—those sorts of stories only devalued the star, and Juliette couldn't imagine Angie wanting that.

"I think you must be wrong," she said gently. "Your mom may not be the easiest person in the world to get along with, but she does want what's best for you. Because, you know, that's what's best for her."

Mercy laughed at this.

"You don't get it. She hates me. For all the years of schlepping me around. For looking just like she did, only I'm famous."

"She doesn't hate you," Juliette said automatically. "Mothers and daughters are complicated. You said so yourself."

"Remember my little dog? Cupcake? My mother said he ran away the night I came here. That he must have tried to follow me. Like it was my fault. Then I found his collar in her purse. She says he slipped it, but I don't believe her. I think she has it because it was from Tiffany's, you know, so she couldn't just throw *that* in the river." Mercy paused for a moment. "I called the police because I don't think Lloyd died from the drugs or because he accidentally strangled himself whacking off. In fact, I know he didn't."

"How do you know?"

Mercy looked at her sideways.

"Guess."

"You think he killed himself?"

Mercy shook her head.

"Well, how do you think he died?"

Mercy paused for a moment, a strange and vivid moment, but when she spoke, her voice took on that childish singsong again and her smile seemed blurry and unreal.

"I think someone murdered him."

"Really?" Juliette said, her tension fading away. Now Mercy was definitely playing some sort of game, she could tell by how closely the young woman was watching her. "You keep saying things like that but you never elaborate. So who? Who would kill Lloyd? Your mother? Carson? Michael? Tell me, Mercy, did you kill Lloyd?"

Mercy laughed and swung her legs up and over until she was sitting shoulder to shoulder with Juliette. "I think maybe it was Carson. Carson hates me," she said.

"So Carson would kill Lloyd Watson because she hates you?"

Mercy only smiled, and for a moment Juliette just wanted to slap her. How could anyone, even a movie star, be so self-centered? Maybe she did know something about Lloyd, maybe there was some sort of weird cover-up to get the insurance company to pay, but it certainly was not going to get cleared up by Mercy Talbot, who was much more interested in keeping everyone watching her while she swayed and bowed on top of fountains and towers.

"Maybe Carson has reason to hate you."

Instead of looking startled or hurt, Mercy smiled slyly. "I know. I slept with her husband. So sad. What a loser he was."

"Wait, you knew? All this time? I thought . . . I mean Michael said you didn't remember."

Mercy shrugged. "It wasn't very memorable, but I'm not so far gone as that. Jesus. I may be a slut but I do try to be a semiconscious slut. And what is protocol when you find out you've slept with the producer's husband? Tell me, Juliette. How would you handle that, back at the Pinnacle? What would Devlin do? He's probably had to deal with the same situation." There was a pause that Juliette refused to fill. "Did you ever sleep with Devlin? You should, you know." Another pause. Mercy shrugged. "Carson should thank me."

Juliette could see whatever drug she had taken enter her bloodstream, dragging rambling languor behind it as it moved. "Carson should thank me every day for the rest of her life. Men who cheat are cheaters. I just got it over with quicker for her. It would have happened eventually, no matter what. Cheaters cheat, it's what they do. We all just do what we were programmed to do until we can't anymore."

"That's not true," Juliette said. "People make choices about what they do. You have a choice."

"Choices. I hate that word. People only use that word when they don't like what you've done. When was the last time you felt like you had a choice? Michael cheats," she said spitefully. "Though maybe he won't cheat on you. He really likes you." Her voice began to fade into sedated self-pity. "I wish someone liked me, but I think maybe it's too late for that." Her head drooped and she slumped against Juliette's shoulder.

Realizing Mercy was about to pass out, Juliette quickly rose and guided her back toward the stairs. Carefully, she half carried her down. When they reached the door, Juliette gave up and simply lifted the girl into her arms; she was shocked at how little Mercy weighed. "If your own mother doesn't even like you," Mercy whispered as she slumped against Juliette's neck, "what's the point anyway?"

A wave of exquisite sadness crashed against Juliette with such force she rocked backward. Mercy's bright hair was against Juliette's mouth, which she set in a grim line, keeping her mind firmly focused on the task of carrying the now inert girl across the yard. It was a question with no bearable answer, which is why Juliette had never allowed herself to ask it.

Chapter Nine

"I AM NOT GOING to live through this shoot," Juliette said, following Gabe through one of the back pastures. Behind them, the tip of the tower was just visible over a line of trees that wound alongside one of the vegetable gardens. It was a blue-domed day, breezy and bright, and everywhere she looked, flowers seemed to have burst from limb and ground that very minute. Despite her frustrated tone, she felt her shoulders relax as the wind lifted her hair and stirred her long skirt around her. She and Gabe were in search of a pregnant sow that had escaped its pen, presumably to give birth somewhere in the forest. Though several of the prettiest interns had offered to accompany him, Gabe had specifically, and repeatedly, asked Juliette to join him.

"You?" said Gabe, peering into a likely-looking bit of gorse. "I thought this was the perfect solution to all our problems. I thought this was your milieu. I just wish the motherfuckers would recycle. How hard is it to separate paper from plastic from glass?"

"Well, I am ready to go on record as saying I have bitten off more than I can chew. That girl is impossible. She practically falls off the tower the other night and she's up the next day in full makeup by seven. Me, I am still woozy two days later."

"Addicts have a remarkable power of recovery," Gabe said. "Until, of course, they don't. Meanwhile, why not let the professionals deal with her?"

Juliette glanced at her cousin to see if he was being sarcastic or not, but his face looked placid enough, if a little flushed, in the sunshine.

"Well, I am. Angie can be in charge of her. Steve Usher can be in charge of her. Not that he seems very effective. I don't even know what she's on, I searched her room that night and I couldn't find anything, except freaking gel caps of all sorts of herbal description. And as far as I know, no one puts their drugs in gel caps; I even squeezed a few to see if they'd been, I don't know, injected with heroin or something. So where is she getting whatever is making her so . . . bizarre?"

"That is the million-dollar question," Gabe murmured.

"Have you talked to her—I mean I know you've talked to her, but have you given her your little pitch?"

"My little pitch? I've told her life does not have to be the way it is, I've asked her if she thinks she could stop using, for a day, for a week."

"And?"

"And she tells me she's not using."

"Do you think that's true? Do you think maybe . . ."

Gabe stopped and stared at her. "I don't think that is even remotely true," he said. "I think she is addicted to drugs and alcohol and therefore is incapable of telling the truth. Don't you even remember?" he said, shaking his head in disbelief. "Don't you remember what that was like, to lie so well and so often that you don't even know what's true? Have you so completely disconnected yourself from the past that you don't even *remember*?"

Before Juliette could respond, he had shaken his head again and sidled over to a stand of blackberry bushes.

"Oops, what have we here?" Stooping, he pushed aside several tree boughs to reveal the sow, the telltale white stripe glowing a bit in the shade. She was on her side, panting slightly, with six piglets fastened to her teats.

"Oooh, look, they're so adorable," Juliette said, allowing the tiny ears, the perfect wee feet, to distract her from the sting of Gabe's question.

"Yeah, probably just about a day or two old." He prodded the mass of squirming piglets with one finger. "Look at the ears on that one, and that one," he said. "I suspected as much. This girl got out a few months ago and it looks like she found true love under the spreading chestnut with some wild boar. Ah, well, there's no accounting for taste, is there, cuz?" He looked up at her. "And how is Mr. O'Connor?"

Juliette paused just long enough to let him know she was grateful he was changing the subject. "Who knows?" she said. "I think he was upset when I left him to go running after Mercy. She truly gets under his skin. Though you wouldn't know, when they're actually working together— watching them through the monitor, you'd swear it was true love. Of the twenty-first and sixteenth century variety." She yanked an orange poppy from the ground, and then another one. "Listen to me, like I'm twelve years old. He's working, that's what he is. He's working and he's absorbed in his work, which is what he should be. I think this movie is taking more out of him than he expected."

"The movie?" Gabe asked. "Or all the women involved?" He took one last look at the pigs. "I guess I'll send some of the interns up to move these guys—it's not safe to just leave them out like this. Wild boars aren't above a bit of cannibalism. Look," he said abruptly, as they headed out of the woods and back into the meadow. "Although I really don't want to tell you this, you have a right to know." Juliette looked at him, and though she was knee-deep in wildflowers and butterflies, a chill ran through her. "Usher offered to buy the place. For thirty million euros."

This was so unexpected that Juliette actually stopped in her tracks. "Jesus," she said. "Gabe. Jesus. That's so much money. I mean, that's a lot of money. Does he even have that kind of money?"

Gabriel gave her a withering look. "Well, I don't think he has it on him in cash. But the man did have six platinum albums. Of glam rock, of course, which is enough to kill me right there. But still, it paid. Besides, he made it sound like he has a few partners in his burgeoning recovery empire. That's why he wants to buy Cerreta. To start a high-end international recovery retreat." He paused to let the words hang in the air for a moment and then resumed walking.

"Wow," Juliette said, hurrying to catch up with him. "That's actually not a bad idea. I mean," she added hastily, "not here, not at Cerreta. But in general, you know, as an idea, something like that would probably really take off. I'm actually amazed no one has thought about it before. What?" she said when Gabriel gave her a look that could only be described as hostile. "Look, I know you got sober in church basements and all that, but that's not for everyone. When Lindsay Lohan went to an AA meeting in Atwater, there were photos of her all over the Internet before the meeting was over."

"Photos she probably authorized. If she didn't take them herself. Look, I'm not going to argue about the spiritual benefit of being in a place like this—why do you think I live here? But sobriety isn't a vacation destination."

Juliette shoved him. She couldn't help it. She knew he was getting on his soapbox, could see him mentally opening the closet where it lived, could hear him dragging it across the floor. But there was no stopping him, not even with mild physical violence.

"Quit it," he said, shoving her back. "I'm serious. This isn't 1868, we don't send people off to Swiss sanatoriums and hope the 'water cure' takes. Mercy is a perfect example of what is wrong with that kind of thinking. Everyone, including you, keeps telling her what a special case she is, how she has to be protected and spoon-fed and chased around, and how's that working out? She's high three days out of five."

He was standing still now, surrounded by green fields and ancient forests, with poppies at his feet and fire in his eyes. Juliette sighed and waited but she didn't have to wait long. "Everyone keeps trying to figure out what's wrong with her, as if that weren't perfectly obvious. She's an addict. She needs to get sober. That's it. No personal recovery attendant, no fancy rehab, no before-and-after pictures. Just one day at a time, starting today. She doesn't need some Tuscan retreat to do it, and neither does anyone else."

Juliette felt a deep and abiding love for her cousin wash over her. He was a pain in the ass, no doubt, but he was such a wonderfully unrelenting pain in the ass. It wasn't the fact that he was probably right, it was his unwavering, unremitting certainty that he was right. Juliette had never felt close to that certain about anything in her life.

"So I'm guessing you want to tell Usher no," she said.

"Damn right," he said.

"In fact, I'm guessing you already told him no, even though, technically, you can't make that decision on your own."

Gabe met her eye, but she thought she detected a reddening in the part of his cheeks not covered by beard.

"Okay," she said, and began to walk again.

"Okay?" He fell into step with her. "That's it? 'Okay'?"

"Yes."

"Oh." Miraculously, Gabe seemed without words. "Well . . . then . . . okay."

In silence they walked through the trees and down the dirt road to the wall that surrounded the castello.

"That's a helluva lot of money," Juliette said, squinting at the broken bits of machinery beside the wall, the sagging *fattoria* roof. Gabriel glanced at her sharply, but she shook her head. "I'm just saying."

Juliette headed back to Casa Padua to call Devlin and see what he thought about Usher's offer, which frankly made no sense to her. That was too much money for a property that would take millions more to renovate. What was Usher's story, anyway? Dev would know that for sure. If nothing else, it gave her an excuse to talk to him, which she felt like she needed ever since Gabe's crack about her making Dev sound like the Buddha. She didn't think Dev was some sort of god. She just knew that the sound of his voice made her feel better. And right now she needed to feel better.

Casting her gaze around the various surfaces in the living room for her BlackBerry, she was suddenly aware that someone else was in the house. Something was unsettled in the atmosphere, and from upstairs there was the distinct creaking that the floor in Mercy's room made when even the lightest step was taken in the space in front of the bureau.

"Mercy?" she called out. Then, feeling the air grow suddenly still, as if whoever was there had frozen in place, she picked up a poker from beside the enormous stone fireplace and quietly made her way up the stairs toward Mercy's room.

"Juliette," said Steve, poking his head out the doorway. "Hullo, hullo. Come in and see if you think I've missed anything." He gestured into Mercy's room. Juliette frowned at him, remained where she was, and although she lowered the poker, she didn't put it aside.

"What are you doing here?" she said.

"I'm doing what is, unfortunately, my job," he said with a wry smile. "Perhaps not exactly what I had in mind when I stood before the scream-ing thousands at Madison Square Garden, but rewarding in its own way. I'm searching Mercy's room, at her mother's request, and Carson's. For drugs," he added as Juliette's expression did not change. "The drugs Mercy is clearly taking, though for the life of me I cannot think where she is keeping them. I wonder if perhaps you could help me . . . give any hints of secret hiding places? This is an old house, with many secrets, I am sure, and while I can't go through it brick by brick, perhaps there are places you know of where a rather ingenious junkie might keep her stash?" He smiled at her appealingly.

"I already searched her room," Juliette said shortly. "I even took sam-
ples of all those herbal medicines she gulps by the handful and sent them
back to L.A. to be analyzed. Just in case." She looked at Usher narrowly.

His eyebrows shot up. "In case what? Someone is secretly doping
her? Someone like . . . me, perhaps?" He rocked back on his heels and
surveyed her admiringly. "Now, why would I do such a thing, Ms. Greyson? In the hope of creating a need for my services?" He stroked his chin.
"Not the worst business plan I've ever heard, but a bit risky, don't you
think? Maybe she'll head to Promises next. Or Betty Ford. Or maybe
she'll overdose like poor Lloyd, which is not, I'll be frank with you, a
ringing endorsement. Well!" He clapped his hands together. "Give us the
worst, then. What did you discover? Are Mercy's St. John's wort tablets
really compressed heroin? Will the very worthy Mr. Delfino be arriving
with shackles in hand? Shall I call my lawyer?"

"I haven't gotten the results back," Juliette said, feeling more than a
little ridiculous but strangely relieved. "But I couldn't find anything. And
I already searched everywhere I could think of. I checked the kitchen,
the fridge, the fireplace, all the loose floor tiles, my room. I even went
through all the toilet paper in the closet, to see if she had stuck anything
in the tubes. That was one of *my* favorite spots."

Usher's laughter rang against the thick, stuccoed walls. "Marvelous,"
he said. "I hadn't thought of that." He clapped Juliette on her shoulder and
the two made their way back to the living room. "I was actually wondering
if you knew who the local dealers were. I know my way around L.A., or at
least the parts of L.A. my clients are familiar with, but I am a babe in the
woods here. Sometimes it actually helps to have a word with the dealer,
you know, or make it worth their while to be a bit short-supplied . . . I
notice a lot of rather grubby young people around; is it possible they could
help me out?" He looked at her with gentle inquiry.

"No" she said. "Not here. Cerreta is utterly drug-free, if you don't
count the wine and the limoncello. Guest, intern, farmworker—Gabe

would toss them out on their ear if he even suspected anything beyond, maybe, a loose joint or two. And he'd know. Believe me."

Usher considered this for a moment. "Where does he think Mercy is getting whatever it is she's on?"

Juliette stopped for a minute and thought hard. "I don't know," she admitted. "And it's funny that he's never voiced an opinion. He's all about voicing an opinion. As you probably know."

"He certainly doesn't like me much," Usher said matter-of-factly. "He made that fairly clear when we discussed . . . well, I assume you know what we discussed." He looked at her sharply, with a question in his eyes.

"Yes," said Juliette. "And you need to know that I back Gabe fully. In his choice of music, and whatever decision he makes regarding Cerreta. It is his home."

"Yes, but it is also your birthright." His tone was businesslike, but then he grinned and drew closer, his face an elfin study of cheerful coercion. "Come on, Juliette, it'd be fun. You know it would. Don't tell me you haven't envisioned this place as something more than what it is. It's got 'luxury getaway' written on it in letters a mile high. Good Lord, the view alone is worth a million pounds. What I don't understand is why you've been sitting on it all these years, slaving away for Eamonn Devlin and whatever bastards currently own Pinnacle International, when you could be running your own show. I understand they're building a new airport in Siena," he added nonchalantly.

She had to smile at his tone, at the outrageous, almost irresistible nakedness of his plea, and she did. But: "It is Gabe's home," she said firmly. "Yes, of course, I've had many thoughts about the future of this place, but he's the one who's done the work, he's the one who gets to decide. And I have to say, I don't think you have a chance in hell, Mr. Usher. It's not so much you he doesn't like, it's your methods. He doesn't think much of high-priced rehab for the rich and famous."

"Or, you regret to add, my wretched Little Book," he added for her. "I know, I know, Mr. Delfino made it only too clear when I tried to give him a few copies for your library. All right, all right, I know when I'm licked. I don't suppose," he added, looking around the room as if he had misplaced something, "you've seen Lloyd Watson's Little Book anywhere, have you? Mercy mentioned he had given it to her, that he had marked some passages for her, and I was hoping to at least have a look . . ."

Juliette shook her head. "I haven't seen Mercy with any copies of your book, except the one Angie carries around and forces on her from time to time."

Usher smote his forehead.

"So much for my influence. And Mercy seemed to be doing so well before this ridiculous film came up. I told Angie it was a bad idea to take her out early, just when she was settling in. But Angie, well, you know." He winked, but then his eyes grew serious. "I had hoped that Lloyd would help her a bit. I had no idea he had slipped. He always sounded fantastic when I spoke with him. And I spoke with him regularly. I honestly thought we had turned a corner."

"Life is full of corners, Mr. Usher," Juliette said. "That's the whole problem."

Usher's mouth twitched with mock solemnity. "I may have to use that in the next edition of my book, you know." Then he sighed. "I suppose I'll go search Mercy's trailer now. Have you had a squint at the inhaler she's always sucking on?"

Juliette laughed. "I took a few puffs myself the other day. Nothing."

He nodded. "Well, I always did love a mystery. Oh," he said, turning around one more time, "if you see that book, or learn of the local drug lord—"

"I'll be sure to let you know."

✳ ✳ ✳

When Juliette returned to the villa, there was a note taped to the main door. *Come see what they've done to your castle,* Mercy had written, adding three *x*'s and two *o*'s. Finding Gabe hunched over his computer, she shoved it at him. "Oh, look," she said, "it's for you."

"Right, that's just what I need," he said with an awkward laugh, "to fall in love with some crazy, needy, addict movie star." He balled up the note and shoved it in his pocket while Juliette watched with mild shock. She didn't think she had ever heard Gabe use the term "in love" in reference to himself.

"Let's go see," she said, suddenly very much wanting to see her cousin in the immediate vicinity of Mercy Talbot.

"I'm busy."

"You're not. Come on. Just for a little while. Don't you want to see what it looks like as an abbey, or whatever they've turned it into?"

"If they wanted an abbey, why didn't they just shoot at the abbey?" he asked, gesturing away from the villa, where, a mile or so down in the valley, the ruins of a twelfth century abbey stood, burned and half buried in morning glories and ivy.

"Because they're going to use that for something else. Come *on,*" Juliette said, tugging at him like she had when she was a child. "Maybe they found the Giotto."

Gabe grinned at her.

"Maybe that's why ol' Steve Usher is so eager to buy this place," he said, relenting. "Maybe he found a secret map or something."

Together they got in his beat-up Peugeot. "That was a crazy summer," he said, pulling out of the courtyard. "That was the craziest summer."

He glanced over at Juliette. She knew he wanted her to continue, but she kept her gaze firmly in front of her.

"Do you think your dad really believed in the Giotto?" he asked. "My folks didn't, not really, but your dad . . . What happened to that old letter he had, the one he always quoted, the one from the contessa? Did you find it, in his stuff, after he died? We should get that back here, put it in the library in a glass case or something."

Juliette shrugged and continued to stare out the window.

Gabriel sighed, a long, painful, pent-up sigh. "You know, Jules," he began, "my parents were——"

"I'm sure it's where it always was," she said, interrupting him. "In that trunk he kept. Which is in storage, back in Waterbury with all the rest of their things." She turned toward him and on her face was a smile she hoped was not too pleading. "I will give you the key whenever you want and you can go through it all, take whatever you want. Really. Whatever you want, whenever you want."

"In Waterbury. In storage," Gabe said, abruptly stopping the car in the last pull-out before the trail to the castle. "You know, it's been fifteen years, Juliette . . ."

"I know exactly how long it's been, Gabriel," she said, pulling herself out of the car and slamming the door. She started walking swiftly away and then stopped. Gabe was still standing by the car. With his hands shoved in his pockets and his shirttails flapping, she could see him as he had been, at ten and twelve and fourteen, before he began refusing to come to Italy, before it became impossible for any of them to come. As she thought of all the things that had happened to that boy, her eyes filled with tears.

"Please don't, Gabe," she said. "It's just too hard for me to think about."

"It doesn't have to be," he said, coming up beside her. "You make it harder than it is. If you'd just talk about it, things would get clearer."

For a moment she let her forehead rest against the fine strong span of his collarbone. He smelled like rosemary and sweat and that spicy Italian laundry detergent Juliette could never find in the States. He smelled like all the summers of her youth. Juliette knew what Gabe wanted to do. He wanted to comb through the charred remnants of their past, he wanted to take the memories they each had, of their parents, of Cerreta, of Connecticut, of the time they had all spent together, what they knew had happened and what they thought had happened, and examine them through the lens of adulthood and sobriety. He thought that by pulling each tangled, gritty thread out of the pile, cleaning it up and smoothing it down, things would take on an order, things would make sense. And Juliette would do it if she thought such a thing were possible, because she loved her cousin and she wanted him to be happy. But she knew it was not.

"They're clear enough already," she said, and began walking into the woods.

The Castle That Only God Knows was nestled deep in the forest and was impossible to find unless you knew where to look. It dated to the fourteenth century, though it was unclear who had begun building it and why they had never finished. It was small, meant to be a private home; an extended family, and all the necessary servants, could have fit comfortably. When Juliette and Gabe were children, they could climb the outside stairs, or scramble up to them from the ramparts, but the wood floors were either missing or rotten with age. Although they had each made dangerous double-dare excursions from window frame to window frame, the trees and the ground alarmingly far below, the two had mostly confined their play to the ground floors, lighting fires and staging battles, trying to imagine who would have lived in each room and why the castle had been abandoned, wondering if a witch had been involved, or possibly a sorcerer.

When they got older, they attempted some repairs, had grand plans of finding that fresco, using the money to restore the castle so they could live there. Just the two of them, alone in the woods. But since it was just the two of them, they did not get very far.

In recent years, Gabe had applied for aid from the Italian government, which sent out workers and supplies whenever the idea of having a castle tucked into a natural reserve appealed to an incoming bureaucrat for a moment or two. Which is to say sporadically. As a result, most of the castle could be viewed safely. Occasionally, Gabe found traces of visiting campers or locals—wine bottles, fire pits, condoms. For a while, he told her now, he considered a locked fence, but then he decided that since it was the Castle That Only God Knows, he had no business fencing it off.

"You should worry more about that gray-water swamp," Juliette said as they scuttled to the side of the fire road to avoid being run over by a golf cart. "Or that quarry in back of Padua. You should fence that."

"I did fence that," Gabe said.

"Yeah, well, the weeds are higher than the fence, then. You should fence it better. Or one of your precious pigs will wind up at the bottom."

"Feel free to talk to your construction crew," he said, refusing to acknowledge her mood. "Feel free to make whatever improvements your little heart desires."

"I'll remember you said that, because I was thinking of putting a spa under the carriage house."

"Fine," he said placidly. "If that means you'll be sticking around to run it. Oh, my God."

The path had made an abrupt left turn and it was as if they had entered an enchanted forest. Where a few days before there had stood the half-finished shell of a castle surrounded by scrub oak and pine reached by a narrow and winding trail, now there rose from behind flowering trees and carefully clipped hedges the stately and formidable grace of what could certainly be considered a medieval abbey. Statues of the Blessed Mother and her infant son, of Saint Joseph and the paschal lamb, glimmered from the courtyard, which was now miraculously paved and behind gorgeous wrought-iron gates.

"It's like Disney World," Gabe said. "I mean, if there was, like, a Renaissanceland in Disney World. Unbelievable. Seriously," he said, walking up the carefully groomed path, "I would have never believed they could do this. We should definitely get them to fence the quarry," he added, turning around and around. "We should get these people to do any- and everything they can. They're fucking magicians."

His wonder was infectious; Juliette felt the last scratchy bit of her temper smooth itself away as she wandered around the set, lost in admiration. It really was astonishing, although as she looked more closely she could see that so much of the magic was just very precise stage dressing. Where one wall or even a corner had been made up to look like part of a working abbey, another was still whiskered with the grass and wildflowers that grew from between its stones and mortar. But still, she couldn't help smiling, remembering all the hours they had spent here, the weeks spent looking for hidden rooms and trapdoors. And here it was, all these years later, truly come to life. There were even, among the milling crowd of crew in their requisite cargo shorts and baseball caps, a handful of white-robed and wimpled sisters, some smoking, others texting, but still, nuns in the middle of the forest.

But even as she was wallowing in the satisfaction of seeing her cousin finally impressed by something, Juliette heard the unmistakable hallmarks of on-set strife.

"No way," said a male voice, clearly strained beyond all endurance and reaching upper registers it was not intended to reach. "I don't care what she says, I am not rewriting that scene again. No, I will not shut up." From out of one of the lower rooms dressed to look like a chapel, Joseph Andrews strode, with Golonski angrily following him. "No. If you want that change, then *you* make it. It's a Ben Golonski film, right? Then, great. Ben Golonski can fix it. What the fuck are you looking at?" he snapped as he passed Juliette. Golonski stopped abruptly and stomped back to the chapel, immediately growling into his cell phone.

From another side of the quadrangle, she could hear Angie's voice raised, then Carson's, then finally Mercy's. "You heard me, Mother," Mercy said as she appeared from a second-floor doorway, unsteadily heading for the stairs, her white shift falling from her shoulders, exposing the pronounced ridges of her clavicles and breastbones. "You're fired. Go home, all the way home, back to Malibu and take your rock star, recovery-addict boyfriend with you. I just can't bear it," she said, throwing herself at Gabe, who had come to stand beside Juliette. "Some things are just past bearing. No discussion, Mother," she said as Angie appeared in white capris and many bracelets, and carefully picked her way down the stone steps, with Steve Usher making placating gestures close behind. Looking up, Juliette saw Carson watching from the shadows of a high arched window, an expression of satisfaction clear on her face.

"Mercy," Angie said, hurrying over, "you stop this right now. You heard what Ben said. The light is going, they need to shoot the scene right now, so you just have to pull it together . . . Here," she said, fishing in her purse and pulling out an inhaler. "This will make you feel better. You're all woozy or something. Did you eat breakfast?"

"No, I didn't eat breakfast, because I'm not allowed to eat breakfast, because you told me yesterday that my ass looked fat in the black pants. Hi, Gabe," she said, fitting herself more securely against him, lifting his arm so it was encircling her. "Do you think my ass looks fat?"

"I never answer questions like that," Gabe said, his voice only slightly less tense than his arm. "My sense of self-preservation is far too strong."

"Well, maybe you should eat something," Angie said, still trying to fit the inhaler in Mercy's hand. "Why don't you take a few minutes, you could even take *five* minutes and relax. Find your focus. I'll tell the others you'll be ready. In five minutes."

"Angie," Steve murmured, drawing her away. "Give her some room. Go take a walk, have a cup of tea, or better yet, why not go back to the villa? Mercy and I need to do a little visualization, I think."

"You will not. Because you're fired, too. I saw what you did, Mother. We're shooting a love scene," she said, turning to Gabe and Juliette. "And I'm supposed to strip, I'm washing myself and I strip, and then Michael, or Roberto, comes in behind me and touches me and, well, you know. Sort of like that scene in that Amish movie with Harrison Ford. So we're doing it, and I look up." She pushed herself away from Gabe, her hands gesturing wildly, her gown all but falling from her body. "And there's my mother. Taking pictures."

"I always document your work, honey," Angie said, reaching over to pull up the shoulders of the shift so that Mercy's breasts were not exposed.

"With your cell phone? Please. Me and O'Connor liplocked, his hands on my tits." She slapped her mother's hands away, her eyes flashing crazy green. "And what the fuck do you care if Gabe sees my breasts, or Juliette, or anyone, for that matter? Or is the problem that they're not paying for the privilege? Where were you going to sell those photos anyway? To Perez or TMZ? Or your new favorite spot, old deadanddying.com?" Angie blanched, and Mercy laughed. "You didn't think I knew about that, did you?"

"Mercy," Angie said, and suddenly her tone was desperate.

"I saw what else was there, you know," Mercy said, her voice reaching high and cracking. "Have you ever seen this website, Juliette? It's very special. Marilyn Monroe's pubic hair and bits of Heath Ledger's sheets, autopsy reports and toxicology reports and everybody's health records. Lloyd's there, too, isn't he, Mom? A lovely photo, taken by someone who clearly thought the world of him . . ."

"Mercy!"

"Someone had their trusty cell phone out the night he died. Wonder who that was. I saw you, Mother, coming out of his room. I know what you were doing. Oh, my God." Mercy moaned, swayed, and turned white. Gabe and Steve grabbed her under each arm, as she tried to catch her breath and steady herself. "Give me the fucking inhaler, Mother, and go back to the villa," she said finally, her voice low and trembling. "Or I swear to God I will shut this fucking movie down, if only for the sheer pleasure of making sure you never make another penny off of me again."

"Go, Angie," Usher said, wading in, his voice kind, his face a study in unflappable sympathy. "It will be fine. We'll sort things out. You're just exhausted, aren't you, Mercy? You know what you need? Carbohydrates. I say to hell with all this slimming nonsense, you're a gorgeous young woman, let's get a biscuit or two in you and you'll be right as rain." Putting his arm around her waist, Usher began leading her away from the castle, toward a small craft services tent, but Mercy refused to let go of Gabe's hand. "All right, Gabriel, will you join us? And Juliette as well? Lovely. Deep breaths, Mercy, my girl, deep steady breaths. No need to get yourself so excited over nothing. You and your mother just need a little break, that's all. Nothing surprising about that. Everybody's been working so hard, and you trying to make big changes in your life on top of that. Now, here we are, sitting down, and let's see about getting that tea, then."

Juliette had to admit Usher was handling the situation beautifully. Mercy sat and Angie went and by the time Michael and Golonski appeared, their faces twin studies of dread and preemptive anger, Mercy was eating a sandwich, while Usher lectured mildly on the importance of creating a clean and healthy chemistry in the body and brain. "And that means eating more than once a week and drinking water, not all this bloody green tea everyone keeps pouring into themselves, which is liquid caffeine, i.e., a diuretic. May keep you slim, but only by dehydration. In the Little Book, I devote several chapters to this very thing and I think they are actually helpful. I remember the time Richard—Gere, that is—and I went to visit the Dalai Lama . . ."

Gabe was scowling, but only slightly; from where she was sitting, Juliette could see that, under the table, Mercy was resting her hand on his thigh as a person might rest her hand on the head of a faithful retriever.

"Everything okay?" Michael said, his eyes going first to Juliette. Almost imperceptibly she shook her head. Though dashing in his ruffled white shirt and knee-high leather boots, he looked old in the late morning light, the skin around his eyes puffy and dark, his mouth pulled small and tight.

"It's fine," Mercy said flatly, not looking up from her sandwich. "I'm sorry I wrecked the shot."

O'Connor looked down at the back of Mercy's head, and the look on his face was so gentle and kind that Juliette's heart thudded in her chest. Crouching beside his costar, Michael put his hand in the middle of her bare shoulders. "Sweetheart," he said softly, "I know how hard these scenes can be, and I know that you and Lloyd had something you and I do not and that things are not going the way you expected." Mercy's eyes filled with tears, several dripped onto her plate, but still she did not move, and neither did O'Connor. "If you meant what you said, if you really don't think you can do the scene, then I'll back you, Ben'll back you." Juliette glanced up at the director standing behind them and almost laughed out loud, so far was Ben from agreeing with this statement. "We'll figure something out." Michael shifted himself into a more comfortable crouch. "It's a movie, princess. Just a movie. Nothing worth losing your head about, certainly nothing worth crying about." O'Connor brought his face close to hers and stroked the top of her head. "You're doing great. You are amazingly great. So you just tell us what you need to make this work. Because we are totally in this thing together." He kissed her temple like a father kissing a beloved daughter and gave her hair another stroke. "All right?"

Mercy nodded, still not looking at him. He waited a beat, then, with a sigh and a pat on her shoulder, he raised himself from his crouch and turned to go. But before he could, Mercy grabbed his hand, and with one fluid motion pulled herself up out of the chair, wrapped one hand around the back of Michael's neck, pulled his face down, and kissed him. Softly at first, then more deeply, passionately.

"No," she said when she finally pulled away into the vacuum of shock that now surrounded her. "I think we should leave the scene as it is. And we better get through it now. While the light's still with us." And, throwing down the napkin she still held in one hand, she walked purposefully back toward the set with a confused but visibly relieved Golonski right on her heels.

After a moment of stunned silence, Gabriel began to laugh. Juliette, who had half risen from her seat when Mercy made her move, straightened her back but was otherwise rooted to the spot, staring at O'Connor, who was staring after Mercy. He pressed his fingers against his lips and turned slowly to Juliette.

"Tell me," he said. "How ridiculous did that look? On a scale of one to ten. No, don't tell me. I'll wait for the critics to tell me." Without another word or look, he stalked off.

"What are you laughing at?" Juliette asked her cousin, slightly nauseated by a rush of mixed emotions.

"That girl," Gabe said, shaking his head in admiration. "She's the most amazing person I have ever met."

The rest of the shoot went remarkably well, or at least that's what everyone said at dinner when the entire crew gathered in remarkably good spirits. The set designer had solved some sort of huge problem which Juliette did not quite understand, ditto the best boy. Michael was holding court with Golonski and Joseph and was in fine movie star form; at one point, he called over a trio of Australian tourists to join them. Mercy seemed more like herself than she had in days. Not that anyone honestly knew what that self was like. She sat at the end of one of the long tables on the patio, talking earnestly to Gabe as if they were the only two people present, and actually eating something, neither herbal supplements nor inhaler in sight.

When Juliette sent a questioning glance at Usher, he raised his palms in a gesture of pleased bafflement. As the interns brought out plates of salami, then rigatoni in wild boar sauce, then chunks of lamb grilled in wine and rosemary, genial conversation rose and fell along the tables, bursting now and then in friendly argument or splatters of laughter. Only Angie was strangely silent, sitting three tables over from her daughter and communing mostly with a bottle, then two bottles, of white wine.

"It does feel odd that I'm finally shooting in Italy and I'm playing a painter," O'Connor was saying. "I mean, the cop is more like it, but it seems a shame I made *The Undisturbed* and *The Second Sicilian* back in the States, with Santa Barbara standing in for Sicily. How much fun would it be to do a mob picture here in the old country?"

"Terrific if you want to perpetrate all those wonderful stereotypes of a don in every piazza that Americans have gorged themselves on all these years," Gabe said.

"Well, they may be stereotypes," Michael said, "but you can't deny that organized crime exists. There was just recently that big piece in the *New Yorker* about the new drug state here, and that journalist who just wrote the book on the Mafia had to leave the country, right? I'm trying to option that book; that's a great story."

"I'm not saying it doesn't exist," Gabe said, "any more than I would say it doesn't exist in Los Angeles or New York. But the assumption that Italy is run by the mob, and that the mob is somehow cool and romantic, that just makes Americans look stupid."

"I'm sorry if I have somehow contributed to the declining IQ of our country," O'Connor said. "Though I did win an Oscar for *The Second Sicilian* . . ."

"That's just my point," Gabe said. "Those kind of movies always get a lot of attention because Americans have this weird romantic relationship with 'organized crime,' not to mention the basic assumption that Italy, or Europe, or Mexico, for that matter, are somehow intrinsically more corrupt. There are rarely any American mobster movies, you'll notice. They're always Italian-American, or Irish-American or Russian, always tied to a decadent European tradition."

"Oh, you're just taking a position, Gabe," Mercy said, with a teasing intimacy that startled Juliette. "You can't argue that what is essentially an international crime problem doesn't have international roots, and some people argue that crime fiction is the only thing keeping certain cultural traditions alive anymore. And anyway, the mobster is just another version of the master criminal. We'd be lost without him. Though it would be nice," she added with a conspiratorial smile, "if the him were a her once in a while. What do you think, Joseph?" She raised her voice slightly. "Why don't you write a mobster movie for me? Since Michael wouldn't let me be in *The Second Sicilian*."

She flashed her wicked smile at O'Connor, who, like everyone else at the table, was clearly dumbstruck by Mercy's sudden excursion into literary theory—Juliette had to wonder who she had lifted that little speech from. But he quickly caught himself, and raised a glass in acknowledgment.

"So," Mercy continued, "stop trying to make Michael mad when everyone is in a good mood for once. Tell us the story of the Giotto instead. You tell it better than Juliette and it is my favorite story ever. Seriously. You should listen to this, Golonski; I swear it's your next film."

Gabe was still stuck mid-rant, not quite sure how the conversation had been so neatly wrangled and, like O'Connor, a bit taken aback by Mercy's burst of oratory. But when she offered him her most dazzling smile and the full attention of her shining golden eyes, his frown faded. For a moment Juliette could see the couple the two might become, each indulging the other's dramatic excesses, stopping each other before things got out of hand. The couple the two might become if Mercy wasn't such a bottomless pit of need. If she wasn't a drunk and a drug addict. If she wasn't a movie star.

Juliette swallowed hard.

With a rueful shrug and a grin that told everyone he knew he was being manipulated, Gabe complied, telling the story of the very pious Contessa

Gabriella, who had funded many of Giotto's local works and introduced him to some of the reigning families. Giotto had, in fact, often visited Cerreta and had, according to a letter from the contessa to her sister, given her a great gift of rare beauty in the Place That Only God Knows. Some family members thought this meant the artist had touched her soul. "And some," he added with a grin, "had a more lewd interpretation." But others, including Juliette's father, believed he had painted a fresco for her, though there was no mention of it in any of the artist's notes or biographies. Still, Gabe and Juliette had spent the better part of an entire summer searching the entire property for it, but it had never been found.

Golonski was captivated, and even Carson was interested enough to look briefly away from her BlackBerry.

"I love the image of two children alone in a ruined castle, searching for a lost masterpiece," the director mused. "I wonder, is there any way we could include something like that in the second act?" He glanced over at Joseph, who literally writhed in anguish.

"It wasn't quite as romantic as that," Gabe said. "We were hot and sweaty and we fought a lot about where to look. I don't think anyone but Uncle Peter thought it was true; my folks just used it as bait to keep us out of their hair."

"I don't see why we can't just have that image, somehow," said Golonski. "Maybe in a dream sequence."

Beside him, Joseph Andrews choked so hard O'Connor had to thump him on the back six times before he could breathe again.

After dinner, Carson corralled Michael and Mercy into the library to "go over a few pages," while Gabe retreated to his office, followed closely by Usher, who seemed intent on establishing a friendship if not partnership. The interns cleared the table and everyone drifted off, leaving Juliette with a very drunk and vaguely weepy Angie.

"Oh, you don't have to bother," Angie snapped, when Juliette asked if she wanted some coffee or a bit more dessert. "You don't have to bother about me. No one has to bother about me. I'm just the mother. Just the incredibly pushy, bitchy, impossible mother. Just the paid help, really. But I'm leaving tomorrow. This time I am really leaving. I've had it with all of them. Let my darling daughter fend for herself for the first time in her goddamn life, let the rest of them deal with her in her natural state if they think I'm the one making trouble. They don't know what trouble is."

With her blond head nodding emphatically and her words sliding together as if they were moving across ice, Angie looked like a drunk in a movie. All she needed, Juliette thought, was a frowsy evening gown and a piano player. Tempted though she was to leave her there, Juliette leaned over her and put a hand under one elbow.

"I think you should probably go on up to bed," she said gently. "It's late and it's been a rather harrowing day. Everything will be fine tomorrow. These things blow over."

"No, it won't," Angie said, not budging. "We've come to the end of the line, Mercy and I. You have no idea," she said, peering up at Juliette miserably. "*She* has no idea. The things I've done for her, the things I do for her. She isn't normal, you know. She never was. As a baby she screamed constantly. For the first six months of her life. Constantly. She never slept. We never slept. And then she didn't speak until she was four. Six months of shrieking followed by three and a half years of silence. She was like a ghost, that kid. She had rashes, she had food allergies, she couldn't bear to wear long sleeves, she refused to put on socks. For years she wouldn't wear shoes. You couldn't get them on her feet, and if you did, she kicked them off. We had to carry her everywhere. When she finally did talk, she didn't talk. Not like a normal kid. She just recited. She would recite everything she had heard that day. Everything. You can imagine. Then she learned how to read and she would recite everything she read. Cereal boxes and newspapers, storybooks and whatever was on the label of the cough syrup. One time we had a barbecue and she recited our tax returns."

At this Angie suddenly laughed, shaking her head, and Juliette laughed with her until Angie's laughter turned to tears.

"We took her to doctors and they told us she had a learning disability. A learning disability! She could read Shakespeare at five! Maybe it was autism, they said, or Asperger's, or hyperactivity. Everyone suggested we medicate her, but I put my foot down. No pills for my baby." She took a gulp of wine. "Ironic, huh? Maybe if I had medicated her then she would not be taking so many drugs now. I don't know. Nothing any of those doctors said explained the way she was. And then one day she said she wanted to be an actress, and we thought, *Oh, good, that's a way to channel it.* Because we didn't realize, she didn't want to *be* an actress—she already *was* an actress. That should have been the diagnosis." Angie lit a cigarette and took a drag. "That was the disorder. She's an actress. Everything else"—she blew a soft raspberry and waved one hand in the air—"it's just the trappings. She's nuts, my daughter. They're all nuts, these people. Every. Last. One. And if they aren't when they start, they are by the time they're done."

"So why did you do it?" Juliette asked, torn between just letting Angie blow off whatever steam she had to blow off and be done with it, and feeling like this drunken sob story was a bit too self-indulgent. "Why take a child to auditions? Why let a child work in the movies? Why keep being her manager if it makes you so unhappy?"

Angie stared at her. "Haven't you been listening?" she asked. "She's my *daughter* and this is what she *is.* She can't do anything else. She didn't go to college, she didn't really finish high school—those on-set tutors are just a joke. I don't think she could name the fifty states or more than three presidents, frankly. Unless she had to in one of her movies. She remembers every line she's ever had in her movies. Because this is all that interests her. Oh, she can still spit back whatever she reads, but she doesn't understand things like math or science or history. It doesn't interest her enough to understand unless she can imagine herself playing it. When she can do that . . . well, you've seen her." Angie shook her head and her features softened. For a moment Juliette could see Mercy in Angie's face, older and harder, but still there. "She's like an angel, or a muse. Something, I don't know, not human. Or totally human. More human than human. It really is a gift, like Mozart or Einstein. She has this rare and wonderful talent, this one thing that she can do, so well, better than anyone, but that's all. That's all there is."

Angie threw herself back in her chair.

"And she's going to ruin it. With her drugs and her fucking around. She burned down our house, for Christ's sake. Like Richard fucking Pryor. Wrecked the car twice, practically killed us. And she thinks she's immortal, that it will all always be right there—the success, the money, the work. She doesn't realize that it's one thing for a male star to screw up—Russell Crowe or Colin Farrell or your buddy Michael O'Connor. They can drink and drug and fuck whoever they want, but for a girl it's totally different. You get older, the roles dry up anyway, even without all this insurance crap. But she doesn't want to think about that, oh, no, and she doesn't need *me*. Because I'm such a bitch. I'm holding her back. Fuck her. I'm holding her *up*. She has no idea the things I've had to do to protect her, to keep her from winding up like Lloyd. Poor old Lloyd," she finished, a sob choking off her final words.

Juliette had heard more than a few drunken rants in her time, so it wasn't precisely sympathy that prompted her to reach over and pat Angie's shoulder, but it was something close. Pity, maybe. Angie might be a monster, but there was a certain desperate necessity in her monstrousness. Exhaustion raked her face, fear bruised her eyes, and Juliette could certainly see the truth in what she said. Mercy was damaged, and damaging. She was selfish, obsessive, irresponsible, self-destructive, and untrustworthy. Still, whenever Juliette thought of her, that sharp little chin, those strange shade-shifting eyes, she smiled. Knowing how destructive Mercy was, Juliette had still brought her here. Like the sun and the wind, Mercy was a force, an inevitable uncontrollable force who could reach through and around all sorts of walls, even those of her own faults, and touch people. Somehow she found the smallest, tiniest cracks and took hold, bloomed, like the flowers that thrived on an old stone wall. That was why she had become so valuable to so many people, the object of so much desire, capable of so much destruction. Something essential about Mercy made you love her.

What must it be like to be the mother of a person like that? Juliette thought. To see your daughter captivate millions without even trying? To see a younger version of your own face on posters and billboards, on the cover of magazines and dominating the movie screen? At times, the envy and fear must be so great that even the most loving mother in the world would choke.

"I think everyone understands what a great job you've done," Juliette said, attempting to coax Angie to her feet and away from what remained of the wine. "It's easier for people who want to work with Mercy to blame you, but they know in their heart of hearts that you're just doing what's best for Mercy. Believe me. They know." Angie gave Juliette a small but grateful smile, of which she took full advantage. "Now, why don't you go up to bed and relax for a change?" This time Angie allowed herself to be lifted and led away from the table, but not back into the villa. Pulling away from Juliette, she headed instead to the wide lawn that separated the back of the villa from the garden.

"I'm going for a walk," she said, straightening herself and walking with surprising steadiness. "In the moonlight. To collect my thoughts. And say goodbye to this place. It really is a very lovely place," she said, sounding suddenly tired and sincere and almost normal. "You were very nice to let us come. I hope we haven't ruined it for you."

"Not at all." Juliette shook her head. "Shall I join you?" She did not want to spend any more time with Angie, but she felt somehow responsible. After all, this woman had just been fired by her daughter. "Would you like some company?"

"No," Angie said sharply. "Jesus. You really are your own worst enemy, aren't you?" She stopped and peered into Juliette's face as if looking for something specific. She did not seem to find it. With a small sigh, she patted her hair into place and fished around in her purse for a cigarette. "If I go," she said after lighting it, "she's going to expect you to take my place. She likes you. She'll tell you she wants to be more like you. And that will make you feel very special." She took a long hard drag and blew out the smoke. "But it won't be true. Mercy likes being Mercy, and in the end she'll just wear you out. So take a little motherly advice. Go back to your old job if you can. Because my daughter is way too much work. Even for you."

Angie looked at Juliette with sadness more than anything, then turned around and walked out onto the lawn. As she finished clearing away the last few wine glasses and crumpled napkins, Juliette thought to herself that everything Angie had just said, every single thing, was probably the God's honest truth.

It was years before Juliette forgave herself for not following Angie—drunk, distraught, irritating Angie—into the blurry dark. Because the next morning Mercy found her mother lying dead at the bottom of the old quarry behind Casa Padua. She shredded the breathless dawn with her screams. She screamed through Juliette's attempts to comfort and embrace her and through Carson's harsh slap to her face. She screamed as Gabe pulled a blanket around her and pulled her onto his lap, as Steve Usher peered over the edge of the quarry and fell to his knees, unintelligible in his distress, and as the police rather slowly arrived. She didn't stop screaming until one of the paramedics who arrived with the police gave her a shot. And then another one when the first one didn't seem to take.

Chapter Ten

J ULIETTE WISHED SOMEONE WOULD give her a shot. Angie's body looked strangely peaceful. Head to one side, one arm thrown up as if in sleep, she was surrounded by the purple trumpets of morning glories. Still, when Juliette saw her, when her brain was able to process what the utter stillness of Angie's form meant, she felt as if she had been suddenly placed in an icy glass box. No sound seemed able to register, though all around her people were talking. It was fairly clear what had happened—walking in the dark, her senses already considerably blurred by wine and anger, Angie had accidentally stumbled against the waist-high wire fence, much of it also covered in the morning glories that surrounded the quarry. She flipped over, falling to her death. It must have been instantaneous; none of the greenery that surrounded her body was disturbed. Her purse lay a foot or so away from the upflung arm. Summoned, as Juliette had been, by Mercy's scream, Gabe had joined the growing crowd beside the quarry at a dead run, and as he tried to comfort the hysterical girl, Juliette could see the memory of her words of warning about the fence register on his face.

She heard them echoed a few minutes later when Carson arrived, just as the ambulance pulled into the courtyard. Surveying the situation—

Angie's corpse, the inconsolable Mercy—she put her hand on Gabe's shoulder and said in a voice pitched low but deadly enough to be heard over the braying of the siren, "If we lose one day of shooting because of this, I will sue you so hard you won't be able to sit down for a month." Then she slapped Mercy's face.

"That's her way of expressing relief," said O'Connor, who had appeared a few steps behind Carson, tucking in his shirt and stepping gingerly in bare feet. "Someone said it was Mercy who had fallen."

"Are these people all insane?" Gabe asked, one arm still around Mercy, whose screams were now ragged and regular, a shattering sub-set of breathing. Before Juliette could answer, the emergency team arrived, followed quickly by the fire department and the police. She was surprised, and unnerved, to see Inspector Di Marco, unmistakable in another dark and perfectly cut suit, his hair silver and sleek as if he had polished rather than combed it. He bowed his head gravely to her before moving to survey the accident scene.

When the police had left and Mercy had been taken sedated to her bedroom, when Carson called for a cast and crew meeting and Gabe disappeared into one of the lower fields where the horse had kicked its way through a wall, Juliette logged on to the Internet and the web-site deadanddying.com. She wanted to see if the accusations Mercy had made against her mother could even be true; for some reason, she felt this was important.

The site's creators had taken the Smoking Gun's template of posting mug shots of the rich and famous one step—or several steps—further. As Mercy had said, here were death certificates and autopsy reports, morgue photos and a gallery of wrecked cars, from Montgomery Clift's to Lindsay Lohan's. Mercy had her own page, as did Lloyd Watson. Clicking on Lloyd's, Juliette saw, along with a gallery of the typical got-cha pictures, the clothes he had died in, the police report, photos of the crime scene, and then a grainy, horrible, and blurred photo of his corpse. Or at least what might have been his corpse. It certainly was the figure of a naked man, on his knees, but with his head hanging forward. It could have been a corpse, and it could have been Lloyd, but it was impossible to know for certain.

Had Angie taken the picture? Some overwhelming emotion had crossed her face when Mercy had accused her of doing so. Was it outrage, or guilt?

Bile rising in her throat, Juliette clicked on Mercy's page. While she didn't believe the most gruesome aspects of the site were real— the clothes, the death certificates, even the wrecked cars on the other pages could easily be fakes—it was certainly Mercy in various compromising photos. Which included a series featuring the star cavorting with the crew in Siena. Juliette still had a hard time understanding why Angie would take photos of her own daughter passed out or falling out of her dress or making out with a cameraman. And why would Angie take a picture of Lloyd after he had died? Juliette could not believe that whatever she was paid would be worth the possible damage the photos would do to the film, not to mention the general horribleness of it all. Even Angie could not be so cold-blooded, could she?

The image of Angie's own corpse rose in Juliette's mind and she remembered a famous photo of a young woman who had jumped from a building and lay nestled in the remains of the car she had fallen onto as if she were sleeping. That's what Angie had looked like; someone, Juliette thought, hysteria gathering in her throat, should have taken a picture of her. A cold wave washed over her as she wondered if someone actually had. Well, she thought, bookmarking the site before closing down her laptop, they'd know soon enough. Then she picked up the phone to call Devlin.

✱   ✱   ✱

"Shall I come over?" was all he said when she told him what had happened.

"What?" she asked, taken aback by his curt tone. "No. I mean, why? Do you think something's going on? I mean, besides what's going on."

Devlin sighed. "I think this sounds like utter insanity. I think you sound rattled and paranoid. You've called me six times in as many days at all hours of the morning, and I don't know what you expect me to do for you from here."

"I don't expect you to do anything," she said haughtily. "I just wanted . . ."

"You just wanted what? What do you want, J.? You run off to Italy to 'collect yourself' without even a hint at whether you'll be back or not. You go silent for weeks, and the next thing I know, you've got Michael O'Connor and an entire movie set in your backyard." He sighed and his voice softened. "Tell me, J. Just tell me. What do you want from me at this point in your life?"

On top of everything else, here was a question she could not anwer. Why was she calling him every single day suddenly? What did she want?

To hear the sound of his voice, that's what. To have him make things right-sized. Dev didn't believe in out-of-control or the end-of-the-world, only in situations to be handled. And when she was in Los Angeles, she did handle them. But always with the knowledge that he was there, just around the corner, which somehow made things easier even if he didn't lift more than a skeptical eyebrow. She closed her eyes and thought of how much better she would feel if Dev were just standing in the next room. Just standing there with that so-how-are-you-going-to-sort-this-out look on his face. She called him because she missed him, but if she told him that, it would make things even more confusing. He was her boss and her friend, and however he defined love, she could not imagine it involved anything approaching monogamy, much less devotion. Just thinking about it made her eyes

sting. Instead she leaned her head against the wall and listened to the
awful sound of her own silence.

"Well, whatever you do, don't fix the fence," Dev said when she
didn't answer. "That would be an admission of liability."

And then he hung up on her.

"I don't understand," Gabe said, examining the fence a few hours
later, after the police had left. It seemed unbroken, untouched almost
except for a small sag at one point where, apparently, Angie had hit it. "I
don't understand how she could have just fallen."

"It was dark, she was drunk," Juliette said shortly. "She could have
tripped on a rock, or just slipped on these loose stones. She had those
damn high heels on, she would have hit the fence just at her waist. Shit,
Gabe, I knew we should have fixed that fence. I knew it after that night
I chased Mercy up the tower . . ."

"Well, unless we had turned it into a wall, I don't see what good it
would have done," Gabe said. "Christ almighty, this is one of the reasons
I hate drunks so much. Drunk drunks, that is. I mean, she wasn't the
greatest mother in the world, but she could have at least tried not to kill
herself right in front of her daughter."

Juliette felt the blood drain from her face; she looked at her cousin
quickly, but Gabe's eyes were on Casa Padua, where Mercy still slept.

"I just hope she doesn't think it was my fault," he said softly, and
Juliette could hear the strain in his voice. "Because," he added, catching
her eye and finding his normal irritated tone, "it wasn't. And I hope that
witchy Carson keeps her liability comments to herself. Or I will throw
her off this property."

"How could this be your fault?" Juliette said angrily. "You don't
control the universe and everyone in it, you know." Her conversation
with Devlin left her feeling pulled tight and thin and she felt suddenly
worried about her cousin's concern for Mercy. Although she had felt a
certain smug satisfaction watching him recognize Mercy's allure, the

thought of him having his heart broken by a woman who was nothing if not a professional heartbreaker did not sit well with her. "And we are not liable, because I made certain that the contract we all signed stated that the production company was aware of the condition of the estate and that we would not be responsible for any injury to persons or property."

"Oh," said Gabe.

"Which means that, in the likely event Mercy is unable to work tomorrow, Carson will have to answer to the insurance company herself. Since she okayed the location. So," she added practically, "we should definitely leave the fence as it is; to fix it now would be admitting fault."

Gabe looked at her narrowly. "Wait, did you just run this by Devlin?"

"No," Juliette said shortly. "Well, I did fax him the contract before we signed it. And the bit about not fixing the fence, that was what he said when I called him today."

She and Gabe were on the porch now and because she could think of nothing else to do, Juliette sat down. Gabe joined her.

"I hope you swore Devlin to secrecy," said Gabe. "I heard Carson and O'Connor sweet-talking the cops about keeping their lips zipped. Carson even intimated to me that I should get a nondisclosure oath from my staff because 'any publicity about this tragedy would just reflect poorly on Cerreta.' I told her I had heard that there was no such thing as bad publicity so I had already called *Entertainment Tonight*. She was not amused."

Juliette looked at him narrowly. "Eamonn Devlin's default setting is secrecy," she said with a brittle laugh. "I saw you talking to our friend Di Marco. What did he want?"

"If I knew where Mercy had been last night. And I did." He looked at his cousin coolly. "She was with me."

"Really?"

"Really."

"All night?"

"All night."

"I wondered where she had got to," Juliette said, then said no more.

"We were talking most of the night," Gabe said, after a pause that he clearly was not comfortable with. "About her recovery. She seems to really want to get sober even if no one else does. Did you know that Steve Usher told her that a reasonable first step was choosing between drugs and alcohol? That it was okay to drink because she had to 'step down' from her addictions? We see how successful that's been. Apparently Lloyd tried to get her to give it all up. I think . . ." He paused, and when he spoke again, his voice was softer, less defensive. "She swears she never gave him any drugs, but she feels pretty guilty about his death, like it was somehow her fault. I told her no one could make or break Lloyd's sobriety except him, but . . ." He stopped and shook his head. "It's too bad, because it seems like he had almost gotten there, you know? She gave me his copy of that horrible Little Book and you should see it. He wrote these hilarious and really insightful things all over the margins. He totally went to town on the bibliography, which is five pages long and chock-full of books you've never heard of. Seriously, Usher should be arrested for being criminally unhelpful."

"Poor Mercy," she said, automatically tuning out Gabe's lecture on the evils of Steve Usher; having seen the anguish on Usher's face as he looked down on Angie's body, Juliette had a difficult time casting him in the role of the villain at the moment. "How is she ever going to survive this?"

"That will be interesting to see," he said. "With any luck, she won't. If by survive, you mean continue to deny the reality of her life so she doesn't have to change. With any luck, she will let herself feel whatever it is she feels without burying it under too many drugs and bullshit. With any luck, she'll finally decide to get help." He gave Juliette a piercing look. "But that may be too much to ask for."

"What's too much to ask for?" said O'Connor, stepping onto the porch. "That they just pull the plug on this wretched film and let us go home?" he said, handing Juliette Angie's purse. "Here, the police asked me to deliver this to Mercy. I guess they're satisfied that it was an accident, which is a minor blessing. I mean, after Lloyd, it is beginning to feel like this project is cursed or something. I mean, God, what a thing to have happen. Angie wasn't my favorite person in the whole world, but still. How is Mercy? Is she still sleeping? Oh, there you are, princess," he said, his voice instantly dropping to a more gentle, almost loving tone, his gaze shifting over Juliette's shoulder to where Mercy stood, blinking against the sun, in the doorway. "How are you feeling, kiddo? I'm just sorry as hell about your mom. It's a terrible thing. Unbelievable, really."

Mercy nodded silently, and held her hand out toward Juliette for the purse, which she drew against her chest and cradled as if it were a doll.

"What would you like to do, baby girl?" Michael continued in a soft voice. "You want us to get you home? You want to talk to your dad? We can get you on a plane tonight, you just say the word."

Mercy did not seem to hear him. She opened the purse and lifted it up to her face, breathing deeply. Watching her, Juliette remembered in a rush the smell of her own mother's purse—an intoxicating mix of leather and White Shoulders, cinnamon gum and the copper of old pennies. Mercy lowered the bag and, rummaging around in it for a moment, found her inhaler. After three long puffs, she looked at Michael with a coolness that added years to her face.

"I haven't spoken to my father in six months," she said. "I don't see why I should speak to him now." She turned to head back into the house. "Tell Carson," she said over her shoulder as she trailed away, "that we can shoot that kitchen scene, if there's still time to set it up. I just need to take a shower first."

"Mercy," objected the three of them in unison; after exchanging looks, the men ceded to Juliette.

"You really don't need to do that," she said. "Not even Carson expects you to work today, or tomorrow, for that matter. You need to take care of yourself or you really will collapse . . ."

Mercy sighed and looked at Juliette with pity.

"How long do you think it will take for my mother's death to hit the media, the Internet? I mean, if it hasn't already? And when it does, how long do you suppose it will be before every paparazzo and entertainment reporter in the world tries to find me and photograph me and interview me, the troubled and grieving daughter? Cerreta may be isolated, but it isn't on Mars."

"She's right," O'Connor said after a pause. "We'll be lucky to finish even if we do start today. It could get ugly."

"We'll get security," Juliette said. "We'll put up a gate at the end of the road."

Mercy gave her a small pale smile.

"You do that, Juliette. Meanwhile, tell Carson we should keep shooting as long as the light holds." And she vanished back into the house.

In the silence that followed this proclamation, Juliette turned instinctively to Gabe to see what his reaction would be, to Mercy's decision and the reason behind it. She did not imagine he would be happy with the idea of a gate or security at the end of the road leading up to Cerreta—it certainly was not in keeping with the eco-crunchy nature of the place and would certainly let any paparazzi, and gawkers, know they were in the right place. But Gabe was still gazing at the space where Mercy had just stood, his face a mixture of admiration, pity, and anger. "What the hell," he said finally, "is in that inhaler?"

"Nothing," Juliette said, taken aback. "Seriously. I checked."

"Check again," said Gabe. "Because my money says she's sucking down a speedball."

✷ ✷ ✷

Juliette managed to take the inhaler to a pharmacy in Siena, and found nothing but albuterol. She emailed Devlin for a local security contact; she wasn't about to call him again and would have rather not emailed, but she needed a name. Almost instantly he replied, sending her a name and a number, told her he was glad she was "finally seeking professional help," apologized for getting off the phone "so abruptly," and asked if Steve Usher was still there.

"Yes," she messaged back, relieved that their communication was back to normal. "But I don't think he will be of much help. He doesn't seem to have much of a network over here. He is," she added because she felt she had to, "sticking pretty close to Mercy. For once."

And it was true. Mercy moved through the next few days like a wraith, sitting in silence between takes staring at nothing or disappearing into her trailer. She smoked constantly, ate rarely, and acknowledged the presence of the makeup artists, the stylists, her costar, the director, or even Juliette only when absolutely necessary. Surprisingly, she allowed Usher to coddle her, to ply her with fortified water, a rainbow assortment of herbal supplements, and a constant low murmur of readings from the Little Book.

Maybe, Juliette thought, this was because Usher had seemed so genuinely shocked and upset over Angie's death. Remembering how the blood drained from his face when he peered down at the body, Juliette had to wonder if there wasn't some truth in Mercy's accusations that Usher and Angie had had more than a working relationship. For once Usher seemed at a loss for words; even the loose-limbed jauntiness of his self-conciously rock-star step had vanished. Moving almost crablike in his floppy linen, he seemed to have aged ten years. But somehow it brought him closer to Mercy. Soon it was Usher making Mercy's needs and requests known to Carson and O'Connor and the rest of the crew, and everyone had to acknowledge he was much more charming about it than Angie had ever been.

Even with an official proclamation of accidental death, a low hum of tension filled the set and quickly seeped all over Cerreta. With little or no argument, Carson had a gate installed at the bottom of the road leading to the castello, and the Italian security firm Devlin had recommended sent over a pair of requisitely thuggish-looking men who wandered the grounds and various live sets. But aside from a backpacker who was carrying a suspicious number of cameras and several telephoto lenses, there was no trouble. Back in the States, Becker quietly announced Angie's death and issued a statement that Mercy was flying to Paris to be with friends and family. Everyone on the set received a personal email from him reminding them of their confidentiality contracts and warning he would "personally take action against" anyone who breeched that agreement, "considering the tragic circumstances."

It may have been an effective news blackout but it didn't help the mood at Cerreta. The normally profane and jocular crew now fell silent whenever Mercy made an appearance. Some quietly offered their condolences, but many exchanged skeptical, judgmental, or even occasionally accusing looks when she passed. In death, Angie was granted a sympathy she had never received in life; among themselves, some of the same crew now discussed how high-handed and ungrateful Mercy had been with her mother. Anyone could have seen how miserable Angie had been that last night, but had Mercy even bothered to try to patch things up? Of course not. No wonder Angie had been such a bitch, with a daughter like that. It was not at all surprising she had gotten so drunk that night; more than a few wondered if Angie hadn't simply hurled herself into the quarry, and why not? Hadn't her own daughter just fired her?

Silent and pale, Mercy seemed to accept that her status was not that of a grief-stricken daughter, or at least not that alone. She drew to the set not only the normal mayhem of a troubled star but something that began to feel like fear. Like an unfortunate sailor whose mere presence appeared to doom a voyage, she was in danger of becoming Jonah. O'Connor was not the only person to use the word "cursed"—it hung in the air like a constant whisper, utterly at odds with the bright skies and fragrant wind of late spring as it shook its skirts out over the Tuscan countryside.

Yet even as Mercy seemed to melt away into silence and smoke, on camera she had never been so vivid, so full of desperate fire or tamped-down passion. As the dueling narratives of the film crescendoed, Mercy was a wonder to watch. Her modern woman battled nefarious forces that would destroy art and lives in pursuit of profit, while in a parallel life, her young nun, hobbled by poverty and the oppression of the times, vainly attempted to deny her earthly desires, seeking in God what she could not have in life.

Soon the work became as much a source of tension as the accident. As Mercy became almost pathologically immersed in her character, Michael O'Connor struggled not to be outshone. In scene after scene, he, too, reached for depths of feeling and layers of complication he had not visited in years as an actor. And while Juliette felt a rush of almost proprietary pleasure seeing him push himself so far and hard, she could also see the toll it took on him, emotionally and physically. More than once, she saw him reach for his own tawny vial of prescription medication and she wondered if it was continuation of the chemotherapy or just pain meds. Any concern he had for Mercy, any thought he might have of Juliette, were soon put aside as he disappeared entirely into the two characters, becoming almost as taciturn and withdrawn as Mercy.

"Juliette, I'm working," he had said with a sigh at one point when she brought him a cup of coffee and attempted a conversation. "I'm sorry, but this is all I can do at the moment."

Juliette found some consolation in the fact that he was not lying. Aware that Becker's Paris story could only hold for so long and fearing that the intensity of the two stars could not sustain itself indefinitely,

Carson and Golonski pushed the schedule, shooting scene after scene, requesting rewrites to accommodate Mercy's increasing abandon, Michael's desperate determination, and the landscape around them. The few times Juliette glimpsed Joseph Andrews, he looked gray and grim, utterly unapproachable, his sole companion a laptop on which he appeared to be writing an entirely new movie.

Golonski, on the other hand, had never seemed happier, smiling and nodding, cosseting Mercy during the shoots, arranging the folds of her costume, stroking her hair, touching her impassive face as if she were a doll. Following his cue, Carson took the opportunity to glue herself to O'Connor's side, position herself as beloved trainer to his prizefighter. Juliette had barely spoken to him since Angie's death, and aside from offering a few regretful smiles, O'Connor did not seem to notice.

It was little comfort that Gabriel seemed to be suffering the same fate.

"Mercy won't even speak to me," Gabe said as he and Juliette stood on the northwest corner of the courtyard, watching the crew set up for a series of scenes involving the bell tower. "Which I kind of get, since we spent a lot of time that night talking about all the damage her mother had done. So she probably feels guilty, which is ridiculous, since the fact the woman is dead doesn't make her less of a bitch. But still . . ."

Juliette nodded, her eyes searching for and finding O'Connor, who was watching a nearby monitor with a look of distinct dissatisfaction on his face.

"And she probably blames me," Gabe continued, "which means she's wrapping herself up in denial, aided and abetted by ol' Steverino. Who, by the way, has offered not only to buy Cerreta but to create a foundation that would allow me 'to take my message all over the world.' The man will not take no for an answer, even though I've given it to him in three or four languages."

"She'll speak to you," Juliette said. "Just don't be pushy. You can be very pushy."

"Caring," Gabe said. "I can be very caring. The longer she wastes with him, the longer it's going to take for her to get sober and on with her life."

"See, that's what I'm talking about, Gabe. Nobody makes any real change in their life just because someone tells them it's a good idea. You really need to watch more television."

Seeing O'Connor rise, looking weary and unhappy, and make his way toward his trailer, Juliette frowned a bit and almost unconsciously began following him. It had been days since they had actually had a private conversation, much less anything more intimate. She knew from experience how hard it was for him to ask for help, at least when he actually needed it, and she wondered how much anyone on the set knew of his physical condition. Since he had come to Cerreta, she realized as she began to walk a bit more quickly, he had not even mentioned the cancer to her.

Meanwhile, Gabe continued to walk beside her, saying things she didn't quite catch because she wasn't quite listening. "You really should take a look at the Little Book," Gabe said, refusing to acknowledge her intention to leave, "if you need a laugh or two. Lloyd's notes are pretty hilarious. I bet Usher wants it back so no one can sell it on eBay. Although if you believe Mercy, he'd be the one to sell it on eBay."

Juliette frowned—there was an unfamiliar note in her cousin's voice. Frivolity, that was it. "Are you high?" she asked. "Or is this just you in love? Because it's really weirding me out." She began moving toward Michael's trailer, into which he had disappeared for once not trailed by Carson. Without missing a beat, Gabe followed her.

"I am ebullient by nature," he said. "Where are we going? You know," he said, his voice rising slightly, "I actually forgot to tell you. I managed to pay down a bunch of debts and get us on a program to pay off the rest. I think you should see it."

"Later," Juliette said.

"Later I have to go into town," Gabe said. "Let's do it now, real quick." He took her arm and all but pulled her away. "Just real quick."

"What is wrong with you?" Juliette replied hotly, jerking her arm out of his grasp and knocking on the trailer door. "We can do it later. I'm not going anywhere."

"Jules," Gabe said, his voice low and pleading, "come on. I don't think you should——"

But it was too late. Upon her final knock, the trailer door had swung open, revealing, if not in full light then at least in no-explanations-necessary silhouette, Michael seated on the sofa while Carson bent over him. She was wearing only a T-shirt.

Juliette didn't pause to see what would happen next; her face flaming, she turned on her heel and left. She heard a voice call her name but she was moving so fast she wasn't sure if it was Gabe's or Michael's. Either way, she didn't care. She didn't want explanations or reassurances or Gabe's infernal lecture about the importance of feeling her feelings. She just wanted to get away, to be alone so she could remind herself, calmly, that she had known something like this would happen, known it all along, it was just a matter of time, and this didn't matter, not really, not at all. She remembered, with a bitter smile, a conversation she had fallen into back in Los Angeles with Michael's most recent ex-wife, who had warned her about getting involved with him and mentioned, most specifically, O'Connor's on-set behavior. Even Mercy had warned her: "Michael cheats," she had said, "though maybe he won't with you."

"Maybe" is not a word upon which to balance your heart. But why should she be any different from the countless other women in O'Connor's past? And why would Michael be any different from her husband? Josh had cheated on her. After ten years of marriage, happy marriage. Even after everything that had happened, Juliette still couldn't quite believe that Josh had left her. You really couldn't count on anyone.

Hadn't she learned the lesson yet? Hadn't she learned that lesson years ago, right here in this very spot, listening to the angry words and the weeping, the roiling silence that followed? There was at least some comfort in the symmetry—beauty and peace were no protection against treachery. Love, romantic love, was a small illusory Eden, its borders defined by betrayal.

Taking the steps of Casa Padua two at a time, she was barely aware of the car pulling into the courtyard, but when it was quickly followed by two more, red lights flashing, she paused. Inspector Di Marco unfolded himself from the first car and smiled gravely up at Juliette. "Signora Greyson," he said. "Where would I find Signor Golonski and Signora Cooper?"

"Is something wrong?" Juliette asked, quickly steadying her voice. From the corner of her eye, she could see Gabe come to a halt a few yards away.

"Please," the inspector answered, with a formal nod. "We will follow you."

Dutifully, Juliette led Di Marco and two police officers through the confusing maze of the set to where she had last seen Golonski. A wild hope rose in her that Carson would be arrested, though for what she could not imagine—while the producer was undoubtedly capable of tipping Angie into a quarry, Juliette could not see why she would. Angie's death only gave Carson another problem to deal with. Where had she been that night? No doubt Michael could vouch for her, she thought bitterly.

Golonski, Joseph, and the cinematographer were bent toward a trio of monitors; as Juliette approached, Carson appeared from nowhere, fully dressed and motioning furiously for Juliette to stop where she was, that it was a live set.

"Cut, cut," Golonski yelled, as the sound of footsteps reached him through his headset. He looked over toward Juliette, his face murderous. "What the hell? Do you mind? We're in the middle of a fucking scene here."

Stepping to one side, she let Carson and Golonski see Di Marco and the two officers behind her, and she took a moment of pure satisfaction in the look of fear on the producer's face. Maybe she had killed Angie after all. But no.

"Mr. Andrews," Di Marco said, motioning the two carabinieri toward the screenwriter. "You are wanted for questioning in connection with the murder of Lloyd Watson. Please come with me."

Chapter Eleven

JULIETTE FINALLY TOOK REFUGE in the library. From its large picture window, she could watch the chaos that lapped at the villa, small waves of humanity and equipment and noise. It was difficult not to feel under siege, even more difficult not to admit, at least to herself, that she had been the one who allowed the attacking army in through the gates.

In the uproar that had followed Joseph's being led to the police car, Golonski, at Carson's urging, tried to continue filming. But when Mercy heard what had happened, she fainted. Michael, who was standing right beside her, had completely missed her as she went down. Her head hit the ancient bricks with an audible crack. Out of nowhere, Gabe appeared, scooping her up and carrying her off, while Carson began shouting into her cell phone and Golonski threw his hands up and stomped off. Michael stood, still in the middle of the set, turning slowly around as if in a daze, as if he didn't know where he was. But when his gaze swept toward Juliette, she slipped away and, skirting the edge of the restless and wondering crew, made her way to the villa and up a back staircase to the library.

Randomly noticing a bowl of apples and a bottle of wine on the long refectory table that stood in the back of the room, she figured she could wait out most of the craziness until darkness fell. Then she could creep away unseen, possibly jumping in her car and just driving away. Maybe Devlin was right. Maybe she should just go home. Except she couldn't go home. Not now. She couldn't leave Gabe in the middle of a mess she had made.

"This was supposed to be my vacation," she said plaintively to the wasp that was trapped in the corner of the window, bumping against the glass as if certain this time it would give way. "My vacation," she repeated, throwing herself onto the couch. She wished she had thought to grab her purse during the proceedings, or at least her BlackBerry. She would very much have liked to talk to Devlin right now, even if it meant admitting that she did feel overwhelmed. She needed his inevitable murmur and derisive laugh. To Devlin, it seemed, all the vagaries of the human heart, all the absurdities of human behavior, were perfectly predictable and rather banal. Life was like the hotel business, he had told her time and again. The trick was imaginative anticipation; if you're never surprised, you're always prepared. Devlin, with his own steely-eyed refusal to dwell on things he had done, was never surprised.

"Have you seen Mercy?"

At the sound of O'Connor's voice, all she felt was a gray fug of exhaustion. She did not open her eyes. She heard him enter the room, make his way across the dry and creaking wood of the floor, felt him settle at the far end of the sofa. Still she did not move.

"Other women have attempted to eradicate my existence in a similar way," he said. "They were equally unsuccessful. I have an unfortunate aversion to disappearing. As you well know, my Juliette." He drew out her name, lingering over the *t*'s and she could see his famous big-screen grin on the backside of her eyelids just as clearly as if they had been open. And when they were, there it was, exactly as she had imagined it. Exactly as she had seen it time and time again in the restless dark of a movie theater. Juliette sat up.

"Let's not," she said quietly. "I'm not in the mood."

"And how could you be, with our friend Joseph Andrews somehow implicated in the death of Lloyd Watson, with Mercy swooning before my eyes as I stood there, incapable of movement?"

His smile was calculated to be infectious, those angled eyebrows high over pools of blue alight with that knowing mischief that had seduced millions for so many years. She closed her eyes again and leaned back against the corner of the sofa.

"Why are you here, Mr. O'Connor? Have you come to confess? To tell me that you promised Joseph you'd star in his movie if only he'd kill Lloyd Watson for you?"

"Interesting theory. Now, why would I do that?"

"Who knows? Boredom? Professional jealousy? Insane rage over ceding your leading-man mantle to a younger man?"

"You're being unkind, my Juliette, which is something you rarely are." He reached out for her ankle. "Why? Are you angry with me? Have I done something to offend you?"

She pulled her leg away, tucked both of them under her.

"Nothing I didn't expect you to do," she said flatly. "Though I can't say I'm impressed by your taste. What does it mean, that men not only cheat on me but with women I can't stand?"

"Cheating," he said carefully in a low voice. "That's a word with all sorts of implications, isn't it?" He paused. She looked at the ceiling and began counting the angels painted there, comely young women all, with pink lips and round breasts beneath their celestial robes.

"Juliette," he said. "Look at me. No," he said, catching hold of her arm and yanking her toward him. "Look at me."

Late afternoon pulsed through the window, and even in that syrupy gold, Michael's face was pale and lined. The skin, stripped of the makeup, seemed thin and papery, the bones of his skull and jaw too prominent. Even so, his eyes were bright blue, so blue that, she realized with a shock, he must be wearing tinted contacts, something she was certain he had never done before. She saw now the very clear imprint of his illness; even if it was in remission, the cancer had done damage. Despite the prominence of his bones, he seemed somehow blurry, as if his face were being worn away, used up like a photograph too often handled or a painting left for years in sunlight. Sorrow jolted her, not personal, not the feeling of a lover or even a friend, but a more universal loss, like one might have for a work of art destroyed or defaced.

As if he could read her thoughts, he abruptly let go of her arm and turned his face away. "I'm playing lover to a girl young enough to be my daughter because I need to prove I can still do it. Which maybe I can't. I'm old and I'm tired and maybe I'm done, but this," he said, motioning toward the set outside the window, "is all I know how to do. There's nothing else. There's never been anything else. I need the work. And for the first time in a long time, I don't know if I can do the work."

Watching him now, Juliette could see that these words were an effort and the effort seemed sincere. But even that made her angry— everything that was going on, and this was what he was worried about? That he wasn't the greatest actor in the world? It seemed absurd.

"So getting a quickie from Carson, that somehow makes everything all right? Shores up the old confidence level?"

"I suppose," he said simply. "For a few minutes. Under certain circumstances. It keeps the demons at bay. For a few minutes." He shrugged. His tone was far too matter-of-fact to be mistaken for an apology. "As I said, I don't expect you to understand. But it had nothing to do with you, nothing to do with . . . us. Which is a very separate thing. Or might be, under different circumstances." He sighed and looked around, at the walls lined to the ceiling with books and bits of Etruscan pottery, at the portraits of Madonnas and dark bearded men. "I should have never come here," he said regretfully. "I should have told Carson we needed to find another location. You need to keep work and . . . life separate. We all do things out of fear, repeat patterns for the comfort of familiarity. I have new fears and very old . . . patterns."

With mild shock, Juliette saw that he expected some sort of sympathy from her; with an even greater shock, she realized that sympathy was in fact one of the things she felt.

"Why were you looking for Mercy?" she asked abruptly. Already she was forgiving him, finding something in his honesty that made up for his betrayal, and hating herself for it. No, they hadn't made any promises to each other, but Carson? If it had been anyone but Carson. "Are they actually going to try to keep filming today?"

After a swift searching look, O'Connor answered as if none of the previous conversation had occurred. "No chance. Carson is utterly immersed in damage control and the crew is being reminded of their confidentiality clauses one more time—she may as well have it tattooed on their foreheads. Golonski, meanwhile, is off to Siena to try to spring his screenwriter; we are, apparently, missing a climactic scene. Which is a problem."

Juliette said nothing.

"And I was looking for Mercy because I was suddenly overcome with an odd sense of concern for her. While I don't want to try to get back into your good graces by resurrecting our sleuthing past, I do wonder just what the hell is going on. Don't you? I mean, why do they suddenly think Lloyd was murdered? And why on earth would Joseph have anything to do with it? I have wracked my already overtaxed brain trying to figure out who would want that poor boy dead, and aside from your theory of my jealous rage, I can think of no one. Can you?"

"I don't have any idea. According to Devlin, it was the insurance company that reopened the investigation, because if it was suicide or an overdose, they don't have to pay. I think they're trying to prove that someone faked the whole autoerotic thing in order to make it look like an accidental death. That is apparently covered, which frankly is a little weird. But why they would think it was Joseph is beyond me."

"Probably because it was his semen on the floor in Lloyd's room."

Shocked, Juliette and Michael swiveled their heads in time to see Mercy, followed closely by Gabe, entering the room. "At least that's what I'm guessing. We were just in the chapel," she said with a wan smile. "It really is peaceful there, although Gabe showed me the special room where the nobles sat so they wouldn't have to even breathe the same air as the peasants—pretty horrible when you think about it. We lit a candle for my mother, and one for Lloyd. I guess I should have lit one for Joseph. But I can't believe he did it alone, which only leaves my mother. Which makes perfect sense, since he does have this weird fixation with me. She probably slept with him, and that's how she got it. Although I don't see her actually planting it; that would be just gross. So maybe it was his idea. Except it's got more written all over it."

"Got what?" Juliette said, her head spinning as her eyes went from Mercy to Gabe, who was watching the young woman with an air of expectation. "What are you talking about?"

"The semen. Which must have been Joseph's, or why would they arrest him?"

"They didn't arrest him," Michael said sharply. "They took him in for questioning."

"Whatever. They'll probably arrest him later. Isn't tampering with a crime scene a crime? And they must think he tampered. Otherwise how could his semen get in Lloyd's room?"

"What the hell are you talking about?" Michael and Juliette asked almost in unison. "And will you please stop saying 'semen'?" Juliette added.

Looking from one baffled face to another, Mercy sat down with a sigh.

"I told you I was the one who found Lloyd's body," she said. "I told you that. And when I found him, with that rope around his neck like he had been whacking off, I knew it wasn't right. For one thing, the rope had cut this huge red mark into his neck and Lloyd would never have let that happen. He was way too into how he looked and we were shooting the next day—everyone in costume and makeup would have seen it. And then there was the . . . word Juliette doesn't want to hear again. On the floor. Totally gross, and I knew it wasn't Lloyd's."

"I am going to regret asking this," Michael said, "but how on earth did you know that?"

"Because it was like two feet away from the body," she said impatiently. When Michael continued to look blank, she sighed again. "Lloyd didn't have that kind of trajectory. He took so many supplements to keep that cut look of his, he didn't have *any* trajectory, actually, and not much in the area of quantity, either. What?" she said, surveying the expressions on the faces around her. "Oh, am I the only person in this room who has ever actually had sex? Anyway, I assumed they would test the stuff for DNA and realize something was wrong. But apparently they didn't; everyone was too fixated on the toxicology report. An actor dies and it's always about the drugs." She shook her head sadly before adding rather brightly, "So I phoned in my anonymous tip."

"You are kidding me," Juliette said. "So you're saying Joseph's DNA matched the . . . what was on the floor of Lloyd's room? How would they know that? How would they get Joseph's DNA?"

"From Carson," Michael said wearily. "Or the insurance company. Joseph has had a heroin problem for years, but he cleans up when he's on set. He just has to pee in a cup once a week to prove it."

Now it was his turn to face the various looks of surprise in the room.

"You'd be amazed at how many cups are being peed into on any given movie set," Michael said. "There are a lot more highly functioning addicts out there than you might think."

"Until they're not," Gabe said. "And they wind up dead, like Lloyd Watson."

"So you think Joseph wanted to make it seem like Lloyd didn't OD because if he had, the insurance wouldn't pay and they'd shut the movie down."

Mercy nodded. "Yes. It's expensive to keep me on a stalled project," she said frankly, "and God only knows what they offered Michael to come on at the last minute."

"Oh, I did it for scale and the opportunity to work with you, my dear," he said with a sardonically sweet smile.

Mercy ignored him. "Everyone's in cost-cutting mode these days, and if it got too expensive Becker might have just sent the whole thing back to development hell," she explained, sounding suddenly like the Hollywood professional she was. "Joseph needs to get his movie made or else his price will plummet. He thinks he would be the next Richard Curtis if only American directors and producers weren't so stupid."

"But I don't understand why Angie would have been involved in trying to make Lloyd's death look like something other than an overdose," Juliette said.

"Or a suicide," Michael added. "Does someone think Lloyd did it on purpose? Was there a note? A suicide will stall a picture even faster than a drug overdose."

"If Joseph's a heroin addict, he may not have been thinking straight," Gabe said. "He may have panicked."

"I actually don't think he's using anymore," Michael said.

"But why do you think Angie was involved?" Juliette asked, turning to Mercy.

Mercy shrugged. "I saw her coming out of Lloyd's room that night, and then those pictures showed up on deadanddying; they had Angie written all over them. At first I thought she was just banging him. She still got off on the whole mother/daughter thing, even though it's been years since I told her I wouldn't do that three-way shit anymore."

Mercy stopped, startled by what she had just said, something she clearly had not meant to share. There was a sudden awful silence. Juliette let out a small gasp and Michael quickly stood up and moved toward the window. Gabe reached out and put his hand on Mercy's shoulder, but his expression did not change. For a moment, Mercy dropped her eyes and a flush crept up her neck, stained her cheeks, but she quickly looked up and defiantly straightened her back. "Not that it was any big secret, those little two-for-ones. At least not among certain circles. Though you never indulged," she added, her voice shaking slightly, "did you, Mr. O'Connor?"

Michael was fiddling with the curtain, his eyes firmly on whatever activity was taking place in the rising twilight below. Turning, he regarded his costar kindly.

"My luck with blondes ran out long before you were born, princess," he said.

Mercy tried to smile, but her mouth only twisted. She dropped her gaze again to her lap, where her hands wrung each other as if she were trying to rub the flesh off them.

"It's okay, Mercy," Juliette said, crouching down beside her and taking those hands in her own. "Like you said, that's all in the past. It's nobody's business. You don't have to talk about it now. You don't even have to think about it now."

Gabe made a sound of protest in his throat.

"That's right," he said. "Just keep it buried inside, just carry it around for a few more years. Feed it drugs and alcohol until it explodes and takes her with it. Jesus. Mercy," he said gently, not making a move toward her, "you are allowed. You are allowed to talk about the things that have happened in your life. You are allowed to tell the truth about it and you are even allowed to do it in such a way that doesn't make any money for anyone."

"Stop it, Gabe," Juliette snapped. "Her mother just died. You always think talking about something makes it better, but it doesn't. Let her grieve however she wants to."

"You can't grieve until you admit what it is you've actually lost," Gabe said quietly. "Angie's death doesn't change who she was, the good and bad. You can't mourn someone you won't let yourself see clearly. When are you going to figure that out?"

"Stop it." She stood up to face him. "This isn't about you. Or me."

"No," Gabe said, and all at once Mercy and Michael were completely forgotten. "I won't. Look at what silence does to people, Jules. It's not just Mercy. It's us, too. It's been fifteen years and we've never once had a conversation about what happened, which made sense when we were both fucked up, but makes no sense now. My parents were in that car, too. My parents died that night, too. They were all drunk, as usual, and probably fighting, as usual, and it finally caught up with them. It wasn't the fog or the music or whatever the hell else the cops said. You and I know what they were like when they were all together, and it killed them in the end.

He drew a deep breath. "There. I've said it. Out loud. And look, the world did not end. It was an awful thing, but it wasn't the most important thing that ever happened to you. At least it doesn't have to be."

Juliette stared at him, opened her mouth to speak, shook her head, turned neatly on her heel, and walked out the door.

For the second time that day, she mounted the steps to Casa Padua, her muscles knitted into preflight tension, determined this time to leave Cerreta, possibly forever, to take her credit cards and what was left of her savings and fly far away, to Paris, to Greece, back to Los Angeles. Anywhere but here, where the ghosts rose from every corner, laughing over their wine, stumbling across the courtyard to fall into bitter arguments behind closed doors. She grabbed her purse, her car keys, and pounded down the steps again, ignoring the sight of Michael emerging from the villa, expelling from her mind the words Gabe had just uttered and all the pain they rained down.

Eyes straight ahead, she strode past the lights and wires, past the monitors, the racks of clothing, the stacks of chairs and crates, the table with its assortment of drinks and snacks, through a stone arch, along a stone wall, and straight to where a line of cars were parked. There, a man stood, having apparently just pulled in. Juliette took one look at him and threw herself into his arms.

"Well, J.," Devlin said, rocking back on his heels but embracing her nonetheless, "I had hoped you would be pleased to see me, but this exceeds even my wildest dreams."

"Let's go," she said, keeping her eyes down so he wouldn't see her tears, pulling him toward the car. "Get in, just please get in. I have to get out of here. I'll explain later. Just please, Dev."

"All right, all right, calm down," Devlin said, his amusement transformed into a wary concern as he got back into the car and put it in reverse. "I'm assuming you're not running from the law. Because if you are, I certainly hope you have your passport on you."

"Yes," she said, gulping slightly. "I mean yes, I have my passport, but no, I am not running from the law. Just my friends and relations. Just my past."

"Ah," Devlin said, and said no more.

She sat back into the quiet of the car, drank in the rich leather smell of the upholstery and the wonderful miraculous relief of having Devlin calmly driving next to her, his profile so familiar, his presence a reminder that there was life outside of Cerreta, outside of this movie shoot, away from Mercy and Michael and Gabe. The simple act of his shifting gears took on an almost magical quality of reassurance.

A few minutes passed, then a few more.

"Where am I headed?" Devlin asked finally.

Juliette shrugged. "I don't care."

Two small towns later, Devlin again broke the silence.

"J., you know I would follow you to the ends of the earth, but I've been in transit for about twenty-four hours now, so unless you object, I'm going to head back to the Coronet. Because I have a feeling," he added, "we're going to be having one of those long and complicated conversations you like so much, and I may need some coffee."

Juliette laughed, giddy with the distance rolling out between herself and Cerreta and the soothing sound of her boss's voice.

"Oh, Dev," she said. She closed her eyes, leaned back in her seat, and put her hand on his wrist, circling it very lightly. "It's been a terrible, horrible day and I've missed you so much. But what in God's name," she said, raising her head and looking at him as if for the first time, "are you doing here?"

"You kept saying you didn't need any help," he answered. "And for once in our long years of friendship, I didn't believe you."

It did not take long to reach the Coronet, though when she reached into her purse to tip the valet, she was annoyed to discover she had somehow picked up Angie's instead of her own. *So much for leaving Cerreta never to return,* she thought, *and now I'm carrying a dead woman's purse.*

But as the temperate hush and discreet luxury of the lobby and then the soft-pile comfort of Devlin's suite washed over her, Juliette felt nothing but blessed relief. It was as if she were finally coming home. There were bowls filled with orchids beside chairs deep and soft, the sofa shone with a silken damask, and the coffee arrived in sterling silver with napkins so large and plush they could have been tablecloths. As they ate panini, Juliette carefully explained all that had happened since Mercy had arrived at Cerreta, her strange moods and midnight ramblings. She told him about Inspector Di Marco and what Mercy had said about the DNA, about Joseph being taken in and how she didn't know what to believe because Mercy lied so often.

"Gabe says you can't trust anything she says because she's an addict, which is definitely true, but then sometimes she does seem to know things, to see and understand things in a way that's almost frightening."

"She is something of a savant, our Mercy," Devlin agreed. "And even a liar is capable of telling the truth, if only accidentally. It's what makes them so irresistible. And how is dear Mr. O'Connor?"

Juliette heard the question behind the question and all she could think of, and only with burning shame, was the sight of Carson in Michael's trailer and how it had filled her with mortification.

"Aging," she answered, with a light vicious laugh, "rapidly."

"Brilliant," Devlin said. "I'm all ears."

Michael, she told him, seemed to have taken on the project to prove something, and it was turning out to be harder than he had anticipated, what with all the various tensions, between himself and Mercy, Mercy and Angie, Angie and Carson, Golonksi and everyone, Gabriel and Steve Usher. Usher, meanwhile, seemed more interested in buying Cerreta than keeping Mercy sober. "Though I wonder if it isn't some sort of ruse, because he's offering so much money, more than it's worth, actually, and he seems to think he could get Gabe to stay, though I don't know why, since Gabe shows him nothing but open contempt most of the time."

"Steve Usher is far more complicated than he ought to be," Devlin said, pouring himself a second cup of coffee. "Many people have expressed concern over how the press always learns so much about those who pass through Resurrection. Certainly he seems more interested in notoriety than anonymity."

"That's true," she said with a laugh. "He's a terrible gossip considering his line of work. He keeps asking Mercy for Lloyd's copy of that damn Little Book and Mercy won't give it to him because she says he'll just auction it off. Which I totally believe, even though it apparently makes him look like an idiot. Still," she added, "out of everyone, I think he was the most sincerely upset about Angie's death."

"That is surprising," Devlin said, and something in his markedly unsurprised tone made her look at him more closely. Sitting in one of the leather chairs, with one leg resting at a right angle on the opposite

knee and an arm thrown across the back of the chair, Devlin was a portrait of a dark-eyed urbane businessman. He may have just gotten off a
plane, driven along Italian highways, and up the dusty road of Cerreta,
but there was not a crease, wrinkle, or smudge on his person. With his
square jaw smoothly shaved and his dark hair combed sleek, he fairly
sparkled with freshness and respectability.

But Juliette knew there was no way he would have left his beloved
hotel just to help her cope, even with the most stressful circumstances.
Coping with stressful circumstances was her best area. With a little sigh,
she looked him straight in the face. "Why are you here, Dev?"

Devlin put down his coffee cup.

"Tell me again what happened the day Angie died," he said.

Eyeing him narrowly—would he never just answer a simple question?—Juliette recounted Mercy's anger and Angie's drunken monologue, told him all that Mercy had said and implied, about how her
mother had been in Lloyd's room the night he died, about how Mercy
thought it was Angie who had taken the pictures that showed up on
deadanddying.com, how she had sold photos of her own daughter, and
more than photos, her own daughter herself.

"If Michael hadn't looked the way he did when she said it," Juliette
said, "I would have thought she was lying. Did you ever hear of anything
like that? About the two of them, sleeping with men, together?"

Devlin gave an almost imperceptible shrug.

"Jesus," Juliette said, sickened almost as much by his lack of outrage
as she was by Angie's actions. "Really."

"People do awful things sometimes, J.," Devlin said matter-of-factly.
"But I am far more interested in what happened to Angie. Do you honestly think she just fell?"

Juliette stared. "What, you don't? But that would mean someone
killed her. Why would anyone want to kill Angie?"

Devlin laughed. "You can't be serious. Who wouldn't want to kill

Angie? I myself have fantasized about it on several occasions, as recently as a week ago."

"Well," Juliette said, grateful to give voice to a thought that had been nagging her, "the only person crazy enough to do something like that is Mercy. And Mercy didn't do it, because she was with Gabe all night. Besides, Angie was leaving, which is what everyone wanted."

"Or so she said."

"Well, all right, maybe she wouldn't have left in the end. But even if Carson or Golonski or Andrews hated her that much, it wouldn't make sense for them to kill her, not with Mercy already on the ledge."

She looked at Devlin intently. "Is that why you're here? Do you know something about what happened?"

"I know I don't like the idea of two deaths on one film set," he answered with maddening vagueness. "And when a woman not known for her naturalistic tendencies goes for a midnight stroll in the forest and falls into an abandoned quarry, well, it does make me wonder. Or maybe," he said with a grin, shifting slightly in his seat, "the idea of you and Michael O'Connor sharing a month-long Tuscan idyll just didn't sit well with me."

At the sound of O'Connor's name, the scene in the library unfolded itself on the surface of Juliette's brain. So much pain exposed by so many in just a few minutes. She had had to leave or she would have just made it worse. So much worse. Gabe thought he wanted her to talk about that terrible night, but he didn't. Because even he didn't know what she would have to say.

She walked to the window, gazed out at the narrow street, empty save for the pale gold of the streetlamp and the shadows it threw, and wondered just what the hell she was going to do next.

"Tell me the rest, Juliette," Devlin said after a moment. "Why were you running away? What were you running from?" When she didn't answer, he rose and came to stand behind her, his hands light and warm on her shoulders. "Just tell me," he said, his voice gentle but insistent, "and be done with it."

But she couldn't even tell Devlin. So she told the window, she told the street, she told the implacable Sienese night. With as few words as possible, she told him about the night her parents died. How the two couples, best friends for years, had been out to dinner, how they were heading home long past midnight across those misty snow-filled fields into the path of a freight train.

"Gabe thinks it's because they were drunk, which they probably were; they were always drunk," Juliette said bitterly. "Drunk and arguing, or drunk and . . ." She stopped, then tried again. "But . . ."

"But?" Dev was still behind her, looking out over her shoulder at the street, his hands steady on her shoulders.

"But my father was driving. My father was driving and I don't see how it could have been an accident." She had never, not once, said those words out loud. "He was not . . . happy." She was so close to the window that her breath fogged the glass. She closed her eyes. "For as long as I knew him, anyway. And the police said my mother was in the backseat. With my uncle. I think my mother always had a thing for my uncle. They used to joke about it, but I think it was real." She shrugged, a movement she recognized instantly from childhood. "I think he did it on purpose. They fought that night, before they left. I remember lying on my bed listening, wishing they would just *leave,* just leave already. He said he was sick of being the 'odd man out.' And she just laughed. I think he hated them all and did it on purpose. He killed my mother and Gabe's parents on purpose."

"You don't know—"

"Oh, for godsake, Dev, how drunk would a person have to be," she asked savagely, "to not see a *freight train?*"

Her eyes were dry and her head ached; she wanted a drink so badly but was stopped by a sense of irony from getting one. Instead, she shivered and leaned her hot forehead against the window, aware of nothing but the sleek cool glass and the warmth of Devlin's hand against her back; she could feel the outline of his fingers.

"Put it down, Juliette," he said quietly. "True or not, it's not your burden and you've carried it long enough." Now both his hands were on her shoulders, and his voice was in her ear. "So just put it down."

"I can't," she whispered, and drew a long painful breath.

"You can," he said, and, gripping her arms, pulled her away from the window, turned her around. "But that's what you're afraid of, isn't it?" He put a finger under her chin and raised it; now his eyes were dark and gently mocking. "However will you survive without that snowy night to haunt you, without all that lovely dark guilt to keep you from being happy?"

"Fuck you," she said furiously, and then she kissed him. Deep and angry, pushing back against all the years of forgetting that rose up, her mother's perfume and the smell of spilled wine, the dusty frightened dark behind some sheltering door, the sight of a car driving away in a cloud of dust.

Up they rose, sights and smells, and she wrapped her arms around Devlin, kissed him so hard she could not breathe, so hard she tasted blood. His hands were on her hair, her face, stroking her, calming her, trying to disentangle himself, but she made a small sound in her throat and after a moment's struggle he gave in and kissed her back, until all those images receded and only the warm wet depths of his mouth remained. For years she had pushed aside his nonchalant flirtation, the almost automatic attempts at seduction, and now all she wanted, all she needed, fiercely, undeniably, was his hands on her, rough and irresistible, his body covering hers, creating a wall to hold back everything that had happened, everything she was feeling. She thought of all the men she had loved, all they had required of her, and she felt an overwhelming urge to strip herself naked and wipe her whole self clean, inside and out. She filled her mind with fire and sank her teeth gently, then not so

gently, into Devlin's neck, ground herself against him; she felt his teeth
on her neck, his thumbs pressing hard into her hips until she groaned.

"Wait," he said breathlessly, pulling away. "Sweetheart, wait, just wait."

"No," she said, yanking him back to her, pushing him onto the bed.
"Don't talk. Not now. Just fuck me. Finally. Just fuck me."

"Christ," he groaned as her mouth found warm naked flesh. He
gripped her arms with bruising fingers and forced her back onto the
bed, his knees jammed hard between her legs, forcing them wide. "Is
this what you want?" he said, looking into her face, offering her one last
chance to turn back. "Are you sure this is what you want?"

"Harder," she breathed into his ear. "Fuck me harder than you think
you should."

He laughed softly and dangerously. With one hand he forced her
hands above her head and with the other tore her blouse open. Teeth
clenched and muscles taut, Juliette cleared her mind of everything but
the thin and brilliant line that divided fear and desire, pleasure and pain.

There was, at last, a warm and throbbing darkness that rose and fell
like gentle breathing, cradled her as it moved. Swimming up through
something like sleep, she moved a leg, an arm. Muscles strained, joints
ached, and she could feel the heat of Devlin's body lying alongside her.
She smiled and imagined a shell, scraped sleek and dazzling by sun and
sand and pounding surf.

"Feel better?" Devlin's voice rose from the dark behind her eyelids.
He chuckled and she felt his mouth on her bare shoulder. "I've been
many things in many beds, J., but never before an exorcist."

"You should try it as a second career," she said dreamily. "Or a fifth
career. Whatever you're up to now."

Juliette did not open her eyes—she knew once she did, whatever
this was, whatever had happened, would be over, and real life, with all

of its tangles and blurry patches, would be right there where she left it. Rolling toward Devlin, she pulled herself onto his chest, blind eyes and seeking hands, until she found his face and kissed his mouth as softly and tenderly as she could. To make up for the rest.

"I've set my mark on you," he said as he examined her arms, neck, and torso with great thoroughness, planting kisses on the places where she knew small bruises were already rising. "Look. Now you're damaged goods, and no one else will want you."

"You're a brute," she answered.

"I didn't invite the beast into the room; you did. Open your eyes, Juliette," he said, with a firmness that bordered on anger. "Look at me."

"Ah, well," she said, opening them and smiling up at him, tracing the admirable slope of one bicep with its own small spattering of welts, "it was a lovely beast. A sweet and lovely beast, and not tame at all."

"You've no idea," he said, pushing her onto her back. "But let's try it my way now"—he kissed her temple, then her ear, his tongue soft and his hands busy—"for variety's sake."

"We should probably eat something," Juliette said an hour or so later, when she finally pulled herself to a sitting position and felt her head swim. "We should definitely drink something or they'll just find our bodies tomorrow morning, dried-up husks of our former selves."

"There are worse ways to be found," Devlin said, "as you know." But he dutifully swung himself out of bed and padded off to call room service.

"Can you imagine?" she said, almost to herself. "Putting a noose around a dead body, pulling it tight." She shivered again and pushed the thought of Lloyd Watson from her head.

"I wonder if Angie had any smokes in that purse," she said, rolling to the edge of the bed and fishing over the edge. "I haven't smoked in years but there's something about debauchery that calls for a postcoital cigarette," she said, finding a pack of Camels in the bottom of the bag. "The tobacco industry must love Hollywood; they're the only people you can count on to smoke anymore."

She pulled a cigarette out of the pack and paused, then lifted the pack to her nose and sniffed. She detected a rose-heavy perfume and mint gum combined with the dark fragrance of the tobacco, and something else, something tantalizingly familiar. Juliette remembered how Mercy had held the bag to her face and breathed deeply, inhaling, Juliette thought with a pang, the essential elements of her mother. Curious as to what these were, Juliette did the same, catching the same scents that clung to the cigarettes, along with the talcy smell of makeup, the metallic tang of loose change, and something else, that other smell, mouth-watering and vaguely chemical, so clear to her she could almost taste it.

"Oh, my God," she said, dumping the contents of the purse onto the bed and examining each compact, lipstick, and aspirin vial. "Oh, my God," she said, looking up at Devlin as he reappeared with the phone still in his hand. "This bag is, or was, totally full of cocaine. Here," she said, holding out the now-empty purse, "you can smell it. But where is it?"

She began undoing lip gloss and flipping through the pages of Angie's Little Book. When she found nothing, she took the bag back, shook it, and began patting the lining. In less than a minute she found it, a small, almost invisible zippered opening along one of the seams. Gently sliding in two fingers, she pulled out three small rectangles of folded paper.

"Bindles," she said. "Good old-fashioned bindles. Italian *Vogue* or I miss my guess," she added, examing the shiny paper. "So that's where the drugs were coming from. From Angie. Unbelievable." She opened the packet and, using her finger, tasted a bit of the white powder. "Nice," she said, and for a moment she was actually tempted. The clarity of that first line, the brilliant rush of euphoria, and the heart-singing certainty it would never end—she would not mind feeling those things now. She looked up at Devlin and smiled wickedly. "Should we do a line or two, just to be sure?"

With deft fingers, he plucked the packets from her hand and walked away; a second later, Juliette heard the toilet flush.

"I believe we've both had quite enough excitement for one day," he said.

"That was probably a thousand dollars' worth of drugs you just flushed," she said.

"Put it on my tab."

"I can't believe it was Angie all along," Juliette said. "It doesn't make any sense. She seemed genuinely convinced that Mercy was wrecking her life with drugs. Why would you put your kid in rehab and then give her drugs while she's working? Why would you bother paying for the services of Steve Usher with one hand," she said "while you were feeding coke to your daughter with the other?"

Juliette looked at the purse; she remembered how insistent Angie had been about finding Marcello, how long she had spent with him, presumably explaining exactly what she had wanted her purse to look like even though it was a simple replica of Juliette's.

"You've gotta love a woman who designs a bag with a secret pocket for drugs," she said, thinking of the young and handsome shoemaker, with two gold earrings like a pirate. Everyone had loved him, Mercy so much that he had visited the castello twice. What else had Angie had made? Shoes and a satchel for Usher. How many secret pockets were in that satchel? she wondered. Juliette pushed away the covers and jumped out of bed.

"First thing tomorrow," she said, throwing herself back on the pillow, "we're going to go see a man about a purse."

Chapter Twelve

IT REALLY IS GORGEOUS here," Devlin said as they drove back to Cerreta the next day. It was late morning and the road from Siena was empty, cutting through fields and forest like a silent gray river. The outlines of tiny ancient fortress towns peered down from forests that bulged and billowed with green; faraway hills were crested with cockscombs of cypress trees and their perfect paintbrush silhouettes. "I can see why you would come here. I can see why you would want to stay."

Juliette sighed. "I don't know what I want," she said. "It's beautiful but it's poisonous, too. You can get lost here, you can forget you ever did anything else but watch the clouds pass, the grapes ripen. You can convince yourself that this is enough."

The car bounced onto the dirt road leading to the villa. "Maybe this is enough," Devlin said.

She looked at him and happiness flashed through her like a bright and dangerous electric current, unleashed only by his still-wet hair, his newly shaven jaw, his arm strong and straight as he gripped the wheel. Even utterly still, Devlin radiated movement, as if this were just a brief pause before he sprang once again into action. She wanted him to turn the car around, or pull it off the road, she wanted him to kiss her as he had last night. She took a deep breath and reminded herself of who he was, who she was, and what was really happening now. There was a reason she had not turned to Dev in the horrible months after Josh left, despite his many fond invitations; she had known him twenty years and in all that time there had never been a woman who mattered to him. Even last night, she had woken to hear him murmuring into his cell phone—it was still daytime in L.A. She had fallen asleep before he returned to bed and when she had woken this morning, he had been nowhere to be found. It wasn't until she was showered and dressed that he strolled in. He had smiled and she had smiled and neither said anything about what had occurred between them. What was there to say? Juliette thought. It had been inevitable that they would sleep together, and so they had. If she pursued the matter, or even the memory, it would only lead to trouble.

"You don't believe that," she said now.

"Don't I?" He turned his dark eyes on her. "I have a house on a hill myself. In Ireland. Maybe I'll show it to you someday."

"I'd like that," she said quietly, and they continued the drive in silence, broken only by Devlin's wry remark that she and Gabe might want to get "this Christ-awful road paved."

The courtyard was full of film equipment, but only a few interns could be seen. One was carrying baskets of basil and early tomatoes toward the kitchen, another maneuvered a wheelbarrow around the lights and ropes of electrical wires. Juliette was surprised. She hadn't seen an intern do anything resembling farmwork since the filming started.

"They're shooting down near the abbey," said the girl with the mohawk when Juliette asked. "I think it's a dream sequence. It's only the principles."

"How quickly they pick up the lingo," Devlin murmured, amused.

"I know," Juliette said. "She's a psych major from Harvard and could not have been more disapproving when the trucks first arrived. Now I think she's dating the production manager. Well, sleeping with her, anyway. This is not a 'dating' situation. So if they're shooting," she mused, "then Golonski must be back, which means Joseph got sprung, which means . . . well, I don't know what that means. Michael might know, but he's working. Gabe might know, but I'm not sure I'm speaking to him. And Mercy, well, I wonder if she's missing what you flushed. I wonder if she even knew it was there."

"Or put it there herself?"

Juliette shook her head. "I don't think so. She has her own bag— several, in fact. That's why Angie's was lying around next to mine."

She stood for a moment, indecisive. "I'm guessing if Mercy is down there, Usher is, too. I think I'll search his room first."

"J.," Devlin said. "I'm shocked. How your standards have fallen since you left the Pinnacle."

"I mean, I think I'll take Mr. Usher some fresh towels and make certain he did not leave his briefcase or anything else of value lying about," she amended with a laugh. "Why don't you go see if there's any breakfast left in the kitchen; we make a mean frittata here at Cerreta."

Usher hadn't left his bag or anything at all lying around. His room in the villa was neat as a monk's cell; the only sign that anyone was staying there were a stack of Little Books on the desk under the window and a pair of shoes peeping decorously out from under the bed. Just for grins, Juliette checked to see if the heels were hollow; they were not.

Hearing the faint sound of footsteps coming up the stairs, Juliette backed out of Usher's room and ran smack into Gabe carrying what looked like a pile of black sweaters.

"What the hell are you doing?" he asked, looking from her back to Usher's room.

"What the hell are *you* doing?" she asked back.

"I'm bringing Mercy a sweater, or some sweaters," he answered, his tone going from indignant to sheepish. "She said she wanted the black one from her mother's room but there are like five black ones so I'm bringing them all."

"How the mighty are fallen," Juliette said. "Haven't you forgotten her latte? And her cocaine?"

"Oh, shut up," he said wearily, then sighed. "It's a mess down there, she's a mess down there, and no one seems the least bit interested in anything but getting as many scenes done as they can today. Like the law is after them or something. Where have you been? O'Connor told me you had run off with Devlin. Did he come to drag you back to the Pinnacle by your hair?"

Juliette ignored him. She wanted to shake him until every painful thing that had ever happened to the two of them fell out onto the floor and she could kick it under the bed. But he was standing there holding a pile of Mercy's sweaters. "Did Golonski bring Joseph back from Florence?" she asked instead.

"Yeah," Gabe said.

"And?"

Gabe's expression grew exasperated. "How should I know? I'm just the hired help. All I know is that he's back and Carson looks like she's going to kill someone and Mercy is cold all the time. Look," he said, shifting his bundle from one side to the other, "I know you're angry at me and I'm sorry about that, but I meant what I said. We need to be able to talk to each other about the past, Jules. The whole past."

"No," Juliette said immediately. "Well, maybe. Sometime. Just not now." She put her hand to her forehead. "Look, can we just . . . not pick at each other for a while?"

For a minute Juliette thought Gabe was going to protest or argue, but in the end he just nodded. "You should come down," he said. "They didn't fix the abbey like they fixed the castle, but it looks pretty amazing. I'm thinking I should apply for restoration funds again. We," he amended quickly. "We should apply."

"I'll be down. I need to collect Dev."

Gabe opened his mouth, then closed it and shook his head. "I am glad you came back, Jules," he said. "Even if," he added, a glint returning to his eye, "you are the world's biggest drama queen."

"You don't know the half of it," she muttered to his retreating back.

Juliette was surprised they had chosen to shoot at the abbey, or what remained of it. Santa Lucia occupied a lovely spot, half a mile away from the castello. Among the trees, what had once been a wide lawn was now a meadow, hip-deep in wildflowers and blackberries, but it was rather difficult to get to. Few outside Cerreta knew of its existence, at the end of a faint, narrow trail that twisted up from the main road. The trail had now been violently carved into a wide path and, seeing it, Juliette was shocked, both by the sudden excavation and the fact that Gabe had allowed it. In a way it was a road that led nowhere—a fire had gutted the place in the seventeenth century, leaving only the living quarters intact. The church was nothing but a memory and a vague outline of crumbling stone amid the sunflowers and morning glories.

As they drew nearer, they could hear the assistant director call for quiet. Locating Carson and Golonski, Juliette approached warily, casting her eye around for Usher. Behind her she felt Devlin stop abruptly. Turning to look at him, she saw his eyes move from the monitor to the scene in front of him.

"Would you look at her," he said with wonder and frank admiration in his voice. "Just look at the girl."

Mercy, in her novice's gown and a light shawl, was balanced on one of the few whole walls of the abbey, the skirts of her gown scalloped beneath her. She was wearing a long blond wig that streamed golden ringlets over her shoulders and her face was turned so it was a three-quarter profile. Even from this distance, they could see her eyes were filled with mute and tortured adoration; on the screen they were almost overwhelming. She was beautiful, beyond beautiful, gazing at O'Connor, who, in tunic and breeches, was sitting under a tree painting her, brow furrowed in dissatisfaction as he plied his brush, oblivious, it seemed, to the intensity of devotion that transformed Mercy's face. And indeed, when he, or the painter he played, glanced up, the look was gone, replaced by a sweet and angelic smile, a smile that would anchor a canvas for the ages, but utterly unlike the deep and love-drenched expression that had been there moments before.

Even Carson drew a sharp breath at the moment, and with a yelp of pleasure Golonski yelled cut. Still on camera, Mercy's smile vanished. The ethereal glow became pallor, her shoulders sagged, and she grew smaller and less substantial. *It's exactly as if,* Juliette thought, *someone has just turned off a light.*

As if on cue, the electricians and camera crew rushed the set, refiguring lights and moving cameras. Michael stood and stretched; his stand-in took his place on the low stool before the painting. Several of the crew helped Mercy down from the wall while her stand-in hopped up. Mercy just stood there for a moment, as if she did not know where she was. Michael was now in conversation with Golonski, but Juliette could see him glance now and then at his costar, his face a study of exhausted, irritated concern. Then Usher appeared, bearing, Juliette noted with amusement, one of the sweaters Gabe had so dutifully fetched. Untangling Mercy from her shawl, he wrapped the sweater around her—she was shivering, though the sun was shining and it was quite warm—and led her toward what could only be called a makeshift living room, a tableau of sofas and cushioned chairs positioned a few hundred yards away in the shade of some cypress trees.

Juliette was about to head over when Carson blocked her path.

"I thought you'd left," she said with open hostility.

"I did," Juliette said sweetly, "but now I'm back."

At the sound of her voice, O'Connor looked sharply their way. See-ing Juliette, he smiled with obvious relief. Then his eyes flicked to Dev-lin, whom he offered a small, gracious, but manly nod.

"We're shooting here," Carson said, taking in the exchange, "and I would appreciate it if you would stay away from the talent. You seem to have a distracting quality that we can't afford just now."

Juliette's smile did not so much as twitch.

"Carson," she said, "I believe you've met my boss, Eamonn Devlin. Dev," she said with an introductory gesture, "this is Bill Becker's . . . assistant. You two no doubt have a lot to talk about. Dev knows Bill very well, don't you, Dev?"

"Ms. Cooper," Dev said, clasping Carson's hand and leaning in to kiss her on each cheek. "How lovely. And in fact, I did just see Bill day before yesterday and he seemed extraordinarily pleased with how things were going out here. It isn't often one sees Bill Becker pleased to any degree," he added, giving Carson a look that was both complimentary and know-ing, "considering, ahem, the personalities involved. And if you are feel-ing any stress, it certainly does not show." Carson's face, which had been startled and guarded at Devlin's appearance, softened, and her eyes took on that vaguely hypnotized glaze Juliette had seen so often around her boss. His brogue, she noticed with a swallowed laugh, had deepened considerably. Released from Carson's attention, she edged quietly away.

As she approached, Mercy barely acknowledged her, though Steve Usher was quite effusive, offering her food and drink, informing her that Gabe had just left a few minutes ago to tend to "something impres-sively farm-related," and would she mind keeping Mercy company and an eye on his bag while he slipped off in search of the loo? She most certainly did not mind, though it was an odd, stunted silence that fell after he made his departure.

"Are you okay?" she asked Mercy, who was running one hand obses-sively up and down a chain she wore around her neck, while the other held the inevitable cigarette, although she did not appear to be smoking it. Mercy nodded. "I took your mother's bag by mistake yesterday, in case you were looking for it." Juliette watched her keenly but Mercy only shook her head.

"Everyone here hates me," she finally said, almost idly, as she smoked and fiddled with her necklace. "Even without my mother around, everyone hates me. I thought it would help, you know, her being gone. I know that sounds terrible, but I thought it would."

She turned a bland face toward Juliette and waited for a reaction. Juliette just stared right back and Mercy turned her attention back to her cigarette and her speech, which once again Juliette sensed she had been waiting to deliver.

"But it doesn't. It's just the same. Even when they're being nice to me I know it's just because they feel like they have to be. Especially now. At least my mother understood that. She never bought any of their bullshit. Which is probably why she did what she did."

Juliette felt a great weariness creep over her, but she asked the question she could see Mercy wanted asked. "What? What did she do?"

"Oh, didn't you hear? I was right; it was Joseph's, um, DNA in Lloyd's room. But apparently there was spermicide mixed into it."

Juliette gave her a blank look.

"From a condom? Jesus, didn't you ever see *Presumed Innocent?*" Mercy asked. "It was my mother's favorite movie, which is why I know it was her idea. She staged the whole autoeroticism; Joseph was just an unwitting . . . donor."

"So your mother slept with him and used . . . That's just disgusting."

Mercy shrugged. "The things we do for love, or money. Or both. She didn't want the movie to be shut down, either. Or maybe she just didn't want the press to find out that Lloyd was using because she knew everyone would blame me. Or maybe she gave him the drugs. Who knows? Either way, Carson is fucked because the insurance company won't pay until there's a 'thorough investigation,' and Bill Becker is furious. So"—Mercy allowed herself a small spiteful smile—"some good has come of it."

"Do you ever miss your parents?" Mercy asked suddenly. "Even after what they did?"

Juliette blinked as her mind caught up with Mercy's words. "Yes," she said, and when she said it, she realized it was true. "Here. I miss them here. I think that's why I stayed away for so long."

Mercy nodded, but then someone called, "Places," and soon the word was ringing all over the set. "I have to go," Mercy said, getting up, slow and unsteady as an old woman. "I really miss my mother, Juliette," she said softly, as if it were a secret. "And I'm pretty sure it's my fault she's dead. Gabe says it isn't, but I think he's wrong. He's not right about everything. But you know that already." And with a small sad smile, Mercy trailed away.

"Usher left his bag but I couldn't do the switch or have a look because Mercy was practically sitting on it the whole time," Juliette told Devlin while they hitched a ride back to the villa on a golf cart. "And anyway, I couldn't really think about that because you will not believe what is going on." Quickly she caught him up on the events. "Mercy is falling apart, I mean honestly falling apart. And frankly I don't blame her. You should talk to her," she said, suddenly inspired. "She loves you. Seriously. Maybe she'll tell you what's really going on."

"You seemed to need me in another capacity," he said, gripping the side of his seat with great alarm as the cart bumped its way along the makeshift road. "Is this safe, do you think?"

"Did you play catch up with the lovely Carson? Was she as big a bitch when you first met her? Or is that Bill Becker's doing?"

"Now, now, J.," he admonished. "She's just ambitious and in a very difficult situation."

"God, you sound just like O'Connor. With whom, I believe, her affections are currently occupied."

Devlin registered her bitter tone with raised eyebrows and she had the presence of mind to blush.

"Right, sorry. Anyway," she continued, quickly changing the subject, "I know Usher's bag must be full of something; when I hefted it, it was way too heavy for what I could see in there, which isn't much. I should be able to make an easy switch if you can manage to keep him occupied."

"That seems to be my sole duty in life these days, keeping people occupied." His words were accompanied by a keen glance that filled Juliette with alarm.

"Oh, Dev," she said, "you honestly don't think . . ."

"Leave it, J.," he said lightly, as he detached himself from the golf cart, which had now stopped. "That's a conversation for a different time. And it's certainly not as if I weren't enjoying myself. Though I cannot believe," he added, flexing his knees, "that this is the preferred method of transportation for people in the film industry. The dust alone . . ." He surveyed the fine silt of white that now covered his pants, before flashing her a smile. "But you let me know when you need another . . . distraction. Now I'm curious as to what's in that bag as well."

Before they had come to Cerreta, Juliette and Devlin had visited the Siena cobbler. After finding the secret pocket in Angie's purse, Juliette was convinced the cobbler was also a drug dealer. Certainly he had the sexy undercurrent of danger down pat. But when they had presented themselves as friends in need of a fix, he had seemed legitimately baffled. "You are with the movie stars, yes?" he asked. "The ones who were staying at the Coronet?" When they replied that they were, he had simply smiled and shrugged. "You should talk to your friends, then," he said. "I cannot help you." Juliette attempted to press him in Italian, but Devlin had told her to "leave it." The cobbler had, however, provided her, at great cost, with a bag similar to Usher's. Juliette's plan was to switch the two long enough to give Usher's bag a thorough once-over.

"It all seems so insane," Juliette said now. "I mean, do we really think Usher was giving Angie drugs to give to Mercy? Why? To keep her coming back to Resurrection? That doesn't make any sense. None of this makes any sense." They had arrived at Casa Padua and she threw herself into a chair on the front porch. "I keep thinking that maybe it is just as simple as Mercy being a drug addict and lying about everything, the way drug addicts do."

"I'd buy that. Except Angie is actually dead," Devlin pointed out, sitting down beside her. "As is Lloyd."

Juliette shrugged. "Well, Lloyd OD'ing and Joseph or Joseph and Angie or just Angie trying to make it look like autoeroticism is enough weirdness for any set. Maybe Angie just fell. The police didn't seem to see anything that would make them think otherwise."

"Perhaps," Devlin said.

"I mean, do you think Mercy could have killed her mother?" Juliette asked. "Gabe said she was with him all night. Although as far as Gabe is concerned," she said to herself, "it would have been justifiable homicide. Still, I don't think he would lie. He's very big on telling the truth. It's one of his major faults."

Devlin was silent, seemingly engrossed in the sight of a black cat picking her way along the roof of the *fattoria,* where, in one geranium-framed doorway, a young man sat strumming a guitar; against the golden weathered stone, he could have belonged to virtually any century. "Extraordinary," Devlin said, breathing deep the sun-warmed scent of rosemary and lavender and some sweet flower that joined them when the breeze blew by. "Just extraordinary."

"I wonder what will happen if the insurance company doesn't pay for that time lost after Lloyd's death," Juliette mused. "I'm actually amazed Bill Becker isn't here in person teaching Carson the meaning of running a production."

"That," Devlin said, pulling himself out of his reverie, "is the last thing anyone needs. But you know, J., for all the extraordinary interruptions, it does appear that the movie is getting made, and from what you've said, it sounds like it could actually be good."

"I know, it's weird. The worse things get, the better Mercy is. She's giving O'Connor a run for his money."

"It's good for him," Devlin said. "He's been coasting for the past few years—*Bluebird* was god-awful—and he's spent the last six months feeling nice and sorry for himself. Not to mention occupying way too much of your precious time."

"You're the one who installed him at the Pinnacle while he was having chemo," Juliette said. "You're the one who told me to keep him preoccupied and comfortable."

"Each word you utter is a lance in my heart," he said with mock drama. "I remember all too well the circumstances that created your intimacy." He paused for a moment and Juliette remembered the strange and unsettling events that had drawn all three of them together—Josh's death, Michael's illness, Oscar season—all of which had sent Juliette running for Tuscany. She was smiling to herself at the irony of it all—here they all were again—and so deep in memory that she missed Devlin's next words.

"What?"

"I said, do you love him?"

Her smile vanished; Devlin was looking at her with nothing more than mild curiosity, as if he had asked her if she happened to know the time. Considering the course of recent events, Juliette found that mildly insulting—she had imagined he would be more than slightly concerned about her feelings for O'Connor. But that was the problem with Devlin; he was so damn sensible about everything, so calm and matter-of-fact. For a moment or two during the previous night, Juliette had imagined he had felt, as she had, carried away. But here he was, asking the obvious question, perfectly prepared, it would seem, for either answer.

"Jesus," she said. "I don't know. Is that why you flew all the way to Italy? You could have just emailed. What kind of question is that anyway?"

She spoke angrily to keep her voice from shaking. It wasn't as if she had expected, or wanted, a declaration of love from Devlin. Women were simply guests in his life; treated graciously for the short duration of their stays, then forgotten. Still, having him look at her as if this were all just a matter of idle curiosity was genuinely upsetting. She had no idea what the previous night had meant, but certainly it meant something. At least it had to her.

"Do you want some wine?" she asked abruptly, then stood and disappeared into the house.

"Here," she said, tossing him a copy of the Little Book as she reappeared, carrying two very full glasses. "Busy your mind with the Steve Usher path to recovery instead. Just don't let him see that. It's Lloyd's copy and Mercy doesn't want him getting his money-grubbing paws on it."

"I'll save it for my bedtime reading," Devlin said, slipping it into his jacket pocket. "Location to be determined later." When Juliette choked, he slapped her on the back. "Oh, look," he said, "the circus has come to town."

And indeed, up the drive and into the courtyard came a procession of golf carts and small trucks, disgorging all manner of crew members, who immediately began unloading lights and impossibly large coils of wire and setting up for a scene outside the tower.

Chapter Thirteen

M ANY THINGS WERE MADE clear in the following hours. Michael arrived at the villa and walked by Juliette without a word, only to send her a note from the depths of his trailer saying: *Point taken. Now what?* Carson invited Devlin to join her in a tour "of the site" as if Cerreta had been conceived of and built for her personal use, and just as Juliette was spluttering her outrage, a PA came panting up to tell her that Mercy needed to see her right away in her trailer.

"Off you go, now, J.," Devlin said, taking Carson's arm and following her lead toward the olive grove. "Can't keep the star waiting."

"Now I understand why you made such a big deal out of taking my mother's purse," Mercy said, tossing the bag at Juliette as she entered the trailer. "I see you helped yourself. I hope you enjoyed it." Leaning toward her, she turned over Juliette's arm, exposing the pale underside where the imprint of Devlin's fingers was still very clear. "My, my, my. Looks like you did. Is he as good as everyone says he is? He never would give it up for me, said I was too young."

Moving through her trailer, Mercy did not appear angry by her discovery, but she did not appear particularly sober, either. A bottle of vodka stood open on her dressing table beside two long fat lines of cocaine—apparently what Juliette had discovered did not represent the whole stash. Juliette sighed.

"I flushed it," Juliette said. "It's not my thing anymore. And I was hoping it wasn't yours, either."

Mercy hoovered one line, then the other, then took a gulp of vodka. Juliette winced. She could almost taste the stinging sweet chemical paste in the back of her throat. Mercy's eyes brightened and she sat up straight.

"Lovely," she said. "It's a night shoot. Up in the tower. My nun's a little trippy because she's in love with the artist so she feels like she's cheating on God. Actually cheating, like God is her lover. What?" she said, catching sight of Juliette's disappointed face.

"You have no idea how much time I have spent wondering how you were getting hold of that stuff," she said. "I'd even convinced myself someone was slipping you drugs secretly because you kept telling me, and everyone, that you weren't doing drugs anymore."

"I'm not," Mercy said earnestly. "Seriously. None of the fun stuff, no Oxy, no meth, and just enough of this. This is just . . . medicine. God, do you think I could get through the schedule we have here, do you think I could do what they're asking me to do, without some sort of help? Even Mother understood *that*."

"And she was giving it to you? All along?"

"Well, she was giving me cocaine. That was the thing. She wanted me to use this but not that, a certain amount and no more. Just like she wanted me to sleep with Michael but not Lloyd, and to make this film but not the one I wanted to do, which was this really cool indie about a werewolf. But when Becker called, Mother had me on a plane like the next day. It will be interesting to see," Mercy added with marked dispassion, "what exactly I do now that she's dead."

"Where was she getting it?" Juliette asked, because after all this time, she really wanted to know.

Mercy shrugged, took another sip of vodka. Juliette had to admit the girl looked much better, more lively and present, than she had down at the abbey, but keeping up with the starlet's many moods was giving Juliette a headache. "I don't know. I never asked her. It's just there, you know, like the Twizzlers and the bottled water. But just enough for work, not nearly enough for fun. Maybe"—she giggled—"it's in my contract."

"Then why bother to go to rehab?" Juliette asked. "Why bother sitting there listening to Gabe for hours? Why come to me? Why bring this entire movie, with all its attendent shit, here, where it doesn't belong?" Her voice was rising in volume and pitch. "Why all the help-me-please bullshit?"

Mercy lit a cigarette and surveyed Juliette perplexedly.

"I went into rehab because Mother said you have to go into rehab once in a while or people will think you don't care. And I do want to get well. I just have to get through this movie first. I'm totally kicking O'Connor's ass," she added, her eyes sparkling with pride. "I mean, I was really scared of acting with him, he's so amazing, do you remember the blind guy in *Anthem* or the mobster in *Crescenta Valley*? I thought he'd wipe the floor with me, but he's reaching, I can see him reaching. And that's pretty incredible, because when he reaches, man, no one can touch him. You missed the stuff he shot this morning, but it was unbelievable—I was ready to throw myself off a tower for him for real by the time he was done."

She lit a new cigarette off the old one and smashed the butt into the twist-top off the vodka bottle. "I think it's going to be an unbelievably good movie, if Golonski doesn't wreck it in the edit. Don't you?"

She seemed so happy now; manic, yes, chemically stimulated, yes— but still it was the best Juliette had seen her since Angie's death. It was as if that young woman who moped beneath the trees earlier today had been banished. For a moment, Juliette envied her, remembered what a rush coke was, good coke especially, which was the only kind Mercy

Talbot would have. The first time Juliette had tried it was after her parents' death. Her roommate had given it to her to help her pull herself together in time for exams. When she felt that first gorgeous bloom of energy and euphoria hit her brain, Juliette had wondered why everyone in the world didn't use the stuff every day, why it wasn't sold at the post office or the grocery store. Surely this was one of mankind's greatest achievements, one that would benefit every living soul on the planet.

It took her a year to discover why this was not the case, and by that time it was too late. She had dropped out of school, hooked up with drug dealers, and moved in with Gabe, who was on his own downward spiral. Looking at Mercy, Juliette marveled that the actress had been able to pull it off for so long. Mercy had had her low points—the accidents, the fire—but no one could argue with her productivity. And here she was, her sometime-lover dead, her mother dead, on a set where 90 percent of the people wished her nothing but ill, with a costar who had ambivalent feelings about her at best, and still Mercy was giving everyone exactly what they wanted, and more. Mercy could see so many things with startling clarity, even as she continued to tell herself the most painfully obvious lie of them all.

"You're something, Mercy Talbot," Juliette said aloud with a sincere and admiring laugh. A wish coursed through her to be ten years younger and not so certain that real life required moderation and nothing stronger than the occasional martini. She would have liked to have sat here with Mercy Talbot, safe in her trailer with no one allowed in unless she said so, drinking and smoking and fortifying herself with sudden bits of stardust, talking about love and sex, men and bosses, even mothers and death. The things people outside Hollywood talked about, the things normal people talked about. For a moment she was tempted. How bad would it be, after all these years? Was it that much different than the bruising, muscle-straining, mind-altering sex she'd had with Devlin? What was so terrible about a little judicious self-medication in a painful world?

Unfortunately, Juliette knew that the price was too high. Look at poor Lloyd Watson; one way or another his need for relief had cost him his life. Look at Mercy herself, who couldn't get well despite all the best intentions and the aid of every recovery group known to man. Which begged a question Juliette thought she had answered: If Usher wasn't the one supplying Mercy with the drugs, why on earth was she keeping him around? A question Juliette now asked.

Mercy thought about this for a moment, spilled out another small pile of coke, tidied it into a line, and snorted it. "I don't know exactly," she said. "He isn't cheap, that's for sure, and he's been asking for a weekly stipend, which is weird. But he really did seem shook up about my mother's death and he's not a bad guy to talk to, you know? He listens pretty well and he's got some great stories. And his program may be silly, with all those little phrases, but at least he understands that sometimes you can't just go cold turkey, that sometimes cutting down is better. It's not so daunting that way. Gabe says it's a daily reprieve," she added, looking wistful, "that an addict is always in recovery, never recovered. I get that, I do, and he's probably right. I mean, I know he's right. But who wants to hear that? It's just depressing. And not all of us have that kind of time, you know. Not all of us can just devote ourselves wholeheartedly to our sobriety."

She uttered these last words with Gabe's precise cadence and intonation; she even got the accent right. It wasn't a mean impersonation, just dead-on, and Juliette found herself laughing so hard, it bordered on hysteria, the real reason for which she refused to contemplate.

"Mercy," she said, wiping her eyes with the back of her hand, "you have to promise me that if you survive this movie, you will take a year off, just take a year off and go somewhere quiet and get yourself clean. Because it would absolutely break my heart if you died."

"Well, that's one heart that would break," Mercy said, sending a jet of smoke angling out of the corner of her mouth. Then she smiled sweetly. "You know, Juliette, I may do just that." She looked at herself in the mirror, tugging at the skin around her eyes and mouth as if she were not pleased with what she saw. "If I survive this movie."

There was a knock on the door. Mercy held a finger to her lips. The knock was repeated.

"What," she said with overdone exasperation. "I'm trying to sleep in here."

"Pages," said a voice, "new pages."

"Slide them under the door."

Several sheets of paper obligingly presented themselves under the door; they were a yellow with a green tinge, like a tennis ball. Juliette handed them to Mercy, who glanced at them and rolled her eyes. "Oh, look," she said, "we've gone neon. It is never a good sign when you go neon."

"Life is so much better when the writer is in jail," Mercy continued, leaning back into her chair. "He cannot leave this shit alone. Golonski should have never let him on the set. He hates me, he hates Michael, he hated Lloyd. Joseph Andrews is the reason God invented email." She sighed again, took a swig of vodka. "You'd better go," she said dismissively, her attention already fully occupied by the script. "These are for tonight and it looks like they've messed with the staging. You should come to the shoot, though," she added, with a surprisingly bright smile. "It's the big climax and all . . . should be pretty dramatic. Bring Dev," she added with a knowing lift of her eyebrow. "That should send Michael into the appropriate mood of despair."

Then she turned her attention back to the pages with a finality that left Juliette no alternative but to leave. As she closed the door, she could see Mercy cutting herself another line. Her head still turned, Juliette bumped smack into Usher as he hurried toward Mercy's trailer, his bag over his shoulder.

"Oh, Juliette," he said. "Michael is looking for you."

She nodded.

"You really need to work on your timing," she said with some amusement and no small amount of contempt.

Michael was not in his trailer. The assistant there said she thought he had gone to craft services to eat. The craft services tent, which now stretched out beside the patio of the villa's kitchen, was empty save for the fragrance of coffee and chocolate cake—it was the production designer's birthday—and a table full of set designers and women from the wardrobe department. One of them said she thought Michael was in the makeup trailer; when Juliette headed to the door, the table rippled with repressed laughter. She wavered for a moment—she suddenly felt embarrassed and ungainly, as if she were being sent on a wild goose chase. But just then a grip walked by. "Michael O'Connor is looking for you," he said. "He's up in his room, I think. At least that is where he said he was headed."

Mounting the stairs, Juliette was struck by how quiet the villa was, though outside she could see the courtyard roiling with preparations. The sun was setting, and as she made the sharp turn from the stairway to the corridor, it slipped behind the hills. What orange glow had remained suddenly vanished, as if snuffed out. Her eyes adjusted to the sudden dimness and Juliette saw a figure in white emerge in front of one of the doors. For a moment her blood froze and she thought wildly about the stories her father had told her of a woman in a long white dress who walked the hallways at night. But then her vision grew clearer and she could see that it was only Carson, sidling quickly toward the opposite staircase. She seemed to be buttoning her white blouse.

When Carson vanished down the stairs, Juliette forced herself to walk toward the door from which the producer had emerged. She stood there, debating whether to knock or not, when it opened and there stood Michael O'Connor.

"Wow," she said. "So did you plan it this way or did I just miss my cue? Because French farce has never been my forte."

"Really?" O'Connor said. "You seem to be following the basic narrative structure quite well. How was Siena?"

"You know what?" Juliette said. "There is only so much I am willing to do, and I'm not willing to do this." She turned and began walking back the way she had come.

"Wait, Juliettte, wait." And in two steps, there he was, towering over her.

"What, Michael?" Juliette said. "What? Do you want to know what happened in Siena? Do you really? Because it's none of your damn business."

"It doesn't matter what happened in Siena. And you're right, it is none of my damn business." He sighed and passed a hand over his face. "And for the record, Carson was just here with new pages. More new pages. Because we can't go three minutes on this shoot without fucking new pages. But that isn't what I wanted to say."

He took a deep breath and in the silence of the empty corridor Juliette was afraid he would be able to hear her heart pound.

"Look, I just want you to know that when I signed on to this project, when I realized you were in Tuscany, I thought for a minute that if I could start again, that if we could start again, then we might actually have a chance, not a big one, of course, me still being me, but a shot—"

"Just stop," Juliette said, horrified not by what he was saying, but by how badly he was saying it. It sounded rehearsed. And though liar and cheat he might well be, Michael O'Connor never ever sounded rehearsed. "Jesus. If that's the best you can do, spare me, and I mean that literally. What happened, happened. As you pointed out, we're all adults. So don't stand there trying to conjure regret, or whatever it is you're doing. Jesus."

"You see?" he said, his voice suddenly torn between laughter and anger. "You see how fucked I am? Can't even make a simple expository speech that I actually mean sincerely. Struggling to make a simple movie, to keep up with that fucking child who's strung out on dope and booze half the time and still doing better work than I am." He took a step back, raised his hands in a helpless gesture. "While you sit there and watch and feel bad. Again. Feel sorry for me. Again. It's absurd and I can't seem to do anything about it."

"Poor you," Juliette said. For reasons she could not explain, she felt the urge to laugh, not in derision but in relief. She realized she meant what she had said—it didn't matter. What had or had not happened with Carson didn't matter. She wasn't sure why, but she did know, with great certainty, that she didn't want to see regret in O'Connor's face, or pain or anger. What was the point of that? What was the point of Michael O'Connor if he was going to behave like everyone else she knew? After all these weeks of watching him brood and frown and struggle to do what always looked so easy when it was done, she'd trade all the apologies in the world just to see a little fuck-'em-all mischief back in his eyes. "I guess you'll just have to learn to live in the mortal world with the rest of us." She patted his cheek. "We'll do our best to make your stay a pleasant one." Then she turned and walked away.

"Wait," he called again after a moment of stunned silence. "So you never answered my note." She paused and looked at him quizzically. She had forgotten his note. "What next?" he asked quietly.

She shrugged and offered him a small smile. "I'm going to take a nap. You should probably do the same. I understand you have a very big scene tonight, and when I last saw your costar she was midway to stoned out of her mind."

As Juliette moved across the courtyard, she could feel the dimensions of Michael's window burned onto her back. She knew he was watching her but she refused to even glance behind her; let him stew. It would be good for him; get him in the mood for his scene. In Casa Padua, she found Devlin asleep on the couch, the Little Book angled open on his chest as if he had been waiting for her. Passing him silently, she went into her bedroom, closed the door, closed the window, lay down on the bed, put a pillow over her head, and did her best not to think of Michael or Mercy or Devlin or anything at all.

When she woke up it was dark. The ache in her shoulders and her head told her she had slept for a long time, and for some reason this made her instantly anxious. Pushing open her bedroom door, she was almost blinded by the lights pouring in from outside, bright white retina-burning stage lights, aimed at and bouncing off the bell tower.

Devlin was sitting where she had left him, awake now and frowning over the book in his hand, flipping from one page to another.

"Have you looked at this?" he said, his eyes still on the pages.

"No," she answered, shivering slightly as sleep retreated and the evening air hit her skin. "What is it?"

"Lloyd Watson's Little Book," he said. "And I think I know why Usher is so hot to get his hands on it. Look at this bibliography." He motioned her under the lamp where he held the book.

"God, enough with the bibliography," Juliette said. "I know, it's long and weird. Gabe went on and on about it. It's probably padded, but I don't see Steve Usher going down in the big bibliography scandal of the century."

"Will you shut up and look at this?"

Juliette joined him on the couch; feeling his warmth, she leaned into him, pulled one of his arms around her, and closed her eyes. Devlin promptly bit her neck.

"Ow," she said, sitting up. "Shit, Dev. What did you do that for?"

"Strange, isn't it, how context dictates sensation? Now would you please look at what I am showing you, which is very likely the reason I traveled ten thousand miles and into your arms?"

Juliette yanked the book out of his hands. The bibliography was indeed quite extensive, five pages long, and full of books she had heard of—the Bible, the Big Book of Alcoholics Anonymous, several unauthorized biographies of Usher and other substance-abusing stars, *Alice in Wonderland*—and many titles she did not recognize.

"Look at the markings," Devlin said, pointing to several entries in which some of the various initials of authors had been circled and the corresponding page numbers of the works quoted. In, for example, the entry for *The Cocaine Wars,* by F. Edward Hinchley, Simon & Schuster, 1987, pp. 263–308, the *F* had been circled, as had 263 and 8. In *Crack Alley,* by Monty L. Pickens, HarperCollins, 1994, pp. 258–302, it was the *L,* the 258, and the 2. Up and down the page the little blue circles went, like the scatterings of some demented code breaker. Juliette tried to turn the letters into words or find a pattern in the numbers, but nothing presented itself.

"Is it an anagram?" she asked, noting several *L*'s, two *F*'s, three *E*'s, a *B,* two *C*'s, and a single *A.* "Do the numbers add up to something?" She flipped to page 258 in the Little Book, but it was bare of markings, and the book ended on 260—there was no 263. She looked at Devlin, baffled. "What am I missing?"

"You've just been out of Los Angeles for too long. 263, F8; 258, L2; 361, D6 . . ." He looked at her expectantly, but she returned the look, even more confused.

"I don't know, Dev. Bingo?"

"Really, J.," he admonished. "Before everyone had GPS, what did we always put in the gift baskets for guests who are visiting Los Angeles for the first time? What do we keep copies of in everyone's office? 253 E5, does that not ring a bell? You have three seconds or I'm afraid you're fired."

Juliette frowned. "That's the Pinnacle's location in the Thomas Brothers' Guide. Oh," she said, illumination dawning. "Oh, my God, the *Thomas Guide.* Wait, what?" Illumination flared, then sputtered out. "The *Thomas Guide?* Does anyone even use that anymore?"

"What's the *Thomas Guide?*" asked Gabriel, who had appeared in the doorway, flushed and out of breath.

"Were you just running?" Juliette asked, momentarily distracted by her cousin's appearance. "You never run."

"You first. What's the *Thomas Guide?*"

"It's a big book of maps for Los Angeles, for all of Los Angeles," she explained. "Pages and pages. You can't really live without it if you don't know the city, and there's a street index in the back. Every address has a page number and a letter number, like E4, that matches up with a sort of longitude/latitude grid. Like any map, really, only you can pretty much find any house or business."

"Or street corner or park or parking garage," Devlin added grimly.

"Right," Juliette said, glancing at him, her eyes narrowing as she tried to figure out what exactly he meant. "And Devlin thinks, and it certainly looks like, there are a bunch of locations marked off in this copy of Usher's book."

"What sort of locations?" Gabe asked.

"How would I know?" Juliette asked. "I don't have the damn thing memorized."

"But I can guess," Devlin said. "Considering that each of the circles occurs in an entry in which a specific drug is part of the title. Page 263 is mid-Wilshire and I'm pretty sure, for example, that this one, G9, is a high-class strip club. You can't see it from the street, you have to know it's there. I have had to give directions, on occasion, to our guests," he added, answering Juliette's raised eyebrows.

"A strip club?" she said. "Why would Usher be including the coordinates for a strip club?"

"Because, my dear idiot, that is where, presumably, a person might buy some heroin," Devlin said, exasperated, pointing to the title in that entry, "as in *A History of Heroin,* by G. Gordon Libby. G. Gordon Libby, Jesus, did no one at his publisher even check any of this?"

"It's self-published," Gabe said. "So that would be a no."

"So you're saying that Steve Usher, recovery guru to the stars, is running some sort of a drug ring?" Juliette asked in disbelief. "How is that possible? Why would he do that?"

"Anything is possible," Gabe said. "And for the money, of course."

"I don't think he's *running* it, exactly," Devlin said. "But he's obviously got a hand in, a bit too far in, it would seem." Juliette fixed him with her fierce what-do-you-know look, and he sighed. "Last week, I got a call from a . . . well, let's just say a former business associate. He very much wanted to know the whereabouts of Mr. Usher. This particular individual is not the sort of man you want looking for you. But I suspect he had been hired to have an interest. There have always been rumors that Usher was not as fastidious as one might hope for a recovery guru."

"What does that mean, exactly?" said Juliette.

"Oh, come on, J.," he said impatiently. "Everybody knows Resurrection isn't exactly a tight ship; why do you think it makes so much money? What other rehab center has tea dances and Oscar parties? What did you think that meant?"

Flushing, Juliette had to admit she hadn't really thought about it all that much. Devlin gave her a look of surprise and mild disapproval.

"Well, it was common knowledge that the staff was prepared to look the other way—not for the actual patients, but for their friends and family. Someone checks in with their entire entourage, chances are not everyone is seeking sobriety. But now it looks like it wasn't just a matter of allowing the stuff in. Now it looks very much like he was involved in selling it."

"And Lloyd figured it out," Juliette said. "That's what Mercy meant when she said Lloyd knew they were a bunch of phonies. So did Usher kill Lloyd?"

"I don't see how, since he was actually in Malibu at the time," Devlin said.

Gabe had grown silent and still. "We've got to go," he said urgently. "Now." He tugged Juliette off the couch.

"Why? What's happened?"

"I don't know," he said. "That's why I came over in the first place. They're shooting a scene in the tower and I heard them arguing about Mercy using a stunt double. Apparently she was insisting on doing whatever had to be done herself. But I just saw them set up this huge sling around the top of the tower, like those nets you put under trapeze artists. And that made me very nervous. Because last time I saw her she was high as a kite, and if it turns out Steve Usher is some sort of drug kingpin, who knows what might happen?"

Outside, the wind had picked up and was surprisingly cold. Cerreta's square, solid bell tower was bathed in a light that turned its warm golden stone silver and made it seem impossibly tall and forbidding, looming against the night sky like a place of judgment. Juliette could see the net hammocks strung just below the battlements and three large inflatable slides like rides at a child's picnic. She could just make out a group of figures on the top of the tower; a camera on a zip line hovered outside the battlements, presumably on remote; another on a crane was manned by the cinematographer.

Carson, Joseph, the production designer, and a group of other people Juliette recognized only vaguely huddled around the monitors. Stepping closer, she could see on the screen what was happening on the roof of the tower. There was Michael in a cape and high boots, Mercy in her full white habit, Golonski speaking to both of them closely, his hands making small chopping motions, while a handful of other crew members milled about, measuring things and adjusting lights. One woman was fixing something around Mercy's waist, tweaking and pulling until Mercy finally shook her off.

"Is this a good idea?" Juliette said, watching as Golonski helped Mercy up onto the low wall that ran around the top of the tower, held her hand for a few seconds, then let go. Even from below it was easy to see how the wind blew against her dress and her hair. "That does not look safe to me at all." At that moment, Mercy swayed and grasped at the air in front of her, as if she might fall. But as Juliette, Gabe, and Devlin gasped, they could see Mercy laugh as if it were a joke and jump down with a dramatic flourish.

"I'm sorry, did you say something?" Carson answered, her eyes on the screen.

"I said, do you think that's safe?"

"No," she said, her voice riddled with sarcasm. "We've loosened every other brick and greased the rest. Of course it's safe. Do you see the nets? Do you see the slides? Do you see the wire around her waist? I know it is a burden to feel you are the most insightful person in the room, but we do actually know what we're doing. With any luck," she said, speaking to Joseph and the cinematographer, "we can get this in a few takes. They've both been unbelievably great today."

"If you don't mind them going totally off script," grumbled Joseph.

"Not totally," Carson said soothingly. "Not in every scene. Not in spirit anyway. But I think Ben's right to let them have a few extra takes to experiment. When the nominations come rolling in, you can take full credit."

Golonski disappeared from the screen and a minute or two later emerged from the tower, hands deep in his jacket pockets, and took his seat behind the monitors.

"Can you hear me?" he said, as he put on his headset. "You all right, Mercy?" Mercy nodded. "Is the wind too much?" Mercy shook her head. "Well, we're going to follow your lead, my darling. So if you feel uncomfortable up there or change your mind about the double, all you have to do is say so. Otherwise, it's up to you and Michael, right?" Mercy nodded.

Taking off the headset, he turned to Usher, who was standing back a bit, in the shadows. "What the fuck is she on anyway? Besides the booze?"

Usher pursed his lips in a small regretful way. "If I had to guess," he said, "I'd say cocaine and opiates. If I had to guess."

"Fan-fucking-tastic. You're pretty useless, aren't you? Though I must say," he added, watching as one camera went close on Mercy's face, with its huge golden eyes and air of tragedy, "she looks amazing. In a haunted, fucked-up kind of way. Which is just what I need. Okay," he said, putting the headset back on. "Give me places."

"Places," commanded the assistant director quietly into his headset, "places."

"Quiet on the set," the stage manager yelled, which made Juliette smile despite her concern. *A movie,* she thought, *they're making a movie,* and an embarrassing shiver of excitement twitched her stomach. The AD counted down, "And five, four, three . . ." and they were rolling.

With the wind whipping their hair and clothes, O'Connor's artist began. He made the case for the secular world, spoke of true love as the one real miracle in a random universe, God's living pledge to his children. There would be no sin, he insisted, in exchanging one vow for another. But Mercy's young nun would hear none of it. She acknowledged her love, her passion, and absolved her lover of whatever sin he might have committed, as she, not he, had made the vow that was broken. She loved God too well to return to Roberto's arms, but she loved Roberto too well to be able to take up the veil again with a shred of honesty. Standing on the wall high above the fatal ground, she evaded his outstretched hands, his pleading words, his anger. She spoke instead of the joy of surrender, which she had now known both with God and man, how one voice cried hold on, and the other, just as strong, called for her to let go. Which one was God?

It was three pages' worth of dialogue, and even before the midway point, when Mercy climbed onto the wall, Golonski called for take after take. Michael stuttered over a certain phrase, changed it, then changed it again, found a certain hollow-voiced anger that seemed to be working. Mercy slid in tone from heartbreak to borderline madness before falling into a high clear monotone that was full of both rapture and exhaustion. Watching her droop between takes, Juliette wondered if her buzz had worn away; at one point, she saw Mercy slip something into her mouth and assumed it had.

An hour passed, then another. They were closing in on three, and everyone was cracking their necks and stomping their feet to get the circulation going. Carson asked Golonski if he had gotten what he wanted, and he nodded. "Almost," he said, then called for one more take. "And have some fun with this one." Mercy smiled, and pulled Michael toward her, whispered something in his ear. He shook his head. She stroked his hair, kissed his mouth, lingering there as if it were painful to part from him, then nodded with a wild beckoning smile. They took their places.

The scene began unfurling like a tapestry brought to life. Though she was cold and bored, though any concern she had had for Mercy's state of mind had long since vanished in the numbing repetition of the takes, Juliette was suddenly riveted. By O'Connor's anguish, his character's increasingly frenzied inability to understand, much less stop, what was happening. By Mercy's luminous zealotry. Wild and gorgeous, her nun walked a knife's edge between transcendence and insanity and it was breathtaking to watch, as if an angel stood on the tower wall, reeling between the madness of sexual desire and divine love. Mercy swayed and shivered, flung open her arms, threw back her head as if she were standing on solid ground, not hundreds of feet in the air. As she neared her climactic lines, she began to walk along the wall, her arms held out from either side, like a child on a balance beam, and her voice took on a singsong quality that made the hair on Juliette's arms rise. When Gabe spoke, she elbowed him in annoyance; she could not bear to miss a word.

"I said," he hissed, "she's walking the wrong way."

"What?"

"Look," he said, taking Juliette's headphones off and yanking her away from the mesmerizing glow of the monitor. He pointed up to the top of the tower, where Mercy's white figure was just visible, heading along the ramparts to the back of the tower.

"There's no net on the back side," Gabe said. "No slide. No nothing. She's supposed to go to her left. She's supposed to walk toward the front."

On the monitor, O'Connor pleaded, fell to his knees, while Mercy stood, her hands held out palms-up like the Blessed Mother, the wind whipping her hair into a halo.

"She's on the wrong side of the tower," Juliette said to Carson, to Golonski. When neither responded, she pulled Carson's earphones off.

"What the fuck?"

"Mercy's on the wrong side of the tower," Juliette said loudly, pointing up. "She's supposed to go stage left, she's moving stage right." When Carson did not respond instantly, Juliette leaned over to grab Golonski, but the producer yanked her arm back.

"She's fine," Carson hissed. "Look at her, she's totally in control. She's got spotters, she knows what she's doing. Just look at her, she's amazing. They're amazing. It will be over in a minute and she's not doing the jump anyway. We'll add that later with CG."

Juliette looked around. Everyone on the set was silent, rapt, everyone on the set could see what she saw, what Gabe saw. It was a multi-million-dollar production, being overseen by professionals, involving some of the top names in the business. No one seemed the least bit nervous, no one seemed the least bit concerned. They were all swept away by what was happening, two actors delivering what might be the performance of a lifetime on top of a bell tower in Tuscany.

On screen, Mercy made her final proclamation. Michael's artist took two small steps forward and held out his hand. Slowly the nun lifted her hand as well, then looked down at him, with one small, anguished, ecstatic glance that turned Juliette's blood to ice. She had seen that look before, on the fountain in Florence high above a sea of paparazzi.

"Mercy, don't!" she shouted, all but throwing Carson to the ground as she shoved her way to Golonski so she could yell into his mic. "Michael grab her, grab her now, now!" The director promptly cracked Juliette across the jaw. Devlin sprang from nowhere to put him in a headlock and they all watched the monitor as Mercy Talbot turned, her face beatific, her posture perfect, bounced on her toes once, twice, then threw herself into nothingness.

Chapter Fourteen

It was, they all agreed later, only by the grace of God that O'Connor managed to catch her without going over the side himself. The wire around her waist might have saved her had Mercy not decided, about seven takes in, that it was driving her crazy and, unbeknownst to anyone, taken it off. When Michael tried to explain how he had done it, what actual physical movements he had made, he couldn't. But somehow he managed to spring from a kneeling position, throw himself against the wide ledge, and hook his hands under her arms just as she went down, down to where there was no safety net, no inflatable slide, nothing but two hundred feet of empty space ending in earth and rock.

Amid screams and gasps, he yanked her up and over the wall, where she promptly collapsed into what could only be called a disassociative state. "I don't understand, why did you do that?" she kept asking blankly, as crew members rushed to cover her and Michael with blankets. Both on the ground and on the tower bedlam ruled. "What the fuck! What the fuck!" Golonski screamed over and over, nodding like a preprogrammed bobble-head until Joseph Andrews finally, and with visible pleasure, slapped him. Twice. Beside them, Carson was strangely silent, staring wildly at the best boy as he vomited into a tub of geraniums.

Not that Juliette had time to notice much; the moment her heart began beating again, she was shoving past everyone to get to the tower. Thudding up the steps, she soon became part of a swarm, bodies panting with adrenaline, fueled with anxiety. She burst out onto the roof and in two steps was by Michael's side. But he held up his hand in a warning gesture, and so she went down on her knees, as close to him as the circle he had drawn would allow. Usher was instantly hovering over Mercy, unhooking his ubiquitous black satchel so he could lift her. But Gabe cut him off with such deadly authority that the rock star fell back, stumbling over Juliette. Determined to remain as close to Mercy as possible, Usher followed Gabe back down the steps.

Vials of Xanax appeared from the pockets of virtually every person present. Grizzled cameramen and burly electricians wiped their pale and sweaty brows, their hands shaking as they passed a bottle that had appeared out of nowhere. Even O'Connor took a swig. He relaxed just a little but still he did not move.

"How did you know?" he asked finally, still not quite looking Juliette in the face. "How did you know she would jump?"

"I saw her face," she said, and when he shook his head in self-recrimination she explained, briefly, the incident in Florence.

"Why would she do something like that?" he asked softly. "Why would she want to kill herself, in front of everyone?"

"I don't think she wanted to kill herself," Juliette said, actually surprised by the suggestion. "I think she was fucked up and carried away and didn't realize she was on the wrong side of the tower."

"I didn't, either." His tone was bitter. "I was so caught up in the scene, in what we were doing, that I just forgot." He looked at her finally and his face was blank with disbelief. "I forgot the camera and the mic, forgot she was a thousand feet off the ground, I forgot she was Mercy Talbot and a total mess, I forgot that we were even making a movie. There was just the wind and the sound of her voice, and my heart was breaking . . ." He looked at Juliette as if she weren't there.

"It's okay," Juliette said soothingly, putting a hand on the back of his neck. "Everyone else forgot, too. Everyone except Gabe. We were all watching the artist and the nun, but he was still watching Mercy."

"When I heard you, for a minute I didn't even know who you were. But I did see her turn and I thought, *Wait.* And then I saw her bounce and I thought, *She's not supposed to actually jump,* but I didn't want to break character when it was going so well." He laughed harshly. "God forbid I break character when it was going so well."

"But you did," she said reassuringly. "You saved her life."

He shook his head. "I have no idea how I did it. It's like I blacked out or something."

"Well, that's okay, because I'm pretty sure they've got it all on film."

"Dear God," O'Connor said, rising to his feet as suddenly as he had sat down. "Somebody better tell Golonski to destroy that, and fast. Or it'll be making the rounds on YouTube, and that's all this poor screwed-up picture needs."

Following him, Juliette tripped over something. It took her a few moments to realize it was the very thing she had been trying so hard to get her hands on. Picking up Usher's black bag, which was surprisingly heavy, she stuck it under her sweater.

As they came to the bottom of the tower, Michael was swallowed by a swarm of crew led by Carson; as they offered him water and wine and ecstatic praise, Juliette stepped back into the shadows inside the tower. Perching on a cask of Vin Santo, beneath the salty silhouettes of pork legs slowly aging into prosciutto, she pulled Usher's bag from under her sweater and felt along the lining until she found the small secret zipper and opened it.

No drugs, no weapons, just a series of neatly wrapped stacks of euros.

He probably could buy Cerreta, she thought, noting the denomination (five hundreds) and trying to do the math while struggling against disappointment. What had she expected to find in there? Ten pounds of heroin? A letter confessing to Lloyd's murder? Mercy had said Usher was asking for a weekly stipend. He had asked if she knew who the local drug connection was. Had Usher been planning to set up shop over here?

She slung the bag over her shoulder and assumed a casual expression as she left the tower, feigning relief when she caught sight of Usher hurrying toward her.

"Oh, good," she said. "I thought I was going to have to search high and low. Here," she said, handing him the satchel. "I guess in all the craziness you dropped this."

Michael must have made his fears known; Carson not only confiscated the memory cards from the cameras, she confiscated the cameras. And everyone's cell phones, iPhones, BlackBerrys, and personal cameras. Anything and everything that could have possibly recorded an image of that moment, she collected, and directed two personal assistants to find and delete any images from that night.

"You all signed confidentiality agreements," she said when a few people protested. "And part of that agreement, if you bothered to read it, was that you not bring any recording device to this shoot. Frankly, I am shocked to see how many of you have disregarded this rule. So you can either let us go through them and return them to you, or you can relinquish them permanently."

Mercy had been taken back to her room in Casa Padua, where she emerged from her state of shock and became coherent enough to shake her head in bewilderment. The new pages had said stage right, she insisted. No, she hadn't thought to look beneath her because the new pages, the ones she had gotten a few hours before call, had said she was to move stage right.

"And I double-checked with Joseph and Golonski," she said. "I asked them if these changes were final and they said yes."

According to the director and the screenwriter, the stage directions had never been changed and phrases like "understandably distracted," "grief over her mother," and "lit up out of her mind" were making their way through the relief-drunk conversation until Mercy, with a snort of indignation, sent a PA in search of the pages. When he found them, they said, most distinctly, that she was to move stage left.

"These are different pages," she insisted. "They're not even the same color. The ones I had were greener. Remember, Juliette, you were there, you saw them . . ."

Juliette shook her head. "I didn't. I mean, I saw new pages, but I didn't read them." She looked at the bright yellow pages, yellow like a tennis ball. "The color looks the same to me, but you did say they had changed the staging."

"See?" Mercy said triumphantly.

"Mercy," Carson began patronizingly, her eyes looking over Mercy's head at Golonski in silent complicity, "you can't blame the script. You were in an altered state. The wind, the scene . . ."

"But you saw me going in the wrong direction." Mercy paused, her face pale. "Why didn't anyone try to stop me?"

To this, there was no answer. Carson and Golonski made replies, unfinished sentences about not realizing she had removed her safety harness, how they had been more than happy to have a stunt double, about being transfixed by her work, how they assumed she was making an artistic judgment call. But the words were so clearly attempts to defend the indefensible that even Carson seemed to lose her poise. Finally, however, she pulled herself together.

"Mercy," Carson said, firmly turning the tables, "you're acting like you fell. But you didn't fall, you jumped. And nowhere in any version of the script were you supposed to jump. Not to mention your decision to take off your safety harness. So why don't you tell us this: what exactly were you trying to do up there?"

With great deliberation, Mercy pulled a bottle of pills from somewhere in the depths of her costume and swallowed two.

"What I'm always trying to do," she said. "Now get the hell out of here. All of you."

With equal parts reluctance and relief, Carson and Golonski filed out. Juliette wavered in the doorway. Gabe, however, sat down in the window seat, picked up a paperback from the adjacent bookshelf, and waved Juliette away. Mercy didn't acknowledge him one way or another but that didn't seem to disturb Gabe in the least. He just leaned back and read his book.

Carson and Golonski were gone by the time Juliette returned to the living room. She could see Devlin in the kitchen pouring wine and slicing something. In a moment he appeared with a plate of cheese and meat in one hand, two glasses of wine in the other.

"I am going to have to make a deal with your cousin before I leave," he said, settling into the couch. "This is the best salami and prosciutto I've ever had."

"It's Gabe's beloved Sienese pork," she said absently. "Though I think the salami may be wild boar."

"Even better," he said, helping himself to another slice. "Who in Hollywood doesn't love a wild boar?"

Juliette sank back into the couch and put her hands over her eyes.

"You all right?"

"Great," she said. "I'm just great. Mercy Talbot almost leaped to her death off my bell tower less than a week after her mother fell to her death in my quarry. If I wanted to turn this into a high-class resort," she said, getting a bit hysterical, "I am certainly not going about it the right way."

"Is that what you want?"

"I don't know what I want." She sighed. "As I think I have made abundantly clear."

"Oh, I don't know about that, J.," he said, and his tone made all manner of things shake loose inside her. She closed her eyes. Hard.

"What should we do about Usher?"

"I don't think we can do much about him, at least not tonight. Unless you think he had something to do with what happened with Mercy," Devlin said doubtfully. "Which seems like a tough thing to pull off, since he was sitting right beside Golonski the whole time."

Juliette shrugged. "I don't know. I think Mercy is sufficiently screwed up at this point to have misread her script. On the other hand, I did see new pages come under the door and three minutes later I bumped into Usher on my way out. Oh, and his bag is full of money. Lots and lots of euros."

Devlin looked at her with admiration. "In the middle of all that, you managed to get your hands on Usher's black bag." He shook his head. "Sometimes I do believe your talents are wasted at the Pinnacle. Well, all things considered, I would imagine Mr. Usher will be stealing away under cover of night. If he hasn't already."

"What?"

"While you all were consoling Mercy, I went looking for him, and he was nowhere to be found. All for the best, in my opinion."

"Are you crazy?" she said. "You think we should let him get away?"

"Let him get away? I'm not the sheriff, Juliette, and neither are you. What did you want me to do? Take him into custody as an officer of Cerreta?"

"We should have called the police, or the feds or somebody."

"The feds," he said reluctantly, "are already on the case." He sighed. "That's the other reason I am here. Things are even more complicated than you think. Apparently someone—Lloyd Watson, I presume— finally gave the DEA something on Usher. Only, when they went to collect him, he had gone off to counsel Mercy Talbot in Tuscany. Where, apparently, he had established contacts with several employees of the Coronet, two Americans and one Italian, who were dealing drugs out of the hotel, presumably to Mercy, or Angie, among other people."

"Jesus, Dev," Juliette said. "Thanks for sharing. How come you haven't said one word of any of this the whole time you were here? Why did you let me run around talking to cobblers and swiping Usher's man-purse when you knew all along what was going on?"

"Because I didn't put it all together myself until I read that damn Little Book. The fact that he's got so much cash on him certainly seems to confirm it," he answered. "And I was sent to sort things out at the Coronet because the Pinnacle overlords have great confidence in my discretion. Oh, don't give me that dark and fearsome look. I didn't tell you because you had enough on your plate and I didn't want you sharing the information with O'Connor."

Juliette opened her mouth to protest and realized she honestly could not. Dev smiled almost imperceptibly.

"Besides," he said, his tone a bit softer, "I didn't really know anything for certain."

"Well, how do you know so much now?"

"Because while you were watching tonight's bit of Hollywood magic, I made a few calls. It seems that the two Americans are in custody and ready to rat out Usher in exchange for not having to go to trial in Italy. But he was careful. He never sold the stuff himself. He just made the necessary 'introductions.' And the feds can't touch him unless he comes back of his own accord—why do you think he's in Italy? He's British, and Italy won't extradite for drug dealing. But the feds aren't his real problem."

"Okay, Dev," Juliette said with a sigh when he fell silent. "So what's his real problem?"

"His real problem is all that money you saw. He didn't just do a runner on the authorities, he did a runner on his business partners. And they aren't so fussy about international law."

"Not to mention all the publicists and agents and celebrities and their lawyers, who will be screaming bloody murder when all this hits the media. The scandal will be huge," Juliette said. "Pretty much everyone's been through Resurrection."

"Good Lord," Devlin said, "I hadn't even thought of that. That's a force as dangerous as, and certainly more vindictive than, any drug cartel."

"So why are you just sitting here? Why did you let him leave? We should go now, we should see if he's still here, and hold him somehow. Isn't that why you came?"

"No," Dev said quietly. "I came to protect my interests—the Pinnacle, and you—and that's what I'm doing. Listen, my love, Steve Usher can deal nice neat packages of cocaine and OxyContin to the rich and famous through his Malibu retreat, but the drug business is the drug business, and at some point not too far up the line there are guys with machine guns and machetes. But if Usher's not here, we've got no problem."

"What about justice?" Juliette cried. "Doesn't this mean he probably had something to do with Lloyd's death? Or even Angie's? You don't think we should call the police?"

Devlin shrugged. "If he had any brains, Steve Usher would call the police and turn himself in. Either way, I'm fairly sure justice will find him soon enough. I'd just prefer it happened elsewhere."

Juliette made a sound of disgust, and he turned on her.

"Use your head, Juliette," he said with sudden heat. "This is Italy. Steve Usher, who is apparently the world's biggest idiot, has double-crossed his American connections and thinks he can set up shop here. No matter who gets to him first, it's not going to end well, and calling the police won't change that. Me," he added, his voice returning to its normal calm cadence, "I'm just trying to minimize the collateral damage. I would rather you and Mercy and Gabe did not wind up like Lloyd or Angie. Mr. Usher can just take his chances."

Juliette stared at him; a small part of her knew he was right, but still, his matter-of-fact tone in the face of all that had happened shook her.

"Sometimes I don't even know who you are," she said.

"That is moderately obvious," he replied coolly.

"I'm going to bed," she said. "I'm very tired and I'm going to bed."

"A fine idea," he said, sitting down on the couch and taking off his shoes. "If you could spare a pillow."

After wordlessly finding and handing him the pillow and the linens, Juliette stood in the doorway, trying to think of something to say.

"Go to bed, J.," Devlin said. "No doubt tomorrow will be a busy day." As if for emphasis, he rolled onto his side and closed his eyes. Which was when Juliette saw the gun tucked into the back of his pants.

Chapter Fifteen

WHEN JULIETTE WOKE UP the next morning, the house was empty. Pulling on some clothes, she hurried out to the villa. The set around the tower had been almost entirely struck; only a few lashings of wires and cords cut through the dust and gravel. Stalks of empty light stands stood here and there in clumps, like sheaves of corn leaning against the wind. The tower, the center of so much angst and anxiety, stood as it always had, solid and serene against the bright blue sky, the stone pale in the morning light. In one of the high windows, a tabby cat arched her back. Swallows darted up and under the eaves of the villa, the improbably sharp angles of their wings dark and precise as punctuation marks.

She found Gabe in the pantry off the kitchen, with a clipboard list in his hand and a look of clear unhappiness on his face as he addressed one of the interns in a voice that Juliette knew all too well.

"I understand that things are a bit loose, what with the craft services people and two sets of chefs, but we still need to keep track of things. At this point, I don't really care where anything goes, I just need to know that it went."

He turned toward Juliette. "Your friends are going to leave in three days," he said, dismissing the intern with a nod. "And I have a sneaking suspicion that all they will leave is sawdust and bare wire."

"Who told you three days?"

"Carson told me three days."

"Where the hell is everyone anyway? I woke up and I was alone in the house."

"Unusual for you these days, I admit," Gabe answered gravely. "But some of us had things to do."

"How is Mercy?" she asked. "And where is Devlin?"

"Mercy is as she ever was," Gabe said. "She spent most of the night hunched over the toilet barfing her guts up, and yet she and Michael are currently doing what I believe is called close-up work. Very romantic. I hope she brushed well. I honestly don't understand how she is still capable of standing, much less acting. I give her points for stamina."

"She only does the really good drugs."

"Yes, well, that helps, I suppose, but still . . ."

"Where are they?"

"They've rigged up a rather impressive studio in the carriage house. All of it with two-by-fours and duct tape, as far as I can tell. I don't think this crew ever sleeps. Things just appear in the morning like magic."

"Magic in the form of like a hundred and ten strapping men and women in cargo shorts who are, apparently, eating their weight in your organic produce. So where," she asked again, attempting to appear nonchalant, "is Devlin?"

"He left early this morning," Gabe said, "in his little rental car."

"Oh," Juliette said.

"He did not say when or if he would return. If that was your next question."

"Oh," she said again. "Well."

"Mr. Usher, too, has left us, apparently. His room is empty save for a stack of those horrible books, which I think he must have left as a joke.

Mercy has been calling him," Gabe said. "She seems surprisingly upset that he's gone. Actually, 'angry' would be a better word. Did Devlin go after him?"

"I don't think so," Juliette said, wondering why Dev had left without leaving a note or a text or, God forbid, waking her up to tell her what he was doing. She thought briefly of the gun—how on earth had he gotten it? But the idea of Devlin hunting Usher down to kill him made no sense, so she put it out of her mind. Was he angry that she had questioned his intentions? That she had him sleep on the couch? Did he think she had just used him the other night, and was there even a remote possibility that this would upset him?

A feeling of helplessness swept over her. She had left Los Angeles to avoid the hamster wheel of internal monologues like this one. She had left Los Angeles precisely so she could stop obsessing about all the varied and seemingly contradictory feelings she had for Michael and Devlin, for the Pinnacle, for Hollywood, for Los Angeles, for her life in general. And here she was, knee-deep in it all once again, having exposed herself in ways that had seemed impossible even two weeks ago. Where would she have to go to find a little peace, a little solitude? Iceland?

"I *said*— Oh, look, it seems I was wrong. Usher has not really left us," Gabe was enunciating when she dragged herself out of her thoughts. "Here he comes, with two new and important-looking friends."

Looking out the window, Juliette watched as Usher lifted his white-linened self out of a big silver car and, flanked by two stocky men in dark suits, strolled through the courtyard, gesturing to the tower and the villa and back to Casa Padua as if he were conducting a tour. As he spoke, he was also conferring with his cell phone, nodding and smiling, and when he hung up he made a follow-me motion with his arm and conducted his friends toward the carriage house, presumably to find Mercy.

"Interesting," Juliette said, more than a bit surprised, as much by Usher's easy manner as by his appearance. So much for Dev's theory that he was fleeing under cover of night.

"What should we do?" Gabe said. "Call the police?"

"And say what?"

"I don't know, that he's an American drug dealer?"

"And this means what to the Italian authorities?"

"Well, at least call Dev. He looks like he might be packing heat. What?" Gabe asked. "Remington Steele, right?"

"Nothing," Juliette said, remembering Devlin's warning about Usher's "real" problem. "I'm going to have a little chat with Steve. You better stay here; you talk too much."

"Oh, no. Wither thou goest, I go."

Together, Juliette and Gabriel made their way to the carriage house, which was indeed chockablock with the now all-too-familiar lights and electrical cords, swarming with texting personal assistants and crew members in boots and shorts. They were between takes, the electricians adjusting the lights and carrying impossibly heavy things around. Usher, meanwhile, was chatting amiably with Carson and Golonski, while his two friends were getting autographs from Michael and Mercy, snapping pictures with their cell phones. He did not seem like a man in danger or on the lam or anxious in any way, and his friends appeared just polished enough to know Steve Usher but dull enough to be investors of some type. Juliette wondered if Devlin had gotten it all wrong; maybe Usher had skipped the country to get *out* of the drug business.

"I like your movies," the taller one was saying to O'Connor. "Not the last couple, which were kind of sappy, but the ones from before. The one about the cop murders I liked and *The Second Sicilian,* and that one you did with Scorsese, what was it called, *The Undisturbed.* You were fucked-up crazy in that one."

He shook his head in admiration. "What's this one about?" he said, taking in the period clothes—which for Michael included a flouncy white tunic and a hat with a feather—with obvious distaste.

"It's complicated," Michael said. "And I don't get to kill anyone. But I hope you like it anyway."

"Ah," Usher said, catching sight of Juliette and Gabe. "Here they are. Just the people I was looking for. Walter, Frank," he said, beckoning the two men over, "let me introduce you to the owners of this marvelous place. These are some business associates from Los Angeles and I've just been telling them how much I've pestered you to sell dear old Serena."

"Cerreta," Gabe corrected.

"Yes. Indeed. But they won't," he said brightly, turning to Walter and Frank, who each extended a hand to Juliette and Gabe. "It's a family property, you see."

"It's nice here," said Walter, the one who had been talking to Michael. "Quiet. Old. I've never seen a real castle before."

"It's not a castle," Gabe corrected, "it's a villa. But," he amended, catching sight of Juliette's face, "there is a real castle. About a mile into the woods. If you'd like to see that. The crew was using it, though."

"We're done," Carson said. "We just need to load up that gate and the statues. You can keep the lawn if you'd like, or we'll remove it, up to you. There's a few trenches that need to be filled in; we'll do that tomorrow. Actually, you and I should take a tour of the grounds tomorrow and make sure everything is as it was."

"I find that impossible to believe," Gabe said. "But yes, I'm happy to survey the damage with you."

"I am still holding out a small hope that you will change your mind, you know," said Usher, anxious to regain control of the conversation. "So if you don't mind, I'd like to take my friends around a bit more, show them the interior of the villa and your marvelous vineyards."

"I'd like to see a real castle," said Frank.

"No one's there today," said Carson regally. "Help yourself."

"Perhaps you would care to join us," said Usher, to Gabriel and Juliette.

Juliette shook her head. "Thanks, but I've got some calls to make. I'm afraid we thought you had left us, Steve. We cleaned out your room and everything. Are you back? Because we'll have your books taken back if you'd like . . ."

"Absolutely, I'm still here," Usher said. "I was just running into Florence on an errand, and to meet up with my friends here. I'm here until the shoot's over. I don't know why anyone would think otherwise."

"Mercy was calling you," Gabe said.

"I know, I know, I had turned my cell phone off. Quite accidentally. But I'm here now." He threw a small wave to Mercy, who was being touched up by the stylists. "Not going anywhere. Just on a tour."

"Our mistake, then," Juliette said, trying to read Usher's overly reassuring tone. "I'm terribly sorry. It was nice to meet you gentlemen. Though we are not interested in selling Cerreta, we're happy to answer any questions you might have."

"Juliette." Mercy shook off the stylist. "Juliette, can you come here for just one minute, please?"

Juliette made her way into the carriage house, where Mercy and Michael were standing in front of a green screen. Michael was staring at the ground, his brow furrowed, while Golonksi talked into his ear; as Juliette passed, he offered her the briefest of smiles, the smallest of waves, before returning to his original expression of deep thought.

"I need to talk to you," Mercy said, twitching inside her costume and breathing vodka fumes into Juliette's face. "Jesus, what is wrong with this thing, it was fine yesterday and now it feels like it was made of steel wool. Seriously. We should go on break in about an hour. Can you meet me? I have to talk to you. About your cousin. Who probably thinks I'm a freak, since I threw up on him like seven times, but there's something important I need to ask you. And don't let Usher leave again, okay? And tell Dev I got his message, all right? And could you get them to give me some real tea, with honey, like we had that first day? It's like no one listens to me in this place." She gave a huge exasperated wriggle. "Can you just look down the back of this and see what's there? I feel like there are a thousand hypodermic needles poking me in the back and you're the only person here who understands anything."

There was nothing, of course, but a fine silk lining, and there was already tea and Cerreta honey on a small table nearby. As she helped settle Mercy into place, Juliette threw a sympathetic glance Michael's way and was rewarded with a bright and blinding smile. Still, as Golonski called action, Juliette backed away, thinking of what Angie had said about the danger of being Mercy's keeper; it would suck the marrow from your bones.

"Did you follow them?" she asked Gabe, when she found him in the toolshed behind the *fattoria*.

"No, I didn't follow them," Gabe said. "And I didn't offer them lunch, either. Usher took them to see the wine cellar. Apparently, they want to buy some wine and have Michael and Mercy sign the labels. I don't know how much stranger this setup can get."

"Mercy wants to talk to me," Juliette said. "She says she *needs* to talk to me, about you, and that you probably think she's 'a freak.' Any idea what that's about?"

"That I finally kissed her last night. Right before she vomited for the first time."

Juliette laughed before she had time to think.

Gabe grunted as he heaved a wheelbarrow into place. "It was a mistake," he said. "Kissing a drunk is always a mistake. I could practically taste the coke. In fact, it may have constituted a slip. I don't know what I was thinking. She just seemed so sad, so normal, for a minute or two."

"That's when they're the most dangerous," Juliette said. "That's when you should turn around and run."

Juliette called Devlin's cell phone again, but he did not answer, again. She called the Coronet and was told he had checked out. She called his cell phone again and left a message telling him about Usher's reappearance and the existence of his two friends. "Are you even still in Italy?" she asked, and hoped the recording wouldn't sound as trembly as her voice sounded in her ears. In a sudden rush of anxiety, she called the Roman police headquarters; Inspector Di Marco was not available, would she care to leave a message? If he had a moment, could he please call Juliette Greyson at Cerreta? Thank you.

Then, after staring at her BlackBerry as if she could will it into ringing, Juliette went to meet Mercy.

Chapter Sixteen

HAVING CONVINCED THE COSTUME department to reline her dress, Mercy, now clad in camisole and shorts, wanted to go for a walk, "away from everyone," she said. "I'm so sick of everyone looking at me, you know? Like they know something secret and horrible about me."

"I don't think anyone's thinking anything like that," Juliette said automatically. "And they have to look at you. You're the star of the movie."

"But they don't have to look at me so much," she said peevishly, picking her way down one of the trails that meandered through the forest from the back of the villa. "We're almost done, you know."

"I heard."

"I don't want to leave, Juliette. I just can't imagine going back to L.A. Not now, not without my mother. There'll be a funeral and I'll have to talk to my dad and it'll be all over the Internet and the magazines and then I'll have to do publicity for this fucking movie and it will never ever end. If I leave here, it will go on and on like it always has until I just drop dead at some film festival or junket somewhere. You have to figure out a way for me to stay. Talk to Gabe. Tell him I'm sorry I puked on him. Tell him . . . I really like him."

"Gabe's been puked on before, believe me," Juliette said wryly. "And I'm certainly not going to tell him you 'like him.' I graduated high school years ago." She paused, then added quietly, "You do? Seriously like him?"

Mercy nodded. "He's like the first actual *man* I've ever met," she said. "I mean, he does things and says things just because he thinks he should, just because they're true. No one I know just says things because they're true or expects me to do something just because I should. It's like he doesn't understand how the world actually works or he just doesn't care. He doesn't even care what I think."

"Oh, he cares," Juliette said.

"Well, I know he cares, but he won't change what he says or does because of it. It's so"—Mercy gave a little shiver—"sexy. So unbelievably sexy. And then I puked on him." She shook her head. "So I have to stay," she said brightly. "To make up for it."

"I don't know, Mercy," Juliette said doubtfully. "I love Gabe and I love Cerreta, but it's not like they've had the best effect on you. I mean, you almost took a header off a tower, not to mention what happened to your mom . . . well, I would think you couldn't wait to get out of here."

Mercy broke a switch off a tree, stripped the leaves from it, and walked for a few minutes in silence. The forest seemed to arch around her, like the frame of a picture. Dust glittered in the golden light, crisscrossed with shadow and birdsong.

"None of that seems real," she said finally. "On location, nothing ever seems quite real, which is why so many people get in so much trouble. But here, especially . . . I guess I'm afraid that if I leave, it will become real. She'll really be dead. Here it still seems fluid. Like it's something that might have happened, but maybe not. I know that isn't true but it just feels better. You know?"

Juliette did. Juliette most certainly did. She pulled down her own switch, stripped off its leaves, and walked in her own silence, grateful for the hill they were climbing and the living, rustling breath of the woods around them.

"Mercy," she said finally after they reached the top. "If I thought you could solve any of your problems by staying, I would tell you to stay. Seriously. But all your crap, all your fear and shame and dread and whatever will show up, right here, every morning, sitting on the end of your bed, waiting for you to wake up. No matter where you are. Even here."

And when she said it, she realized it was true. Which meant it didn't really matter where she, Juliette, went, either. It all followed her, too.

"I think you're wrong," Mercy said blithely. "I think you *can* start over. And I think it helps to be in a new place to do it. In a new place, you're a different person. Or at least you can be, if that's what you want."

Juliette was about to continue her protest when Mercy stopped.

"There's the castle," she said, pointing off the trail, down the slope. Juliette was surprised; in the past it hadn't been visible from this trail. The production crew must have taken down some trees or bushes, must have cleared some of the undergrowth that surrounded it. Gabe would probably have a fit when he realized that. What was the point of having a hidden castle if it wasn't hidden?

Mercy meanwhile was sliding down the hill at an alarming pace, moving through the woods silently and almost invisibly like a dryad. "Come on," she called over her shoulder. "I want to show you something. There's a door . . ."

Juliette had to make an effort to catch up with her, but even with her long legs, she couldn't. Mercy was lounging against the outer wall when Juliette emerged, flushed and breathless, from the woods. As she always did when she spent time alone with Mercy, Juliette felt she had entered a sort of parallel universe, a place without rules that was both tantalizing and unnerving.

"How do you move so fast?" she asked.

"Magic." Mercy laughed. "Didn't you know? These woods are thick with it. And my own brand of pixie dust." She cocked her head to one side, her eyes bright, and laughed again her beguiling wicked laugh. "You're so pretty, Juliette. With your hair all over the place and those green, green eyes. You should marry Dev, you know."

"Mercy," she said warningly.

"You should marry Dev, and I will marry Gabe, and we could live here, in this castle, and run Cerreta as an educational foundation that also happens to be a world-class hotel. Seriously. We should. We could. Because I think I found your Giotto."

And with that she disappeared through a break in the wall that Juliette and Gabe had always called, for some reason she could not remember, the priest hole.

"There's a door," Mercy said, drawing Juliette into what must have been, and what had indeed been filmed as, the kitchen. It was larger than most of the rooms in the castle, with two levels of shelves built into the stone along two of the walls. A five-foot-high fireplace stood at one end. The prop department had left the terra-cotta oven they had used in the shoot, as well as the bundles of flowers and herbs hanging from the ceiling. The floor had been swept and a large iron pot had still hung in the fireplace. Again Juliette was struck with a wave of almost painful nostalgia. How many picnics had she and Gabe shared in here, how many small smoky fires had they built, promising themselves that this time they wouldn't bother going back to the villa, to their parents? They would live here, in their hidden castle, forever.

"Look," Mercy said, tugging at Juliette's arm and pointing to a small wooden door in the corner formed where the stone oven met the wall. "This was covered by a pile of bricks."

"Mercy," Juliette protested.

"And they wouldn't let me go down while we were filming." She pulled open the door and disappeared inside. "Wow," she said as the darkness engulfed her, "it's really dark in here."

"It's a pantry," Juliette said. "There's nothing in there but spiders."

"I should have brought a flashlight," Mercy said. "Let's find a flashlight. I bet the crew left one around here. I saw some Giottos when I was in Florence, you know. His people actually look like people, even the saints."

"Mercy," Juliette said. "I don't want to go grubbing around in there. I've been in there a hundred times and it's not there. It's not anywhere. I'm pretty sure my father made up the whole thing. To keep us busy. So we wouldn't be underfoot while they drank themselves into a stupor. Or to make himself believe there was something wonderful here because what he had wasn't enough. Was never enough."

Suddenly Juliette could see her father, his brown eyes shining as he fingered the letter and leaned over her and Gabe, discussing the various places the painting might be, just as if he believed in the future, though he so clearly did not. Her lungs grew tight and her stomach soured and she remembered how often she had felt this way as a child. Overwhelmingly anxious, waiting for the next bad thing to happen, the next screaming fight, the next weeks-long silence. She didn't want to be here looking for something that didn't exist, had never existed, not with Mercy, not ever again. "Let's go back. I want to call Devlin again and there's no reception out here."

"He'll be home in time for dinner," Mercy said, pulling Juliette out into the courtyard. "What? He left me a message to tell you he would be home for dinner. Don't look at me like that. Just five minutes, we'll explore for five minutes. Wait," she said, becoming suddenly still. "Did you hear that?"

Somewhere outside the castle walls men were talking. "Shhh," whispered Mercy, crouching now, and pulling Juliette along with her into one of the front rooms where the windows looked out onto the forest beyond the castle walls. "If it's Golonski, let's pretend we're wild boars. What do they sound like?" She was smiling and trembling in the dim light, still hunched like a child in a cupboard during a game of hide-and-seek. Despite all the memories and desire to get away, Juliette had to smile. Mercy's excitement was infectious and the simple action of pressing herself against the damp cool wall and peeking through the window made Juliette's heart beat harder in childish anticipation.

But it wasn't Golonski, or at least not as far as she could see. Outside, Steve Usher was showing the castle to the men Juliette had met that morning. They looked up at the turret, admired the gate, gazed around at the woods, nodding and silent as Usher chattered on. Juliette couldn't hear exactly what he was saying, but enough—"just perfect," "pay through the nose for privacy"—reached her that she figured he was still pitching them the place, which made her very nervous. You couldn't steal an estate, so she wasn't quite sure what Usher had in mind, but she could see he hadn't given up. The three were now walking along the trench that Carson had mentioned, and Juliette, tiring of the game, was heading for the door when she heard a sudden intake of breath and Mercy yelled, "Hey, asshole," and rushed past her.

Following her around the curving wall and through the entrance, she encountered a most unexpected tableau. Usher was on his knees on the edge of the trench. The man called Walter held a gun to his head, the other was pointing his gun in the direction of Mercy's yell. All three men were momentarily frozen, their faces turned toward Mercy as she marched out of the castle, despite the fact that Frank's gun was pointed now at her.

"What the hell?" she said. "What do you think this is? *Miller's Crossing?* Get up, Steve. You're ruining your pants."

Obediently, Usher began to rise. Walter shoved him down.

"You cannot be serious. What, do you owe these guys money?" Mercy asked. "He's got the money. Just take it and leave. If it's not enough, I'll write you a check."

"Mercy," Juliette said, sidling up to her, "I don't think it's just about money. I think they're trying to make a point." She could not imagine a scenario in which this would end well, certainly not one in which they would actually be allowed to go, but she figured it was worth a try. "Let's go."

"It has to be about money," Mercy said. "Look at these guys. It could only be about money, drugs, or prostitution, and . . ." She stopped and looked at Usher, illumination dawning on her face. "And it's not prostitution, is it? Shit. Lloyd was right. I can't believe it." She threw back her head and laughed. "He totally said more people went to Resurrection to get high than to get sober and I thought he was just being paranoid. So let me guess," she said, strangely at ease. "You've been running drugs out of Malibu and now you want to do it here and these guys aren't happy about it."

Usher looked at her, stricken. "So, I'm sorry, so you didn't *know*? Until just now? But I thought Lloyd had told you. You had his book and everything."

"What book?" Mercy said. "Lloyd never told me anything about you. I mean, he wasn't your biggest fan, that's for sure . . ."

"But I thought you were the one who had contacted the DEA."

"Me?" Mercy asked, astonished. "I didn't know you were dealing drugs. I knew whatever it was you were trying to do there didn't work— I mean, look at me—but I figured it was because of, you know, the yoga on the beach and lame equestrian therapy."

Walter and Frank laughed appreciatively.

"I resent that," said Usher, with a remarkable amount of dignity considering the circumstances. "Equestrian therapy is very popular and effective and Resurrection has as high a recovery rate as any center. Which isn't very high, I admit, but it's not like we don't help people. We do. We just also offer certain services to the nonaddict as well. If you would only read my book—"

"Shut up about the book," Walter snapped. "Without the book, none of this would have happened."

"The book," Mercy said. "Oh, that book, Lloyd's Little Book. He did say it was all in the book, but I didn't pay any attention. He said a lot of things when he was messed up, and he was messed up a lot. Which wasn't my fault, you know. I didn't give him any of my drugs."

"Of course you didn't," Steve said, still speaking just as if he were not on his knees in the mud with a gun at his head. "You didn't have to. There are drugs in this world; it was up to Lloyd whether you use them or not."

"That's true, you know," said Frank. "You need to take personal responsibility."

"Shut up, Frank," said Walter, who, clearly awed by Mercy's presence, seemed to be struggling to grasp the situation.

"If my clients wish to become and remain sober," Usher continued, "I am committed to their sobriety. One hundred percent. That's why his threats were so personally hurtful to me . . ."

"Which is when you should have picked up the phone, called our mutual friend, and explained the nature of the problem," said Walter, attempting to take control. "Instead of relying on your own big ideas and squirrelly outside contacts."

"If I had told 'our mutal friend' that our mutually beneficial operation was about to blow up in my face, it would have been the last call I ever made."

"Probably," Walter conceded. "But it would have saved a lot of time, and Lloyd Watson would still be alive. He had a pretty promising career, if you ask me."

"Wait," said Mercy. "This is crazy. You work for who?" she asked Walter. "His supplier? Who is what, a drug lord? Who has people *killed*?"

"That's right, princess," Frank said. "Where do you think all that coke you snort comes from anyway? Saks Fifth Avenue?"

"Shut up, Frank," Walter said again, before turning his attention back to Mercy.

"Could you put the gun down for a second?" Mercy said. "Just a second?"

"Listen," Walter said, not lowering his arm, "I think you'll agree that we're doing everybody a service here. We'll be gone in a few minutes and you heard the lady; they're filling in this trench this afternoon."

"I'm not going to let you kill someone just because he's an asshole," Mercy said, raising herself to her full height and summoning some long-ago action hero role.

"An asshole?" Walter said derisively. "Why do you think your buddy Lloyd's dead? Why do you think your mom's dead? Because this guy doesn't understand the nature of the business, that's why. There's a chain of command and he ignored it. He still thinks he's a rock star."

"Come on, Walter," Frank said. "Let's get this over with." He looked from Walter to Mercy to Juliette in a way Juliette most decidedly did not like. Neither, it seemed, did Walter.

"You know what, sweetheart?" he said, looking at Mercy. "I like you. I like your movies, though you really need to quit doing drugs and put on a few pounds. So I'm going to give you to the count of three and if you move fast enough, we'll pretend we didn't see you and you pretend you didn't see us. You're good at that, right? Pretending?"

Something in his voice told Juliette that the offer was sincere but good for a very limited time only. She grabbed Mercy's arm, but Mercy did not move. Straight and tall, she stood frozen.

"You killed my mother," she said softly, her eyes on Usher's face. "You *killed* my mother?"

"No, no, no," said Usher. "Well, all right, technically, *yes*. I did. But I didn't mean to. It was an accident. I was quite devastated when I found out she was dead; she had tried so hard to help me with my Lloyd problem. But it was dark that night and I was very upset. When I saw her running down the path like that, well, to be honest . . ." He paused and cleared his throat, then added with a little laugh, "I thought it was *you*."

In the echoing silence, Usher rushed to explain. "I am sorry, you know, because I am fond of you, too. Honestly I am. And I did want to help you. But you just wouldn't let the whole Lloyd thing go and you kept dropping these disturbing hints that you knew what had really happened, that he had shared so much with you, and you were so coy about giving me his Little Book—"

"I thought you were going to sell it on eBay or something," Mercy said, choking. "I thought my mother had somehow set up the whole hanging thing so no one would know Lloyd and I were using again."

"But you kept saying that people had killed Lloyd and were trying to kill you . . ." Usher said, plaintively.

"I didn't mean it *literally*," Mercy sobbed. "I'm an actress. I'm *dramatic*."

"Ah, well," said Usher, settling his rump back on his heels with an air of studied casualness, "the root of all great tragedy is usually miscommunication. Just as with poor Juliet. Not you, my dear," he added, with a nod in Juliette's direction, "the Shakespearean character."

"You're not even sorry," Mercy said, her voice full of tears and fury. "Look at you. You killed Lloyd, you killed my mother, you thought you were killing me, and you don't even sound *sorry*."

Usher pursed his lips and blinked in his amiable way.

"Mercy, my darling, you and I both know at the rate you're going, you'll be dead in a year, two at the most. You don't care, so why should I? And your mother, well, how upset are you really? On a scale of one to ten."

With a fleet and sudden movement, Mercy was standing inches away from Usher and miraculously Walter's gun was in her hand.

"Upset enough," she said, pointing it at Usher's head.

"For godsake," Juliette said, suddenly panicked that the girl would accidentally pull the trigger. "Mercy, I'm pretty sure that's real."

Real and so close to Usher's head, there was no way she would miss. When Mercy didn't respond, Juliette mustered the same tone she had used to get Mercy out of the fountain. "You're being ridiculous. Put it down before you wind up killing him." She moved toward the starlet and the one called Frank broke his silence.

"I think you should just hold it right there, honey," he said, his gun now trained on Juliette. Seeing the barrel, the hole at the end of the barrel, Juliette stopped in her tracks, her mind a quick-frozen lake of involuntary fear. In the movies, everyone was always so calm when a gun was pointing at them; in real life, she just hoped her bladder wouldn't betray her.

"Go ahead, honey," Frank said softly, speaking now to Mercy. "Why not? You deserve it and no one will know. We'll certainly never tell."

"Wait, wait," said Walter, pulling out his cell phone. "Let me get a shot of this."

"This is ridiculous," said Usher. "Stop it, Mercy, before you hurt yourself. Oh, great, now they have a photo. How's that going to play in the blogosphere? Why don't you ever *think,* Mercy? They're not really going to kill me, they're just trying to scare me. If they were really trying to kill me, they never would have brought me back here, they would have just shot me and dumped me somewhere."

Walter smiled. "Except we wanted to see the movie stars. It may be old hat to you, but that Michael O'Connor, I've been watching him since I was a kid. And when will I get a chance again? So we figured, why not?"

For some reason, the insanity of this explanation helped a bit. Juliette felt her veins thaw, felt the earth beneath her feet again, the true dimensions of her body.

"Mercy," she said, and took a step.

Mercy lifted the gun and shot it into the air. It had a silencer that made a soft benign popping sound. Not even the birds were disturbed.

"You can go if you want," Mercy said, not taking her eyes off of Usher. "If you don't want to watch. But you should go now." And she aimed once again at Usher's head.

"Put it down, Mercy," said a voice. Turning her head, Juliette could see Devlin standing in the trees less than thirty yards away. Frank's aim now wavered between Devlin and Juliette and Mercy. "The police are on their way," he said. "They're coming up the road right now. Europe may not extradite for drug dealing, but it will for murder. So you don't have to worry. He'll go to jail for the rest of his life."

"It's not enough," Mercy said, not moving the gun or taking her eyes off Usher. "He'll get off. People like him, people like me, we always get off. You know that. I'll even get off. Temporary insanity. Becker will cover it up for me. Just like someone will cover up for him." She steadied her hand.

"Don't," Devlin said. "I'm telling you. He isn't worth what happens next. Even if you don't get caught, you can't kill someone and just walk away. You can still be happy, Mercy. Everything that's happened so far are just things that happened. But not this," he said softly. "This will be something you *did*. I promise that you can still be happy. But only if you put the gun down."

For a moment, Mercy wavered. For a moment, she turned her enormous eyes toward Devlin and they were green-gold like the forest, drenched and shining in her white childlike face.

"My mother's dead because of me," she said in a little voice. "How happy do you think it will get?"

As Mercy lifted the gun, Juliette cried out and lunged for her hand. Two shots rang out, impossibly loud, horrifyingly loud, and then came the desperate sound of men in great pain, and blood seemed to be everywhere. Frank's hand erupted as he dropped his gun with a scream, and Usher fell back onto the ground, writhing and keening as blood poured from his left shoulder. Walter grabbed at Mercy just as she looked down at the gun in her hand, terrified and confused, and threw it far away as if it burned her.

But the bullets had come from Devlin's gun, not Mercy's, and another shot threw Walter reeling back, screaming as he clutched his shattered knee and splattered Mercy with blood. As if in a dream, Juliette watched as Devlin kept his weapon trained on the two men. For a moment she felt only fear, expecting the bite of a bullet herself, for he looked like someone she did not know, someone capable of anything. From far away, Juliette could hear the dropping wail of a European siren take hold of the forest.

"Gentlemen," Devlin said, "you have less than a minute. If you are capable of flight, you might consider it. J.," he said impatiently, jerking his chin toward the dropped weapon. But she could only stare at him in confused horror and in the end it was Mercy who hurried over and picked it up. Not that she had to fight Frank or Walter for it; they took off as fast as they could considering their wounds, crashing through the woods. But already the trees were filled with more men and more guns, with noise and harsh voices, led, most improbably, by Gabe and Inspector Di Marco. Mercy began to visibly shake and Juliette automatically put her arms around her. With Mercy Talbot's head tucked beneath her chin, she watched as a stretcher appeared to carry off Usher, still screaming in pain, and then as Walter and Frank and Devlin were led away, flanked by men in uniforms. When she began to protest, Devlin raised his hand to silence her—he was not wearing handcuffs, she was relieved to see, but even when she said his name, he kept walking and got in one of the cars. He did not turn to meet her eye.

Chapter Seventeen

IN THE MIDST OF the subsequent chaos, Mercy became a paragon of clarity. Back at the villa, she neither swooned nor grew hysterical, did not slip off to do a line or surreptitiously pop a pill. She answered Inspector Di Marco's questions in a quiet, measured voice. She told them about seeing her mother leaving Lloyd's room the night of his death. She told them about her affair with Lloyd and the photos that showed up on the website, about how Lloyd had seemed disgusted by his stay at Resurrection and had mentioned on several occasions that Usher wasn't really interested in getting anyone sober because the real money was in the repeat business. She even told them that her mother had regularly supplied her with cocaine and pain medication that she got, apparently, from contacts she made through Usher.

"I guess that means you should arrest me," she said.

"On what charge?" Di Marco said gravely. "I see no drugs in your possession at this time."

"But I want to tell the truth," Mercy said passionately. "I don't want to keep any more secrets. I want to make sure he doesn't get away with it, that I don't get away with it. Because it was my fault, really, that she died. My fault . . ." Her voice trailed away but she raised her chin and straightened her spine. "I would have killed him, you know. You could arrest me for that."

"I do not want to arrest you for anything," he said. "You have done nothing wrong," he said now, "at least to anyone else. To yourself . . ." He shook his head regretfully. "You need to be less harmful to yourself. But unlike you, your mother knew what sort of man Steve Usher was and she chose to deal with him regardless."

"Is that why . . . . did my mother kill Lloyd?"

He shook his head. "No. Lloyd Watson was killed, strangled, by someone Usher hired; we arrested him yesterday. Apparently Usher was aware of the investigation into Resurrection and had been considering coming to Italy, to Tuscany, for some time. He had made offers on several properties in addition to Cerreta. I think he had some romantic idea of somehow becoming involved with the Mafia." The inspector grimaced. "Lloyd had threatened to go public and Usher panicked."

"So my mother didn't have anything to do with his death?"

"No," he answered with a kind smile. "Not his death. I imagine she knew he was using drugs again, perhaps she was even supplying him with them in the hopes that he would stop pursuing Usher."

"I knew she was sleeping with him," Mercy said, her voice cracking.

"Perhaps," said the inspector. "Though it's just as likely that Usher enlisted her by pointing out that if he went down, so would everyone who had ever gone through Resurrection. Which would not have reflected well on you, or her. Either way, I don't think she realized how far Usher would go until she found Watson's body that night. Then she realized she had to protect Usher to protect you. Or at least the movie. A tragic death by overdose or even sexual deviation, a film can recover from those. But a murder? That would have shut everything down."

"But why make it so strange and dramatic?" Juliette wanted to know, thinking of the semen. "Why go to such disgusting lengths?"

The inspector shrugged. "I can only imagine she was playing to the paparazzi as much as the police. And she wanted to get Bill Becker involved in keeping things quiet, so the more grisly details, the better."

"Mother was always one step ahead of the paparazzi," Mercy said sadly. "So what will happen to Usher now? I mean, assuming he survives."

Di Marco made a wry face. "He will survive, that one. It was a clean shot through the shoulder, a real"—he smiled his small, careful smile—"Hollywood shot. I think the American authorities have enough to bring him to the U.S. for trial now, and I would imagine Usher will decide he is safer now in custody than out of it."

Juliette looked at him curiously. "You have been so tenacious about this case," she said. "Why? Did you suspect something from the very beginning?"

The inspector shrugged. Once again he was wearing a beautifully cut suit; it moved in perfect fluid lines with the gesture. "Me, I love the movies. Film stars dropping dead in my country is bad for tourism. And"—he shrugged again—"when people start hearing rumors about a drug dealer who is considering relocating, well, this is Italia. Such a person would have more to deal with than the police. That we do not need."

Carson appeared in the doorway, flushed and breathless. "Mercy," she said, relief written on her face. "There you are. Where's Michael? Where's Golonski? Where is everybody?"

"There's been a shooting," Juliette said. "Steve Usher has been arrested and—"

"I know all that," Carson said. "But that was an hour ago. Bill Becker is on his way. Right now. His driver just called me; they're coming up the driveway."

"And?" Mercy did not even look her way when she spoke.

"And I want to make sure we're all on point. I don't want any of the . . . things that have happened to distract from the amazing work we've—you've—done. Under such distressing circumstances, too. I think we've all behaved remarkably well, all things considered." She offered Mercy a smile that was both sympathetic and admiring. Juliette wondered if she had practiced it in the mirror. Mercy took one look at Carson and snorted.

"Fuck off," Mercy said quietly. "No, wait. I'll make you a deal. You match Becker's contribution to Gabe's foundation and I won't tell him how you almost let me jump off the top of the tower. Convince him to double it, and I'll think about not breaking down in the *Vanity Fair* interview my mother set up before we left."

A look of fury crossed Carson's face, but she caught it and contained it.

"I'm happy to help preserve this lovely place in any way I can," she said. "Do you think you could join us in the living room when you are done here?"

"Certainly," Mercy answered with a grave and queenly nod.

Juliette used the pause that followed to ask a question that had long been nagging at her.

"Inspector," she said, "who makes the suits you are wearing?"

Di Marco looked at her quizzically.

"You have the most beautiful suits," she said, laughing. "And I just can't place them."

"Ah," he said. "My suits. I was hoping you would ask. My son makes my suits. I happen to have some of his business cards. Perhaps," he said, handing her a stack with a twinkle in his eye, "you could recommend him to your friends."

After Di Marco left, Juliette found herself sitting in the library, staring out the window, trying to get the sound of the gunshots out of her head, to erase the image of the sudden, horrifyingly bright blood and the way Devlin would not look at her when he left.

"I can't believe I missed all the excitement," said O'Connor, coming into the room and sitting down beside her. "Drug dealers and feds, an eleventh-hour confession, and a shoot-out in a castle. I thought you and

Mercy were going for a walk to discuss your love lives; if I had known you were going to bring down a drug kingpin, I might have joined you."

"It's not funny, Michael," she said. "It was terrifying and awful. I mean, Usher killed Angie, and he killed her because he thought she was Mercy. How screwed up is that? And Mercy went crazy and Dev, oh, my God, you should have seen him. He didn't even blink. He shot those guys and he didn't even blink." She closed her eyes. "I don't even know where he is now. They took him away even though he was just trying to keep Mercy from blowing Usher's head off, and Di Marco won't say if he's in trouble or what." She buried her face in her hands. "And it's all my fault. I never should have brought Mercy here. I thought it would help and I just made everything worse for everyone."

"Yeah," O'Connor agreed. "It really is your fault that Steve Usher was selling drugs through his recovery center and that he decided to kill a former client to keep it quiet. It's your fault that Usher is such a fuckup he can't even get himself whacked without making a big messy scene about it. As for Dev, well"—Michael's tone became a bit less sarcastic—"he's a big boy, he makes his own decisions. If he wants to play the white knight, he knows how it works."

Juliette heard both bitterness and sympathy in his voice, but after all that had happened, the teeter-totter pulse of her relationship with O'Connor seemed unimportant, part of another person's life. "I just wish I knew where he was," she said with a sigh.

"He's in the chapel," Michael said. "At least that's where he said he was going when he got out of the car."

Juliette looked at him in surprise.

"I actually didn't miss all the excitement," O'Connor said. "Though I didn't have front-row seats. I joined the posse on its way into Siena to make sure there was no misunderstanding about Devlin's role in what happened. I don't like to mention it," he added with a grin, "but I do have quite a following among Italian law enforcement."

"So everyone understood that he . . ." Juliette found she couldn't even say the words. The sound of the shots filled her head, the bloody eruption of Frank's hand, Usher falling back with a horrible yell.

"Was acting in self-defense. Or yours and Mercy's defense. The important thing, I've found," he said, leaning his head back and looking at the ceiling, "is clearing things up before anyone enters anything into a computer. Truth is a fluid state until some bureaucrat hits the save button."

"That's very nice of you," Juliette said. "No, really," she answered his raised eyebrow. "You didn't have to do that, didn't have to get involved."

"I don't know that I did much beside drive him home," O'Connor said with a sigh. "Devlin seemed to have things under control when I got there. But it was the least I could do. I owe the man. Without him, I never would have found you." Lifting her hand to his lips, he gave her his famously wicked grin.

Juliette couldn't help but laugh.

"Are you ever serious, I wonder?" she asked, though she did not withdraw her hand. "Or do you save that for the camera?"

Michael sat up and returned her hand to her. "If I chose this particular moment to be serious, Juliette," he said, "I believe it would break my heart." Before she could answer, he stood. "In the chapel," he said again. "And now, I'm needed in makeup. Though I am beginning to understand how those poor bastards felt on *Apocalypse Now*."

Juliette found Devlin in the chapel, sitting in the front row, looking up at the crucified Christ, the shining eyes rolling heavenward, the blood still dripping vividly from the figure's side and hands and circle of thorns.

"Only the Mexicans outdo the Italians when it comes to the blood and gore," Juliette said, sitting down next to him. "Although I don't know— where do ancient Irish crucifixions stand in terms of ghastliness?"

"There aren't any," Devlin said flatly, his eyes still on the altar. "All our cathedrals and abbeys were destroyed by the British." As Juliette tried to come up with a response to this, he sighed. "It's very peaceful in here," he said. "Very quiet. A good place to contemplate the sins one shares only with the Almighty."

"Yes," she said, inhaling the dark sacred smell of cool stone, old dry wood, and resin. If she closed her eyes, she could find a note of incense—when she was a child, a priest came to Cerreta on Sundays to say mass for the few families that still lived on the property, heard confessions once a month. Because the chapel was so small, Juliette was expected to sit perfectly still; she remembered secretly carving grooves into the layers of wax that had built up on the short pews to keep herself from twitching in boredom, how the wax had collected, dark and sticky, beneath her nails. "I haven't spent any time in here for years," she said.

They sat in silence for several long minutes. Juliette stole a few looks at Devlin's profile. There was nothing to see but the face she had known for so long, lost in thought but still as familiar to her as her own. More so, since she looked at it all day long back at the Pinnacle. He seemed so distant, so quiet and solemn, so unlike Dev that guilt rose inside her like nausea. He was probably furious with her, and he had every right to be. First she left with little explanation and no promise of return, and then she dragged him into a situation from which he literally had to shoot his way out. She had to do something to fix things; although she had no idea what sort of relationship they would have, could have after all this, she couldn't bear the thought of him hating her.

"I'm going to come back with you to L.A.," she said abruptly, although she had not had this thought, or even an inkling of this thought, in the seconds before she spoke. "I just need to tie up a few ends here; we could go by the end of the week. I mean, if you want. To wait."

"I'm leaving tonight," he said quietly. "I'm flying out of Rome first thing tomorrow, so I'll spend the night there."

"Oh," Juliette said. "Well. Okay. Do I have time to pack?"

"There's no reason for you to rush back," he said in a quiet, steady voice, his eyes still on the altar. "Corporate is actually looking for some help opening the new hotel in Paris. In all the excitement, I forgot to mention it."

Still he did not look at her. Juliette's neck and shoulders tightened and she felt as if the temperature in the chapel had dropped twenty degrees.

"You're going to Paris?" she said.

"No," he said. "Not me. I was thinking of you. It seems like a good opportunity for you."

"You don't want me to come back?" she asked, the words almost choking her. "You don't want me to come back at all?"

"They'd only need you for a month or so," he said, still not looking at her. "It would be temporary. It would be Paris. Where, I believe, Michael's shooting his next film. I mean, unless you're planning to stay on here. Which would make sense."

"Is that why you don't want me to come back? Because of Michael? Because if that's the case, then you need to know—"

"That's not the case," he said.

"Then what?" she asked. The distance in his voice made her feel desperate. Two minutes ago, she hadn't even thought of returning to Los Angeles; now it seemed she could never be happy unless she went this very minute, unless she could reassure herself that nothing had changed, or at least nothing important. "Are you angry that I got you involved in all this? Because I really am sorry, though I don't know what we would have done—"

"I'm not angry," he said, cutting her off in the same quiet voice. "I'm just . . ." He paused, and finally looked at her. "I'm just not sure where we go from here."

"You mean what happened in Siena? Well, you don't have to worry, I mean if you're worried. I don't expect you to . . ." Juliette stammered.

"That's not what I meant, and you know it," he said. "That we can deal with, or not, as we choose. I'm more concerned about what happened after. In the woods."

He paused, waiting for her to speak.

"What were you thinking when I shot Usher?" he asked when she did not. "When I shot those other men?"

Juliette swallowed hard. From the moment she saw Devlin sitting in the chapel, what had happened in the woods had become simply impossible. Or like something that had happened years before, to another person.

"I thought you did it because you had to," she said automatically, banishing the image of him firing the gun, how horrible it had been, the shocking violence of it, the noise and blood. "You did it to keep Mercy from killing Usher, which she probably would have, if only accidentally. And to keep those guys from killing us. I don't think you should feel bad about it. I mean, it must be awful to shoot someone, but there was nothing else you could have done. And no one died."

Devlin surveyed her with a coolness that unnerved her.

"I don't feel bad about it. It didn't bother me in the least," he said. "I'm glad the shots were clean, but if they hadn't been, I would have been fine with that, too. I was, as I told you, protecting my interests."

"Well," Juliette said, refusing to understand what it was he was trying to tell her, "you wound up saving Usher's life. Even if Mercy hadn't killed him, those other two would have. But it's over now, so there's no reason to dwell on it."

Devlin sighed and rubbed his brow with one hand. "That's not the point, J."

"You did what you had to do," Juliette said. "I get it."

"No, you don't," he said. "Because you're sitting there already pretending that it didn't happen. Or that some other version of it happened."

"I'm not."

"You are. It's what you do. I saw your face when I shot Usher. You looked at me as if you didn't know who I was. You looked at me as if you were afraid I'd shoot you next."

Juliette felt her mouth go dry. Devlin's voice was steady, his face unreadable, and that had been exactly what she had thought. "I didn't think you would shoot me, Dev. I was just totally freaked out. Guns were going off, people were falling down and screaming. It wasn't like it looks in the movies. It was kind of awful."

"Yes," he said softly. "I know. You said there were times when you don't even know me."

"I said that because I was angry—"

"You said that because it's true."

There was a long silence.

"I know what people say about me back in L.A., the rumors of my dark and dangerous past. Hell, I encourage them." He shrugged. "Women like it, the big suits like it, and it's good for business. It's not all rumor, J. But it's not glamorous, either. I meant what I said to Mercy. There are things that, once you've done them, make happiness difficult. Not impossible, as it turns out, but difficult."

"Dev," she said, putting a hand on his arm.

"No," he said, jerking his arm away as if he had been stung. "Good Lord, J. I don't need that, I don't need you to *heal* me. I just don't want to ever see that look on your face again."

"You won't," she said, desperately wishing she could end this conversation, roll back time, and erase the scene in the woods so they could be who they had been together just twenty-four hours ago. "That's what I've been saying. It happened. It's over and I don't need to think about it anymore."

"Yes, you *do.*" He stood, practically knocking down the pew in front of him, his voice harsh and frightening in the musty silence of the chapel. "You do need to think about it," he said more calmly. "Before you come back. That's what I'm saying. I'm not ashamed of my past, but it is real. I've always wondered why you've never asked about it, about where all the rumors come from. Women usually do."

Juliette looked at him, genuinely surprised.

"I didn't care where the rumors came from," she said. "And I didn't think you wanted to talk about it. That's one of the things I love best about you. You don't need to *talk* about everything. You accept things the way they *are* and just do what needs to be done."

He shook his head, but he was smiling a bit and looked like Dev again. "Go to Paris, J.," he said softly. "Or stay here. Sort out what you need to sort out. Come back when it isn't some sort of grand gesture. I'm past the point in my life where I appreciate them."

Chapter Eighteen

IT WAS AMAZING, REALLY, how quickly and efficiently the shoot wrapped up after Bill Becker arrived. He seemed to bring what was left of Hollywood with him, and not just the macrobiotic chef and three personal assistants, who immediately set up what looked like a technological command center in the library. Computers, flat-screens, consoles—Gabe took one look at what had once been a rather stately and certainly historical room, and did a complete about face.

"Now we're fucking NASA? He's here for three days? It looks like he's got federal funding. No," he said, waving away Juliette's assurances, "it doesn't matter. God only knows what the end result of this experiment will be but there's no point worrying about it now."

Carson walked around white-faced but smiling. She had spent two long hours holed up with Becker on the day that he arrived—his profanity, much of it so choked with anger it was incomprehensible, slammed through the windows and ricocheted around the courtyard like gunfire. Whoever could, fled to their respective domiciles and sat hunched on their beds quietly gossiping and making dire predictions like kids at camp. Those crew members who were taking down the various sets did so in cautious silence and clouds of cigarette smoke.

But after he saw footage, Becker's demeanor changed. He became so amiable it was as if he had been replaced by a different man. Juliette watched with bitter amusement as he introduced himself to the staff and the interns, wearing a retro-striped button-down shirt that he could have lifted from Tony Soprano. Slapping backs and kissing cheeks, he moved his enormous bulk with surprising grace, greeting cast and crew like a newly elected president at a victory party. Still shaken by Dev's abrupt departure and shocked anew at the way in which filmmakers could put the concerns of their industry above life, death, and just about everything in between, Juliette had gone out of her way to avoid greeting Becker, a man she had never liked. Yet speaking with her seemed to be high on his agenda, and when he caught up with her, as she was rearranging one of the garden sheds in a field far behind the villa, he embraced her like a long-lost uncle.

"I knew as soon as I heard your name that this would be the best decision I ever made," Becker announced. Except for the uncharacteristic sheen of sweat on his face and increasingly visible scalp, he could have been standing in the lobby of the Pinnacle, rather than in a dusty little hut, rank with the smell of pig fodder and fertilizer. "Fate, I said, fate sent you to me when I needed you most."

"Yes, well," Juliette said, extricating herself awkwardly from his embrace. "It's all been rather harrowing for everyone. Particularly Mercy."

Becker gave her a knowing look, rummaged in his pocket, and produced his cigar. "Ah, yes, poor Angie. Such a tragedy. Losing a parent, any parent, is always difficult. But you know, I think Mercy will not only survive her loss, she'll emerge even stronger and more focused. Already she strikes me as more mature." He lit his cigar and peered at her through the smoke. "Death has a way of clarifying things, don't you think, Ms. Greyson?"

Juliette shook her head. As always happened when she was in the presence of this man, she was torn between disgust and admiration—

Becker was the coldest, most callous person she had ever met, and considering the city in which she worked, that was saying something. But he had a way of speaking unspeakable truths with such utter lack of apology that she couldn't help feeling envy, even respect. Having survived his own rather notorious fall, Becker seemed unafraid of consequence or opinion; his worldview was not hers, not by a long shot, but at least he had one, and stuck by it.

"Some things, Mr. Becker," she said gravely. "Other things just become even more . . . tangled."

"But that's what makes life interesting," he said. "The untangling. Some of us," he added with a knowing squint, "can make that our life's work. Anyway"—he jabbed the cigar back in his mouth—"it's going to be one helluva movie. And that's what we're all trying to do, right? Create a little lasting beauty in this chaotic and indifferent world?"

He stepped out of the shed and squinted into the sunlight. "And if that bastard Golonski fucks it up in the editing room, I will kill him myself."

Whether it was Becker's presence or just everyone's desire to finally be done with the film, the few scenes that still had to be shot proceeded like clockwork, without incident. O'Connor was the very model of a movie star, cracking jokes with the crew and teasing Mercy as if he were her older brother. Mercy, meanwhile, was prompt, professional, and subdued; she also appeared, for the first time in a long time, to be totally sober.

"She's not, of course," said Gabe, when Juliette made this observation to him while the two oversaw the creation of Cerreta gift baskets that Carson had ordered for the principal cast and crew. "Frankly, at this point she couldn't just quit and expect to finish things; she'd be too far gone into withdrawal. But she does seem to have found some level of mood maintenance, which is probably worse for her in the long run than the DTs."

"What are you talking about?" Juliette was exasperated. "Look at her, she's functioning, she's lucid, she's sleeping. I wish I could say the same thing. Considering everything that's happened, it's a fucking miracle."

Gabe shook his head and repositioned a bottle of olive oil.

"Miracles like that you pay for on the back end," he said. "She'll start thinking she can control her disease and all the craziness will start again, only this time worse."

"Or maybe she's actually taking everything she's learned seriously."

A look of doubt passed over Gabe's face, but when he opened his mouth to speak, he caught himself, took a deep breath, and said, "Maybe. Maybe you're right."

Those four words took such an obvious physical effort that the two of them burst out laughing.

"She wants to stay here," Juliette said finally, wiping her eyes with the back of her hand.

Gabe nodded, fanned out packages of sliced salami as if they were playing cards. "I know," he said quietly.

"And?" Juliette looked at her cousin curiously.

"I told her I don't have your talent for caregiving. Or your tolerance for backsliding."

Now it was Juliette's turn to shake her head. "You are so full of it. You'd walk barefoot over broken glass for her if she asked."

Gabe shrugged. "I know. Which is why I need rules. Without rules, I would run amok. Just like Mercy. Which is why maybe I can help her."

Juliette turned his words over in her head for the rest of the day. In a way, she and Gabe had chosen similar methods to cope with life—he had the orderliness of his program and the unending cycle of work on

the farm, she had the Pinnacle, with its caste system, its code of silent
knowledge, and the ceaseless demands of the service industry. Neither
she nor her cousin did well with idleness. But as for rules, well, the few
rules Juliette had—don't fall in love with an actor, don't sleep with
Devlin, don't talk about the past, don't go back to Cerreta—she had not
simply broken, she had shattered.

She had come to Italy to find the slim living spine of things, to cut
away the dead and dying branches of her life in the hopes of discovering
whatever was still green and vital in her. But she hadn't expected to be
stripped down to the root, to discover that the weight she carried was
almost entirely of her own creation. Something inside her brain lifted
like a low-hanging bank of clouds, revealing a wider, a limitless, sky.

So when she went to O'Connor's room to bring him more towels,
when he opened the door bare-chested, his hair wet from the shower
and the smell of soap still rich in the air, she allowed herself to consider
the possibility of doing something simply because she wanted to do it.
She did not trust O'Connor like she did Devlin, but with low expecta-
tions came a certain measure of freedom. Loving Devlin, she realized
now, would be a delicate and complicated endeavor. He was not simply
a rock amid stormy seas, he was the sea as well. Compared with Devlin's, O'Connor's needs were simple. He was content with her simply
showing up.

"Hi," she said, not moving.

"Hi," he said, one eyebrow hitched high. "Have you come to say farewell? I saw Devlin beetling his way out of here. I assumed you would
not be far behind."

"No," she said. "I'm not going back to L.A. At least not yet. I've been
asked to go to Paris. For a month or so. To help open a new Pinnacle."

"Paris?" he said softly, and she could see he was surprised.

"Look, I know it's been . . ."

"Complicated?"

"Complicated," she echoed. "For both of us. And maybe the whole thing is just impossible, after everything that's happened, but——"

He kissed her, of course, just as she knew he would, and maybe, she thought, it was enough for love, this limited certainty, these sudden small moments of joy. She put Devlin, with all his surprising contradictions and requirements, out of her mind and let herself feel happy. Only happy. Just for a few moments. Michael pulled her close against him and she wondered if there was a chance they could stitch something together out of just this, something that would bear the weight of even a little bit of time.

Chapter Nineteen

I MPOSSIBLY, AT THE END of three days, all of the equipment, the lights, the trailers, the cameras, the dollies, the tracks, the props, the foliage, and all the miles and miles of electrical cords and wire were gone. All through the night the trucks roared in and out of the courtyard, up and down the dirt road until morning broke, and even the sound of the birds seemed muted and cowed.

The silence had woken Juliette and she was walking in the garden behind the villa. Now amid the wildflowers grew topiary and rose trees and all manner of lilies—at some point, the crew had planted all of the flowers and shrubs that had been used to decorate the abbey and the various sets around the villa. It gave the silent walled-in place a wild and gorgeous look, like an outdoor hothouse or a child's imaginary garden.

"I can have them taken away if you like," said Carson, coming up from behind. "The production designer thought you might like . . . a memento."

"Most of them will die anyway," Juliette said, not sure how to take the other woman's tone. "They don't belong here, the soil's wrong, and the light. But," she added, softening, "it will be very beautiful for a little while."

"Oh, I think you'll be surprised," Carson said amiably. "The climate here is a lot like L.A. Very forgiving. All manner of things can thrive. You're lucky," she said. "Not everyone has such a refuge. You should stop feeling so sorry for yourself."

Her elbows were on top of the low wall and she was leaning into the breeze, her golden hair fluttering behind her, her face serene as she gazed over the vineyards and forests, the houses and fields. She was very beautiful and sure of herself, and Juliette hated her.

"Our parents were hit by a train," Juliette said harshly. "That's why Gabe and I have this place. Because our parents died when I was nineteen."

Cason nodded and did not take her eyes from the view. "I know. My parents are dead, too. Or at least my dad's dead. My mother has Alzheimer's; she's in a home. She doesn't know who I am, or who she is, for that matter. She might as well be dead. She would wish she were dead, if she remembered how to wish."

Juliette swallowed. "I'm sorry," she said. "That must be very hard."

Carson shrugged. "Every fucking thing is hard. Or hadn't you noticed?"

To her own surprise, Juliette laughed. Carson looked at her speculatively, then she laughed, too.

"So what is your deal with Devlin?" she asked. "Just out of curiosity."

"No deal," Juliette answered shortly. "He left."

"Sometimes leaving works," Carson said. "Especially when the person you're leaving has so many loose ends to tie up." She gave her a sideways look. "I hear you're going to Paris. That should be fun."

"Thanks," Juliette said, a little doubtfully.

"If I had known you and Michael were such a big deal, I wouldn't have . . . well, no, I probably would have anyway." She gave Juliette a dazzling smile. "Life is short, right? You've got great taste in men."

"Oh, yeah," Juliette said. "I like them damaged, promiscuous, and emotionally unavailable."

"Me, too," said Carson with apparent sincerity. "It makes them much better kissers, for some reason. And the damaged ones at least have something interesting to say when you talk to them. But then, I'm not looking for monogamy. It's hard to have more than one relationship at a time, and right now I'm in a dysfunctional but highly productive and fairly promising marriage with Bill Becker." Just then her iPhone beeped. "As I say," she said, looking down at it, then lifing it to her ear. "Thanks for the laugh, and the movie, Juliette Greyson. Oh, and for the record," she added over her shoulder as she walked away, "my money's on Devlin."

Juliette stayed in the garden for a few more minutes, thinking that of all the extraordinary things that had happened in the past few weeks the fact that Carson turned out to be almost likable may have been the most surprising. But Dev she couldn't think of, Dev who just up and left, who looked at her as if there were some big secret to life that she just didn't understand. Who made her feel like it was her fault that she hadn't begged him to reveal all his carefully guarded secrets. Not that he had ever offered her much information. She thought of how calm he had been when she had told him about her parents, about her father, how he had just treated it as any other piece of information, had tried to absolve her of all the guilt and misery.

He would have made an excellent priest, she thought sourly. He had looked so at home in the chapel, his fingers steepled in prayer. Which was just one more thing she hadn't known about him, even after twenty years—who would have thought Eamonn Devlin believed in God, much less confided in Him? For a moment, Juliette let herself imagine Devlin as a small boy back in Ireland, making his first Communion, in a white cassock as an altar boy, or going to confession to recount all the sweet and sticky sins of youth, things you believed you could not ever tell anyone without getting in trouble. Then you grew up and discovered there were secrets so big you had to keep them even from God Himself. Which was impossible, of course, because, if there was a God, He had to know everything without you even telling Him; confession was for the benefit of the confessor. God already knew.

"Oh," said Juliette, standing absolutely still as a tiny thought took hold, then bloomed inside her. "Oh, my Lord."

Pounding into the villa, she stuck her head in every room looking for Gabe. She found him in his office, hunched over the computer; Mercy was curled up reading a book on the sofa nearby. "Come on," she said, literally jerking him out of his seat. "You, too," she said to Mercy, because she felt it was the least she could do for the girl after all she had gone through.

Past the kitchen she pulled them, through the hallway, up the two flights of stairs, down the corridor, and into the chapel.

"What?" Gabe said, panting and flushed. His voice sounded loud and bruising in the silent room.

"Ssshh." Juliette looked around at the walls, with their bland white stucco and the crucifix above the altar. "If it were on one of the walls, everyone would have seen . . ." Her gaze met the confessional, which was really an ornately carved box standing against one wall to the side of the last row of pews. "The place only God knows," she said, and she met Mercy's eyes, which opened wide in recognition. Together they walked over to the confessional. Juliette leaned against it and gave a heave. It did not move.

"Jules, it's attached to the wall," Gabriel said. "You're going to give yourself a hernia."

"It has to be here," Mercy explained as Juliette poked and pried, trying to see if there was some way of separating the wood from the wall. "Don't you see? The place only God knows."

"We thought it was the castle because of its name," Juliette said, "but the place only God knows is your soul. And where do you bare your soul? Geez, Gabe, you should have figured it out, you're gassing on and on about it all the time. Confession."

She opened the wooden door and ducked in, kneeling on the worn purple velvet cushion, facing the intricately carved screen that separated the supplicant from the priest. All around her was the dim oppressive feeling she always associated with religion. She closed her eyes and thought of Giotto and his pious patron the contessa, who would have had different emotions about it all.

Behind her she could feel Mercy vibrating with approval. "If I wanted to give someone a gift," she whispered, "I would put it where she could see it every day."

On Juliette's right, a wall of wood paneling rose; behind it was the wall. Sliding her hand along the edges of the panel, she searched for a seam or a knob. Resin gathered under her nails.

"What are you doing in there?" Gabe shoved his head into the confessional.

"Looking for a latch. To see if this wall will roll away, or something."

"What, like a power window? I don't think—"

"Why don't you look under the seat?" Mercy said.

"Don't be ridiculous," Gabe said. "I think we would have noticed—"

"Nothing," Juliette said. "All those years and we noticed nothing." For, sliding her hand under the seat, she had found a small lever. She pushed it and, unbelievably, a small crack appeared in the paneling.

"Ratchet it," Gabe said excitedly, shoving his way in, "keep ratcheting it. Here, I'll do it."

"Get away, you'll break it," she snapped, shoving him back with her shoulder. "Mercy, sit on him or something." Mercy obligingly shoved Gabe onto the small seat and perched on his lap while Juliette, on her knees, carefully pulled the small wooden lever back and pushed it forward again. The panel slid open farther.

Slowly and carefully she worked the lever, and inch by inch the panel receded, revealing images. A wall, a garden, a tree in full bloom, the hem of a dress. No one spoke or breathed, and there was a child's foot, the wing of a bird, and soon they were looking at a portrait of the Blessed Mother sitting in a garden with the young, naked Jesus standing before her, his arms raised to be lifted into her lap. Three feet high and as many wide, the fresco's colors were still rich and vivid, the expressions on the two faces stern but joyful, full of love, with no thought to the future or the past. Above them the sky was blue and full of birds and their halos shone gold even in the confessional's dim light.

"It's our garden," Gabe said, when he could speak. "It's the garden behind the villa." And Juliette could see the familiar wall, the tall chestnuts, the cypress trees in the distance, the wildflowers in the grass at the Virgin's feet.

"It's beautiful," Mercy said, reaching out a hand to touch it, then stopping for fear it would crumble. "So beautiful."

"It's real," Juliette said, her voice trembling. "It's been real this whole time."

They sat for many minutes looking at the painting that no one had seen for centuries. Here it was, a thing of lasting beauty in a chaotic and indifferent world, a bit of immortality daubed onto a wall in a house where so much living and dying had occurred. She thought of all the hours and days she and Gabe had spent searching for it, of her father's insistence that it was there, of her dreams of finding it and making him truly happy for once. If her father had seen it, if her father had found it, would things have turned out differently? She saw Mercy's fingers entwined with Gabe's, the love and hope in her shining eyes. She felt her cousin's shoulders rise and fall with his breathing, how solid and strong he was, how easily he could be happy. Still. Now that they knew it had been real all this time.

The air in the confessional grew hotter and damp with their breath, and sounds began seeping through the chapel, voices and footsteps in the nearby library and the corridor.

"What should we do?" Gabe said, whispering now.

"I don't know," Juliette said, suddenly shaken, realizing their glorious discovery was also a huge responsibility. "I guess we should tell someone. Find some wonderful art historian, or whoever's in charge of preserving the Giottos in Florence and Siena. The colors alone . . . I've never seen any so bright."

"No," Mercy said firmly, pushing Juliette out of the way so she could reach the lever and begin closing the panel.

"What do you mean, no?" Juliette said. "You're the one who was so hot to find it, even more than we were."

Mercy continued to work the lever.

"Maybe someday," she said. "But not right now. You think a film crew is bad? Try a bunch of art historians. Believe me, while I was researching my part I talked to a few, and they made Bill Becker look like a kindly social worker."

"Mercy," Juliette said, irritation creeping into her voice; after all, Cerreta was hers and Gabe's.

"I know it's not my decision, but . . ." The panel closed with a click. Mercy turned and looked at them pleadingly. "Please, please. Leave it safe. Leave it here. For a little while. It's so beautiful and . . ."—she groped for words—"it will drive people crazy. Everyone will want it, or a piece of it. And they'll make it something it's not. They'll try to make it more than it is and wind up making it less. Please," she said, her voice falling to a whisper, her face luminous in the dim light, and Juliette knew exactly what she was saying.

"All right," she said, and beside her she felt Mercy relax. "All right. We'll keep it a secret. For a little while."

In the end, Mercy stayed and Juliette left. After the last of the various rental cars and limos pulled away from Cerreta, after Becker had handed Gabe a check for an amount so large it actually rendered him

silent for a full five minutes, the three of them—Gabe, Juliette, and
Mercy—stood in the courtyard, swaying a bit in the vacuum that had
been left behind. Everything looked miraculously the same, only different—the repainted doors shone more cheerfully, the dirt had been
carefully groomed, the garden was full of now-wilting but still lovely
flowering plants, and far off in the woods a new well meant that no
guest would go without a shower again.

"So," Juliette said, turning to smile at her cousin, the smile vanishing
as she saw that Mercy, pale and sweaty, was leaning over as if she might
vomit in the dirt. She moved to help her but Gabe held up his hand.

"You should go lie down," he said kindly. "And drink lots of water."
Mercy nodded mutely and began to walk slowly toward the villa, giving
a small anguished smile as she went, a smile that did its job. "I'll come
sit with you in a bit," he said, and she kept moving.

Looking at Juliette, he shrugged. "I told her it wouldn't be fun, but she
says this is what she wants. She's going cold turkey, day one. She did call her
father, which is something. He's flying in tomorrow." He shrugged again,
but Juliette could see pleasure and fear battling in his face. "We'll see."

"You're a good man, Gabriel Delfino," she said, putting her arm
around his shoulder. "And I'm proud to be your kin."

"So what are you still doing here anyway?" he said, shifting uncomfortably beneath the embrace and the compliment. "I figured you would
have left with O'Connor."

"No," Juliette said. "I'm going back to work. The general manager
of the Pinnacle Paris was overjoyed at the prospect of my helping them
open; I'm flying there tonight, start tomorrow at eight a.m. Michael's
in Paris already. I'm sure I'll see him, but I'm actually looking forward
to going back to work."

"You didn't get much of a vacation."

"I don't seem to do so well on vacation," she said with a laugh. "All
this silence and beauty and sunshine." She shuddered ironically. "I've

always found the whole serenity thing highly overrated. But here's hoping it works for Mercy."

Which was why, when Juliette finally made her way down the drive, through the new gate, and onto the main road, she had traded her rented Mini Cooper for a black Ferrari. She wore a white-blond wig and big black sunglasses, hunched herself small and young behind the steering wheel, and drove as erratically as she dared in the hopes it would look like she was running away from something. It must have worked; the paparazzi followed her all the way back to Florence. She lost them before she hit the airport, but still, she gave them a few photos to offer the websites, the magazines. She figured it would buy the starlet a few days, maybe a week, and that was something.

Acknowledgments

THE ESTATE CERRETA is based on Spannocchia, a similar though not identical *tenuta* in Tuscany where my family and I have spent many wonderful days. Though no murders or moviemaking have been committed there, the lovely people who run it are engaged in a grand experiment of conservation and preservation that we should all support. Information is available at www.spannocchia.com and www.spannocchia.org. I would like to thank Randall Stratton, Francesca Cinelli, and Erin Cinelli in particular for their friendship and for allowing us to share their vision.

I would like to thank my editor, Kerri Kolen, for her faith, keen eye, and unflagging sense of romance; and my agent Lauren Pearson, for her patience, imagination, organization, and ability to take a bundle of loose ends and turn it into a gorgeous bow.

I would also like to thank early readers of this book, including my most wonderful and patient husband, Richard Stayton; and my friends Betsy Sharkey, Chris Joseph, Kate Arthur, and Michael O'Neill. Your comments and confidence were invaluable.